The Code

The Codebreaker Girls is Ellie Curzon's second novel for Orion Dash. Ellie's debut novel, *Under a Spitfire Sky*, is also available from Orion Dash, and a number of short stories by Ellie Curzon have been published by *Woman's Weekly*.

www.elliecurzon.co.uk

The Codebreaker Girls

Ellie Curzon

First published in Great Britain in 2021 by Orion Dash,
an imprint of The Orion Publishing Group Ltd.,
Carmelite House, 50 Victoria Embankment,
London EC4Y 0DZ

An Hachette UK Company

1 3 5 7 9 10 8 6 4 2

A CIP catalogue record for this book is
available from the British Library.

ISBN (Paperback) 978 1 3987 0915 7
ISBN (eBook) 978 1 3987 0294 3

Typeset at The Spartan Press Ltd,
Lymington, Hants

www.orionbooks.co.uk

CC: For my wee gals and Mr C, with love.

HB: For Beryl (1921–1991), who loved to drive.

And for Sheila (1934–2020),
who was evacuated eight times.

Chapter 1

An early morning mist still lay over the fields as Rosie drove into the village. She couldn't dawdle, not with the long drive to London ahead. Overnight, bombs had fallen on the railway lines out of the city and no trains could get through.

She pulled up at the one pump that stood outside Cottisbourne's petrol station. She wasn't surprised that her polished, stately Humber was the only vehicle there.

'Rosie!' Nancy hurtled out of the little building, her plait streaming behind her. She closed her small hand around the handle of the petrol pump and asked, 'Am I filling her up?'

Rosie admired Nancy's enthusiasm. The girl was only ten, but insisted on helping her grandparents at the petrol station. Life in Cottisbourne must be quiet for her after the bustle of London, but Nancy made the best of her evacuation. She already knew the village better than Rosie ever had, from the church spire to the huts of Cottisbourne Park to the RAF base from which Spitfires headed into the cloudless sky. Nancy would make a good spy one day, if she kept her skill for being in the right place at the right time.

Rosie cranked down the window to speak to her. 'Yes, please, Nancy! I've got a long drive ahead of me.'

'Where you off to?' Nancy appeared at the window and held out her hand for the keys. 'Tea with Mr Churchill?'

Rosie placed the keys in Nancy's palm, then she drew off

her Mechanised Transport Corps cap and put it on Nancy's head at a jaunty angle before she needed to ask.

'Sadly, Mr Churchill's busy today! I'm going to be bringing a very important man to Cottisbourne.' Rosie arched her eyebrow and stage-whispered, 'A major-general, no less!'

'A major-general,' Nancy repeated. She skipped away to the rear of the car and called, 'I hope he don't mind ghosts!'

What on earth?

'Ghosts?' Rosie leaned out of the window. 'I'm sure a major-general won't be scared of ghosts. *If* they exist! I'm not sure they do, you know.'

'You reckon?' Nancy cocked her head to one side before she declared with unshakeable confidence, 'Cottisbourne Park's got a ghost or two. I've heard them.'

'Have you?' Rosie kept an open mind, even though she'd never seen a ghost. 'You *heard* them, rather than *saw* them? So it wasn't someone running about with a sheet over their head?'

'In the barn where Prof Hale found that old French motor,' she replied. 'The one with all the junk and the rats' nest. There's all sorts of funny noises behind the walls and it definitely ain't the rats.'

Rosie knew the barn well, an exhausted old farm building full of junk courtesy of the family that had once lived at Cottisbourne Park. *That old French motor* was a Citroën Type A, over twenty years old, and Professor Hale let Rosie tinker with it in her spare time.

'I can't say I've ever heard any funny noises in the barn.' Rosie frowned, trying to recall if she'd ever heard anything beside the wind blowing through the gaps in the broken window panes. *That's probably it.* 'It might just be the wind, you know. And besides, there's all sorts of funny noises in the countryside that you'd never hear back in London.'

2

'And that's the truth!' Nancy laughed. 'You have a listen next time you're in there. You'll hear them!'

'Right, I'll do that, Nancy!' Rosie hid the laughter in her voice. She wasn't in the business of mocking children. It was much better to let them imagine whatever they wanted to, than limit them with mockery. 'I hope the ghosts like mending cars. I could do with them giving me a hand!'

'That's what I'm here for.' Nancy appeared at Rosie's open window. She gave a neat salute and said, 'She's full up and ready to go. Tell Mr Churchill I said hello, Rosie!'

Rosie took back her cap and put it on. 'I will indeed say hello to the PM. You be good!' She tweaked Nancy's cheek.

Good? She'd be creeping through the secret places of the village in no time.

'I'm off ghost hunting,' she assured Rosie. 'Safe drive, Rosie!'

Rosie tooted as she pulled away, not strictly MTC rules, but it always made Nancy smile. And Rosie carried Nancy's smile with her as she headed out of the village towards the main road and onwards to London.

Chapter 2

The drive up to London didn't take too long. The Humber Snipe purred as Rosie sped along the nearly empty roads. Apart from the occasional military staff cars she passed, it was easy to forget there was a war on while driving in the countryside.

But as soon as London's outskirts swallowed her, signs of the war were everywhere. Far too often, like a missing tooth in a smile, a row of houses would be interrupted by a gaping hole where a bomb had fallen. Forlorn wallpaper flapped in the spring breeze, and mantelpieces hung over empty space where floors had once been. Soot marked the brickwork where fires had blazed, and broken, blackened rafters stuck out like snapped ribs.

The wreckage from the Blitz still surrounded them, and for the past few months, the bombs had started to fall again. Not in the number they had before, but any bomb that fell was one bomb too many.

People walked along the pavements, unbowed but tired. Who could get a proper night's sleep when the sky threatened to open and unleash hell?

Rosie drove up through south London, past Waterloo station and over Westminster Bridge. By some miracle, the Houses of Parliament and Big Ben were still standing, but only just, after suffering repeated attacks.

She turned and headed up Whitehall, where the

government buildings were banked up with sandbags and the windows criss-crossed with tape. There was bomb damage here too, the white stone pitted and worn.

As Rosie passed the entrance to Downing Street, she couldn't resist saying, 'Good morning, Mr Churchill! Nancy says hello.'

Moments later, she arrived at the entrance to Horse Guards Parade. There were no soldiers mounted on horses outside the gates today, no tourists standing about with Box Brownies to take their snaps.

Rosie stopped at the gate and wound down her window to speak to the guard.

'Good morning! I'm here to collect Major-General Sir Kingsley-Flynn.'

She could only say his name with great effort. Hale had kept referring to the major-general as Bluff, and that was now all she could think of. Wouldn't do to say *that* at the gate.

'You're expected,' the guard replied. 'Go straight through. I'll telephone the major-general's office to let him know you've arrived. Your name, Miss?'

'I'm Driver Sinclair,' Rosie said, proud that she had a rank. Not a very lofty rank, but even so, she had a uniform and a job to do. 'Thank you!'

Rosie drove slowly through the gates. The courtyard was empty and she carried on under the arch and out onto the parade ground. Bombs had even scourged this place, leaving pockmarks on the grey stone.

She felt a pang of excitement. Driving onto Horse Guards Parade? How many people were ever allowed to do *that*? But she hid her grin, trying her best to look serious, as she piloted the car towards the main building which looked more like a grand mansion than an army headquarters. She brought the car to a halt, then climbed out.

Her heart was hammering. She couldn't fight off the feeling that she was intruding and that at any moment a red-faced guard would appear and shout at her to go. She drew on her experience from the stage and told herself to *pretend* to be brave, because it would make her *look* brave, and headed towards the building. As she approached, the door opened with some force and a man strode out, followed closely by another, who scurried after him with a case in each hand.

Major-General Sir Kingsley-Flynn – Bluff – looked just as important as he'd sounded. He wore the most immaculate uniform Rosie had ever seen, and his height and his broad shoulders made him seem more formidable than ever.

Rosie was just thinking to herself that his moustache was particularly impressive, of a type that few men could carry off, when she remembered to snap him a salute.

'Good morning, sir,' she said. 'I'm your driver today, down to Sussex.'

Rosie had never met a major-general before and she had never seen such a whipcrack of a salute before either. He could've had someone's eye out with it.

'Driver Sinclair, good morning!' Bluff replied with a brisk, no-nonsense bark. 'Let's load the luggage and be on our way, what?'

'Of course, sir.' Rosie opened the rear door for him. She'd given the car a good sweeping out the evening before, and she was proud it was fit for a major-general. 'It should be a quiet drive down.'

'Let's hope it stays that way.' Bluff took off his cap and climbed into the Humber. He peered around Rosie and said to the young man who was carrying his bags, 'Thank you, Private. Once my bags are stowed, that'll be all.'

Rosie went round to the back of the car and opened the boot for the private. She glanced at him as he lifted the suitcase into the car, wondering if she could read anything in his manner or expression that would tell her just how formidable the major-general was. Would he thunder at her if she jolted him by going over a bump in the road?

But how terrifying could he be? After all, Hale had said the major-general was an old friend, and Hale was such a good egg that she couldn't imagine him being friends with someone who wasn't. Hale had chatted so amicably about the man and Bluff wasn't exactly a nickname to fill anyone with fear.

The young man gave nothing away though. He put the cases into the boot without a word before leaving Rosie with a polite nod. That was that then. Just Rosie and the major-general.

She got back into the car, and pulled away in an arc across the parade ground, heading back under the archway towards Whitehall.

Rosie wished she could ask the major-general where all the horses had got to. They must've been taken to the countryside, but Rosie's MTC training had hammered home the rule that drivers were not to engage in chatter and tittle-tattle with their important passengers.

Instead, Rosie glanced quickly up at the major-general in the rearview mirror.

Bluff. Hale's old friend Bluff.

He wasn't looking at her, but instead was scanning the contents of a letter that he held. His expression was grave and after a moment he glanced up towards Rosie's reflection, then back down to the page.

Rosie wondered, not for the first time that day, what on earth a man of the major-general's importance would be doing at Cottisbourne Park. She knew it was a signals station, and she knew that from the sheds in the Park's grounds, they were eavesdropping on the Nazis. She knew it was highly sensitive, urgently secretive work. A great many important people had sat just where Bluff was sitting at that moment, and yet she couldn't shake the feeling that something was up.

The tide of the war was turning, after all. What if the outlook wasn't as hopeful as Rosie had thought?

'How long have you been at Cottisbourne Park?' Bluff asked, catching Rosie by surprise. It wasn't very often that her illustrious passengers made conversation.

'Since forty-one,' Rosie replied. 'Nearly three years now. Have you visited before?' She cringed inside at her question, but she was curious to know, certain she would have noticed a man like Bluff at the Park.

'My work has taken me to many places,' he replied, 'but not to Cottisbourne Park until today. Professor Hale and I are old friends.'

'Oh, yes, he told me.' Rosie smiled. 'I'm very fortunate to work for Professor Hale. I've always thought he's a nice chap.'

Nice chap?

Rosie cringed again.

'A splendid chap,' Bluff assured her. He was younger than Professor Hale though. Young for a major-general, certainly. He must've had quite the career to earn the crossed sword and baton already. 'So, Driver Sinclair, what do I need to know about Cottisbourne Park that nobody else will tell me?'

Rosie couldn't restrain her chuckle. 'Well, no one will tell you about the Citroën Type A I have the pleasure to be doing up in the barn. And I doubt they'll tell you how seriously certain people take the chess club. I'm not sure they'll tell you about the panto I help to put on each year, but I'm sure you'll hear about the dances. They're *legendary!*'

Dances. As if a major-general would come to one of our dances in the old ballroom with the creaky floor.

'Dances, eh?' He chuckled at the very thought of it. 'Anybody I need to look out for?'

Rosie shook her head. 'They're a quiet bunch at Cottisbourne Park. Heads down, pencils scratching away. Everyone's very friendly! We're all working towards the same thing, aren't we?'

'One would certainly hope so,' was the major-general's reply before he fell silent again.

The silence made Rosie uncomfortable. She swallowed, her throat suddenly dry. She kept her attention on the road ahead, driving slowly around the holes in the tarmac blasted by the bombing.

Were there people who weren't working towards the same thing? Who could possibly support the wreckage they were faced with, poor old London and every other city and major town blown to bits but limping on?

'We're a happy family at Cottisbourne Park,' Rosie said. 'I do enjoy working there. It's like a little village.'

'The best of the best,' Bluff replied.

That was certainly the reputation of the codebreakers of Cottisbourne Park, where the best brains, logisticians and linguists had been assembled to crack the codes that came out of Europe at a rate of knots. Rosie probably shouldn't know as much as she did, but they really *were* a family, united by their signatures on the Official Secrets Act, and now and then, people talked.

'They're certainly that,' Rosie said with pride. 'I'm

honoured to work there. I must say, I feel rather dim sur-rounded by so many geniuses!'

'Genius can be overrated.' Was it Rosie's imagination, or was there a hint of a smile in the major-general's tone? 'And they certainly don't have much time for soldiers.'

Rosie glanced up at him in the mirror again. 'You'll be very welcome at the Park. But... well, I've seen other soldiers get short shrift!'

He quirked one eyebrow and told her, 'Just let them try, Driver Sinclair, just let them try.'

Rosie tried not to laugh. Who indeed would dare to disrespect a stately man like Major-General Sir Kingsley-Flynn? Then again, she could think of some. While there were plenty of humble geniuses at the Park, there were one or two people she could think of who walked to their sheds at the start of each shift with a certain swagger.

'I bet you'd give *them* short shrift!' she remarked.

Though what business could a major-general in the Household Cavalry have at Cottisbourne Park anyway? He didn't strike Rosie as a codebreaker and she'd met enough of them. There was something about the codebreakers, whether they were bookish and shy or confident and brash, that she had started to recognise. She didn't see it in Major-General Sir Kingsley-Flynn.

He was a man of action. He was like a coiled spring.

Rosie drove past another bombsite, a huge space with a water-logged crater at its centre. It looked as if it had once been a factory. But they would soon be in the suburbs, then out into the countryside once more.

'Where are all the horses?' Rosie asked him, the question out before she could stop it. 'The ones who were at Horse Guards?'

'Having a darn sight better time of it than the chaps who

used to ride them,' he replied. 'We'll see them back again one day, Driver Sinclair, of that I have no doubt.'

She liked the confidence in his voice, the certainty that life would go back to normal. Sometimes it felt as if it never could. She realised then that she'd needed to hear a man like Bluff say so.

And she was pleased that the horses were safe.

'Whitehall looks ...' Rosie sighed. 'Well, I hadn't been up to London for a while. It looks so strange with all those sandbags everywhere. And no horses outside Horse Guards. Just think, Churchill was only around the corner!'

'And in a devil of a bad mood,' Bluff confided with just a trace of humour. 'I'm looking forward to breathing some fresh air again. Oh, to be in Sussex when the sun is shining!'

Had he had Churchill's ear over breakfast? Rosie didn't dare ask.

'There was a lovely mist this morning. Very picturesque,' Rosie told him warmly. She was fond of her adopted home. She'd travelled through often enough in her past, but she'd never thought she'd stay there for as long as she had. 'Sussex must be waiting for you and is ready to put on a show!'

She met his gaze in the mirror again and this time, Rosie had no doubt that the major-general was smiling.

Chapter 3

Rosie drove through the village, then out into the lanes and up the drive to Cottisbourne Park. It still had something of its grandeur, the lime tree-lined driveway much unchanged, she imagined, from times gone by. She almost had to swerve as Joe Fleet rode towards her on his ancient bicycle. He raised his hand in apology and cycled on. Across the lawn, she saw the huddled shape of Dr James Brett, sitting on a picnic blanket. His head was bowed, his attention fixed solely on the book in his hand.

The mellow stone facade of the large house appeared up ahead, its leaded windows twinkling in the bright spring light, the wisteria starting to blossom on the vines that wreathed the building.

And there, right outside the front door, was an ambulance.

Rosie slowed as she reached the top of the drive.

'Oh, heavens, someone must've been taken ill,' she said.

'Nothing serious, I hope,' her passenger said breezily. 'I really am looking forward to seeing our Professor Hale again, Driver Sinclair. He speaks very highly of you.'

'Does he? How very kind of him!' Rosie craned her neck, trying to make out the figure in the doorway. But it didn't look like Professor Hale's secretary, Jean Fenning. 'I'll drop you here and take you in. I am sorry, sir, there doesn't appear to be anyone waiting for you. Must be to do with the ambulance, I'm afraid.'

'I wasn't expecting a ... what the devil?'

In the grand doorway Rosie could now clearly see the figure half-turned towards the house, one hand raised and his finger jabbing at something or someone unseen. It *looked* like Professor Swann, but Professor Swann wouldn't look so unkempt, his shirt dirty and his hands ...

It isn't dirt.

A stone of dread dropped into Rosie's stomach at the realisation that the furious figure in the doorway *was* Professor Charles Swann of St Vincent's College, Cambridge. And Professor Swann's elegant hands and Savile Row shirt were red with fresh blood.

'Professor Swann's been injured!' Rosie pulled up with more of a swerve than she'd have liked. But at that moment, all thoughts of smooth driving for the benefit of her distinguished passenger had fled. She was a cog in the machine that was Cottisbourne Park, and everyone who worked there was her extended family. Rosie pushed open the car door and hurried towards the house. 'Professor Swann, what's happened?'

Charles turned to look at her, his expression momentarily bewildered. Then he blinked, set his chin into its familiar imperious tilt and said, 'There's been an incident, Miss Sinclair. I ... An accident, perhaps?'

Rosie tried not to purse her lips too much at hearing Charles refer to her once again as *Miss*.

She saw movement in the shadowy entrance hall behind him. Someone hurrying off. Wasn't that Dr Zalewski?

'An accident? You must've cut yourself very badly.' Rosie wondered where the ambulance's medical team could have got to, when Charles was stood there so bloodied without their help. 'I've got first aid training, Professor. Let me look.'

'No!' Charles held up his hand and shook his head. 'The medics are attending, Miss Sinclair. It's no place for a girl.'

'Is it a place for a major-general?' Bluff asked, earning a rather narrow look from the professor, his composure seemingly returned. 'Perhaps you'd care to tell me where I can find your director, Professor?'

Charles shot Rosie a glance then nodded. 'We'd better speak privately,' he told Bluff.

Rosie didn't take offence. So many conversations went on here that she wasn't party to. It was all part of life at Cottisbourne Park.

'I'll take your things to your room, sir,' Rosie told him, as she retreated. 'Professor Hale's secretary will show you up later, I'm sure.'

'Thank you, Driver Sinclair,' he replied. 'And thank you for a very pleasant journey.'

Rosie saluted. 'Don't mention it, sir!' Then she turned on her heel and went back outside.

As she took the suitcase from the boot, Rosie couldn't help but look over at the abandoned ambulance. She'd driven them in London at the start of the war, and she couldn't look at them now without being reminded of the bell clattering as the sirens moaned, the sobs of the injured, and the iron scent of blood.

How could there have been an accident at Cottisbourne Park? It was a haven. No place for blood and ambulances.

She headed back to the house, the major-general's suitcase in her hand.

Then Rosie heard wheels on the gravel, and turned to see Caroline, Charles' sister, riding up on her bicycle.

Oh, heck. I'll have to tell her.

'Is it true?' Caroline leapt from her bicycle, the wheels still spinning as it fell onto the gravel. She dashed up the steps, her face white as she took Rosie's arm and asked again, 'Is it? Tommy's at the gate and he said... Professor Hale?' And her face crumpled at the name, tears welling in her eyes.

A cold finger of fear ran down Rosie's spine. She dropped the suitcase.

Not Hale. Please not Professor Hale.

'Professor Hale? Caroline, what is it? What about Professor Hale?'

'He shot himself!' The words fell into themselves in a panicked babble. 'Tommy says he's dead!'

'Shot himself?' Had she heard Caroline properly? But she had, hadn't she? She'd said Hale was dead. She'd said he'd shot himself. 'How? Why would he? I saw him this morning. He was drinking a cup of tea at his desk. He ... he ...' Rosie shook her head. 'It must be someone else. It *can't* be Professor Hale!'

It was a horrible mistake, Rosie told herself as a sleek black car drove up the driveway at the sort of speed Professor Hale always took a very dim view of. It barely seemed to have stopped before the doors opened and three men climbed out, each as soberly dressed as the other in dark suits and hats. Rosie had seen men like these before, when they arrived for their monthly briefings with Professor Hale. Whenever they left, he would always tell her with a mischievous smile, *those fellows drink a lot of tea for chaps who don't officially exist.*

Their sudden arrival made Rosie shiver, and it seemed to drag Dr Brett from his reverie too. He closed his book and stood, pausing only to gather up his rug before he hurried across the lawn towards the huts and out of sight.

Maybe something *had* happened to Hale after all. But he couldn't be dead. He simply *couldn't* be.

They didn't seem to notice Rosie and Caroline as they made for the door.

'It can't be Professor Hale. It can't be. It can't,' Rosie whispered under her breath, but her sense of dread was unrelenting. It was a small relief when she saw her friends, Sarah and Maggie, approaching arm-in-arm around the corner of the building.

They both looked stunned. News had travelled across the Park already, then.

Sarah pulled her cardigan tightly around her. 'I just can't believe it. You've heard about Professor Hale? It just doesn't feel real. He *is* Cottisbourne Park. What'll we do?'

At her side, Maggie blew her nose into an embroidered handkerchief. She drew to a halt at the sight of the new arrivals and lowered her gaze to the ground, blinking back tears.

Caroline stepped mutely aside as the men entered the building, finally offering the women a nod as they did. Only then did one of them stop and ask, 'There's a storage barn on the estate. Where will we find it?'

'It's all right, Driver Sinclair.' Major-General Sir Kingsley-Flynn strode into the foyer. He greeted the men with a nod. 'Follow me, gentlemen.'

'The barn?' Rosie watched the men go. The barn she'd spent so much time in working on the car. She'd joked with Professor Hale, told him she'd take him for a spin in the Citroën just as soon as it was roadworthy again. 'Caroline, your brother ... I saw him just now. Covered in blood.'

Sarah and Maggie blinked in surprise at that.

'Oh, heck,' Sarah murmured. She exchanged a glance with Maggie, then the two women hurried to join their friends. At the door Maggie craned round to look into the now empty foyer.

'What an awful thing,' she murmured.

Would Charles have shot someone? Would he shoot Hale? Rosie had heard him crowing once, declaring that he'd be a darn sight better than Hale as director of the place, but surely he wouldn't have shot him?

'*Charles?*' Caroline shook her head. 'What are you ... Rosie, *no!* You mustn't say that! Charles would never ... how could you!'

'He was covered in blood!' Rosie insisted. 'You didn't see him! Oh, God, he must've been there when it happened!'

Maybe Hale wasn't dead. Rosie wanted to hold onto that tiny sliver of hope for as long as she could.

'What the bloody hell are you saying?' Charles called as he stalked along the corridor from which Bluff had appeared. 'How *dare* you tell the Sprat I'm mixed up with this? You've got some nerve for a jumped-up bloody cab driver, missy!'

'She wasn't saying that, Charles,' Caroline said through her tears. Her words faltered at the sight of him though, the blood darkening on his shirt as it dried. 'She wouldn't—'

'No, she bloody wouldn't!' Maggie snapped, straightening her back as she leapt to her friend's defence. 'She's in shock!'

'I don't even know what's happened!' Rosie protested. 'Caroline said that Professor Hale ...' Rosie couldn't say it. She swallowed down a sob and Maggie put her arm around Rosie's shoulders. 'All I know is that there's an ambulance parked outside, and you're covered in blood, and the men from the ministry have turned up, and Caroline said ...' Rosie tried once more to say it, but the words stopped in her throat.

Charles nodded, the gesture sharp.

'He shot himself,' he told them in a clipped voice. 'Bullet through the brain. The coward's way.'

Rosie trembled and rubbed her arms, trying to fight the

cold that was consuming her. She shook her head vehemently. 'Professor Hale's not a coward. He wouldn't shoot himself. Why would he?'

But then, why was the major-general here? No, he was Hale's old friend. It was all a horrible mistake. It had to be.

Chapter 4

Rosie passed the day in a haze. She tried to carry out her usual tasks, but every time she began to forget what had happened, the fact of Hale's death rushed back at her like a slap across the face. She spent her breaks with her friends, but with everyone still in shock over Professor Hale's death, no one had very much to say. But at least they could find some strength and comfort just by being in each other's company.

Normally, Rosie would've dealt with her despair and worry by fiddling with the Citroën, but she couldn't go into the barn, and she wasn't sure she ever wanted to set foot in there again.

Inside, she wandered. No one seemed to notice her aimless path as she ventured through the wood-panelled corridor of the old house. How she longed for her friends to finish their shifts, if only so they could share a pot of tea together and try to fill the silence.

She paused for a moment outside Hale's office, but the thought of never hearing his cheerful, 'Do come in, Driver Sinclair!' again nearly made her sob.

She left the house through a conservatory that had been appropriated for a tomato-growing contest. She'd laughed that it was their very own Kew Gardens, and Hale had laughed too.

Someone will need to look after his plants.

Rosie shook her head and wandered into the grounds. Once, Cottisbourne Park had sat in acres of carefully manicured land, but once the codebreakers had outgrown the old house, the grounds began to be covered by one shed after another housing the different teams. There was always at least one person in each shed all day long, covered by three eight-hour shifts. Nothing could be missed.

So had anyone seen Hale going to the barn? Had anyone seen Swann?

But then, as Rosie wandered the cinder paths between the sheds, she saw people bowed over their work. Sarah and Maggie were at their usual desks by the windows of hut five. They looked up and gave her a quick wave, then their focus returned to their task. Even the death of their director couldn't allow them to pause.

She spotted Joe Fleet return on his bike. He left it propped up against the wall of his hut. He was in a hurry, but at the door seemed to remember the sadness that hung over the Park, and his haste vanished. He looked over to Rosie with a nod before heading inside the hut.

A group were smoking outside hut four. The usually jovial Sid Chandler was among them, tamping down the tobacco of his pipe. His desolate expression told Rosie that he knew about Hale. News travelled fast through Cottisbourne Park.

She reached the garage where she tucked up the Humber each night and tried to occupy herself sorting through some things. There wasn't much sorting to do, though, as Rosie kept the garage as neat as a pin.

She always gave the car a rub down after a drive, and kept the chamois leather and brushes in an old boot-blacking box. She crouched down to open it and after drawing out the chamois noticed something underneath it, a white oblong that she'd never seen in there before.

An envelope, with her name written on it.

In Hale's handwriting.

Rosie's heart skipped as she saw it. What if it was his farewell to the world? Her hand shook as she took it from the box. She carefully opened the envelope and unfolded the note.

There was Professor Hale's sprawling, ungoverned handwriting, as though a spider dipped in ink had run this way and that over the page. There was a blot of blue ink beside that morning's date, where his old fountain pen had no doubt gone rogue, as it so often did.

My Dear Driver Sinclair,

I hope you won't ever read this letter but if you do, we've trouble at t'mill, as they say. Mole trouble, if you follow, and not in the tomatoes.

Bluff can sniff out a mole from the other side of the county, so one can but hope he'll work his magic. The only fly in the custard is the small fact that I think our mole may be onto me. If he is and he does something about it before you deliver Bluff to Cotts, be my voice for the major-general. He's not half so fierce as he seems.

Nothing worse than a mole in a country garden, Driver Sinclair, and you know Cotts better than anyone. If I meet a sticky end, I'll be counting on you and Bluff to bring the blighter in.

You really are a splendid fellow tinkerer, you know. And keep watering my toms!

With every good wish

Roderick Hale

'They killed him,' Rosie whispered, fighting back her tears. She ran her fingertip across the paper and said, 'Don't worry, Professor. They won't get away with it.'

★ ★ ★

That evening, Rosie sat in the quiet of the Park's ancient chapel, Hale's letter stowed in her pocket. She had told no one what she had discovered. On the couple of occasions she'd seen Bluff, he hadn't been on his own, and she didn't know who she could trust. Professor Hale would have expected his death would bring those dark suited ministry men, yet his letter had made no mention of them, and their visits always left him annoyed, which was quite an achievement for a man so placid. He wouldn't want them to know what he had written.

She had lit a candle for him, not knowing what else to do, and from the narrow pew, she watched the single flame dance and flicker against the darkness. She stared and stared as if an answer would appear, until after-images glowed before her eyes.

'How far that little candle throws his beams...' said a voice from the doorway. 'Would you rather be alone, Driver Sinclair?'

Rosie turned at Bluff's voice. She smelt pipe smoke, and a wisp of it wreathed his silhouette in the doorway.

And she knew that line. She'd stood on several stages and said it.

'So shines a good deed in a naughty world,' Rosie replied, the words falling out before she could stop herself. She shook her head, trying to forget her carefree days in the theatre before the war. 'I don't mind company, Major-General. You're welcome to come in. I lit a candle for him … for Professor Hale. For your friend.'

'That's very kind.' He walked along the aisle to the place where the candle flame danced, then took off his cap and bowed his head for a moment. He tucked the cap under his arm and asked, 'Do you mind if I sit?'

Rosie had been so addled after the events of the day, that she had quite forgotten protocol. Remembering it now, she shot up from the pew and saluted. 'Not at all, Major-General.'

Bluff waved away the salute with a gesture of his hand.

'I think you've earned a night off the formalities, Driver Sinclair.' He nodded to the pew. 'Please.'

Rosie dropped the salute, then she sat back down on the pew, her back a little straighter than before. 'I'm so sorry about what's happened. Professor Hale was looking forward to seeing you.'

'And I him,' Bluff said with a sigh. 'Professor Hale regarded you as a friend, Driver Sinclair. I'm terribly sorry for your loss.'

Rosie wrinkled up her nose as she tried not to cry.

A friend. I've lost my friend.

She sniffed as she reached for her handkerchief. The letter crinkled against her fingers. Bluff would believe her, wouldn't he? Surely he'd know Hale's handwriting anywhere. 'It wasn't his time to die.'

Bluff put the stem of his pipe between his teeth and for a time they sat together in silence. He kept his gaze on the candle, watching the dancing shadows it threw over the wall and ceiling and when he finally spoke again, his voice was soft.

'It's very peaceful here.'

'It is.' And it made it all the more horrible that Hale's life had been ended with a bullet. 'I never thought anything bad could happen here.'

'It wasn't his time,' he repeated. 'Not when he was so concerned with the moles in his tomato patch.'

Rosie's hand instinctively reached for the letter from Hale. Her pulse thundered in her ears.

'I wanted to speak to you earlier. I ...' *I can trust Bluff. I can.* 'I found something.'

'The professor was most concerned with the gardens,' Bluff said. For a moment he was silent, then he took the pipe from his mouth again and settled his gaze on her. 'Would you mind awfully if we went for a drive?'

'Not at all,' Rosie replied. They couldn't trust anyone, then. They couldn't even whisper in the chapel. 'I'll show you Cottisbourne at dusk. It's a lovely way to see it.'

'Splendid!' He rose to his feet so sharply it was as if the king himself had just strolled into the chapel. With one step Bluff was in the aisle and he gestured for Rosie to go ahead of him. 'After you, Driver Sinclair. Lead the way.'

Rosie got up from the pew. She went over to the candle and reluctantly blew it out in case the blackout started before they got back. But she wasn't abandoning Hale. Maybe, just maybe, she and Bluff would find his enemy.

Chapter 5

As they walked from the chapel to the garage, Rosie pointed out the sheds they'd passed and told Bluff who was working where. Daylight stretched on for so long at this time of year that the blinds weren't yet down as the evening shift settled to their work. In case anyone was listening, she described each person based on who they'd played in the panto, or what they'd done backstage.

'Dr Plumer from Trinity Cambridge, he was a prompt. And that chap just going into Shed Six, he's Professor Woodward from Christchurch Oxford – or Baron Hardup in *Cinderella*, as he's also known. Sid, he's from the Tech in Manchester, he helped move the scenery. Dr Stuart did the music. And my friend Sarah – Dr Woods – made the costumes. And Maggie painted the scenery.'

'And who were you in *Cinderella*?' he asked, his tone convivial now they were outside again.

'I was the director,' Rosie said proudly. '*And* Principal Boy! Prince Charming at your service. Professor Hale joined in too. Did he tell you?'

'Widow Twanky, I believe,' Bluff chuckled. 'That world-class education paid off in the end.'

'Oh, he did tell you then! He was fantastic.' Rosie sighed. 'Poor old thing.'

They reached the converted stable that served as the Humber's garage. Rosie was supposed to pick up her passengers at the house, but Hale wouldn't hear of anyone running around after him. He'd be here at the shed come rain or shine whenever there was a trip on the agenda, sometimes even before Rosie was. The thought that he'd gone, washed over Rosie afresh and she longed for Nancy's world of adventures in the meadows and ghosts in the eaves. It seemed like a simpler place.

Rosie opened the double doors and went to bring the car outside. Her gaze fell for a moment on the boot-blacking box, and she pictured Hale kneeling down to hide his note inside it. One of the last things he'd ever done.

She pushed the thought away and drove the car out into what had once been the stable yard where Bluff was waiting for her. She hopped out and opened the passenger door for him, just as she always had done for Hale.

Bluff frowned, then nodded towards the rear door and barked, 'The members of the MTC generally afford some level of respect to a visiting major-general, Driver Sinclair. Even in Sussex.'

Why was Bluff suddenly insisting on formality?

'Sorry, sir. I forgot for a moment. Professor Hale always sat in the front.' She banged the door shut and opened the rear door, saluting Bluff.

With a sharp salute in return, he climbed into the car, but not before he'd muttered darkly, 'Things have become very shoddy in these parts. Very shoddy indeed.'

'Sorry, sir.' Rosie closed the door after him, then went back to the garage to lock up. As she turned the key, she tried to think of how affable Bluff had been on the way down, and how gentle he'd seemed in the chapel. Not to mention how amused he'd appeared to be when she'd told him about the panto. And now he was snapping at her. It stung.

He'd lost his friend, though. Maybe that was why?

Rosie returned to the car and climbed in behind the wheel. She turned to look at him, sitting in stately fashion in the back of the car. She was reminded of how important he was, and how comparatively insignificant she was. The rank of Driver was only equal to Private, after all.

'Anywhere you'd like to see in particular?' Rosie asked him. 'There's a spot up on the hillside with a lovely view of Cottisbourne Vale.'

'Wherever you see fit,' he replied, imperious. He was looking out towards the house, where shadows moved in the windows and where here and there, Rosie noted, some shadows stood still. Somewhere, someone knew exactly what had happened to Professor Hale.

Rosie drove down the driveway, the lime trees casting long, evening shadows. She pulled out onto the main road as smoothly as she could, and took them on a brief tour of the village. She drove Bluff past the parish church, the pub, the Post Office, the telephone box, the bakery, the greengrocer's, the butcher's. Then she carried on past the doctor's house, and the cottage hospital. Then came the petrol station, and Rosie wondered if Nancy had gone to bed yet or if she was still at large in the village somewhere, engaged in adventures of her own making.

'And that's Cottisbourne,' Rosie told him. 'Aside from the airfield, of course.'

'If we're safely out of sight of prying eyes, pull the car over,' Bluff said, the stern quality gone from his voice. 'I'm far happier sitting in the front, but it doesn't do to let our friends at the Park see anything other than a stuffy major-general, old before his years.'

She was impressed by his acting – he'd certainly convinced

27

her. Bluff evidently didn't mind her seeing his friendly side, then.

Rosie slowed and pulled over by a gate leading into a field. She didn't even have time to open her door before Bluff was out of the car, no hint of ceremony about him now. He climbed into the passenger seat and announced, 'That's better. Far easier to talk, don't you think?'

'*Much* better,' Rosie agreed.

She pulled back onto the road. After a short distance, she turned off onto a steep lane that took them up the hillside. The Humber didn't complain, the engine humming sedately as Rosie drove.

'This is one of my favourite places,' she confided. 'I feel like the only person in the world up here.'

'It looks like a fine place to drink a toast to a great friend,' was Bluff's conclusion. 'One might chance a pipe in chapel, but brandy seems to be inviting a thunderbolt.'

Rosie nodded towards the road ahead. 'Just a little further, just beyond the trees. There's a couple of little standing stones up there. No one seems very bothered by them, but someone must've cared enough long ago to bring them up here.'

She hadn't brought anyone up to see the stones, but Professor Hale knew that they were there, because Professor Hale knew Cottisbourne like a local. He walked for hours around the village and on one of his walks, discovered the two stones. *Romeo and Juliet*, as he had called them.

The trees parted and Rosie pulled up by the old stone wall.

'Professor Hale liked it up here too,' Rosie told Bluff. 'I'm sure he must've told you about his walks? Rain or shine, snow or ... well, hail.'

Bluff smiled and opened the door. He drew in a lungful of

28

air then climbed out of the car and said, 'He never seemed to age, did you know him long enough to notice? Perpetually fifty-something with a mischievous look in his eye.'

'You're right, he didn't appear to age in the three years I knew him.' Rosie got out of the car too and smiled as she saw the fields stretch out beneath them. The world could still be beautiful, despite the horrible things that went on in it. 'How did you know him? Dare I say it, but I doubt you were schoolmates. You're quite a bit younger than him, aren't you?'

Bluff gave a hearty laugh, the sort of laugh that suited a broad-shouldered major-general. He wagged his finger at Rosie and told her, 'Oh, I don't hear that very often, Driver Sinclair. I'm also perpetually fifty-something. The only trouble is, one's actually just turned forty.'

That *was* young for a man of his rank. Which meant he had done something impressive to earn it.

'Goodness me!' Rosie gasped in surprise. 'You're quite an important fellow, aren't you? And Professor Hale trusted you … so … So I can as well.'

The major-general reached into his pocket and took out a silver hipflask. As he looked out over the village beneath them, he unscrewed the cap, breathing deeply once more. The air smelled like spring, fresh and dewy with the approaching evening. It was like a different world to London.

'Professor Hale was my tutor when I was a wayward youth,' Bluff admitted, much to Rosie's surprise. Major-General Sir Kingsley-Flynn didn't seem particularly wayward. 'I wouldn't stay put at Marlborough long enough to learn anything, so summer schooling was required. Professor Hale was the gent for the job, several less personable gents failed miserably.' He held out the hipflask to Rosie. 'A toast to our friend, Driver Sinclair? He wouldn't want tears if there could be brandy instead.'

Wayward?

Rosie looked Bluff up and down, the immaculately dressed senior officer, then she took the proffered flask.

'To Professor Hale,' she said, and took a tiny sip. She didn't know a lot about brandy, but she knew enough that this was luxurious stuff. It must've been hidden in a cellar somewhere since before the war. She passed the flask back to Bluff.

'To Professor Roderick Hale,' Bluff announced as he took the flask. 'Without whom there would've been no major-general, only *Bluff*.' With that, he took a long drink. It struck Rosie then that this was the way to remember the professor. No tears for him, but a very fine brandy taken in the fresh Cottisbourne air. Bluff turned to look at Rosie and asked, 'Now, Driver Sinclair, what do you have burning a hole in your pocket?'

He noticed.

Rosie glanced over her shoulder. There was no one up here, save Hale's old friends Romeo and Juliet, slumbering in the meadow, grey and ancient.

'He left me a note. In the box I keep my chammies in.' Rosie reached into her pocket and drew out the note, still in its envelope. The sight of Hale's handwriting caused her a pang. She passed it to Bluff.

Bluff took the letter almost reverentially. He looked down at the writing, then back to Rosie and their gazes met as he took the paper from the envelope. His expression was un-readable as he scanned the contents and Rosie said nothing, waiting for his conclusion.

She watched him anxiously. Wasn't this evidence that Hale couldn't have taken his own life?

'Cottisbourne Park has a mole problem.' Bluff's words

were conversational. 'They'll do real damage if they go un-checked. Wreck the healthiest garden, you know. Professor Hale was of the opinion that you were made of the sort of mettle that goes into sniffing out a mole. It's part of the reason he wanted us to meet. Did you know that?'

'I had no idea,' Rosie admitted, trying to absorb this new information. Hale had trusted her more than she had thought. 'None at all. No idea about moles, no idea that Professor Hale thought I could do anything more than drive a car and put on a panto.'

Bluff took out his pipe and weighed it in his hand as he said, 'I specialise in cleaning out the garden, if you're with me. I can't say too much more at the moment – there are signatures needed before I can – but Professor Hale had a strong suspicion he might meet with an accident. If he did, he told me that the only person he'd stake his trust on at Cottisbourne Park was you.'

Rosie pointed to herself. '*Me?* The only person at Cottisbourne Park he could trust? Oh, Lord … I don't know what to say. I feel rather humbled.'

But what did it mean beyond humbling words? Was there a part to play for Rosie in securing some sort of justice for her lost friend, or did that rely on those mysterious *signatures*?

'I'll be taking charge of Cottisbourne Park until we steady the ship.' That didn't come as a surprise somehow. 'And I'll need a pair of trusted eyes and ears, just as our friend says in his letter to you. Would you be willing to work with me to tidy the garden, Driver Sinclair?'

Rosie thought of how content she'd been at the Park, how she'd felt part of a family. But like every family, there were quarrels and bad feeling simmering under the surface. Ordinarily, she would never have wanted to turn against the people who she'd spent the last three years of her life

31

with, but one of them, it seemed, was a mole, and it stood to reason that the mole had killed Professor Hale.

She nodded. 'Yes, I'll work with you, Bluff. I'll help you root out the mole.'

'I'm afraid you'll have to talk to the men from the ministry about the paperwork.' Bluff smiled as he touched a lit match to the bowl of his pipe. 'But I'm very glad to have you in my corner. Your references are suitably glowing.'

The men from the ministry. It seemed there was no escaping them.

'I'll sign whatever I need to,' Rosie promised him. 'I led a rather aimless life up until the war started. I'm glad you think I cut the mustard!'

'I have a nose for these things,' he assured her. 'And so did the prof. If he says you've the makings of a gardener, you've the makings of a gardener. Officially, you'll still be a driver, I'm afraid. I hope you understand.'

'It's the perfect cover.' Rosie raised an eyebrow conspiratorially. How had she gone from being a driver to a spycatcher's assistant? 'We can come up here whenever we need to speak and be certain no one's listening. Unless they've climbed into the boot!'

'And it goes without saying that I'll be terribly stern back at HQ. Needs must on occasion.'

'I won't take it personally,' Rosie assured him with a grin. 'We're playing our roles, aren't we? I'm used to that!'

Bluff held out his hand to Rosie. 'Welcome aboard, Driver Sinclair.'

Rosie took his hand and shook. 'I won't let you down, Major-General Sir!'

Hale would be proud of her tonight, Rosie knew, and she'd make sure whoever had killed him was winkled out. He deserved that at least.

Chapter 6

Rosie was in the middle of pinning up her hair the next morning when someone banged on her door.

And banged again. And again.

She hadn't slept very well as she had kept dreaming about Hale, running away from her across the grounds of Cottisbourne Park. Every time the dream had visited her, Rosie had woken up and was in tears. But she was aware of another presence in the dreams, a tall shadow cast across the lawn, a friendly sort of presence.

Bluff.

And presumably, it was Bluff banging on her door.

Rosie's room was above the garage, her quarters once the home to the grooms who had looked after the stables. To brighten it up, she had covered the walls in postcards and theatre posters, and strewn it with cushions and scarves. It was home. *Almost.*

She hurried down the stairs to reach the wooden door at the bottom, doing her best to get her hair in some sort of order as she went.

'Morning, sir!' she said brightly as she opened the door.

But in a moment she realised that this wasn't Bluff. She had never seen the man in the doorway before. He was square-jawed, and very well-dressed in a pin-sharp charcoal grey suit. His overcoat and hat co-ordinated in a way that Rosie rarely saw anymore.

He really makes his clothing rations stretch.

'Oh! I'm sorry, are you lost?' Rosie asked him.

'I look after the gardens for the War Office,' he told her in a voice so smooth it sounded like it should be crooning on a stage somewhere. 'Mr Wyngate. Good morning, Driver Sinclair.'

Gardens. The mole in the garden.

She saw again Hale in her dreams, hurrying away out of reach.

'Good morning, Mr Wyngate.' Rosie leaned out through the doorway and looked left and right, hoping no one else was about. She lowered her voice and asked, 'You want to speak to me about gardening?'

'Would you accompany me to the house?' It was an invitation, but not the sort of invitation Rosie would actually have been able to decline. 'Just the matter of tidying the late professor's affairs.' With that he took a step back, gesturing for Rosie to step outside.

Rosie patted her head. 'This is rather awkward. I haven't got my cap, sir.'

'Then fetch it, Driver,' Wyngate replied. 'Double quick.'

Rosie turned and hurried up the stairs. She felt as if she'd been in the wings, about to go on stage without a crucial piece of her costume. She grabbed her hat from the wobbly card table she used as a dressing table and put it on, then she ran back downstairs. When she appeared outside again, she gave Wyngate her best salute.

'Ready now, sir!' she announced.

He didn't return the salute before he set off towards the house, so Rosie assumed he must be civilian. Or that he was supposed to be civilian. Which meant, in Rosie's experience driving for Cottisbourne Park, that he was probably MI5. He certainly wasn't the first man from the security services to visit, but he was the first to request an audience with her.

And she was more than willing to speak to him, and tell him whatever he needed to know so that they could find Hale's killer.

It wasn't far to the house, and Rosie had to remind herself that Hale wouldn't be sitting at his desk behind one of the polished wooden doors anymore. The house felt different, muted and shadowy, as if it was mourning him too.

Cottisbourne Park was still waking up as Wyngate opened a side door and entered ahead of her. The night shift would be preparing to hand over to the day, and the day shift would still be dressing for breakfast. Rosie wondered how Bluff had settled on his first night and whether his sleep had been any better than hers. Somehow, she doubted it.

'Nice old pile, this,' Wyngate commented. 'One big happy family?'

'Oh, very much so!' Rosie said with a grin. Then she thought better of it and said, 'For the most part. Gosh, I don't suppose you mind me asking, but I'm parched. If there's a cup of tea on the go, I wouldn't say no! I haven't had my breakfast yet.'

Then she realised where she was. The old scullery. Its single window was high up on the wall and barred as if they were in a cell. It smelt of damp and the whitewashed walls were tinged with a faint sheen of green where mould was taking hold. There was a scratched table in the middle of the room, flanked by two plain chairs that looked like they had come from a kitchen.

'Oh, dear, we are rather stuck for spare space here,' Rosie said, embarrassed by the spartan office Wyngate had ended up with. 'Sorry they've given you the scullery!'

'I requested it.' Wyngate closed the door behind them. 'Sit down, Driver Sinclair.'

She was surprised, given how elegantly Wyngate dressed. Surely he'd have wanted an office like Hale's?

Rosie sat down on one of the chairs, taking care as it stood unsteadily on the floor's uneven stone flags. She sat up as straight as she could, her hands folded neatly in her lap.

'I have an interest in names.' Wyngate took off his coat and hung it on the back of the door. It looked incongruous there, so finely tailored against the peeling paint. He hung his hat there too, smoothing down his brylcreemed hair as he said, 'Don't you think names can be interesting, Driver Sinclair?'

'I suppose so.' Rosie thought of Bluff and remarked, 'Real names, nicknames . . .'

Wyngate nodded. He took the seat opposite her. 'You were on the stage, I believe?'

'Oh, I was, yes! Mummy made sure I had an actor's name right from the off.' With a flourish, she said, 'I'm Rosalind Sinclair!'

And what was Bluff's name? It couldn't *actually* be Bluff, could it?

No.

'Rosalind,' he repeated with a thin smile. 'Robert and Sylvia Sinclair's little protégé. Will you go back to the stage when the war ends?'

'I hope to.' Rosie wondered for a moment how he knew her parents' names, until she remembered she'd named them as her next of kin on the forms she'd signed when she'd joined the MTC. And in the same forms, she'd mentioned that she'd been working in her parents' travelling repertory company before the war. 'I do rather miss the stage, but then again, there's a lot to be said for staying in one place for longer than a month at a time.'

Wyngate nodded. 'I've always been rather intrigued by stage names.' He blinked a little too innocently and asked, 'Does your father call your mother Sylvia at home? Or is she Margery to family and friends?'

Rosie stared at him in surprise. It had been a very long time since she'd heard anyone call her mother anything but Sylvia.

'*Margery?*' The name felt very odd in Rosie's mouth. 'How did you know that? Mummy really doesn't like being called Margery. She's Sylvia Wood, and that's that.'

'I make it my business to recognise names, especially when they cross my desk more than once.' Wyngate leaned forward in his chair and knitted his hands atop the pitted surface of the desk. 'Your name, Driver Sinclair, has crossed it three times in the past few weeks. That's either very worrying or potentially very promising. What does the girl from Weston-super-Mare think about that?'

Rosie twisted her hands, unnerved.

How did he know so much about her?

'I'm not *from* Weston-super-Mare exactly. I just happened to have been born there,' Rosie explained. Although she wasn't about to go into detail. If he'd seen her birth certificate, then he knew full well that her full place of birth was The Theatre Royal, Weston-super-Mare. She was relieved that her father hadn't been tempted to add *Ladies' dressing room* to it. 'And as for my name crossing your desk, I really can't think why it has. I haven't done anything out of the ordinary, I've merely driven about as I do usually. Unless it's because of what's happened to the dear old professor?'

'What exactly do they do here at Cottisbourne Park, Rosie?' He offered her another of those mirthless smiles. 'What goes on?'

Hale had told her often enough not to tell anyone what

she might pick up on regarding the Park's business. Even though Wyngate was from the ministry, she still wouldn't say a word.

Rosie gave him her stock, tight-lipped response. 'I wouldn't know, I'm only a driver.'

At her reply, Wyngate frowned. There was something in it that seemed exaggerated, almost a pout. He sat back in his chair, still frowning.

'I'm with the ministry. There's nothing you can't tell me.'

'With respect, sir, I've never met you before,' Rosie replied, steel in her voice. She glanced at the door. No tea was forthcoming, it appeared. Her gaze returned to Wyngate.

He nodded. 'Then I'll tell the girl from Laburnum Crescent what *I* know, shall I? Then we'll all be on the same page of our scripts. We've signed the Act, after all.' There was that smile again. 'People at Cottisbourne Park work on the codes that the rest of the service doesn't even know exist. A pest in this particular English country garden would be potentially catastrophic.'

'I'm sure it would be, if people here were doing what you say,' Rosie said, trying her best not to let her nerves sound in her voice. She unclenched her hands and smoothed her skirt over her knees. She pictured the forms she'd filled out on joining the MTC, giving *Laburnum Crescent* for her address. The place she'd called home when it hadn't been a boarding house somewhere. 'But as I said, I couldn't comment, because I don't know.'

'Did Professor Hale kill himself, Rosie? I don't want to know what the major-general told you, I want to know what you think.'

'Why do you care what I think? Does my opinion matter when I'm only the driver?'

Rosie wasn't about to share her suspicions with anyone.

Oh, Wyngate no doubt did come from the ministry, but she didn't like being taken to a room that looked like a cell. And besides, how did she know *he* wasn't something to do with the mole? She might've wanted to help when he'd first appeared, but he had unsettled her too much with his uncanny knowledge about her.

'He was very fond of you, what on earth could you have had in common?' He pushed back his chair and stood. 'Was there something between Professor Hale and you? You can tell me, Rosie, I'd understand. Older fellow, man of the world ... *actress*? It wouldn't be the first time a driver had overstepped her territory.'

Rosie's nostrils flared in annoyance. She'd heard that bilge before, the insinuations that MTC girls were all dropping their draws for whoever they were driving. And of course, her previous profession was synonymous with *floozy* to some people. But she wasn't going to allow Mr Fancy Pants from the ministry to rile her.

'He was like a kind uncle,' Rosie replied, her words clipped. 'Nothing more, nothing less.'

Wyngate leaned forward, his palms braced on the table top. He met her gaze and whispered, 'Did he kill himself because he'd let slip some pillow talk? And you passed it along to someone that you shouldn't?'

Rosie clenched her jaw. She wanted to give him a piece of her mind, but she quelled her threatened eruption. The horrible little scullery was so chilly, and when the tap over the butler's sink began to drip, she was reminded of her thirst and how much she wanted a cup of tea, and that breakfast would soon be over.

'How can you say that, when he's not even cold in his grave?' Rosie passed the back of her hand across her eyes.

She would've cried, but she was too proud to do so in front of the man from the ministry.

'Cottisbourne Park has a mole problem.' Wyngate slapped his palm against the desk, his voice a furious bellow. 'Someone is passing secrets back to Germany and I want to know what you know! This is a hanging offence, Driver! And mark me, there'll be no batting your eyelashes and walking away!'

And what about blackmarket tailoring?

But Rosie knew better than to mention it.

'You can shout at me all you like, but it won't change the fact that I haven't a clue who'd be a mole here.' And that, at least, was true. But she wasn't going to tell him about Hale's letter.

Rosie never knew what Mr Wyngate's next play would be though, because as the words left her lips the door flew open and a furious voice asked, 'What the devil are you doing in my scullery with my driver, Wyngate?'

Rosie nearly fell backwards off the chair in surprise at the sight of Bluff, who had burst in, in shirtsleeves and braces, a dollop of shaving soap still on his chin. Rosie had never thought she'd ever see the major-general in anything less than full uniform.

She nearly called him Bluff, and saved herself just in time.

'Major-General!' Rosie leapt up from the chair with a salute. There was that whipcrack return from Bluff as Wyngate started back in surprise.

'Driver Sinclair, breakfast is being served,' Bluff told her. 'Mr Wyngate, take a seat. You and I shall have a conversation about protocol.'

Wyngate looked entirely wrongfooted for a second, no more, then he answered Bluff with a nod.

'Protocol,' Wyngate repeated, casting a glance at Rosie that seemed full of suspicion. 'Amongst other things.'

Chapter 7

Rosie strode out of the room, but once she was outside in the warm spring air, her resolve failed her. She leaned back against the wisteria-shrouded wall, her legs unable to hold her up any longer. She reached for her handkerchief and pressed it to her face, her sobs silent until she couldn't hold her desolation and fear back any longer.

The Park's morning sounds of birdsong and distant voices became inaudible to her, lost behind her keening as she cried. All she could see in her mind's eye was Hale's kind face, frozen in time like a photograph, and fading, fading as she tried to hold onto it. Wyngate's cold smile began to appear, disembodied like the Cheshire Cat's, encroaching, the rest of his face rapidly taking over until the man from the ministry replaced Hale entirely.

How dare he say those horrible things? And Professor Hale not even in his grave.

Rosie wanted to help Bluff, she wanted more than anything to catch the mole and find Hale's killer. But how many people thought that she and Hale had been carrying on? What would they make of her despair?

Oh, look, there's Rosie, weeping over her lost love!

But then love affairs were never very secret for long at Cottisbourne Park, where everyone lived and worked so closely together. She was hardly the only person who had shed tears over Hale's death.

Surely no one else would think she and Hale had ... Rosie couldn't give the horrible thought any further space in her mind. She turned her face to the wall as her sobs wracked her, the sweet smell of the wisteria oddly out of place in a world blemished by so much evil.

A small hand fastened around Rosie's and she heard Nancy say softly, 'Don't cry, Rosie.'

Rosie looked down and saw the little girl from the petrol station. Despite her tears, Rosie smiled at her. The world wasn't entirely without light.

'Thank you, Nancy. You know, something very sad has happened. A friend of mine ...' Rosie considered her words for a moment. 'A friend of mine has passed away.'

'I know,' Nancy whispered. 'It's all over the village.'

Rosie stared in surprise. 'How do they ...? What have people said?' Maybe this would be useful to know, and a very handy way to discover it. Bluff couldn't exactly march into the village and question people in the queue for the butcher's shop.

'Nana says you can't keep nothing secret round here.' She blinked up at Rosie, her eyes red from crying. 'You and me'll find out what happened, Rosie. We'll get the bugger!'

Rosie ruffled the top of Nancy's head. She hadn't realised that Nancy would've felt touched by Hale's death. But then Nancy had heard Rosie talk about Hale and had met him on a few occasions when Rosie had needed to fill up the tank while driving him. Hale had been so friendly and avuncular, so kind, that inevitably his death would leave a hole in Nancy's life.

And besides, Nancy clearly didn't think Hale was murdered either.

'We will,' Rosie said, determined. 'We *will*, Nancy.'

'And we'll get that old French motor back on the road

for him.' Nancy sniffed deeply and blinked again. 'What was your brass like yesterday? Is he the boss now?'

'He's a nice chap.' Rosie thought of the major-general bursting in on Wyngate and couldn't help but smile. He cared, and that was something she didn't always see in the people in uniforms who came to Cottisbourne Park. 'He was an old friend of the professor. And soon, maybe we can all go for a ride in the Citroën. Would you like that, Nance?'

The little girl nodded, a smile pushing its way through her wobbly lips.

'Do you think he'll kick me off the base?' Nancy gave Rosie a playful nudge. 'I'll always find a way back in. Lucky my name's not Adolf!'

'As long as you don't go into any of the sheds where people are working,' Rosie told her, just as she had done before. 'I don't know what Blu— the major-general would say.' Rosie glanced back towards the door, wondering if Bluff would appear while Nancy was there.

'That snotty Professor Swann don't like it,' she replied. 'He always chases me off. I was having a look at the Citroën the other day and he comes thundering in and tells me to hop it. If I was back home, my dad'd give him what for!'

Rosie frowned. Not only because Charles had elbowed out Nancy, but because that was now twice he'd been in the barn. What business did he have there? Once when Nancy was there looking at the car, and again just after Hale had been shot.

Rosie crouched down and took both of Nancy's hands. She lowered her voice. 'Nancy, promise me, if you see Professor Swann, hide. I'm not sure he's a very nice person.'

Nancy was silent for a moment, as though letting the warning sink in. When she spoke again, her voice was a knowing whisper.

'I'll keep out of his way,' she assured Rosie. 'Even when I'm hunting for ghosts.'

Hunting for ghosts.

Rosie wondered if Professor Hale would now be added to their number.

'That's it, Nancy. Even then!'

'Least his sister's all right,' Nancy decided, nodding across towards the house, where three figures were emerging. 'She don't walk round with her nose in the air.'

'Caroline's lovely. Oh, and there she is,' Rosie realised as the figures came nearer. She noticed Hale's secretary, Jean, accompanying her, along with Sarah. 'And Miss Fenning and Dr Woods.'

Caroline waved a greeting towards them, then wrapped her cardigan around her body and quickened her pace. She really couldn't be more different from her elder brother, who wore his *son of a cabinet minister* credentials on his face. Charles Swann knew his value to the war effort and applied it to the rest of the world, from the Cambridge college he lorded it over to his section at Cottisbourne Park. Professor Swann might once have been as charming as he was handsome, but years at the top of the tree had robbed him of the need to charm anyone. Now he stuck his chin into the air and strutted around the park like a king at his court. If anyone would be promoted to the empty seat Professor Hale's death had created, it was the uncrowned emperor of Cottisbourne Park.

And wouldn't that make him the prime suspect as Professor Hale's assassin?

Rosie tried to suppress the shiver that ran through her. She got back to her feet and waved to the women.

'Morning, you three,' Rosie called.

'And our favourite little secret agent!' Caroline beamed.

44

'Just getting some fresh air before I'm shut into a shed with three chain smokers for the next eight hours. My dream job!'

Jean grimaced. 'Not my idea of fun at all!' She stroked Rosie's arm. Dark circles ringed her eyes and Rosie suspected Jean had been too upset by what had happened to get much sleep either. 'How are you, Rosie? It's so hard to get my head round. That's he's ...' Her glance darted to Nancy and she whispered, '...gone.'

'I know. Doesn't seem real, somehow,' Rosie replied.

'And the major-general looks a little more fierce than Prof Hale,' Sarah confided. 'We're not *really* military. He can't understand what we do here, can he?'

'He's not been shipped out here to milk cows,' Nancy said. 'Something was already going on if you ask me!'

'It'll certainly be different working for a major-general instead of a professor,' Jean remarked, with a rather surprised glance at Nancy. Had Hale not mentioned his suspicions to Jean, then?

'He's very nice,' Rosie assured them. 'He'll make sure we're all shipshape!'

But Caroline looked uncertain. Her face was pale when she whispered, 'Charles won't like that at all. He's certainly the most accomplished man here. I'd be surprised if he isn't promoted to director.'

All it would take was a word from Mr Swann senior in Winston Churchill's ear, presumably, and Professor Swann would finally rule the roost.

Rosie wondered what it was like to have the sort of background that allowed money and position to pour into your lap. And to expect it, as well, as Charles seemed to. Thank goodness Caroline didn't share her brother's entitled arrogance.

Jean nodded, but there was something uncertain in her

expression. Rosie wouldn't have been at all surprised if she didn't like Caroline's brother very much either, and didn't relish the thought of being at his beck and call.

'He *is* very good at his work,' Jean remarked after a pause. 'Stands to reason he could well replace Professor Hale.'

'Daddy would definitely want that,' Caroline told them. 'I don't suppose you could get a safer chief for the Park than the son of the Minister of State.'

But he was covered in Hale's blood.

Rosie closed her eyes for a moment, trying to push the image away. Maybe he'd tried to revive Hale when he found him. The blood she'd seen didn't have to be incriminating.

'Oh, no, you couldn't find a safer pair of hands,' Sarah agreed.

Rosie glanced at Nancy, hoping she wouldn't announce what had happened in the barn when Charles had found her in there. But Nancy was a clever old stick, she wouldn't say anything about Charles in front of his sister.

'I'm sure we'll find out who's replacing Professor Hale soon,' Rosie said. 'I doubt the major-general will disturb the work here too much in the meantime.'

'I just don't know if this is a place for soldiers,' Caroline sighed. 'But we'll have to wait and see, won't we?'

'I'm sure he understands.' Rosie smiled gently. 'I doubt he'll have us marching up and down at seven in the morning, bellowing and carrying on!'

Sarah laughed. 'I'd like to see him try!'

Rosie looked at her watch. 'Do you think they'll give me some breakfast if I go now?'

'The porridge is a bit suspect this morning,' Caroline warned. 'But at least that means there'll be plenty left!'

'As long as it's food, I'll eat *anything* right now,' Rosie said. 'I'll see you all soon. Take care, won't you?'

'And you,' Jean replied. Nancy shot Rosie her customary salute.

'See you later, Driver,' she said before she dashed off towards the trees that bordered the park. How different her life was here to London, but she certainly brought something of the city to Cottisbourne Park.

'There goes the Artful Dodger,' Jean remarked.

'She's harmless,' Rosie assured her. 'She'll always find a hole in the fence.'

'Right, the bombe awaits.' Caroline stuck her hands in the pockets of her cardigan. 'And so do the chainsmokers. I'll see you all at lunch.' With that she and Sarah strolled away in the direction of the huts and the clack-clacking machines that soundtracked their day.

Jean patted Rosie's arm again. 'Letters to type, phone calls to make. I'll see you later.' Then she went back into the house, leaving Rosie to go to the canteen.

Caroline was right, the porridge wasn't all that appetising, but it filled a hole. Rosie glanced at the handful of staff sitting at the other tables in the canteen, who were finishing their breakfasts. Dr Brett was there, his toast going cold as he read his book, apparently oblivious to the room around him. Rosie received a few sympathetic smiles and nods, before one by one they left, though Dr Brett never looked up from his book even as he strolled from the room. She was alone with her last spoonful of porridge and the dregs of her tea.

Around her, the canteen ladies began to clear away what was left of breakfast. Soon they would be preparing for the morning tea break, but from their hushed whispers Rosie knew what they were discussing. Everyone would be discussing it, and why wouldn't they? For the work they did, life here in this oddly academic outpost of Sussex was quiet, serene almost. It wasn't every day that the Director of Cottisbourne Park was killed.

She dreaded to think what rumours might take flight, and heard again Wyngate's insinuations. But only an outsider to the Park would say something like that, she was sure.

Professor Hale had been murdered, and someone at the Park had done it. Nancy might come and go as she pleased, but an adult couldn't do the same without someone noticing.

There was something about the approaching heavy tread in the hallway outside that identified it immediately as Major-General Sir Kingsley-Flynn. Perhaps it was the brisk one-two of his footsteps, but Rosie knew a second before the door opened that Bluff was on his way. There were no shirt sleeves and shaving cream now, but an immaculately-pressed uniform that was a world away from Professor Hale's corduroy and tweed. And he'd missed breakfast.

What a welcome to Cottisbourne Park.

Rosie swallowed the last of her porridge and dabbed her lips in readiness.

'Driver Sinclair.' Bluff strode over to Rosie's table, his expression dark. 'We've discussed protocol once, are we to discuss it again so soon?'

Rosie knew what this meant. It was time for her to play a role again.

'It... it would appear so,' she replied hesitantly. 'I'm sorry, sir.'

The clattering of pots and pans grew noticeably quieter, but Bluff gave no indication that he'd noticed as he boomed, 'Salute your senior officer, Driver Sinclair!'

Rosie shot up from her chair and saluted. 'Major-General Kingsley-Flynn, good morning, sir.'

Bluff returned it and told her, 'My office, Driver!' He

turned on the heel of one polished shoe and strode away with a command of, 'At the double!'

'Yes, sir!' Rosie pushed her chair under the table before hurrying from the canteen.

Bessie, one of the canteen staff, caught Rosie's eye as she left the room and shrugged her shoulders. She clearly didn't have time for brusque military gentlemen and their strict protocols. Though Rosie was already beginning to suspect that there was rather more to Bluff than his by-the-numbers military bearing might suggest, this was a part that she had to play. She followed in his wake along the corridors of Cottisbourne Park towards the office that had been Professor Hale's, watched by former residents who peered down from their canvases over their ruffs or from beneath their powdered hair. They'd likely never seen anything quite like it.

And neither had Rosie.

She might've appeared in productions with actors playing high ranking officers, but meeting someone like Bluff in the flesh was really quite something.

They arrived at the door of what had once been Hale's office. The sound of Jean's typewriter clattering away echoed along the corridor. She looked up from her work with a start as Bluff opened the door and crossed her office towards that which was now his.

'We're not to be disturbed, Miss Fenning,' he told Jean as he passed her desk. Then he opened his office door and Rosie caught sight of Wyngate waiting inside, his eyes on them as they approached.

Rosie's heart sank.

Oh, not him again!

'Mr Wyngate ...' Rosie nodded. 'Good morning.'

He took off his hat as Bluff closed the door behind them and replied, 'Good morning, Driver Sinclair.'

Rosie tried to find something in her MTC training that would inform how she should behave in this situation. But nothing came to mind, because the etiquette of how to behave after an interrogation had never come up. She spotted a chair, one that Hale had happily let her occupy, but she knew she shouldn't assume that such niceties from Hale's tenure would continue. At least, not while Wyngate was in the room.

'Seems so odd without Professor Hale here,' Rosie remarked. She noticed that the silver-framed photograph on his desk had already disappeared, tidied away by Jean, Rosie suspected.

'I can well imagine,' Bluff told her, his tone notably less brisk now he was out of the earshot of their colleagues. 'Sit down, Driver Sinclair. Mr Wyngate, have a seat.'

Rosie took the chair that Professor Hale had always gestured to her to take, a comfortable, upholstered wooden chair that Rosie had joked was her throne. She wanted to make the same joke now, but wouldn't in front of Wyngate. The man from the ministry sat on the second chair, considerably less aggressive now they were no longer in that grim little scullery.

Bluff took off his cap and threw it onto the green leather surface that covered his oak desk, where it landed beside a sheaf of paper. Then he knitted his hands behind his back and said, 'I hope you'll forgive the theatricality, Driver Sinclair, but it *is* necessary.'

'I understand,' Rosie said. 'And I don't mind, really. It's nice to have a crack at acting again, even if it's not on a stage.'

'Before we continue, I'm afraid I'll have to ask you to read and sign a document.' Bluff pushed the sheaf of paper towards Rosie across the desktop. 'I know you've already signed the Official Secrets Act, but this is addendum to that.'

'The Official Secrets Act becomes a little muddy when the secrets don't officially exist,' Wyngate explained, with the barest hint of a smile. 'This is the unofficial official addendum.'

Rosie began to slowly flip through the typed pages. Bluff had told her there would need to be signatures before he could tell her anything else, and her stomach turned somersaults as she was now on the edge of a precipice.

Bluff settled into the huge leather chair that had seemed to dwarf Professor Hale. It didn't quite have the same effect on the major-general.

'Take your time to read it,' he replied. 'I'm afraid there aren't any punchlines.'

The document's gist was that Rosie was to be party to things that she wasn't to breathe to another living soul until her dying day. And even then, Rosie expected there to be a clause that should she mention anything once she'd passed through the pearly gates, the men from the ministry would still come and find her.

She reached the last page where a dotted line awaited her, and she paused for a moment before she signed, frozen by the enormity of what she had become entangled in. She looked up at Bluff, sitting in Hale's chair, and she thought of the pain he must feel at losing his old friend. She had no option but to sign, and add her efforts to Bluff's and find Hale's killer.

Rosie flourished her signature along the dotted line and dated it. She had come a long way from signing autograph books at the stage door.

She laid down the pen. 'There we are. Signed.'

Wyngate left his seat, the wooden chair creaking as he

stood. He leaned over the desk and picked up the pen then added a scribble next to Rosie's signature. She couldn't make out what the initialled signature said, but she was certain it wasn't a *W.* Perhaps Mr Wyngate was only Mr Wyngate to certain people.

'That's the paperwork completed.' He rolled the papers into a cylinder and returned to his seat. 'I'll let the major-general fill you in. You're under his direct command now.'

Rosie nodded. *Under his command?* She felt rather guilty admitting it to herself, but it was exciting. Horrible as it was to lose her friend, the thought of being trusted and allowed into the inner circle was something she had never expected. A driver in the MTC, under the command of a major-general. And no one outside this room would ever know.

'I'm sure you already know that Cottisbourne Park is in the business of listening. Decoding,' Bluff told her in a low voice, as though Jean might have her ear pressed up to the door. 'But it's also in the business of encoding, which you might be rather less aware of. The Park houses our brightest people. Each one handpicked for the job.'

Rosie decided to be honest with Bluff, seeing as she was being entrusted with so much.

'I must admit, I did know about the decoding,' she said. 'Not that anyone told me in so many words. But the encoding? I hadn't known that. Although it makes sense.'

'Professor Hale handpicked the encoding team himself,' he went on. 'And he had certain other roles that I suspect you may not have been aware of. He and Mr Wyngate are long-time associates.'

Rosie glanced at Wyngate – or whatever his name was – from the corner of her eye.

'A great deal goes on here,' Rosie said. 'I imagine I might know some of the encoding team and not have a clue!'

'Professor Hale was always on the lookout for people to join my teams,' Wyngate told her. 'When I said your name had come across my desk a handful of times, that was true. The professor was of the opinion that you have the makings of an undercover operative and recommended you to me.'

'And to me,' Bluff added. 'I'm in the business of keeping moles out of our gardens and the prof was sure you had the same skills. When he invited me to Cottisbourne, you were the only person here that he believed he could trust without question.'

Rosie looked over to the door to Jean's office. Couldn't he trust his own secretary?

'He never breathed a word of that to me. I'm very surprised by all this, I must admit. But if you decide that I can do it, then I won't let you down, I promise.'

Bluff knitted his fingers atop the desk blotter. 'I've been tracking a particular mole, *Prospero*, for nearly two years. We've finally isolated him to Cottisbourne Park and we were closing in, but Professor Hale suspected that Prospero was onto him. That's why he asked me to come down.'

Prospero.

Rosie recalled the Cavendish Players' performance of *The Tempest*. She had played Miranda and her father had taken the role of Shakespeare's iconic magician. He had put his heart and soul into every performance, electric as he swooped across the stage in his shimmering velvet cloak.

How dare the mole call themselves Prospero!

'You've been tracking them for two years?' Rosie said, surprised. 'Has someone managed to trace Prospero's signal to Cottisbourne Park?'

'No.' Bluff shook his head. 'It's been a very slow and delicate operation to get here. Prospero changes his frequency constantly and broadcasts in short bursts, sometimes nightly, but sometimes a week or more can pass and he won't send more than a few seconds worth of morse. Our listening stations can't home in on his location and that was one more way we knew he had to be in our business.'

'Did Professor Hale leave any clue as to who this Prospero character might be?' Rosie asked.

'No, and the mole's led us a merry dance,' he replied. 'Every time our people crack a code, the Germans somehow know about it and change to another, leaving us chasing them. If that weren't bad enough, Prospero has shared our own highly classified information with the Axis powers too. That helped us tighten the net – precious few operatives have been on the codebreaking and encoding team – but it means that he's cost some very good people their lives.'

Bluff's gaze dropped down to his knitted hands for a split second, no more, but that second was enough for Rosie to realise that this was personal for him. Had he lost other friends because of this so-called Prospero, not just Professor Hale?

'I see.' Rosie wished she could reach across the desk and touch his hand to offer him some comfort and sympathy. But Wyngate was there, and besides, maybe Bluff had his own way of coping with his loss. With a heavy heart, dreading the names she might see on it, Rosie asked, 'Do you have a list of suspects?'

'We do.' Bluff nodded. 'As far as the park will know, Professor Hale took his own life and you've all been saddled with a by-the-book Colonel Blimp until his permanent successor can be selected. In fact, I'm going to be looking to weed the garden, if you will. Rosie, I need you to keep an ear to the ground. If you see or hear *anything*, no matter how small, I want to know. It goes without saying that this is very dangerous work, but the risks to you are minimal.'

Rosie nodded. 'I understand. We're dealing with someone who's armed, for one thing. And desperate not to be caught.'

They'd be hanged for treason, Rosie knew. Motive enough to kill Hale in order to avoid the noose.

'It's imperative that Prospero thinks we've fallen for his ruse,' Wyngate told her. 'And it was imperative that my department knew what you were made of before we agreed to the major-general's request to bring you on board. I like to think that I'm usually more of a gent than I was this morning.'

Albeit a gent with black market clothing coupons.

'I should hope so.' Rosie quirked her eyebrow at him. 'And you never did get me a cup of tea. I know, I know, you had to be sure. I'm glad you realised that I can be trusted.' She turned back to Bluff. 'So ... who's on this list?'

This time the piece of paper came from Wyngate himself, slipped from the inner pocket of his sharply cut suit. Without a word, he placed the single sheet on the desk in front of Rosie.

Rosie closed her eyes, trying to delay the moment. She swallowed and picked up the list.

And just as she feared, she knew every name on it.

Dr James Brett.

Professor Nicholas Jones.

Sidney Chandler.

Dr Douglas Stuart.

Joseph Fleet.

And the last of the six:

Professor Charles Swann.

Rosie took in a sharp breath and put the list down.

'I know them. I can't think of any reason to suspect any of them, except ...'

Bluff nodded her on as he said carefully, 'Except?'

'Professor Swann.' Rosie looked up at Bluff, wondering what he'd think. 'Everyone thinks he's a shoo-in to replace Professor Hale. And ... he was covered in blood! He found Professor Hale, but what if the reason he was covered in his blood was because *he* killed him?'

'Professor Swann's father is Minister of State at the War Office.' Wyngate sounded almost incredulous, as though he couldn't imagine such a thing. 'His sister works here, Driver Sinclair. He found Professor Hale's body yesterday, that's how he came to be bloodied.'

'Nevertheless. He *is* one of only half a dozen people who have had the access that we *know* Prospero used to his advantage. Each of them could be our man, and each of them would be a possible candidate to take the professor's place if something happened to him.' Bluff settled back in his chair, his head cocked to one side. 'Give me your thoughts on each of those men, Driver Sinclair. You know them better than we do.'

'Well ...' Rosie picked up the list again. She hated the thought that one of these men was a mole and a murderer. But justice had to be served. 'Starting at the top ... Dr Brett's a quiet sort. Reads a lot. Often sits outside at lunchtime, even in the winter, all wrapped up. I've seen him looking at snowflakes with a magnifying glass. Professor Jones, he's in the chess club. To be honest, I think chess is his one passion in life. He keeps himself to himself. Sid ... sorry, Mr Chandler. Friendly chap. Helped with the set painting for the panto, changed the sets between scenes. Very chatty. I can't imagine he'd ... I just can't. Dr Stuart likes to play the piano. You can hear him in the rec room sometimes, and everyone dances! He's ever so good. Got a girlfriend in one of the other huts called Gladys Barker. Mr Fleet ... likes crossword puzzles, and he's talked to me about cars sometimes. Bit of a motor-racing fanatic by all accounts. Then ... then there's Professor Swann.'

Rosie turned to look at Wyngate. How would he react to what Rosie had to say about *him*?

'The minister's son.' He reminded her. 'His grandfather, *Lord* Swann, sits in the Upper House, Driver Sinc—'

Bluff silenced Wyngate's complaints with a sharp look. He shook his head and told them both, 'Nobody's lineage means they're free of suspicion. Give us your thoughts, Driver.'

'I'm very good friends with his sister,' Rosie admitted. 'You should know that before I say anything, but I don't think it makes me particularly biased. I have to be honest with you ... I just don't like him. He's very full of himself. The other men on this list, some are more gregarious than others, but to a man, they get on with their work and don't demand accolades. Professor Swann is ... dare I say it, he's one of the most arrogant, self-important people I've ever had the misfortune to meet.'

Bluff smiled. 'I'm afraid to say that Professor Swann isn't alone in the world of codebreaking in having a particularly healthy opinion of his own abilities.'

'That doesn't surprise me somehow.' Rosie put the list down on Hale's ... Bluff's desk and smoothed out the creases in the paper. 'So ... what do we do?'

'I have to get back to London.' Wyngate cast a glance at his wristwatch. 'I'll leave this in your capable hands, Major-General. Driver Sinclair, you're simply here to inform, not to involve yourself.'

'Mr Wyngate, I believe you're exceeding your portfolio,' was Bluff's polite but firm rebuttal. He rose to his feet and held out his hand to Wyngate. 'It's been as much of a pleasure as always.'

Don't involve yourself.

Did he suspect she would?

'Don't worry, I'll do as Major-General Kingsley-Flynn asks,' Rosie replied.

If Bluff wanted her to involve herself, then it had nothing to do with Wyngate. To her surprise, once he had shaken Bluff's hand, Wyngate turned and offered his hand to her too. Rosie hadn't expected that.

'Prospero won't know what's hit him,' he told her. 'I wish you both the best of British.'

'Thank you, sir!' Rosie beamed at him as she took his hand. 'You can count on me! Watch out, Prospero, your days are numbered!'

And with a last nod of acknowledgement for Bluff, Wyngate took his leave. Perhaps he was about to take another name and scream at another driver too. It was certainly an unusual way to earn a living.

Once the door closed behind him, Rosie turned her attention to the list again. She saw the men named on it pass before her eyes as if they were on a carousel. 'They hang traitors, don't they?'

'In my experience,' Bluff admitted. 'If the traitor doesn't save them the trouble.'

'It's just … these men. I can't imagine them doing this. Killing Professor Hale. Selling secrets.' Rosie bit her lip, then asked Bluff, 'Can you tell? When you meet a mole, do you know, deep down inside? By instinct?'

He nodded, his expression grave. 'Sometimes. I hadn't seen my career going in this direction, Driver Sinclair, yet it appears I have a talent for it. *Gardening* as Mr Wyngate and his colleagues would say.' Bluff sighed and picked up his cap, examining the ornate trim on the peak. 'Prospero has cost me some friends. And I intend to flush him out.'

'Why do they do it?' Rosie stared at the paper again

until the names on the list began to dance and spin, the letters coming loose and rearranging themselves in endless, nonsensical, garbled strings.

'They all claim to have their reasons. The important thing is that we don't jump to any conclusions,' Bluff replied. He took out his pipe and a small leather tobacco wallet. As he spoke, he began to pack the bowl. 'And that we get to the bottom of this quickly. I don't know this place at all, but you do. As far as the team here know, you're saddled with a curmudgeon of a military chap who knows nothing about codes, let alone moles. But the tide of the war could rest on this. The information coming in and out of Cottisbourne is absolutely vital.'

'Golly.' Rosie fidgeted in her seat. *Can I do this? Am I good enough?* 'All right, I'll help you. Whatever you need to know, whatever you want to find out, I'-ll find a way to the truth. Whoever's doing this, however it might seem on the outside, however it might pain me to think it – they're a bad'un, and we have to stop them.'

'First things first. Let's see how our boffins take to being told they're under military command for a little while.' Bluff lit the pipe then set his cap dead straight on his head and offered her a little smile. 'What do you think, Driver Sinclair? Stern and patrician enough?'

'Oh, very much so!' Rosie nodded. 'You're ever so good at this! I do think your being here has rather put the cat among the pigeons. People here don't like being under the thumb of the military. It *is* rather scholarly and quiet, and I don't think half of them ever iron their clothes, and most of the time go about trailing their shoelaces because they're off in another world. I rather think they assume you'll demand they polish their boots and that you'll drill them on the driveway before breakfast. You know, I once saw some poor chap walk to his shed, and his shoe was squeaking, and someone banged open a window and shouted at him to keep the noise down!'

Bluff laughed, but assured her, 'I won't have everyone up at six for drill. But it won't do our mole any harm to wonder if I will. Prospero appears to be rather confident of his own intelligence, and that sort can often underestimate everyone else.' He dropped his voice to a whisper to confide, 'They have a special lack of respect for those of us who wear uniform. It won't do any harm for him to think I'm of the opinion that things have got very shoddy indeed around these parts.' With that he smiled and added sternly, 'Cottisbourne Park needs bringing into line, Driver.'

Rosie saluted him. 'Very much so, sir. I'm glad you're here to whip everyone into shape! What a shabby old show!'

'And who knows where the future may take you?' He returned her salute. 'Perhaps you'll become a gardener too. The prof certainly thought you had the talent for it.'

And she had never even guessed that Hale might be involved in anything beyond the world of Cottisbourne Park. Yet he had seen something in her that made her trustworthy, not to mention a possible candidate for life in the world of men like Mr Wyngate. Rosie had been his driver and his friend, but she had no idea that he'd been involved in espionage in any sense. Which probably meant he was very good at it indeed.

And somewhere in Cottisbourne Park, the man who had murdered Hale and sold out the country was wondering if he was about to be found out.

Six names, six men.

'I can't say I ever thought I'd end up doing something like this,' Rosie admitted. 'But then again, I never thought I'd become a driver, either. The war's changed a lot of things, hasn't it?'

'Everything,' Bluff replied. There was a note of wistfulness in it, but she could hardly blame him. It was a wonder he could trust anybody at all. A moment passed, then Bluff gave a decisive nod. 'Right. Let's tell the boffins that I'm the boss. Then we'll wait for the storm.'

Chapter 8

Rosie spent most of the day in what was Hale's office, going through the personnel files of the six suspects. As they worked, Rosie thought of other people at the Park who the six were connected with, and she and Bluff looked through their files too.

In Dr Brett's file, Rosie found a letter to Professor Hale complaining about the quality of his blankets, with a carbon copy of the professor's apologetic reply. Dr Stuart's file contained a letter to Hale saying that he was planning to create a cipher based on the musical scale, and an idea for passing messages into occupied territory by using encrypted sheet music.

There wasn't anything else of note, and Rosie wondered if spycatching was as exciting as it had first sounded. But as she watched Bluff work, she saw his undimming determination, like a bloodhound after a scent.

That evening, Rosie led Bluff to the far end of the ball-room, the scene of several dances since Rosie had arrived. Its chandeliers were swathed in cobwebbed blankets, looking for all the world like gigantic insect nests suspended from the ceiling. The room had elegant plaster mouldings on the walls of dancing figures in classical drapery, but they were burdened with several layers of dust, and the long French windows were criss-crossed with tape. A dais stood at the end which would offer Bluff a commanding view of everyone in the room – and they a view of him from the rows of chairs that Jean had set out that afternoon.

Footsteps echoed in the corridor, and Rosie glanced at Bluff.

'Here they come,' she whispered.

'Take a seat, Driver Sinclair,' he told her sternly, no doubt just in case anyone was within earshot. 'This won't take long.'

Rosie took a chair and positioned it in a corner near the front. She sat down and watched as some of the finest minds in Britain came into the room, some shambling along, cleaning their glasses on their shirts, others striding confidently. One of the women had brought her knitting, which was poking out of the pocket on her skirt.

Rosie allowed her gaze to roam, but she had spotted five of the six suspects on the list come in and they now all sat in different parts of the room. Dr Stuart anxiously tapped his toe, while Professor Jones daydreamed out of the window at the rose garden and the vegetable patches beyond. Sid was chatting with a group of men, while Dr Brett hadn't bothered to take a seat and was instead brushing the dust from one of the mouldings with his handkerchief. Joseph Fleet was sitting in the row behind Caroline, leaning against the back of her chair as they chatted.

When Charles Swann strolled into the ballroom, his head was bowed in deep conversation with Bartosz Zalewski. She remembered again the blood on Charles' hands and the rust shades as it dried on what had been an immaculate shirt. As they crossed the threshold the two men parted. Bartosz weaved his way through the chairs to join his colleagues from hut seventeen, whilst Charles took his time to go along the rows, exchanging handshakes like a star meeting his public. He eventually came to the front row and the members of his own team. Hut two was the most vital team on the base, Rosie knew, even if she didn't know why. And Charles Swann was the most vital man on the hut two team.

Rosie nodded to Bluff and whispered, 'I think that's everyone who can be spared for now, sir. Ready when you are.'

With a curt nod, Bluff cleared his throat. The noise died down, but the chatter didn't stop until he barked in a voice that seemed loud enough to rattle the windows, 'Let's have some order, Cottisbourne Park!'

Some of them quietened at once, whereas others responded like sulky schoolchildren and huffed and folded their arms. Sarah giggled behind her hand. Dr Brett sat sideways in his chair, staring at Bluff from the corner of his eye. Professor Jones had nearly leapt out of his skin, roused from his dream of who-knew-what. Dr Stuart anxiously ran his hand through his hair and it stood up on end until he started to slick it down. Sid was one of the last to stop talking and rolled his eyes as he sagged against his seat, muttering something to Joseph. Charles, however, continued to chat in that plummy drawl of his.

'...been in a bloody asylum. What if he'd shot one of us instead?'

Rosie couldn't help it. She snapped her head round to look at him, but then so did several other people.

'Goodness me ...' Sarah muttered under her breath.

Someone else loudly cleared their throat and the legs of more than one chair scraped against the floor. Charles didn't even pretend to care. He folded his arms and set his bright blue gaze on Bluff, not a trace of respect in his expression. That swaggering, ironclad confidence would make a man think he could get away with anything.

'I know you're all very busy, so I'll keep this as brief as possible,' Bluff told his audience. 'First things first. There

64

will be a memorial service for our friend, the late Professor Hale, at the village church on Sunday morning. Everyone at Cottisbourne Park is welcome to attend.'

A murmur whispered through the room, and several people nodded sadly. Jean, sitting near the back, took her handkerchief from her sleeve and dabbed at the corner of her eyes. The suspects' expressions, their gazes fixed on Bluff, didn't change.

'The War Office will name Professor Hale's successor in good time,' Bluff went on. Rosie stole a glance at Charles, recognising the slight hint of a smile that played on his lips. He believed that job was as good as his already. 'And I'll be standing in as acting Director until they do.'

Rosie hadn't heard such an impressive gasp ring through an audience since the Cavendish Players had staged *A Doll's House* and Rosie, as Nora, had swept away, walking out on her husband and children. She noticed a lot of unimpressed head-shaking, and a couple of hands were tentatively raised before disappearing again.

Turmoil ran through Charles' team from hut two. They had evidently assumed that Charles would replace Professor Hale, but even if Bluff hadn't been temporarily heading up Cottisbourne Park, any of the other five suspects could have stepped in. Charles was merely the only one who was willing to publicly stake his claim.

'What?' one of them snapped, and another declared in a growl, 'I should bloody cocoa!'

'That's outrageous!' Charles exclaimed. 'What qualifications could a Bally *soldier* have to run Cottisbourne Park? I speak five languages. I can strip and build a bombe with one hand tied behind my back. *I* am leading the team on the Endeavour code. How dare you?'

A murmur began to run through the crowd again, building

and building until it turned into a mass of irate voices. Was Charles going to stage a mutiny?

'We're not part of the military!' a man called. 'Shame on you, taking over this *civilian* operation!'

'Hear, hear!' someone else shouted. Rosie's gaze darted across the room. The other five suspects looked just as annoyed as everyone else at that moment. In fact, the only person who looked entirely calm was Major-General Kingsley-Flynn.

'The suspicion in Whitehall is that the boffins of Cottisbourne Park have become rather ill-governed over these past few months,' he told them sternly. 'A touch of military discipline will do this place no harm whatsoever. I don't speak five languages, Professor Swann, but with a bark like mine, I don't need to.'

Rosie looked across the restless audience and spotted a hand raised. Dr Brett's, no less.

'Sir?' Bluff pointed towards him. 'Your name?'

'My name, Major-General, is Dr Brett,' he replied in his precise manner. 'And I should like to say a few words.' Dr Brett got to his feet. He was still holding the handkerchief he'd been using to dust the mouldings on the wall, and only now put it away in his pocket. 'I'd like to begin by saying how very saddened I have been by the death of Professor Hale. And I should like to say, also, that you, Major-General, are quite right. This place *has* become rather shabby. Not old Hale's fault, I hasten to add. I don't know why he did what he did, but I do think the Park could do with a firm hand, Major-General, and it strikes me that you're just the chap for the job.'

'Typical Oxford nonsense,' Charles scoffed. 'They always did lie down under the cosh.'

But Bluff gave a nod of thanks and said, 'Thank you, Dr

Brett. It hasn't escaped my attention that the Park is home to some rather forceful personalities, but we all share the same goal.'

'Jolly good!' Dr Brett said and took his seat, with a glare aimed at the back of Charles Swann's head. The woman sitting next to Brett demonstrated whose side she was on by turning her back on him. He had clearly aired an unpopular opinion.

Another hand was raised, a woman sitting near the front. Rosie knew Valerie, as she had been a keen instigator in the tomato-growing contest.

'Madam?' Bluff asked. Charles looked over his shoulder to see who was waiting to speak, his face white with unvented fury.

'Miss Valerie Fieldgate,' she said, shooting to her feet. Her fists were balled deep in her cardigan pockets. 'Professor Swann is quite right. This isn't a military outpost – this is Cottisbourne Park. We have very fine minds here, *very fine indeed!*'

Rosie tried not to wince at Valerie's impassioned emphasis.

'And very fine minds cannot survive under the stifling boot of military rule!' Valerie went on. 'We will not have it. We will not march about, we will not be drilled, and we will *not* wear uniforms!'

She shot Rosie a venomous glance, and Rosie was shocked. She'd got on perfectly well with Valerie before, and had no idea she felt so strongly against her uniform.

'Nor do I ask you to, Miss Fieldgate,' Bluff explained. 'But if you *were* in my troop, you'd know better than to address a major-general with your hands in your pockets.'

Valerie's fists headed further down inside her cardigan as she replied, chin held imperiously aloft, 'I should rather we had one of our own at the helm, not a Sandhurst bully!'

Then she sat down, and flashed a smile at the men of hut two. Rosie was sure they'd laugh about her as soon as they were back in their lair. Charles gave her a nod of thanks, then said, 'Hear hear, Miss Fieldgate.'

'Alas, Miss Fieldgate, a *Sandhurst bully*, as you so ably put it, is apparently what you have.' But there was nothing bullying about Bluff, Rosie could already see that. 'Any further questions?'

'Thinks he's bloody Churchill...' a man whispered loudly, but Rosie didn't spot who'd said it.

No one else raised their hand. If Dr Brett had not spoken for them already, then Valerie certainly had. Bluff had just opened his mouth to speak when one elegant hand was raised, a gold signet ring catching the afternoon sunlight.

'Professor Swann.' Bluff smiled. Charles needed no introduction, it seemed. 'In English, if you please.'

Everyone's attention turned to Charles. Valerie smiled at him with admiration, nodding eagerly. He rose to his feet like the prime minister approaching the dispatch box, that imperious chin held high.

'My father is Minister of State.' Charles' voice was icy. 'My grandfather sits in the House of Lords. *His* grandfather served in Pitt's ministry. Even my sister – the Sprat – learned all she knows about this business from me. How dare you presume to walk into my world and throw your weight around? It takes brains and ingenuity to do what we do, not boot polish and braid!'

His gang from hut two nodded energetically. Valerie gazed at him in admiration, as Maggie rolled her eyes at her. Around the room, murmurs of assent could be heard. The other suspects nodded too, all except Dr Brett, who appeared to be an outlier when it came to approving Bluff's tenure.

'Professor Swann, I'm perfectly well aware of your

impressive family connections. I can assure you that Mr Churchill speaks of you with a great deal of pride and respect.' Charles cast a regal glance at his followers and across the ballroom, Caroline clasped her hands together with affectionate pride. But she would always be *the Sprat* to her brother. 'You are, however, exceptionally busy with Endeavour and about to get busier still, as you and I will discuss. You'll be too busy winning the war to run Cottisbourne Park, believe me.'

Rosie suppressed her grin.

Touché, Professor Swann!

Bluff's words had affected many other people in the room. *Winning the war,* that was what they were all here to do. Even the mole – although they clearly wanted to win the war for the other side. There was a great deal of nodding now as they had swung round to agree with Bluff.

'Nevertheless, I want my complaints noted,' Charles spat. 'And I want that little bally urchin from the village off the grounds once and for all. She's a threat to national security and Professor Hale might've indulged it, but I won't!'

Nancy.

Rosie hadn't mentioned her to Bluff and she turned and looked up at him.

'Oh, don't be a meanie, Charles!' Maggie scoffed. 'I doubt the Germans are recruiting little English kids!'

'You'd be surprised who Jerry is recruiting,' Charles said as he resumed his seat.

'I'll make enquiries, Professor,' was Bluff's reply. 'From to-morrow, I'll be having meetings with the senior operatives in each hut. In the meantime, you all have my gratitude and that of every man, woman and child in this land. If anyone wishes to speak to me privately, by all means do. Dismissed, Cottisbourne Park!'

The audience noisily rose to their feet, chairs squeaking against the floor as they left. Sid, a pipe between his teeth, stayed behind with Sarah and a couple of other men to help Jean stack the chairs away.

Rosie went up to the dais to speak to Bluff. 'Sir, that went … as well as could be expected, I suppose. I do apologise, people can be so rude. And I suppose you want to know what Professor Swann meant by the *little urchin*?'

Sid and the others had gone and Bluff and Rosie's feet echoed across the wooden floor as they headed for the door.

'There's a little girl in the village called Nancy. An evacuee,' Rosie explained. 'She came down from London to live with her grandparents. They run the petrol station in the village, you see, so I've got to know her over the past few years. She treats Cottisbourne like a playground. She's always rushing about *somewhere* having adventures. I doubt there's any fence you could put up around the Park that would keep her away.'

'It simply won't do,' he barked, striding on alongside her. 'There's far too much coming and going for my liking. Perhaps what we need *are* a few more soldiers to keep things shipshape!'

Rosie remembered that Bluff was being stern on purpose, but maybe he really *did* have a problem with Nancy's frequent appearances at the Park.

'Sir, if I may, I have told her that on no account must she go into the huts, and as far as I'm aware, she never has. They're staffed constantly, so someone would have seen her if she had.' Rosie smiled gently at Bluff. 'And Professor Hale was very fond of her and kept a bag of boiled sweets in the car in case we met her at the petrol station. She's ever so upset about his passing.'

'Boiled sweets?' His voice was filled with horror. They paused at the door to Jean's office. 'My office, Driver Sinclair.

70

At least *you're* in uniform, I might yet have some authority at Cottisbourne Park.'

Bluff threw open the door and stalked into Jean's office. As he passed her desk he told his inherited secretary, 'Kindly go along to the stores, Miss Fenning, and gather suitable supplies for the desk of a major-general. Then telephone Horse Guards and arrange for the delivery of my trunk. If I'm here to stay, I can't do it on three shirts and one tin of boot polish!'

'Of course, sir.' Jean scribbled a note on her pad, then rose from her desk. 'Will there be anything else?'

'Not at present,' he replied. 'But I'm sure I'll think of something.'

Jean hurried away. Once the door was shut behind her and the sound of her footsteps had receded, Rosie headed into what was now Bluff's office.

'I don't suppose you mind me taking this chair?' She gestured towards the one she had sat on earlier. 'I always used to joke to Professor Hale that it was my throne.'

'Please.' He gestured to the chair, then took off his cap and put it on the desk. 'Well, what did you make of that little performance from our boffins? The *Sprat*?'

Rosie sat down with a sigh and removed her cap as well, placing it on the chair where Wyngate had sat earlier. 'Honestly, if I had a brother who called me the Sprat, he'd have got a toe in the rump a long time ago. Caroline's told me she used to have to hide from Swann when she was little just to get away from him. Pinching her, pushing her in the lake...' Rosie shivered. 'You know, it's funny... Dr Brett seems glad you're here, but is he only saying that to throw off suspicion?'

Bluff settled into the chair, his expression thoughtful. 'There's the question... I'm going to talk to each of the senior hut operatives over the next few days. It's a bind, but one can hardly call half a dozen and leave the other napping. Some of it's relying on the old nose, but once in a while someone lets something drop. It's the whiskers, you know, they lend one a useful air of the unimaginative establishment.'

'You do have a very impressive set of moustaches,' Rosie said with a grin. 'I'll keep my ears open in case I do hear anything. I didn't see anything off in the others' behaviour. Sid helping out stacking the chairs is quite normal for him, really. Always ready to lend a hand.'

He nodded, then murmured thoughtfully 'As for Nancy... where was she yesterday when the prof was killed?'

'Gosh, I really have no idea. She was working at the petrol station when I left Cottisbourne first thing, and I didn't see her again until this morning.' Rosie looked at Bluff's cap. The spring evening light made the gold embroidery on the visor glitter. 'She did tell me though that she'd seen Swann at the barn. He shouted at her to go away.'

'If she finds her way onto the park, that might end up being to our advantage,' he mused. Then he bunched his hand into a fist and rapped the knuckles atop the blotter. 'And of course, Driver, should anyone ask, I'm an absolute tartar of a commanding officer, agreed?'

'Oh, you most definitely are,' Rosie assured him. 'The strictest of the strict. And don't worry, if Nancy says anything, I'll let you know. Although it might be hard to separate reality from what she's made up. Her latest game is hunting ghosts!'

'Ghosts?' Bluff gave a rather rueful laugh. 'Driver Sinclair, if there were ghosts to be seen, my childhood home is the place to find them. Sadly, I heard nothing so much as a rattling chain when I was a lad in the middle of Buckinghamshire.

To look at the old place, you'd expect it to be stuffed with ruff-wearing phantoms.'

Rosie tried to picture Bluff's childhood home.

Turrets. Surely it has turrets.

'Well, that's just it,' Rosie said, 'she's convinced herself there's ghosts in the barn.'

'Ah, the barn.' Bluff drew in a deep breath, a veil of sadness settling over his gaze. 'Have you been in there since Professor Hale's death? I saw the car he was so proud of yesterday, when ... you were working on it together?'

'I haven't been back in there. Not yet. Of all the places for him to be killed ...' Rosie attempted a smile. 'You saw the car? What do you think of her?'

'I think she's splendid. Exactly like the car he had when I first met him all those years ago. Will you continue on the renovation?'

'Nancy thinks I should,' Rosie told him. 'And she's right, I should, shouldn't I? For Professor Hale. And for his friends. He'd want me to, wouldn't he? And I do enjoy tinkering about with it.'

'I think he would.' Bluff smiled and added, 'A good deed in a naughty world, as a wiser woman than I said last night.'

'Portia,' Rosie said. 'One of my favourite roles. My role as a driver in the MTC has been fun, but I do miss Shakespeare.'

Was it Rosie's imagination, or did Bluff's eyes light up? 'You're an actress, Ro— Driver Sinclair?'

'Yes! Rosalind Sinclair of the Cavendish Players.' She smiled at him. Had he nearly called her Rosie? 'I've always been on stage. I took my first curtain call when I was an hour old.'

'Well, wayward young Bluff would've been quite starstruck. Do you know, I once ran away from home and spent a quite obscene amount of money on hotels, playhouses and

73

the finest food in the city,' he beamed, his face filled with remembered mischief. 'Tell me, what's your favourite role? You must have one.'

'Was that during your wayward period?' Rosie chuckled. 'Well, I *am* rather fond of Portia. And Rosalind, strangely enough.'

'I was a very adventurous fifteen-year-old, as well as a wayward one. The theatre's been my weakness ever since,' Bluff assured her. 'I saw an exquisite outdoor production of *The Merchant of Venice* in Gloucester just before the war. It was a golden summer evening, the sort of evening when one starts to plan for a life after the army. The sort of evening when anything might be possible.' He leaned forward and dropped his voice to a low murmur to confide, 'And the most exquisite Portia too, though I'm sure your own is at least her equal.'

Rosie was surprised to hear a soldier speak as Bluff sometimes did. He had a gentle soul beneath the uniform.

'They must be very fond of *Merchant* in Gloucester. We performed ours there in thirty-eight!' Rosie felt the glow and pull of Bluff's nostalgia. The world before the war. The world that had gone. Not that it had been perfect by any means, but ... 'It was an outside performance in the grounds of a big house, I remember.'

'And do you know, Driver, as Shylock sharpened his blade, somewhere in the distance the thunder began to rumble.' He shook his head. 'Entirely coincidental, obviously, but what a moment. Not a drop of rain, just that foreboding rumble up in the clouds.'

Rosie replayed the moment in her mind as Bluff spoke as it dawned on her that she and Bluff had met before. Almost. 'That's funny ... the same thing happened in our production! You must've been in our audience. Oh, how splendid!'

74

The most exquisite Portia!

'Antonio with the unfortunate beard?' he asked. But what *wouldn't* be unfortunate next to his military moustache?

'Yes, that awful beard!' Rosie laughed. Then she smiled fondly at Bluff and said, 'You really thought I was that good? *Really?*'

'I've seen more than my share of Portias. You were far and away the best.'

'Oh ... I don't know what to say.' Rosie grinned. 'You should have come and said hello after the show.'

And was it Rosie's imagination, or did Major-General Kingsley-Flynn blush? She was certain of it.

'I've got a poster from that production in my room above the garage,' Rosie told him. 'I'll bring it down with me tomorrow to show you, if you like?'

'That would be splendid!' Bluff nodded keenly. 'Driver, I hope I won't embarrass you by saying this, but ... There've been times over the last few years that I've been in hot water and I've always taken myself back to that summer evening in Gloucester and remembered that sunset over the stage.' He smiled and reminded her, 'How far that little candle throws his beams, eh?'

Over the years, Rosie had heard audiences tell her that her performances had touched them. But to hear a soldier like Bluff say it, meant more to her than she could adequately put into words.

'I'm so glad,' Rosie said. 'Some people say that theatre is just a fleeting thing. That it doesn't last like a film does. But that's not true, is it? Because it stays with you. That moment, that evening ... it doesn't fade.'

'Even in the North Sea, with nothing but the stars to light the way.'

Where on Earth has the war taken you?

But Rosie wouldn't put him on the spot and ask.

'A happy memory to carry with you wherever you go.' Rosie laid her hand on his desk, reaching for Bluff's. She brushed the tips of her fingers against his, then folded her hands in her lap.

'I have an evening of telephone calls to Whitehall,' he sighed. 'And two days of meetings with resentful boffins. After the prof's memorial on Sunday, shall we go and look at the Citroën together? I think he'd want you to continue.'

'I'd like that. I'm sure he would. If you like tinkering with engines, then I'll let you have a go too!' Rosie reached for her cap. 'Well, I best leave you to the telephone.'

Bluff nodded. 'Keep your ear to the ground, Driver, and don't forget that poster of yours!'

Rosie saluted him. 'Don't you worry about that, Major-General, I won't forget!'

Chapter 9

Now that she was off duty, Rosie went back to her room. The Humber had gone precisely nowhere today, and Rosie hadn't been a driver at all.

She peeled off her uniform as she headed up the flight of stairs that always smelt vaguely of petrol. Once she was in her room, she hung up her hat and her jacket, and draped her wide leather belt over the back of a chair.

Her room had been rather spartan when she'd first moved in, but Rosie had stuck picture postcards on the walls of places she'd visited, and posters of productions she'd appeared in. She'd spent long winter evenings in her room with the girls from the Park, looking through the collection and swapping memories of the places they'd known in the sunnier days before war came; old, historic towns, picturesque coves with stunning cliffs, sweeping natural vistas, seaside resorts and endless golden beaches.

Rosie crossed the room to the spot where she'd pinned up her poster for *The Merchant of Venice*. The play's name was in huge swirling letters, with a small image in the corner of figures in Renaissance costume. Underneath, it read, *The Cavendish Players at Gloucester Botanical Gardens*.

Thinking of Bluff, Rosie ran her hand across the poster.

'You have no idea how much it means to me,' she whispered to the empty room, 'that you of all people thought my Portia *exquisite*. That little candle threw its beams a very long way indeed.'

As Rosie changed out of her uniform and into her favourite dress, she wondered what would have happened if Bluff *had* come up to speak to her at the end of the performance. *A dashing officer, asking for my autograph*... She tried to remember seeing Bluff in the audience, but wondered if he'd sat near the back. If he'd been in the front row, she couldn't have avoided spotting him.

How different life had been then. There had been no spycatchers or moles in her life, unless they came out of a script. And there certainly hadn't been any murders. She shuddered at the thought of it.

Poor Professor Hale.

But at least they had the list. The net was closing in on the mole, the killer. And Rosie had to remind herself that she needed to be subtle. It wasn't a game. Whoever it was had killed, and God willing, they'd catch them before they killed again, either by a gun or by their treachery.

'Rosie!' She recognised Maggie's cheery voice a moment before her friend knocked on the door. 'Are you at home? We're off to the pub!'

'I'll be down in a sec!' Rosie ran back down the stairs and opened the door to Maggie, who was waiting with Sarah and Caroline.

'I'm *so* sorry about Charles this afternoon. Beastly!' Caroline said as soon as Rosie emerged. How different the siblings were. 'We girls are off to the Boar's Head to toast our lovely old prof. Will you come?'

'I'd love to! Thanks for asking me along,' Rosie said. The camaraderie was one of the things she loved about working at Cottisbourne Park. 'I'll go and get my things. Do pop

78

up, girls. And Caroline, you *don't* need to apologise for your brother.'

'I feel as if I should,' Caroline said as the women followed Rosie up the stairs in a swish of skirts. 'Everyone's talking about it. Well, about the major-general really, you know what it's like around here.'

'Gossip travels fast,' Maggie said.

Rosie looked in her make-up bag for the oddments she'd managed to get hold of. She leaned towards the blotchy mirror that hung over her sink to touch up her face. 'Charles wants to be in charge, but I suppose the major-general had a point – he *is* very talented, and it would be a waste for him to be shuffling papers at Professor Hale's desk.'

And he certainly wasn't going to be put in charge if there was any risk of him being a mole. But Rosie did her best not to dwell too much on that thought in Caroline's presence.

'Suicide…' Sarah sighed. 'Poor old prof. I wonder what drove him to it?'

Rosie wondered what to say. She wasn't going to tell Sarah the truth, even though it pained her to lie to her friends.

'You know, that's just how it can be,' Rosie said with a shrug. She leaned closer over the sink as she drew on her lips in carmine red. 'Someone can seem perfectly happy, untroubled, but deep down they're hiding something very, very sad. I should expect that's it.'

Caroline nodded and peered at her reflection over Rosie's shoulder. Rosie had only ever seen Caroline wear make-up once, when they celebrated new year at the Boar's Head and her friend had really pushed the boat out. Charles and his cronies spent the evening teasing her until the girls found her in the toilet, scrubbing off the make-up as tears ran

79

down her face. Her brother was a bully, never more so than when surrounded by his friends and with an audience of ladies to impress.

'Would you like some make-up?' Rosie offered. 'It is a bit old now, but I had so much in my theatre kit! Still works, though. I'll be your make-up lady for this evening if you like!'

'I don't know ...' Caroline bit her bottom lip, but Rosie could see that she was tempted. She glanced to Sarah and Maggie, who nodded encouragingly. 'Oh, why not? Charles teases me anyway, I might as well give him something to tease me about.'

'Don't worry, I won't make you look like Snow White's evil stepmum!' Rosie guided Caroline to sit down on the edge of her bed. She took out her powder puff and dusted Caroline's face. 'I wonder if the pub'll be busy tonight?'

'I saw Joe Fleet peddling off half an hour ago on that rickety old bike of his,' Maggie chuckled. 'No prizes for guessing where he's off to. He bats his eyelids at Lil on the bar all night, but she likes the Spitfire boys.'

'Did I see Joe chatting you up in the canteen earlier?' Sarah asked Caroline as Rosie carefully dabbed some makeup onto Caroline's face. 'I saw him chatting to you earlier. I thought, *I'll have to ask Caroline about that!*'

'*Me?*' Caroline laughed. 'He wasn't chatting me up, he was asking me to look at part of his cypher. My Russian's rather better than his and guess what?' She dropped her voice to a whisper and confided, 'Charles couldn't solve it. He had to send him to me!'

'Charles *I-can-speak-five-languages* Swann was bested by his sister? Wonderful!' Rosie moistened her mascara brush under the tap, then ran it back and forth over the dark pad of makeup before stroking it against Caroline's eyelashes. 'Still, *I* like to think that Joe was being a flirt.'

'Stop it!' Caroline shrieked through her laughter. 'Oh, poor old Charles. He really *should* be in charge, you know. What's that Major-General like, Rosie? Everyone feels terribly sorry for you being co-opted as his factotum. Jean says he barks at you as though you're on the parade ground!'

'He does! But that's what military people are like, isn't it? At least, I've always assumed so.' Rosie smudged some rouge onto the back of her hand, then used her big brush to give Caroline's cheeks a rosy tinge. 'It's not the same as working for good old Professor Hale, of course, but I doubt Kingsley-Flynn will be here for very long. Especially if he's not very popular with everyone here. He won't get the best out of people by shouting a lot!'

And at the thought of that, Rosie felt a little pang. She'd miss him when he moved onto his next mission, Rosie realised, even after two days. Bluff had already made an impact, just as she had on him on that summer stage in Gloucester.

Rosie finished off Caroline's make-up with some carmine for her lips, then she took her hand mirror and held it up to her. 'There we are!'

Rosie wondered if there'd be another show one day, and Bluff would be in the audience, and this time he'd come to see her afterwards. And they could talk about Cottisbourne Park.

'Goodness,' Caroline breathed. 'I wouldn't know myself if not for my necklace. I look like a Swann at last. I'm almost glamorous!'

'You look smashing,' Rosie assured her, as she put the mirror away. 'Now let's get down to the pub.'

★★★

The Boar's Head was full when they arrived, with an assortment of men in tweed jackets courtesy of Cottisbourne Park, and pilots in blue from the airbase. Smoke rose up from pipes and cigarettes, and the pub was lively with the murmur of relaxed conversation.

Rosie spotted Joe at the bar, trying to talk to Lil. She was leaning against the bar taps in awe as a pilot seemed to be telling her about an aerial battle, his hands describing loop-the-loops and explosions. At the sight of him Rosie thought of Bluff in his wayward teenage years again, running away to London and running up bills in hotels and theatres as he lived the high life. It was a world away from the man who had become a major-general at forty, but Rosie fancied that there was still more than a hint of that wayward lad about him. Hale certainly hadn't tutored it out of his charge, whatever Bluff's parents had hoped.

The women went over to the bar, and from their vantage point, Rosie identified more people from the Park. Unsurprisingly, Valerie Fieldgate wasn't among them, but Sarah called a greeting to George Carter, who worked in the hut next to hers. And beside George, Rosie spotted Sid.

She looked around, trying to appear casual, wondering if she'd see Charles. But although some of hut two were there, unsuccessfully trying to chat up a pair of women mechanics from the airbase, Charles was not.

'What can I get you, love?' Lil asked, tearing herself away from her RAF admirer.

'Halves all round, please,' Rosie said. Beer wasn't what it had been before the war. It was so light now that Rosie wondered if it could strictly be called beer at all.

'Me, drinking beer!' Caroline smiled, then whispered to Rosie, 'Can you believe I'd never been in a pub before the war? Ma and Pa don't agree with girls in pubs.'

'You hadn't?' Rosie wasn't entirely surprised. She'd grown up playing with her dolls in theatre bars, and the idea of someone's parents keeping them out of pubs seemed bizarre to her. But then, Caroline was a young lady, and young ladies didn't go to pubs. 'Oh dear, and now you've been corrupted by Cottisbourne – and me! What do you make of this particular circle of Hell? It's not too bad, really, is it?'

'I love it,' Caroline admitted with an apologetic shrug. 'I really owe all of this to Charles, you know. He convinced Pa to let me go to Newnham, or I would have probably been married off to one of Pa's political pals by now!'

'That doesn't sound fun at all.' Rosie winced. 'I do hate the way they use their wives as props. Standing dutifully by, waving and smiling. Not that your mother does, of course. I mean, she's supportive of your father but...' Rosie took a breath, trying to walk away from the hole she'd just dug for herself. 'Besides, you're doing an important job here, Caroline. I'm glad you're around.'

But Caroline gave Rosie's hand a gentle squeeze and assured her, 'She does, Rosie. She plays bridge and hosts tea parties and is the absolute model of a cabinet wife and a future viscountess. Ma's fab, but she's definitely Pa's political prop!'

Relieved that she hadn't insulted Caroline's parents and offended her, Rosie remarked, 'Not your idea of fun, then?'

'Not a bit! They've already got Charles earmarked for the Home Office, you know.' She grimaced and whispered, 'Future PM, Pa says. Handsome, charming – when the mood takes him – and a genius to boot! There's only one little sprat in the Swann household and it isn't Professor Charles.'

'He might be lined up for great things, but he really shouldn't call you *Sprat*,' Maggie said. '*Why* does he call you that?'

'We have a lake in our grounds,' Caroline said matter-of-factly, as though everyone did. 'When we were children, he told me we had sprats swimming in the lake. I leaned over to see them and he pushed me in. I've been little Sprat ever since. He made my life miserable. Our house had priest holes and little hidden spots everywhere that I never told Charles about. I hid whenever I heard him coming after that!'

'I hope you could swim,' Sarah remarked, sipping the beer that Lil had slid across to her.

'I don't have any siblings,' Rosie said. 'I'm not sure if I'd have liked to have an older brother!' Although Rosie hoped that if she'd had one, he wouldn't have been like Charles. A nice, kind brother who looked out for her, that's what she would've wanted. Not an arrogant bully like Charles Swann.

Caroline picked up her glass and took a dainty sip, as though it was an afternoon sherry. She shrugged one shoulder and said, 'I forgave him once I'd dried out. Charles has always been that way, you see. Terribly competitive and terribly confident.'

Lil had gone back to talking to her airman and Joe looked rather lonely. Rosie stepped back from the bar a little and said, 'Evening, Joe.'

'Evening,' he replied morosely. 'Sad old business with Professor Hale, isn't it? And now we've got that sergeant-major marching about the place.'

'Major-General, you mean,' Rosie prompted. 'But yes, it is very, very sad about Professor Hale.'

And you might be the one who did it.

It hurt Rosie to think of it, but someone at Cottisbourne Park had killed Professor Hale and that same someone had betrayed the country again and again, and each betrayal chipped away at what they were all struggling towards. One of the six names on the list lived in the Park, drank here in

84

the pub, ate in the canteen and laughed and joked with their comrades, or commiserated at the news of another ship lost, another plane downed, even as they warned Germany that their codes had been intercepted. Worse than that though, they passed secrets back too. And with Rosie and Bluff's efforts, they'd flush out the mole who had turned on his friends.

'Thanks for the help earlier,' Joe said to Caroline, raising his glass. 'Really appreciate it.'

'Oh, that's all right.' Caroline blushed beneath her makeup. 'Sometimes it's all down to how one's mind works, isn't it?'

'Have you got a bit of slap on, love?' Lil trilled. 'You look gorgeous. You'll be fighting off the Spitfire lads!'

Rosie nudged Caroline playfully. She wondered if Caroline had ever had a boyfriend. She'd never heard her mention anyone, and Rosie could only imagine what Newnham College was like. Nuns probably had more of a social life than the girls who studied there.

The pilot who'd been talking to Lil gave Caroline a wink and said, 'You're a smasher. You'll be painted onto the side of a Spitfire before the week's out!'

'Look out Berlin!' Sarah laughed. 'Here comes Caroline!'

'Lucky old Berlin!' Joe remarked.

Rosie would've raised her eyebrows at Joe's flirty remark, but the suspicion hanging around Joe stopped her. The pub's door opened at that moment, admitting more pilots who flowed in as a sea of blue. They went over to the bar where Lil happily awaited them.

As the pilots mobbed the bar the little Cottisbourne party went over to their colleagues, but everything had changed now Rosie knew the secret of Prospero. Was this what Bluff felt like all the time?

Detached. A fraud. A watcher.

Sid got up from his seat, offering it to Caroline. 'Can't have a lady standing,' he said. 'We should toast the mighty professor!'

'We'll miss him dreadfully,' Caroline said gently, blinking rapidly to fend off her unspilled tears. 'A true gentleman.'

Rosie now questioned the wisdom of encouraging Caroline to wear make-up. The whole lot'd be smudged if everyone started to cry.

'To Professor Hale,' Sid said, holding up his glass.

'To the Prof,' replied George and the girls as one.

'To dear old Professor Hale,' Rosie said, her voice barely above a whisper, cracking under the weight of her emotion. She thought of Bluff. He should've been here too, but then they'd drunk their toast to Hale yesterday, at the top of the hill he had so loved. Rosie and Bluff, with only Romeo and Juliet to see them.

And in a funny sort of way, she had the feeling that their old friend would have approved.

Chapter 10

Rosie headed back from the pub, arm-in-arm with Caroline and Sarah. Maggie walked on Sid's arm, and they laughed as Joe unsteadily rode by on his bike. Rosie strained to hear Sid's conversation but nothing he said sounded suspicious in the least.

She said goodbye to everyone and went up to her room. She had nothing much to report back to Bluff, and was worried she'd let him down, and Hale as well. Neither Joe nor Sid had said anything remotely incriminating.

But that was *something* to report, at least.

Rosie unpinned her hair and let it fall loose. She stood by her window, the last of the late spring light filling her room with its burnished glow.

She looked across the yard to the house. Some of its residents had drawn their curtains, but some were still open. She noticed movement in one of the windows and recognised who it was. A pinpoint of light glowed in the bowl of Bluff's pipe where he stood at the window of what must be his room, looking out over the park. He reached up and took the pipe from between his lips then lifted the sash and leaned his hand on the sill, taking a deep breath of the night air.

Rosie wondered if he had spotted her. But she liked this, watching Bluff. Unobserved by him, perhaps. She leaned against the window frame, and wondered what was on his mind.

Hale. The mole. Men from the ministry.

Or was he thinking of an evening before the war, before everything changed? When he'd sat in the glow of a summer evening and watched a play.

He didn't look so much like a major-general now, his cap and tunic discarded and his tie hanging loose around his open collar. He didn't look very fearsome either, and certainly not like the curmudgeonly military man he had convinced the codebreakers of Cottisbourne Park that he was. But had he got the mole fooled too?

Rosie wished she could call across the yard to him, but what if someone heard? The stern officer would never stand for such shabby behaviour. But Rosie was undaunted and gave him a wave.

Just a tiny twitch of her hand, which could be mistaken for nothing.

He hadn't seen her, Rosie decided as Bluff put his pipe between his lips again. As he did though, he gave the briefest wave in acknowledgment. Nobody who saw him would have had a clue.

Rosie gripped the window frame to stop herself from waving back. The big, joyful wave that she wanted to give him, a wave that would have filled the window, wouldn't have been suitable for a senior officer to receive at all.

She smiled instead, and twirled the end of her loose hair around her finger. Bluff's reply was a polite nod, courtly almost, and Rosie thought again of that summer night in Gloucester that they hadn't even known they'd shared. Maybe they'd share another one day ... another stage, another show when the war was over.

We will. We'll see each other again.

Rosie was certain.

She stayed beside the window, not wanting to go. And yet she couldn't throw up the sash and wish him goodnight.

The sound of footsteps hurrying through the courtyard echoed through the night. The tread was fast, urgent, and it sounded like a man. Charles Swann emerged from the shadows of the grounds, towards the house, hurrying away from the barn where Professor Hale had met his death. He glanced this way and that, but didn't look up. Rosie caught the slightest hint of movement as Bluff took a step back from the window, the better to watch the harried professor pass.

Rosie followed Bluff's lead and took a step back too. They couldn't afford for a suspect to spot them. Why was Swann in such a rush?

Passing something on?

But why was he coming from the direction of the barn?

When Rosie looked back towards Bluff's room, she could feel his eyes on her even though she couldn't see him clearly in the shadows. With another ghost of a wave he began to knot his tie. Bluff was heading to work again.

Going after our suspect.

Rosie nodded. She pulled a cardigan on over her dress and crept down the stairs, her heart thundering in her chest.

Just imagine, catching Charles red-handed!

She opened the door at the foot of the stairs, then came outside and locked it behind her. She was out in the night and the smell of petrol gave way to the heady scents of the night-flowering plants that dotted the Park. There was no sign of Bluff, but Rosie heard those tell-tale footsteps in the night again. Charles Swann was coming back.

Rosie took her key out of her pocket again. She'd have to unlock her door and go …

Her key fell from her hand and hit the paving stones with

a clatter. She crouched down to pick it up, scrabbling for it in the encroaching darkness.

A pair of polished leather brogues stopped a foot or so from Rosie's nose. Then Charles Swann swooped down and plucked what Rosie knew must be her lost key from the ground.

'What're you up to, creeping about?' Charles asked as he stood. 'Off for an assignation or was it one too many milk stouts with the Sprat?'

'The Sprat?' Rosie got up to her feet. She did her best to rein in her nerves and keep her voice steady and her gaze unwavering. 'You mean Caroline? I'm getting some fresh air, not that it has anything to do with you. Why? What are *you* up to?'

'What business is that of yours?' Charles held out his palm, in which Rosie's key rested. 'Nice girls don't creep about after dark, Miss Sinclair. *Actresses*, perhaps.'

Rosie snatched the key from his hand. She wasn't going to waste her breath with a thank you. Not to *him*. 'And nice men? Do *they* not creep about after dark either?'

'I left my wallet in the rec room,' he snapped. 'Does that satisfy your curiosity or will our glorious leader have me court-martialed at dawn?'

Rosie didn't believe him. She shrugged. 'How should I know if the major-general plans to start punishing people for being forgetful?'

'Good evening, *Miss* Sinclair.' He turned and strode away towards the huts, though whether to sleep or scheme Rosie daren't guess.

Rosie pocketed her key. He was up to something. Out of the six suspects, Charles Swann was the one who Rosie trusted the least.

She wondered where Bluff had been headed. Charles

had been coming from the direction of the barn, so Rosie decided to head that way, although the thought filled her with trepidation. After all, Hale had met his end there.

She crept through the hurrying darkness, taking the shortcut she always used to get to the barn. The large, black-painted wooden structure crouched on the path ahead, a huge dark shadow hunkering in the evening half-light. At the sight of it, Rosie was haunted by a sensation of unease. The barn had never unnerved her before, but it had changed from the cluttered, dusty place where she had liked to idle away her spare time, to the place of her friend's murder.

The broad double doors, where heavily-laden hay wagons had once lumbered in, were unlocked, as usual. Rosie pushed one side open, unsure of what she would see inside. She thought she'd see *something*, some sign that a man had died here. A shadow of Hale on the air, a space that could never be filled.

But there was nothing there besides the familiar, reassuring scent of dust and old straw, and the tang of petrol exhaled by the old car.

Rosie gasped at the headless figure silhouetted by the small window opposite. She took a swift step back. After a breathless moment in which Rosie was certain her heart had paused, she swallowed and took stock.

It was only Madame Vionnet, the dressmaker's dummy, with her split seams leaking sawdust onto the floor. She and Nancy had dressed her up in a frilled blouse and long skirt from half a century before, which had tumbled out of a rotten wardrobe that was now home to a family of rats.

Rosie tried to chase away her fear, clinging to the memory of that silly, careless afternoon.

She came further into the barn. When she heard the flap of the pigeons that roosted in the roof, Rosie's heart skipped again. But as the pigeons cooed contentedly, she was reminded again of the happy times she had spent here, Hale helping to polish the car's lamps as Rosie had worked on the engine.

The floor had been swept. Rosie had never seen it so clean in the whole time she'd been at the Park. Whatever had been useful – chairs, sofas, tables, wardrobes, coat-stands, bookcases – had long ago been pilfered to furnish the huts. No one had really bothered with the barn after that, until Rosie and Hale had begun work on the car. All that remained were stacks of tea chests and old barrels, and the sticks of furniture too decrepit to be mended and which would become firewood by winter.

What a place to die. Shot and left among the relics. Grief welled up again in Rosie and she wiped away her welling tears with her fingertips.

'Oh, Professor Hale ...' Rosie whispered.

A torch beam swept the darkness and Bluff whispered, 'Rosie, is that you?'

Rosie turned towards the source of the light. 'Major-General? Yes, it's me. I'm sorry I'm not in uniform, I'd just got back from the pub.'

'I didn't expect you to ...' He stepped out of the shadows. 'Are you all right, Driver Sinclair?'

Bluff wasn't in full uniform. It made Rosie feel slightly less embarrassed. He'd put his tie on, but wasn't wearing his tunic or his cap, and his sleeves were rolled up. So he did relax now and then.

Rosie glanced away from Bluff, awkward now, and stared down at the swept floor. She shivered. Was this where Hale had been found?

'I'm sorry, sir ... it's rather a shock, being in here again. After ... after what happened.'

'I can well imagine,' he assured her gently. 'It's not the return we planned, I know. Would you like to go back to your quarters?'

'No.' Rosie shook her head. She was determined to be brave, for Hale's sake. 'He's up to something, isn't he? That man.'

Bluff nodded. 'It looks like it,' he replied. 'But I can't be sure what. He was in here though, I could still smell that cologne of his.'

Rosie sniffed. 'Sort of spicy?' It wasn't subtle, like Bluff's sandalwood scent. 'He caught me, leaving my room. He seemed angry that I'd seen him. He said he'd left his wallet somewhere, but I'm not sure I believe him.'

Bluff nodded thoughtfully, then turned and laid his palm on the Citroën, which shone in the dim beam of the torch.

'I don't like to think of anyone creeping about in here,' he admitted. 'I had a mind to padlock the place, but that might scare Prospero off.'

'It might…' Rosie whispered. She went over to Bluff's side. 'At least the car's still in one piece. There's nothing else here though, apart from mountains of old junk. And that's how some people might even describe this old thing.' Rosie affectionately patted the bonnet.

'The prof told me you'd finally got her up and running not so long ago? Still a way to go, but the heart's beating again.'

Rosie nodded, remembering Hale at the wheel as Rosie had watched the engine shudder into life. If only she could bring back her friend so easily.

'Oh, yes, sir, the engine goes. I just want to do some final tweaks so she's roadworthy.'

'I have no mechanical nous at all,' Bluff admitted, which surprised Rosie. 'It's all magic to me.'

'Bet you never thought Portia would be handy with a spanner,' Rosie said. 'I always used to help Daddy work on the van – it carried our props and costumes about, so it was rather crucial, you see. Being an amateur mechanic came in handy, didn't it?'

'Very handy indeed,' he told her with a smile. 'Do you think you'll be able to face working on the Citroën again? I know this is where we lost our friend, but I know how much he loved this car and how much he valued your friendship too.'

Rosie glanced across the cluttered space, then looked up at Bluff. 'Before I do, will you tell me, sir, where Professor Hale was found? Only, I'll keep wondering.'

He cast the torch beam up towards the hayloft, which bristled with old farm machinery and discarded sticks of furniture. Rosie had never climbed the narrow ladder that ascended up to the loft, but now it carried with it a sense of foreboding, as though the murderer was still there.

'He was up in the hayloft,' he said gently.

Rosie frowned. Hale couldn't have gone up there by accident. He'd been doing something. Going after the mole?

'Thank you for telling me. It's hardly a nice thing to know, but I'd rather know than try to guess. Poor old Professor Hale.' Rosie stared at the ladder. 'Why on earth did he go up there? And why did Professor Swann?'

'Professor Swann heard the gunshot,' Bluff explained. 'Or so he would have us believe.'

'And came running…' Rosie recalled the polished brogues and pictured Swann walking through the dust and cobwebs in the barn. 'I *will* carry on working on the car. For Professor Hale. And maybe one day, we could take her out for a spin?'

'I might even be able to lay my hands on a petrol coupon or two.' Bluff patted the car and swung the beam back over its bonnet. 'We'll take her up to see Romeo and Juliet and drink another toast to our friend. And to new friends, perhaps?'

We're friends?

'New friends.' Rosie nodded. She liked the thought of that. 'Oh, yes, let's drink a toast to new friends. And if you … I don't know if there is, but if there *is* a Mrs Kingsley-Flynn, she's welcome to come for a spin in the Citroën too.'

There must be a Mrs Kingsley-Flynn, surely? Or a Lady Kingsley-Flynn, more to the point? She'd be poised and elegant and she'd never have had her hands in a car engine nor donned overalls and painted scenery either. Rosie could almost picture her, and the woman she imagined would be entirely out of place in a dusty old shed filled with junk.

'There are several Mrs Kingsley-Flynn's on the family tree and a healthy number of Lady KFs too,' Bluff said with a smile. 'But none of them are married to me. One doesn't tend to meet one's soul mate when one's on the road to becoming a major-general with H-Cav.'

'Oh … sorry. I hope you didn't mind me asking. I wasn't …' Rosie stopped. She was digging another hole. Acting was fine, she spoke other people's words. But when she had to come up with her own, she sometimes tripped over them. 'You must've seen such a lot of the world.'

'Don't apologise. I *have* seen a lot of the world, but not always under the happiest conditions. I intend to change that after the war though. I've a yearning for travel.'

Rosie wouldn't press him on what he'd seen. That was the trouble with war. If you got to see the world, it was hardly looking its best. 'Just anywhere or have you some plans? You know, I'd always travelled about. I'd never been in one place longer than a month before I came here!'

'Wherever the wind blows me. I don't have any plans at

all, which is very definitely *not* me.' And yet maybe it was. The war was teaching everyone things they hadn't known before. 'And what about you, Driver? Is there a Bassanio waiting for his fair Portia to return?'

'No,' Rosie replied. 'I haven't even *found* my Bassanio! That's what comes of touring about, pretending to be someone else every evening.'

Bluff was only being polite of course, because he was a polite sort of fellow.

'Perhaps it won't be Gloucester next time I see you on stage.' Bluff swept the torch beam over the barn again, then extinguished it at the distant sound of propellers scything through the clouds. For a moment Rosie held her breath, but the siren didn't sound. One of their own, then. 'Perhaps it'll be Broadway!'

'I don't know about that...' Rosie replied. She felt the tug of nostalgia. 'So many people have come and gone from the Players over the years. Some ended up in the West End, and some of them even got into film and radio plays. And I've sort of... stayed where I am.'

'You're a fine company of players. Well-drilled, to my experienced eye. I wouldn't be surprised if the Cavendish Players don't become something to be reckoned with once all this is over.' The plane was passing overhead now and Rosie recognised the sound of a Spitfire. Probably one of the local boys coming home. 'And if you ever need a stage in Buckinghamshire, there are considerable grounds and a rather forbidding moat at the old family pile. Consider it at your disposal. It'll make a change from mother's bloo— bally operas!'

'Thank you! You know, I'd very much like to take you up on that, sir!' Rosie was sure Hale wouldn't have minded them talking about the future. He used to tell her that she should always think about what she would do when peace came, whatever that peace looked like. 'Mummy and Daddy are talking of retiring, at least from running the company. We always perform at the same places, and it's time ... well, after the war's over, God willing, we can play in Buckinghamshire. As long as your mother doesn't mind us nudging out the opera!'

He laughed and assured her, 'I think they'll be delighted to host such a prestigious company. I imagine running a theatre company isn't all that different from running a troop, is it? Lots of shouting, impressive costumes and everyone needs to be in the right place at the right time.' Bluff leaned closer and whispered mischievously, 'That's a Sandhurst education distilled.'

'That is pretty much it! Sorting out billets, working out schedules, keeping everyone in line.' Rosie chuckled and added, 'And all the drinking and you-know-what-else-ing is probably a lot like the army as well, I reckon!'

'I'm a respectable major-general, Driver Sinclair,' was his too-stern reply. 'I wouldn't know anything about drinking and you-know-what-else-ing. I was born in this uniform.'

'Well, *I* wouldn't know about that either!' Rosie tapped the side of her nose. 'I'm too busy learning my lines!'

'You and I are going to see Prospero in handcuffs,' Bluff said. 'And he'll answer for killing our friend.'

Rosie's gaze wandered up towards the hayloft. The last place Hale had known in this life, where he had died among the dusty cobwebs and the detritus that generations of the Park's inhabitants had left behind. Had he seen his nemesis? Did he get a look at them before they pulled the trigger and ended his life with a bullet?

'We will, Major-General Sir. Oh, my word, we *will*.'

'I don't usually work with an associate, but I'm glad to

have you in my battalion.' He looked up as though only just noticing that the night had fallen silent again. 'I can't see you to your quarters for obvious reasons, but I want to be sure that you're safely back at barracks. Would you light a candle in your window as a signal? Blow it out after sixty seconds and it should go unnoticed.'

'A candle?' Rosie had a couple in her room, in case the electricity went. 'Of course. It'll throw its little beams across the courtyard to you, don't you worry.' She patted his arm. 'I'm glad I'm in your battalion too.'

'Fall out, Driver Sinclair. Consider the next two days yours to enjoy whilst I'm shut in my office weeding through Cottisbourne Park,' Bluff told her with a smile. 'Sleep well.'

Rosie glanced back at the car. 'In that case, I don't suppose you'd mind me working on the Citroën? At least you'll know where to find me if you need me. I'll reclaim this place for Professor Hale.'

'I think it's a marvellous idea,' he said. 'And if your young friend finds her way through the fence and wants to help, she has my permission to do so.'

'She'll be only too glad.' Rosie drew her cardigan around her, preparing to leave the barn and go out into the night. 'Sleep tight, Major-General Sir Kingsley-Flynn! I'll see you soon.'

'Over the courtyard,' he chuckled. 'Goodnight, Driver Sinclair.'

Rosie waved to him as she left the barn. It was only once she was on the cinder path heading back towards her room that she recalled something that she hadn't paid attention to at the time. When Bluff had first spotted her in the barn, when he'd seen her overcome as she'd walked into the place where their friend had been murdered, he'd called her Rosie.

Not Driver Sinclair.

'Rosie and Bluff!' Rosie whispered as she unlocked her door.

She went back upstairs and took a candle stub from the drawer. She lit it and went over to the window with it, then looked across the courtyard to Bluff's room. Silently she counted down the sixty seconds. Ten remained when Bluff's window opened and she saw the red glow of his pipe bowl in the darkness.

They were both safe for tonight.

Chapter 11

In daylight, the barn wasn't so bad. Or at least, Rosie told herself so. For a start, Madame Vionnet didn't make her jump out of her skin. She merely stood, the unseeing witness to a murder, beside a lampstand with a bent, stained shade.

As Rosie bent over the Citroën's engine, she ignored the old building's occasional creaks and groans, and the whistle of the wind through the cracked panes and the gaps in the roof where tiles had been lost. Nancy might believe in ghosts, but Rosie refused to. The living were frightening enough.

Professor Hale had helped Rosie rescue the Citroën from under the piles of old rubbish it had languished under for years. There'd been half a chicken coop in the back, and sacking over the seats that had crumbled as soon as they'd touched it. They'd rescued the wood from the old tea crates, freckled with woodlouse holes, that had been piled on the roof, and even found a set of bent cutlery tied up with string under the bonnet.

They'd rolled the car forwards into the middle of the space, and there the Citroën stood, facing the barn doors, awaiting the day she'd be back on the road.

Rosie rolled up her sleeves and busied herself, taking things apart, cleaning them, oiling them, putting them back together again. As she worked, she thought about Professor Hale. She didn't, as she'd feared she might, dwell on the events of the hayloft, but thought instead of the Hale she'd known, happy and hearty, and larger than life. The man who'd be very pleased indeed to see her working on the car that would've been his pride and joy.

When he died, Hale had been in the midst of tracking down the owner of the car, so determined he was to buy it. Yet nobody seemed to know whose name was on the paperwork, as though the Citroën had simply been left there one day and forgotten until Rosie and her friend stumbled upon it. Nancy had been beside herself when Rosie showed it to her and suddenly the restoration found itself not only with a mechanic in the shape of Rosie, but with a very willing garage owner's granddaughter too. Supplies weren't easy to get, but having Nancy's grandparents to call on certainly made things a lot easier as the old Citroën began to slowly come back to life.

Rosie had already patched up the holes in the car's fabric roof and washed and cleaned the body work. The burgundy paintwork gleamed again, and would look fantastic if Nancy's grandparents could get her some wax. All she had to do was remove the last few bits of straw and clods of earth, and the engine would be singing.

Professor Hale would be proud.

Rosie glanced up at the hayloft, but forced her gaze away. *No, I mustn't think of it. I mustn't.*

'Hard at it?'

Who the heck?

Rosie gasped in surprise and looked up to see Joe standing there. It wasn't unusual for him to drop by and chat about the car, but now that he was on the suspects' list, Rosie wasn't sure she wanted to be alone in the barn with him.

'Yes, I wanted to carry on doing it up,' Rosie said. 'I think it's what Professor Hale would've wanted, don't you?'

'No doubt about it,' Joe replied, nodding. 'He thought a lot of this car, did the prof.'

'Just can't believe he'll never see it on the road,' Rosie sighed. She tried not to sound accusing, but it was hard. Joe wasn't a stranger to the barn, and this was where Professor Hale had been killed. 'But I'll think of him when I eventually get to drive it.'

'And he'll be looking down at you, pleased as punch,' Joe assured her. He looked around the barn, sweeping his gaze over the car and Rosie and, finally, the place where Professor Hale had died. 'Well, I'd better leave you to get on. I'll see you later, Rosie.'

'Bye, Joe.' Rosie waved to him, before turning back to the car. What was it they said about murderers coming back to the scene of the crime? But did Joe really have it in him to kill Professor Hale?

The afternoon shadows were growing longer when the barn door opened and Nancy skipped over the threshold. Rosie was relieved to see Nancy; at least *she* wasn't on the suspects' list.

Nancy looked as though she'd been adventuring, and it filled Rosie with happiness. Nancy's hair had escaped its plaits, whilst there was dirt smeared on her cheek and one of her knees sported a fresh graze, not that any of it seemed to worry the little girl. As Nancy was fond of saying, she'd been through the blitz, so the Sussex countryside was nothing.

'Hello!' Rosie said, glad to have a visitor. She grabbed a rag and rubbed at the oil on her hands, not that it would've bothered the girl who helped out at a petrol station. 'What have you been up to today?'

'I've been up at the farm mucking out the stables. They gave me a massive bacon sandwich to say thank you.' Nancy trotted over to the car. 'And I got a letter from Mum!'

'Is she well?' Rosie asked her. She couldn't imagine how hard it was for the children who had been sent miles from their parents for their own safety, leaving their parents in the line of danger. Although Rosie had lived an itinerant childhood, at least her parents had always been there. 'Here, let me tidy your hair for you.'

'She's doing all right.' Nancy turned so Rosie could plait her hair. 'She saw Mr Churchill crossing Green Park and he wished her a good morning. What d'you think to that?'

Rosie crouched down and untied the ribbons from Nancy's hair, before starting to re-plait it as neatly as she could. 'Did he indeed? It sounds as if he was in a good mood!' Unlike the morning she had collected Bluff from London. 'I'm glad your mother's all right. I've been busy on the car, you'll be glad to know. We'll take her out for a drive soon, I promise.'

'Grandpa says he'll have the wax in the next couple of weeks.' Nancy scuffed the sole of her shoe on the floor as Rosie worked. 'How come we can't get wax for your motor, but your major-general mate has no trouble getting it for his tash?'

'You've seen him?' Rosie wondered where Nancy had managed to get a peep at Bluff. She tied the first plait firmly, then started on the next. 'Maybe the military have a special reserve of wax for officers cultivating a moustache! They can't have untidy 'tashes in the army. It simply won't do.'

'I saw him this morning when I set out for the farm. He was walking up in the top fields, having a proper good hike.' Nancy looked back at Rosie over her shoulder. 'What's he like?'

Rosie could picture Bluff striding across the fields, his long legs easily carrying him through the tough grass.

'He wants everyone to think he's very stern, and they all

believe him,' Rosie whispered. She knew she could trust Nancy not to say anything. 'And he's told me that if you want to help us find out what happened to poor Professor Hale, then you're welcome to. But you must be very, very careful.'

Nancy beamed. 'Did he really say that?'

'He did! You mustn't worry about Professor Swann shouting at you, but you must avoid him if you can.' Rosie tied off the last plait. 'There you are, all ready to spy.'

'I came by the barn yesterday to see if you were here, but it was all shut up.' Nancy spun on her heel. 'I'll tell you a funny thing though? When I tried to open the door, the inside bar was down. Whoever was knocking about didn't want anybody else coming in.'

Was it Professor Swann again?

'What time was this, Nancy?'

'About four, I'd say. Must've been, because when I got back to the garage, Nana was just locking up.'

'Four. Right.' Rosie had been in Bluff's office then, going through personnel files. She'd report back to Bluff. They might be able to find out where each of the six suspects had been at the time. 'That's very helpful, Nancy. Well done.' Rosie went over to a tea chest near the car and nudged aside the lid. 'Do you know what I found in here the other day, Nancy? I've tidied it up for you as best I can. I was going to give it to you the other evening, but…' *But something rather horrible got in the way*.

Nancy's eyes grew wide and she pottered over to join Rosie, silent with anticipation.

Rosie reached inside and from the curls of shavings, she brought a wooden cross out of the chest as carefully as she could, untwisting the string that dangled from it as she did. Then came the little wooden figure attached to the strings, and Rosie laughed as she danced the puppet around Nancy's feet.

'Look! It's a dancing lady!' Rosie said.

She had touched up the scratches as best she could, and had tied a scrap of fabric around the puppet to give her a dress, which flared about the figure as she moved. Nancy's eyes grew wider still and she clapped her hands together with childish excitement.

'She's amazing!' Nancy exclaimed. 'What's her name?'

Rosie thought for a moment, then told her. 'Portia. And she's yours if you'd like to have her.'

'Portia,' Nancy repeated in an awed whisper. Then she put her arms around Rosie and hugged her tight. 'Thank you, Rosie. She's the best puppet ever!'

Rosie hugged her back. She hadn't had brothers or sisters, and she had been the only child in the Cavendish Players. Although Rosie was an adult now, Nancy was like a substitute sister for her, and Rosie hoped Nancy saw her as the same.

'Here, shall I show you how to make her dance?' Rosie asked. Nancy nodded, her gaze fixed on the puppet.

'When I grow up,' Nancy said, 'can I join your theatre shows? Mum and Dad love the theatre, it'd be amazing if they could come and see me and you in a show.'

'Maybe!' Rosie said.

She took Nancy's hand and closed her fingers around the wooden cross, then together they made Portia jig across the floor of the barn. Nancy gave a delighted laugh and the sound of it sent a surge of pure joy through Rosie. This was what they were all fighting for, for little girls like Nancy and villages like Cottisbourne. The likes of Prospero were outnumbered a million to one, no matter how much sadness they spread.

Once Nancy headed home for tea, carrying Portia in a narrow wooden box that once had contained a whisky bottle, Rosie went to the canteen for supper. Stew again, but when did they eat anything else?

As she lined up in the queue, she wondered how Bluff had got on, and she surveyed the room in case any of the suspects were there. Professor Jones had brought a chess board into the canteen and was playing himself. He sat in silent contemplation of the pieces laid out in front of him and finally moved a piece. Then he turned the board around and started again.

Dr Brett was on his own at a table in the corner, a book propped up against his glass of water as he ate. Dr Stuart was deep in conversation with a serious-looking young woman whose attention seemed to be more on the embroidery hoop in front of her than on the piano-playing doctor at her side.

There was simply nothing suspicious about them. Unless that made them even more suspicious.

Rosie sighed to herself as the queue shuffled forwards, then she spotted Bluff. He was standing beside the door that opened onto the kitchens, talking to Tommy, the grounds-keeper. Not chatting, definitely *talking*. The two men made an unlikely pair, Bluff so tall and straight-backed, his khaki uniform immaculate, the ribbons that commemorated un-spoken acts of valour the only splash of colour. Tommy was a man of the soil, twenty years the major-general's senior, small and wiry, his overalls dusted here and there with fresh earth and ancient paint stains. Before the war he had manicured the ornamental lawns and cleaned fountains of fallen leaves, plucking deadheads in the rose garden and shaping the topi-ary lanes. Now he kept the grounds of the codebreaking station shipshape, a caretaker until normality resumed and there were no more soldiers or professors in Cottisbourne

Park, the family who had graciously surrendered it having moved to their highland hunting lodge to see out the war. They were evacuees too in their way, Rosie supposed.

She wondered what they could be talking about. Rosie wasn't sure about Bluff being interested in gardening tips. At least, not the kind of gardening that involved actual plants and moles that weren't in human form. But Tommy would spot people coming and going, and that gave Rosie pause. He was a very useful person to know.

Rosie looked away, trying not to draw attention to Bluff's conversation, but irresistibly her gaze was drawn back to the man who was so different from everyone else at Cottisbourne Park. He was different to everyone she'd ever met, come to that. So straight-backed and stern in front of Swann, but with more than a hint of that wayward young man he had once been. He was an unusual sort of major-general, that was for sure.

He was playing a role, and he was playing it very well. And that, Rosie realised, was exactly what an effective spy-catcher needed to do. Because the mole was just the same, disguised here at Cottisbourne Park, playing the part of a dedicated codebreaker while all the while selling out their own country and everyone in it.

And there was Bluff, attracting glares and rolled eyes from the people at the Park over their lunch. From people who wondered how Rosie could work with someone strict and cantankerous. Catching spies, it seemed, wouldn't win you friends. She wondered what it meant for life outside of Cottisbourne Park too. Did Bluff have a home to go to that wasn't the moated family pile, or did he have an austere barracks room? Or were a major-general's quarters plush mahogany with the light scent of tobacco and leather overlooking Horse Guard's? Rosie couldn't imagine.

And did he have any friends who didn't wear a uniform?

'Welcome to the barracks,' the woman waiting in the queue behind whispered to her friend.

Rosie resisted the temptation to turn and glare at them.

'He's doing a good job,' the young man who was queuing behind the women admonished. 'It's not one any of us would want, that's for sure.'

But someone did, and where was Charles Swann now? Up to something, no doubt.

Chapter 12

The next day, Rosie went back to the barn to work on the car. Her trepidation on returning to the site of her friend's death vanished when she saw the old farm building. It was a welcome, familiar sight, the paint peeling away to reveal mellow, weathered wood. Musty herb robert and vivid dandelions clustered around the door, and morning glory twined its way up the handle of a rusted pitchfork. A wood pigeon sat on the ridge of the roof, its deep, echoing coo reminding Rosie of the calls from the woods behind the garden back at home.

When she went into the barn, her gaze first alighted on the box where she had found the puppet for Nancy, and she smiled. Such an innocent thing, a toy that must have been loved and played with by a child years before, forgotten until Rosie had resurrected it for another.

As she walked over to the car, her gaze wandered to the hayloft, and her heart plummeted as she thought again of Professor Hale. But she had told Bluff she would reclaim the barn and she would keep on working on the car for their friend. To abandon the dusty old building and the car inside it now would allow the mole to win.

And God willing, the mole will be brought down.

Rosie put down her bag, then she creaked open the bonnet and carried on with her work. Her initial melancholy as she thought of Hale never seeing the car on the road wore away as she reminded herself that she was still working on it for him – for his memory, at least.

She wondered, as she scraped caked-on mud from another bit of the engine, how Bluff was getting on, but perhaps no news was good news. He hadn't been in his office when she went to find him that morning, so she hadn't been able to pass on Nancy's report.

And she hadn't dared to leave a note on Bluff's desk in case the mole found it first. Rosie hadn't been able to speak to him in the evening because she couldn't risk the gossip that might circulate if someone had seen her going to his room. She didn't see him at the window after night fell either and for some reason, the darkness of the bedroom over the courtyard seemed almost as foreboding as the hayloft where their friend had met his death. Nothing could have happened to Bluff, she'd told herself, he was just working late.

Only as Rosie was finally going to her bed did she happen to find herself, quite coincidentally, at the window again. This time a tiny candle flame glowed across the expanse of darkness and through the open sash she'd caught the barest hint of pipe smoke before it was lost on the night breeze. Now in the sunlit barn she thought again of the candle that burned first in her window and then in Bluff's. A light in the dark to tell a friend that all was well, small as a cotton bobbin, but in its own way, as bright as a bomber's moon.

Rosie lost herself in her work. There was something very calming about fixing things, of ensuring everything was spick and span and in its proper place. Perhaps that was how Bluff sometimes felt about his gardening work. Fixing things by rooting out the mole, and normality – albeit the wartime version they had lived with these last few years – would reign again.

The door of the barn creaked slowly and a small, wooden face appeared. The puppet's body followed, a length of lace now tied around her shoulders, providing a shawl to complement her dress. As Rosie watched, Portia performed a dance for her, her wooden feet clicking on the floor of the barn as Nancy's small hands brought her to life.

Rosie laughed, the unexpected dance routine a welcome and pleasant surprise. She clapped enthusiastically as she said, 'Oh, bravo, Portia, what a splendid dancer you are!'

Nancy stepped around the door and bowed as she told Rosie, 'She says thank you. I've been telling her all about London and Mum and Dad and…' Nancy blinked rapidly, then dashed her hand across her eyes and warned, 'I'm not crying!'

'I'm sure Portia is excited about seeing London one day. And isn't that a pretty shawl?' Rosie went over to Nancy and crouched down to give her a hug. She didn't want to draw attention to the girl's tears. Sometimes a hug was enough.

'They've dropped bombs on London again,' Nancy whispered as she wrapped her arms around Rosie in return. 'Nan and Granddad said I needn't worry as it's only a few scrappy bits of junk they're flying, but … my mum's in London. And I want Dad to come home, but he's over there looking for Hitler.'

'It's all right,' Rosie whispered, although how much assurance could she really give her? 'Your dad'll be home soon. He'll find Hitler and give him a good kick up the behind.' Rosie laughed gently, then she tightened her hug. The bombed-out streets of London that she'd driven down only days before came back to her mind. 'It's not a big scary thing like it was last time. Your mum got through that without a scratch, didn't she?'

Nancy nodded. 'Yeah, she did. She said when they went

down to the shelter, they all took their typewriters and kept working.' She laughed then and sniffed back her tears. 'Hitler wouldn't want to come up against my mum and her typewriter neither.'

'He'd end up with a headache!' Rosie chuckled. 'That's the spirit, Nancy. You and your mum and your dad will all be together again one day.'

'I'm not crying,' Nancy reminded her. 'How's the motor?'

'I know you're not,' Rosie assured Nancy with a smile. She released Nancy from her embrace and led her over to the car. 'She's coming along very well. Would you like me to start her up?'

'Can I sit in her?' she asked. 'You been syphoning petrol out of the Humber?'

'Just a little!' Rosie tapped her finger against the side of her nose. 'Yes, of course, hop in! One day we'll go out for a ride in her, I promise.'

Nancy clambered into the passenger seat and sat there with her legs outstretched, Portia perched in her lap. She gathered her cardigan around the doll, cocooning her safely.

'Off to the seaside!' Nancy trilled, her voice alive with excitement.

Rosie hopped up into the driving seat. Making sure the handbrake was on, she turned the key. Nothing happened at once, and Rosie turned to Nancy with an embarrassed shrug. She turned the key again, and the car coughed. Once more, and another cough, then a splutter, and finally the engine murmured into life.

Rosie laughed. 'And we're off to the seaside!'

Nancy gave a cry of excitement, waving her hand as though she were a queen greeting her public. She bounced on the seat, then told Rosie, 'You should be sorting the Spitfires at the base! You're brilliant!'

'Oh, I don't know about that!' Rosie chuckled. If she was out early, she sometimes saw the mechanics who worked at the airbase riding to work on their bikes, their hair protected under brightly-coloured scarves. 'They must have fun, don't you think? I wonder if they ever go up in the planes! But we shall have the most fun of all on our trip to the seaside. Did you bring your bucket and spade?'

Rosie loved playing with Nancy, indulging in the land of make-believe that had once been her bread and butter.

Nancy nodded. 'And my little paper flags to stick in the sandcastles!' Her hand, which had still been waving, suddenly stopped and shot up into a salute as the tall, immaculate figure of Major-General Sir Kingsley-Flynn strode purposefully into the barn. Still holding her salute Nancy dropped her voice to a whisper and asked, 'Are we in trouble?'

'Oh, we'll ask the major-general if he wants to come with us. Maybe he'll buy us ice creams and candyfloss?' She leaned out of the open window and saluted him, glad to see him again. Over the sound of the engine, she called, 'Hello, sir! Listen to her go!'

'Afternoon, Driver Sinclair, Driver Sinclair's chum…' He furrowed his brow as Nancy lifted one of Portia's arms and knocked it against the puppet's head to give a salute from her toy too. 'And afternoon to Driver Sinclair's chum's chum too. Well, Driver, she sounds splendid!'

'Doesn't she?' Rosie revved the engine a little, but as she did, she heard something a little raspy in the engine's noise. She turned the key and the car settled back into silence. 'Hmm… a couple more tweaks required, I fear. What can I do for you, sir?'

'One can spend too long sitting at one's desk,' Bluff replied. 'I thought I might steal ten minutes or so and see if you needed someone to wield an oily rag.'

An oily rag? In that *uniform?*

'If you wouldn't mind. We need to get to the bottom of that raspy noise.' Rosie looked him up and down, pin-sharp and immaculate as ever in his uniform. 'Although I don't have any overalls for you to borrow.'

Bluff was already unbuttoning his tunic when he gave Rosie a look that might have been withering to some people, but to her was simply wry. In the few days she'd known him, she'd already discovered that the major-general's carapace was anything but humourless.

'A major-general doesn't require *overalls*,' was his lofty reply. 'He simply shouts any raspy engine noises into submission.'

'Glad to hear it.' Rosie hopped out of the driving seat and went round to look at the engine. 'By the way, there's some news.'

Bluff darted a glance towards Nancy, who was dancing Portia across the car's dashboard, humming a tune to her. He rolled up one sleeve and whispered, 'Is that Professor Swann's *urchin*?'

'It is, yes. My little friend Nancy,' Rosie replied. Then she lowered her voice. 'She's the one who's got the news. She said she tried to get into the barn the day before yesterday, and the door was barred shut. From the *inside*. I never bar it, and as you know, we were together in your office at the time.'

'Barred?' Bluff whispered. 'Could you tell if anything had been disturbed?'

'I'm not sure,' Rosie admitted. 'And Joe popped into the barn yesterday. He was talking to me about the car, but I thought you should know anyway.'

'Oh gosh, sorry!' Caroline stood on the threshold of the barn, her smile fixed in place as she found herself confronted with the no doubt unexpected figure of the major-general. 'I was just having a cuppa and I heard the engine!'

'Caroline, hello.' Rosie gave a wave. 'Major-General, this is Miss Caroline Swann. Caroline, Major-General Sir Kingsley-Flynn.'

'Ah, Miss Swann.' Bluff offered Caroline his hand. 'Illustrious stock indeed.'

'Daddy and Charles?' Caroline blushed as she shook his hand, then nodded. 'Daddy always jokes that war's become a family business! Not that he jokes about the war, you understand, but … well, he's at the ministry and Charles and I work here at Cottisbourne.'

Caroline had never struck Rosie as the most confident woman at Cottisbourne Park, but faced with Bluff, that became painfully clear. She looked like a deer in the headlights, discussing family matters with a major-general when all she had been looking for was a cup of tea and a few minutes with her friend. But she didn't know Bluff as Rosie did. To her, he was the granite-faced soldier.

Rosie wanted to say something that would put Caroline at her ease, but she didn't want to blow Bluff's cover. Even without his tunic on, he was formidable.

'Caroline pops in sometimes when I'm working on the car,' Rosie said. 'I bring my thermos, you see, and we have a chat.'

'And I sit here goggle-eyed, watching Rosie work her magic,' Caroline admitted. 'I'm utterly hopeless with anything like this. What did I say, Rosie, when you were tinkering about with the engine? Mechanics might as well be magic to me! I even have to ask Charles for help if I get a puncture on my bike, which annoys him terribly.'

'I remember the last time that happened!' Rosie remarked. 'He was crouching over a bucket and swearing away at the tyre as he tried to find the puncture.' And saying some pretty choice things about his sister, too. What an arse poor Caroline had for a brother. 'Well, don't worry, I'll fix it for you next time.'

'No sign of the ghosts today, I hope?' Caroline asked Nancy as she climbed out of the Citroën, walking Portia ahead of her. 'Oh, Nancy, what a pretty puppet! Does she have a name?'

'Portia,' Nancy told her proudly. 'And she's not scared of ghosts neither.'

'The ghosts are being pretty quiet at the moment,' Rosie said. 'I expect they'll go soon enough if the car's too much for them and find a nice ruined castle to haunt instead.'

'I don't believe in ghosts,' Bluff advised Nancy, as matter-of-fact as if she was one of his troops. 'I've lived in some frightfully old places and I've never seen a thing.'

Nancy lifted Portia's head to her ear, then nodded. She cocked her head to one side and told Bluff, 'Portia says you haven't lived in the *right* old places. There aren't ghosts everywhere or there'd be no space for people!'

'Well, perhaps Portia could tell the ghosts to push off.' Caroline shivered and looked around the cavernous barn as she drew her cardigan around herself. 'I for one don't want to hear anyone rattling their chains!'

'Oh, they don't rattle chains.' Nancy leaned back against the car. She reminded Rosie of Bert at the garage, holding forth with unshakeable authority on whatever subject had caught his attention. Like grandfather, like granddaughter. 'Not round here, anyway. Sometimes they talk, but they don't talk like we do, and sometimes they sort of... *click*. It's a funny sort of noise really.'

'Click?' Rosie glanced into the engine of the car. Maybe something was loose inside it. That would explain Nancy's click, perhaps, and the rasping noise she'd heard when she'd run the engine. 'Maybe it's this old girl?'

But Nancy shook her head.

'No,' she said. 'I don't think so. I heard up in the hayloft...'

At the mention of the hayloft, Caroline pressed her hand to her mouth and stifled a little sound of anguish. She shook her head and stammered, 'I'm sorry, I just... one allows oneself to forget and then there it is again. Our prof, so overcome with distress that he... he...'

Rosie stroked her arm, consoling. 'It's all right... He must've had something dreadful on his mind to do what he did. And he's at peace now.'

There definitely had been something dreadful on his mind – a mole at Cottisbourne Park. But Rosie kept her counsel.

'I have to go back,' Caroline sighed. 'See you at supper, Rosie?'

'You will.' Rosie gave her an encouraging smile. 'And next time you get a puncture, let me know!'

'I will. Cheerio, Nancy, and lovely Portia too.' Caroline stroked her hand over Nancy's hair, as gentle as her brother was brash. 'Good afternoon, sir.'

And with that, she hurried from the barn and the memories of what had happened there.

'Right.' Bluff clapped his hands together. 'I have ten minutes and a yearning to pretend I know something about engines. Driver Nancy, you're in charge. Now, Driver Sinclair, how do you want me?'

'Hold this!' Rosie passed him her spanner, then she pointed into the engine. 'There's a metal plate just there. All I need you to do is unscrew it. There's some bits and bobs underneath it which might be causing our problems.'

'Get to it,' Nancy demanded, laughing. 'Or we'll have you on a charge!'

So Bluff threw his tie back over his shoulder then bent into the engine bay and did as he was told.

Rosie was impressed by his strength as he worked at the bolt.

'That's it, you've got it!' she said. Professor Hale had been like a favourite uncle, avuncular and a little bit silly, but Bluff was altogether different, in a way that Rosie couldn't quite put her finger on. But she knew that she liked it.

He did have very fine arms. Not that Rosie had noticed. Not too much. Because of course, how could she not notice that Bluff was a very well-built man. Tall, broad, but muscular.

'There!' Rosie said, leaning over his shoulder. His sandalwood cologne filled her senses for a moment. 'Now just take the screw off carefully – you don't want to drop it into the engine!'

'Exactly what I was thinking,' he assured her. Then he turned his head and whispered, 'Not really, but I suspect you knew that.'

'I didn't like to say,' she whispered in return. 'But excellent spanner skills, there! I'll just go and get my gloves and I'll lift that panel off. Might be a bit warm after running the engine.'

But Rosie didn't move away at once. She was standing so close to him that she could almost feel the tickle of his whiskers on her cheek.

For a moment Bluff was silent, then he confided, 'I can't change a tyre either, you know. But I can tack up a horse with my eyes closed.'

'Can you?' Rosie gasped in surprise. 'I wouldn't want to go anywhere near a horse with my eyes closed. But then, I expect it's not too scary for a brave chap like you.'

'Household Cavalry,' Bluff breezed. 'It tends to make one rather useful on horseback.'

'I bet it does!' Rosie said, in admiration. 'You must miss the horses. There's some on the farms around here, of course, but I don't think they're much good for riding.'

'When this is all done, perhaps you and I might take a ride together? Or a drive?'

'Oh, I'd very much like that.' Aware of a warm blush taking over her face, Rosie turned her head away for a moment. Would he notice? Rosie glanced back at him. 'A ride and a drive. Both would be nice indeed.'

Bluff smiled and held up the unscrewed cap as he said, 'Both sounds splendid to me, Driver Sinclair.'

'You can pop it down just there. I'll ... erm ... get my gloves.' Rosie stepped backwards to where she'd left her bag. Her open tool box was sitting there, her gloves laid on top.

She picked up her gloves and decided to bring the hammer with her too. A big beast of a tool, but Rosie suspected the car might well benefit from a wallop. She came back over to Bluff and paused, staring at the hammer. 'That's odd. It's scratched. I don't remember it looking like that before. Oh, well ... that's tools for you!' She propped the hammer head down against the side of the car, and waved the screwdriver at Bluff. 'Let's see what's going on under there, then!'

Nancy came to peer into the engine bay, standing up on tiptoe beside Bluff. She glanced up at him and said, 'I'm going to be a driver when I grow up. That or a spy. Don't know yet.'

'You could be both,' Rosie told her. She leaned in and stared down at the old workings inside the engine. 'Ah, I think I've found the problem. Looks like a bit of an old bird's nest has got wedged in there.'

'She'll be good as new soon,' Nancy assured Bluff. 'If

you're lucky, maybe Rosie might take you for a drive. Only if you're lucky though.'

'We were on our way to the seaside earlier,' Rosie said. 'Do you want to come along too?'

'Will there be fish and chips?' Bluff asked. Nancy gave an enthusiastic nod. 'Then I'd love to.'

Chapter 13

Rosie peered out across the courtyard at Bluff's bedroom window. Night had fallen but there was no sign of him.

No Bluff, no pipe, no candle.

She started to get ready for bed and went to take off her watch. But her stomach lurched when she realised it wasn't on her wrist.

Her parents had given it to her on her twenty-first birthday. For a moment, she was convinced it was lost forever, until she recalled that she must have left it in the barn as she always took it off before plunging her hands into an engine.

Although Rosie was sure it would survive a night in the barn, she wasn't sure she could survive a night without it. She always laid it on the little table beside her bed in front of a photo of her parents playing Oberon and Titania. She always said goodnight to them. And without her watch...

She knew very well she was being superstitious, but such was the mindset of an actor.

Rosie picked up a torch, and hurried down the stairs and out into the night. There was no Charles Swann lurking in the shadows as far as she could tell, and she ran towards the barn, the weak beam of her torch doing little to light her way. But then, Rosie knew the way to the barn better than anyone. She could have found it with her eyes closed.

An owl hooted as Rosie reached the barn. She saw its white shape taking wing as it swooped towards the trees in the distance. People used to think they were ghosts, Rosie once read.

Something creaked in the evening breeze, the old beams of the barn, Rosie suspected. Not Nancy's ghosts.

The unlit barn was unnerving at first. Rosie nudged open the door and went over to retrieve her watch. She balanced the torch under her arm as she put her watch back on but the torch began to roll out of her hold and hit the floor.

For a second there was no light, and Rosie tutted at herself for feeling scared. The torch illuminated itself a moment later, pointing up to the hayloft.

Rosie shivered.

Poor Professor Hale.

And then she spotted something. Green fabric.

Not just green. Khaki. A figure in khaki lying up there in the hayloft.

There was only one person aside from herself who wore khaki at Cottisbourne Park.

Bluff.

And he was lying motionless on the floor of the hayloft.

Her heart in her mouth, Rosie ran to the foot of the foot of the ladder and called up to him.

'Blu— Major-General! Are you all right?'

Bluff didn't move and in the darkness the silence deepened, disturbed only by another low creak from the old barn.

There's no such thing as ghosts.

Rosie climbed the ladder with one hand, holding onto her torch with the other. She played the beam over Bluff and the hayloft, her mouth dry as she realised with inescapable dread that the mole had struck again.

'Major-General! Sir! Wake up!' she called, but he still didn't move.

Rosie reached the top of the ladder and heaved herself

into the hayloft. She'd been up there a few times keeping Nancy entertained, but she'd never been up there at night, and especially not with a murderous spy on the loose.

This was dangerous. Bluff had warned her. And now he was lying on his back in the place where his friend had died.

Rosie's MTA first aid training came back to her and, crouching beside Bluff, she checked for signs of life. She found Bluff's pulse, but then her training failed her and she began to cry. She dropped down onto the hayloft's floor and brought Bluff into her lap, cradling his face.

'Major-General? Can you hear me? You can, I know you can. Just show me, Major-General, show me you can hear me!'

Something about the night seemed alive, as though there were unseen eyes on Rosie. She shivered, fear prickling at her scalp. A man had been murdered in this very spot and now someone had come back for Bluff. Someone who might still be here.

'Bloody hell...' Bluff murmured in a voice that had caught in his throat.

Relief flooded through Rosie and her tears stopped. 'Bluff! Oh, you dear man, whatever happened? It's Rosie... do you know where you are?'

Bluff's eyes opened and he blinked up at Rosie. She saw the effort it took him to focus before he said, 'Did someone... my head...'

Rosie realised what she'd said to him. *Bluff*. He wouldn't have noticed.

She couldn't see any bleeding on his face. If his head was hurting, it must've been on the back. 'Where does it hurt?'

'Someone clobbered me,' Bluff replied. He blinked several times in quick succession, as though that might help him clear his head. 'Did you see anyone?'

'No, I didn't. Not a soul.' Rosie stroked his face again, then lifted his head a little so she could feel the back. Something warm and wet met her fingertips, and she withdrew her hand carefully. She was sure it was blood. 'Did you follow someone here? Is that why you were hit over the head?'

Bluff reached up and pressed his fingers to the back of his head. He winced, then murmured, 'Heard someone barring the door...'

'Just as Nancy said.' Rosie took her handkerchief out of her pocket and dabbed the back of Bluff's head. 'So you came in... and... was there someone up here, in the hayloft?'

'I almost caught him, I'm sure,' Bluff said, his expression pained. 'He must've heard me... threw down the door bar. I was only a few seconds behind him, but he'd disappeared into thin air.'

Bluff made an effort to sit up, before abandoning it and sinking back onto Rosie's lap. 'Someone was creaking about up here. I climbed the ladder and... wallop.'

'You were out cold,' Rosie told him, concerned. She glanced over her shoulder. Someone had been here. The mole was still active and dangerous. 'Shall we get you to your room, and I'll fetch my first aid kit and clean you up?'

'That's a lot of trouble for you.' He pushed himself to sit up. 'Before he hit me, I'm sure... shine your torch over in that far corner.'

Rosie helped him to sit up. She shone her torch over into the corner. Some old harnesses and tack, thick with dust and cobwebs, were hung in the way, concealing what lay behind until Rosie's torch penetrated through a gap and she saw it.

A heap of straw, a couple of blankets. They looked fairly new, as far as she could tell. They didn't look like they'd been reclaimed from the clutter that filled the old barn.

'Is that...' Rosie stared. How could she have come into

this barn so often and not notice *that?* 'It's a bed, isn't it? Someone's made a bed up here!'

'Just a minute …' Bluff caught Rosie's hand. He steered the torch down over the floor and there she saw a long, rough piece of wood that looked as though it had been part of the roof beams once upon a time. 'I'll wager that's what he hit me with.'

'The bloody b—' *Bastard*. 'Bounder,' Rosie finished. 'He could've hurt you ever so badly. Oh, what a vile human being!'

And although Bluff was conscious now, Rosie was very worried that he might be hurt elsewhere. He was still holding her hand around the torch.

'Let's come back after the memorial tomorrow, in day-light,' he decided. 'I need a very stiff drink. Would you care to join me?'

'I would.' Rosie smiled gently at him. A drink with Bluff? Albeit a rather concussed Bluff. 'As your nurse, I prescribe a tot of brandy or rum, or a nip of whisky. It's the best medicine. Right … let's get you to your feet.'

'What brought you back here?' There was no suspicion in the question though, and his hand was still holding hers.

'I left my watch. I always take it off before I work on the car, and I left it behind.' In truth, because she had been distracted by the conversation she and Bluff had had over the engine. 'Mummy and Daddy bought it for me for my twenty-first. It sounds silly, but I like having it near me.'

Bluff smiled and asked, 'Did you find it?'

'I did! Just where I left it. Isn't it just as well I forgot it earlier?' Rosie helped Bluff to his feet. 'Will you be all right on the ladder? If I was a big, strapping lad, I'd put you over my shoulder like a fireman!'

'I think I'll be all right,' Bluff assured her. 'Luckily I have a thick skull!'

They went over to the ladder and Rosie went first, climbing down as quickly as she could. Bluff followed rather more gingerly, as though he was having to think very carefully about where to place each foot. It was hardly surprising if he'd been hit with the length of wood that they'd seen in the hayloft. Rosie could only imagine what might have happened if she'd arrived a moment later.

'I wonder if the blow on my head is clouding my thinking,' he admitted as he reached solid ground. 'Might it have just … fallen? It's a rickety old place.'

And he gave a discreet wink.

Playing along, Rosie pretended to agree. 'Oh, that must be it! Just unfortunate that you should've been standing underneath it at the time.'

'I'll come back in daylight, but one should consider every eventuality.' Bluff put his hand to the back of his head again, then turned to look back at the hayloft. 'I wonder …'

'What is it?' Rosie asked him. Bluff shook his head and gestured to the door. Despite herself Rosie felt a jolt of relief. She'd been in here long enough for one night.

'You can lean on me, if you need to,' Rosie offered. 'Have you aspirins in your room? Anything I can use to clean that cut?'

Bluff nodded and pulled the barn door shut. The key had long since been lost, but just closing the heavy door offered a fresh wave of relief. Whatever ghosts walked there, tonight they could do so alone.

Rosie slipped her arm around Bluff's waist and slowly guided him to the house. The mole wouldn't be stupid enough to try again tonight, would they? Especially not when they would be against two people, even if Bluff was unlikely to pose much threat to anyone with his sore head.

Cottisbourne Park was in darkness but in the huts, work would be continuing, the bombes working and Professor Swann's Endeavour machines toiling to decode the messages being sent from Berlin. It was strange to think that such important and secret tasks were going on out here in the quiet Sussex night. Rosie barely knew the tip of the iceberg, but even that was enough. They might not have faced bullets or the front line, but the people here were still fighting the war.

And it made Rosie glad that she'd taken the job. It had seemed from the advert that it wasn't too taxing at all, and she'd felt rather guilty when they'd interviewed her. They hadn't been able to tell her what the job entailed until she had been selected, and had signed the Official Secrets Act.

And now, here she was, helping to find a mole, and helping a wounded major-general limp his way back to his room.

They reached the house and went inside. Rosie heard distant voices. There was always someone awake, someone working at the Park. As they made their way upstairs and along the hallway though, the night fell silent again. Bluff suited Cottisbourne Park somehow, as only a man who'd grown up in a house with its very own moat could. Yet he'd run away from it, wayward and looking for mischief. He'd certainly found it here.

The setup of Bluff's bedroom didn't surprise Rosie. The metal bedstead had been buffed to a shine, and the bed had been made neatly, without a crease. There was little personal clutter anywhere, aside from a bottle of brandy and glasses beside his brush and comb on the dressing table, some toiletries by the basin, and on his nightstand a small travel alarm clock. And in the corner, a gramophone with a shiny brass horn.

'I'll sit you down on the bed,' Rosie told him.

'I'm really very robust,' Bluff assured Rosie, and she could believe it too. But everyone needed looking after now and then. 'Brandy?'

'I'd love one,' Rosie said. 'Let me pour the drinks, and you sit yourself down.'

'Look at this room.' Bluff began to unbutton his tunic as he spoke. He sighed and opened the wardrobe, inside which Rosie caught a glimpse of more immaculately pressed khaki and nestled among it, an unexpected flash of scarlet mess dress. 'Austere. The war has made everything austere, even for a major-general.'

'It's very neat,' Rosie offered, trying to sound buoyant. But there was no way to avoid it. It *was* a very austere room. Rosie busied herself going to his sink where she'd spotted a flannel. She dampened it under the tap. 'Now let me look at that wound.'

She guided Bluff to sit down on the edge of his bed and leaned around him to get a look. As she wiped away the blood, she found a cut on his scalp, which was beginning to bruise under his hair. But it wasn't deep, and could be bandaged easily enough. She'd seen similar injuries during her days driving ambulances in the Blitz, caused by flying debris from bombed buildings.

'You've got a cut,' Rosie told him. 'But I don't think you need stitches. Just a bandage. It'll heal. And aspirin for your headache, of course.'

'A bandage?' Bluff tutted. 'At least my cap will hide it. I don't want to give Prospero the satisfaction. Fallen roof beam, my foot!'

'Oh, you might only need the bandage for tonight. Just

to stop it from bleeding. Would you like to see the village doctor, just in case?' Rosie suspected she could guess the answer that a seasoned soldier like Bluff, a man used to bumps and cuts, would give.

'Oh, I don't think we need trouble the medic,' he assured her. 'A bed in a hayloft ... what do you make of it?'

'I really don't know. Someone slacking off and looking for somewhere to nap?' Rosie suggested. She went over to the sink and rinsed out the flannel before wringing it out and hanging it over the edge of the basin. Then she went back to Bluff. 'What with them sleeping in the huts they work in, I suppose someone wanted to get away from it all for a bit of peace and quiet. Although then again ... there's other things people do in bed besides sleeping, if you know what I mean.' She raised an eyebrow.

'I'll have to tell Wyngate about this. I *know* Prospero was in the barn when you arrived. He had to be, he couldn't just vanish into thin air.'

'But how did he get out? There's only one entrance. I don't know ...' Rosie thought for a moment. The barn wasn't in particularly good condition, and it gave her an idea. 'Unless there's a loose board somewhere that he could squeeze out of.'

Bluff wouldn't be able to do that, Rosie realised. Not with those broad shoulders of his.

'And all the time you and the prof were working on the Citroën, you had no idea someone else was using the place,' he mused. 'I noticed the bank of straw when I went up to the hayloft on the morning I arrived, but ... well, there were more pressing matters. And the blankets rather give it away now, don't they?'

'Just a little.' Rosie shook her head. 'It takes a lot to leave me scandalised, but really ... I was working on the car while

someone's love nest – literally a nest of straw and blankets!
– was right above my head. I had no idea. Perhaps when I'd
been up there before, the blankets had been stashed away, so
I wouldn't really have noticed the bed. And to be honest, I
was keeping an eye on Nancy while she was playing. Ladders
and children aren't a good mix.'

'Do I really need a bandage?'

'Even soldiers need bandages sometimes.' Rosie leaned
over him again and had a look at the wound. She hated
seeing someone strong like Bluff brought low. She wanted
to make everything better. 'The bleeding's stopped, though.
Would you be more comfortable without it?'

Bluff looked up at her and smiled. 'I'm a terrible patient,
Rosie. I should've warned you.'

'I can't say it surprises me!' Rosie chuckled. 'Tomorrow
morning, I could pop round with my first aid kit and dab
some iodine on your cut? Although I suppose you might
not like that!'

'There's a first aid kit in the bathroom,' he said, grudging
as a child with a grazed knee. 'If I need iodine, then I shall
endure iodine. You're nicer than the usual army medics, so
perhaps it isn't quite as bad.'

Rosie went to the bathroom, which was well-furnished
with a fascinating array of grooming products, and returned
with the green-coloured tin decorated with a blood red
cross. She put it down on the bed next to Bluff, but before
setting to work with the first aid kit, poured both of them
a brandy.

She handed Bluff his glass, then as she poured iodine onto
the cotton wool warned him, 'This'll sting a bit.'

He gave a curt nod. 'I've had worse, I suspect. Weeding can
be a dangerous job.' Bluff pinched his thumb and forefinger

to the bridge of his nose and closed his eyes, suddenly weary. 'I can't let Prospero slip through the net again, Rosie.'

'They're close. Too close, even,' Rosie said. 'Walloping you over the head tells me that they're scared. Because you're onto them. Now ... here comes the sting.' And she dabbed the cotton wool against his cut.

Bluff said nothing, but she saw him wince and he took a deep gulp of brandy. So iodine could still shake a mole-hunting major-general? It could have been so much worse though. Prospero didn't mean this as a warning, Rosie was certain. It was meant to be final.

And Bluff must know very well that such was the case. Thank goodness Rosie had gone back to the barn when she did, or it would've been so much worse. Another body in the hayloft. Rosie hated to even think of it.

'There, you're all cleaned up now.' Rosie tidied away the first aid box, then she moved the chair that sat by the wall over to the bed and picked up her glass as she took a seat. 'Shall we raise a toast?'

'To ...' Bluff looked thoughtful. 'Theatre. And forgotten watches.'

'Theatre! And forgotten watches.' Rosie touched her glass to Bluff's. 'And to you and me. To Rosie and ... erm ...' *I don't know his name.* 'Major-General Sir Kingsley-Flynn.'

Bluff took a deep breath and murmured something that she couldn't quite catch. *His name?* In that moment he looked like a little boy being asked if he'd scrumped an apple.

Rosie grinned at him. 'You'll have to learn to project your voice,' she teased. 'They won't hear you in the back row!'

He fixed her with a comically withering stare and said, 'Torquil. And that's probably the greatest secret of the war as far as you're concerned.'

'Goodness, I must've got very high clearance!' Rosie

chortled. Then she pursed her lips together, suppressing her laughter, and patted him on the knee. *Torquil, bless him.* 'It's a very nice name. Very traditional. Are you named after someone in your family?'

'It was my great-grandfather's name, but I rather prefer Bluff.'

'How lovely to be named after someone like that!' Rosie smiled at him. 'I'm named after someone who doesn't even exist. But ... Bluff suits you more than Torquil. It's a good name.'

'A relic of my wayward days.' And Bluff looked rather pleased about that. 'I ran a card school at Marlborough. I ran one at Sandhurst too. Absolutely *rinsed* Monty in Tunisia.'

'You *didn't!* You naughty chap!' Rosie sipped the brandy. It was very good, so she took another sip. 'Well, one evening we'll have to play. Although we'll only be gambling with buttons and pebbles.'

'An actress *and* a driver?' He quirked one eyebrow. 'You'll clean me out.'

'You'll never crack my poker face. All your buttons shall be mine!' Rosie unleashed her best villainous cackle, honed from the annual panto. Then she gasped. 'Oh, heck, what if someone hears me in here?'

'I have no neighbours,' Bluff assured her. 'That's precisely why I chose this room.'

'Just as well ...' Rosie took another drink. 'Seeing as I'm your loud theatrical friend!'

Bluff raised his glass. 'To loud friends!'

Rosie laughed. Loudly. The sort of laugh she hadn't done for a while. Once she'd reined it in, she said, 'You wouldn't get a laugh like that in the Household Cavalry, surely?'

'That's a state secret, Driver Rosie.' Bluff laughed, a booming sound that filled the room. Of course it did though, she couldn't imagine a man of Bluff's size having anything less than a major-general sized laugh. 'H-Cav can be full of surprises.'

'Your laugh is louder than mine!'

Rosie took the last sip from her glass. She was used to bedroom socialising. It happened all the time on the road with the theatre company, as no one ever had a sitting room of their own to lounge about in. But they were frowned on at Cottisbourne Park, and if the actress was known to have drunk luxurious brandy in a senior officer's bedroom, she could get into a lot of trouble. MTC girls were supposed to behave.

She put the glass down on the dressing table and moved the chair back to its original place.

'I best be off,' she told Bluff. 'You need your sleep after getting thwacked. If it starts to hurt very badly or if it bleeds again, you will tell me, won't you? I'll come and patch you up again.'

Bluff rose to his feet and nodded. 'You have my word. Thank you, Ro— Driver Sinclair, for everything.'

Rosie gave him an ironic salute. With a grin, she said, 'Don't worry about it, Torquil. Goodnight. Lock your door, won't you, sir?'

He nodded, returning the salute. 'And I shall await the signal from your candle.'

'Of course, sir.' Rosie hesitated at the door. She had the oddest feeling that she should hug him. The poor man had been injured, after all, and she didn't want to abandon him. But he could look after himself. He was a major-general after all. 'Goodnight.'

Rosie closed the door quietly behind her, then headed back to her room. The night seemed to be filled with threat and she kept her senses on alert as she crossed the courtyard, listening for rogue footsteps. She locked her door behind her and moved the empty oil can she'd left downstairs in front of it. It might make a clatter if someone tried to get in. Then she ran up the stairs and lit her candle at the window. An answering flame shone in the window across the courtyard, and she saw Bluff smile as he bent to extinguish it.

Goodnight, Torquil.

Chapter 14

The organ played a solemn tune as Rosie filed into Cottis-bourne's church with the other staff from the Park. Hale had been a popular man, and everyone who could be spared was walking with heads bowed, black bands on their arms, into the church.

Rosie sat a few pews back in the corner with the girls. She hoped she'd be able to see the reactions of any of the suspects who might be present. As she looked around the church, with its marble and stained glass memorials to the family who had once lived at the Park, Rosie remembered coming to the church with Hale at Christmas. They had energetically sung the carols and tried not to laugh when Nancy's angel wings left a trail of feathers in the nativity play. She saw his smile so clearly in her mind that its absence felt like a punch to the stomach.

You bloody awful person, whoever you are.

There were people from the village too, where Professor Hale had collected friends just as he did amongst his code-breakers. There was the postmistress and the landlord, the butcher and the lad who delivered the milk. There was even Nancy and her grandparents, Portia sitting neatly in the pew beside the little girl.

Rosie gave Nancy a wave and mouthed, *hello.* As she did, she heard the creak of a door at the back of church and the vicar made his way down the aisle, his chasuble flowing behind him.

A creak.

Rosie heard again the creak of the barn the night before and realised what she had heard. Not the sound of old wood settling, but instead a door.

But there was only one way into the barn.

As far as I know.

Bluff followed the vicar along the aisle to take his seat in the front pew. His cap was tucked beneath his elbow, his back poker straight and though Rosie looked, there was no trace of the injury to his head. If Prospero was sitting among the congregation, would he be annoyed to see the major-general looking so chipper? Would his face give him away if so?

The vicar opened the service and they started to sing 'Lead us, Heavenly Father'. Rosie glanced around, everyone holding up their hymn books as they sang. And as she looked, she spotted something.

Joe Fleet had a bandaged hand.

She hadn't noticed it in the pub. A shiver went through her, which she hoped anyone who'd noticed would put down to the chill in the old church. Across the aisle, Charles Swann glanced towards Rosie for a second, no more. Then he returned his gaze to the hymn book, a slight smile on his lips.

After the hymn, everyone took their seats again, and the vicar spoke. His words were full of sympathy for Hale. He didn't condemn the man who almost everyone believed had taken his own life. He stressed the fact that times were difficult, and stated his wish that should anyone else begin to slip into despair, they would seek help and consolation. He finished by sharing his own memories of Hale, who he had seen sometimes around the village. The vicar had clearly liked him.

Was there anyone who hadn't, apart from the mole?

Perhaps Prospero didn't dislike the professor at all, and Hale had simply got in the way. Somehow that seemed even worse, that a human being could dispose of another for no reason but to save themselves. But how could Prospero possibly understand friendship or camaraderie? What motivated someone like that?

Rosie watched Charles from the corner of her eye. Of all the suspects, he seemed the most callous. Professor Jones, she noticed, was wiping away tears. Rosie couldn't imagine Charles Swann crying over anything. When Bluff stepped up to the lectern to speak, Charles tipped his head back and gave a theatrical sigh. He looked at Rosie again, making sure she had seen him before he returned his attention to Bluff.

Charles couldn't bear the limelight sliding away from him. He reminded Rosie of certain actors she'd encountered over the years who sighed and rolled their eyes when someone else had their moment. But the thought of Charles holding forth about Hale struck Rosie as disgustingly insincere. He wouldn't be able to say the words without a grin as he thought about plonking his rear down at Hale's empty desk.

But why was he smirking at her? What on earth was he hoping to achieve?

Did he see me with Bluff last night?

Rosie bit her lip. Would he tell people? But she had nothing to be ashamed of. Not a thing. She'd gone back to the barn to fetch her watch. There was no assignation, because she and Bluff were only chums.

Rosie wouldn't rise to it. If he *hadn't* seen her, that smirk might mean *I'm Prospero and you'll never catch me!*

And Rosie was determined that he would be wrong.

Rosie left her window open before going to sleep that night, to enjoy the warm spring evening. The hymns from the service had played in her head, until she had started to dream and a choir of Prospero suspects, ludicrous in choirboy gowns and ruffs appeared, Charles still smirking as he sang.

The next thing Rosie knew was a snatch of dream. A bonfire from her childhood, the scent of burning wood filling her senses, the fireworks shooting upwards, silent although everyone was shouting.

Shouting.

Rosie was wide awake at once. She sat bolt upright, hurriedly blinking away sleep. She could still smell the bonfire, still hear the shouting.

She got out of bed and stumbled to the window. There was a figure in the middle of the courtyard.

Sid.

And he was hoarsely shouting for help.

'Fire! The barn's on fire! Help! Wake up, for God's sake!'

The barn? Oh, no, the car!

'I'm coming down!' Rosie shouted.

She dragged her cardigan on over her pyjamas and pulled on her shoes, then ran outside. The courtyard was busy with a dozen other residents of Cottisbourne Park, and their numbers were increasing all the time. They looked dazed and bleary, some in dressing gowns, others wearing outdoor coats or cardigans over their pyjamas and nightdresses as they headed towards the barn. A plume of smoke was already rising into the sky, shimmering into nothingness against the moon.

One of the firehoses was already unfurled and ran alongside the house. As Rosie ran towards the sound of crackling flames Douglas Stuart, whose name had appeared on Bluff's list, dashed past her, a second firehose unfurling behind him as he ran.

'Driver Sinclair!' Tommy, the groundsman, called Rosie's name over the hubbub. 'Rosie!'

Rosie waved. 'I'm over here!'

'Have you seen Nancy?' He pressed one hand to his side and bent to catch his breath. 'Bert saw the smoke and when he went out to the garden to see what was up, he found the kitchen door open. No sign of little Nancy! He thinks she'll have come over here.'

'*Nancy?*' Rosie froze with horror. She stepped towards Tommy and saw Bert, Nancy's grandfather standing beside him. The usually jovial man looked gaunt with worry.

'She was talking about your car in the barn before she went to sleep,' Bert told them, his frightened eyes turned to the barn. 'What if she's in there?'

Rosie gasped. 'We've got to get inside!'

Rosie fought her way through the crowd standing around the barn. Smoke belched from the half-open door. She'd seen firemen in the East End risk their lives in the Blitz, running into burning buildings. But did she have their same courage?

She cupped her hands around her mouth and called the little girl's name. 'Nancy! Nancy, are you in there?'

Then she turned to see the line of men holding the firehose, heading towards the barn, and saw Bluff among them.

'Major-General! Nancy might be in there!' Rosie shouted.

'Nancy?' Bluff asked, relinquishing his grip on the hose to another man. Rosie recognised Sid, whose name had been there on Bluff's list. Would Prospero really be so white with worry, let alone so eager to help? *And where is Charles Swann?* 'The little girl?'

Rosie nodded. 'Yes! She's not at home!'

Bert hurried over, gripping his cap to his chest. 'My little granddaughter! She was talking and talking about the car at tea time, saying you'd all drive to London and see her mum!' He swallowed as he stared at the building in front of him. 'I can't think where else she would've gone.'

Smoke poured from the barn door, belching thick and black into the night as tongues of flame lashed out from the roof, illuminating the darkness. Bluff took a deep breath and nodded, then turned to address the men with the firehose.

'There may be a little girl trapped inside!' he told them in that Sandhurst bark that he deployed now and then. 'You chaps follow me in and get those flames doused!'

Sid nodded. 'Right you are! Come on, men. Follow the major-general!'

Rosie saw fear on their faces, but only fleetingly. They set their jaws and as one took a step closer to the barn.

Rosie joined them, holding onto the firehose. She squared her shoulders and took a deep breath, preparing herself to go into the inferno. She wasn't going to let her little friend down. 'Don't worry, Nancy, we're coming in!'

'Rosie, no,' Bluff said urgently. 'It's not safe. I promise I'll find her, but will you stay here with Bert? He looks ready to fall down.'

Rosie glanced round at Nancy's grandfather. He was unsteady on his feet, his eyes half-closed.

'Rosie, is that you?' Sarah called in surprise, running up in her siren suit, Maggie at her side. 'You're not going into the barn, are you?'

Rosie bit her lip. Maybe they were right. Reluctantly, she relinquished the fire hose. She caught Bluff's glance and nodded. 'But you must find Nancy. You *must*.'

Then she went over to Bert, and put her arm around his shaking shoulders. Sarah and Maggie stood beside them.

'I promised to look after her!' he whispered.

'It's not your fault,' Rosie told him.

Oh, God, it's mine.

'Come on!' Bluff pulled the barn doors open wide, dropped his head down and dashed into the smoke. Sid and the other men surged on behind him, water shooting into the barn from their hose.

Bluff was a natural leader. How many other men would be followed into a burning building?

'Take care, for heaven's sake!' Rosie called. She couldn't bear to think what might happen. It was only a day since Bluff had been bludgeoned over the head in the barn. And now he was heading into flames.

It was no coincidence that the barn was on fire. Whose work could it be other than Prospero?

'Oh my!' Caroline was at Rosie's shoulder. One hand was clamped over her mouth, the other tying her dressing gown belt. She stared wide-eyed at the scene as though she couldn't believe what she was seeing.

And your brother might be responsible, Rosie realised.

'Nancy might be in there,' Rosie whispered. 'The major-general's going in to look.'

Bert let out a sob, then covered his mouth with his hand. Rosie couldn't imagine how terrified the poor man must be.

The flames that had flickered up through the roof of the barn were diminishing though, replaced by thick, jet black smoke as the men doused the fire. Caroline clutched Rosie's hand, her grip tight as they watched the open door, nobody daring to speak now the word of Nancy's presence had started to get round the crowd. She even saw some people coming from the direction of the huts, summoned by the cacophony.

'Is that ... oh, he's got her!' Maggie exclaimed. She pointed towards the barn, where a soot-dusted figure had emerged, a small bundle in his arms.

'Nancy!' Bert took a step forwards, but he stopped, as if he was too scared by what awaited him.

She has to be alive. She has to be!

Rosie thought again of Nancy in the nativity play, an angel with her pigtails askew.

'Let me go and see,' Rosie said. She slipped her arm from Bert's shoulder and took her hand from Caroline's and ran towards Bluff. 'Major-General, is she ...?' Rosie couldn't form the words.

'She's all right,' he whispered. Nancy gave a shuddering sob and cuddled against Bluff. In her arms, held tight as a newborn baby, Rosie caught a glimpse of Portia. 'A little bit overwhelmed, I think?'

Nancy sniffed. She buried her face against Bluff's shirt and whispered hoarsely, 'I'm not crying, Rosie, honest.'

Rosie called back to Bert. 'She's all right!'

At her words, Bert sagged with relief.

Rosie stroked Nancy's hair. 'Oh, Nancy, you silly sausage! What were you doing in the barn?'

'I want my mum,' she whispered. 'I'm ever so sorry. Rosie.'

'I think we should pop her along to sick bay,' Bluff told Bert. 'Just to be sure.'

'Of course.' Rosie knew how dangerous smoke inhalation could be. Nancy needed help that Rosie couldn't give.

'I'll come along with her,' Bert said as he approached. 'I won't leave her side.'

From inside the barn there came a shout. 'Fire's out, sir!'

'Would you mind taking Nancy along to sick bay?' Bluff

asked Tommy, then glanced back towards the barn. 'Rosie, if you could go along as well and I'll join you when we're done here.'

'I'll come too.' Caroline stroked her hand over the little girl's hair. 'We girls must stick together, eh, Nancy?'

Rosie was glad she was there. It might help a little that although Nancy's mother couldn't be with her, she had other women around her.

'See you soon, sir,' Rosie said. He gave a nod in reply and bundled Nancy over into her grandfather's arms. She clutched his lapel in one hand, still holding Portia tight with the other. This time, Rosie knew, Prospero had crossed the line.

Chapter 15

The nurse who worked in sick bay took charge of Nancy. Rosie sat with her friends in the tiny waiting room as she watched Bert follow the woman in her white uniform down the corridor. It must've been a horrible surprise for her when she usually dealt with cuts and scratches and sore throats. And quite a novelty to deal with a child.

Rosie flipped through a magazine as she waited, puzzling over a knitting pattern for a jumper. What did the jumble of letters and numbers mean? It was yet another code to be cracked.

'What happened, Rosie?' Caroline murmured. 'Nobody would... it was an accident, wasn't it? It must have been.'

'I'm sure it was,' Rosie replied. She couldn't tell Caroline what she really thought. 'Someone might've wandered past smoking and thrown aside their cigarette, and... It's funny – although not much – I was so worried about the car going up in smoke, but as soon as I realised that Nancy might be in there, I didn't think about it at all. I hope it's survived the fire, but the main thing is that Nancy's all right.'

Maggie nodded as she said, 'That's the important thing.' At the other end of the hallway a door opened and closed and Caroline dropped her voice to a whisper to tell Rosie, 'Gosh, he looks like he's been through the wars!'

Bluff had arrived. Rosie hopped up from her seat and saluted, giddy with admiration for him. He looked like he was in need of a good bath, his face sooty and his usually well-groomed hair sticking up in clumps. His clothes were grey with soot, dishevelled and messy.

All in all, Rosie decided, he was allowed to look untidy for once. He was the hero of the hour, after all.

'Good evening, sir.'

'Good evening, Driver, Miss Swann.' Bluff saluted in return. 'How's our patient?'

'She's still with the nurse,' Rosie replied. 'I don't think she's called for the doctor, so that could be a good sign. When I was driving ambulances in the Blitz... the first few minutes were when people...' Rosie shook the memory away, of a lifeless figure on a stretcher. 'I think she's going to be fine.'

'Splendid.' Bluff leaned his back against the wall, exhaustion showing on his face. He passed one hand over his hair and closed his eyes. When he opened them again, Rosie saw that they were red from the smoke and her heart went out to him. 'The car escaped unharmed. The same can't be said for the barn, of course.'

'I should've cleared out all that clutter long ago instead of fiddling about with the car,' Rosie scolded herself. 'But I'm glad the car's all right.'

A door opened at the end of the corridor and Bert appeared, beaming.

'She's going to be fine, the nurse says!' he announced. 'Ain't that grand?'

'She's made of strong stuff.' Bluff stood up straight, no trace of his exhaustion showing. 'Will you take her home tonight? I'd be happy to drive you.'

Of course he wouldn't ask Rosie to do it. That wasn't Bluff's way at all.

'Yes, that's the plan, get her back in her own bed tonight.'

Bert nodded. 'And that's *ever* so kind of you, sir. I wouldn't say no to a lift at all.'

'You don't object to my borrowing the Humber, do you, Driver Sinclair?'

'No, sir, not at all. I'll come with you,' Rosie said.

The door at the far end of the corridor opened again, revealing the nurse pushing Nancy and Portia in a wheelchair.

'Isn't this fun?' the nurse said. Rosie wondered if the wheelchair was more to keep Nancy entertained, rather than because she had trouble walking. She looked a lot more lively now, a bright smile on her face at the sight of her friends.

'Not as good as our French motor, is it?' Nancy called, brave all over again. Her voice was still hoarse, but it could have been so much worse. 'Wait until I tell mum about this!'

'You'd better not, or she'll have my hide!' Bert joked.

'Oh, Nancy,' Rosie sighed. 'Whatever were you doing in the barn so late at night?'

'I was missing mum and dad,' Nancy admitted sheepishly. 'So me and Portia decided to play at driving to the seaside with you and the major-general, only I fell asleep in the car and when I woke up...' Her bottom lip quivered. 'When I woke up, it was all smoky and I couldn't find the door handle, so I got down on the floor of the motor, but... but there was too much smoke and...'

Bluff nodded, the look on his face one of admiration. He held out his hand to Nancy and said, 'Congratulations, Driver Nancy, on showing such courage in the face of danger. I'm very impressed indeed.'

Nancy smiled and took Bluff's large hand in her little palm. She shook it, telling him, 'And Portia as well. She wasn't scared.'

146

'And Driver Portia too,' said Bluff. 'Driver Sinclair has certainly trained her protégés well.'

Rosie saluted him, which was perhaps a little ridiculous when she was wearing only pyjamas and a cardigan, but the occasion definitely warranted it.

'Thank you, sir. I only accept the finest recruits, as you know.' And she winked at Nancy.

The nurse insisted on pushing Nancy to the garage where the Humber waited for them. Rosie ran ahead to fetch the keys from her room, and hurriedly threw on some clothes. She didn't want to embarrass Bluff with her pyjamas a moment longer.

Once she got downstairs, they were waiting by the garage doors. Nancy was quiet again, curled up beneath a blanket, her eyes closed. The exhausted women had finally taken themselves off to bed now the danger was passed, but Bluff was watchful as ever despite his smoke-dry eyes. At the sight of Rosie he raised his hand in greeting.

Rosie waved back. 'Let's get this little girl home.'

They got into the car, Bluff in the driving seat with Rosie beside him, and Bert in the back with Nancy. It was a short journey through the slumbering village to the house Nancy shared with her grandparents. As the narrow beam of the masked headlamps illuminated the neat garden, the front door opened and Rosie saw Nancy's grandmother on the step, her hands worrying anxiously at one another.

He drew the Humber to a halt and whispered to Bert, 'Can you manage, sir?'

'Oh, yes, Major-General.' Bert nodded. 'And thank you. Not many men'd do what you did this evening. Proper self-less, you were.'

'Oh, I'm sure they would.' He smiled as he climbed out of the car and opened the back door for Bert. 'I'll ask Tommy to pop over tomorrow and add a bolt at the top of that kitchen door for you if you like. You've got a little Houdini there.'

'She'll drag a chair over and climb up to draw back the bolt, if I know her!' Bert replied. 'Like she does to get at the biscuits, when we have 'em.'

He waved to his wife, then reached into the car to pick up Nancy and bundled her into his arms. 'Come along, you silly thing. Your nan's waiting for you.'

Nancy murmured something in her sleep, but she didn't wake. Instead she snuggled to him like an infant, Portia tight in her embrace. Bluff gave Bert a nod and whispered, 'Good evening, sir. Sleep tight, Nancy.'

'Night night everyone!' Bert replied, as if he was tucking them all into bed. He turned and headed into his house where his very relieved wife awaited him. As soon as he had gone, Bluff let out a long, tired breath. Was it Rosie's imagination, or did those broad shoulders visibly sag?

Rosie leaned across and said to him, 'Come on, hero! Time for you to head home and pour yourself a well-deserved brandy.'

'I'll drive you back.' Bluff climbed back into the car and closed the door. 'My mind's racing, I'm afraid. No point lying in bed staring at the ceiling.'

'Would you like to go for a drive?' Rosie suggested. 'I haven't taken the car out for a couple of days, so we can spare the petrol.'

He nodded, glancing towards Rosie to ask, 'Shall we go up and see Romeo and Juliet?'

'Why not?' Rosie replied.

The Humber moved smoothly through the sleeping village, then took the steep hill with ease, as it always did. In minutes, Rosie and Bluff arrived at the top of the hill, with the two standing stones sleeping nearby. Rosie loved it up here, looking out over the village and the lush countryside that surrounded it. She and Bluff climbed out of the car, a breeze ruffling Rosie's hair as she drew in a welcome breath of fresh night air.

'This is better. *Much* better!' Rosie sighed. 'You know what, sir? You're a bloody great big hero, and I'm proud to know you.'

He shook his head. 'I'm not a hero. Anyone would've done it.'

'Not just anyone. You didn't even hesitate.' Rosie smiled at him. 'You had no idea what it was going to be like in that barn, yet you thought of Nancy and … she wouldn't be alive now if you hadn't gone in there.'

'She was huddled up in the car with that doll of hers,' Bluff said softly. 'I thought she … it must've been the smoke. I thought she was dead, Rosie, that Prospero had killed her. I telephoned Wyngate before I came to the sick bay, but our hands're tied. Any suggestion of military police and Prospero will realise we're onto him, so don't be surprised if you start to see new faces amongst the groundskeepers and caretakers.'

'Oh, sir, that must've been awful for you, to see her like that. Whatever was she doing …?' Rosie sighed. It had been a very close call. Far too close. 'I feel like it's my fault, that I encouraged her to go into the barn. And look what nearly happened. But I'm glad you've spoken to Wyngate. I really am. And what a good idea, to hide the military police in the grounds like that.'

'Don't blame yourself, this is all down to bloody Prospero.' Bluff stretched his arms above his head and yawned. 'We'll move the Citroën tomorrow. It can share the garage with the Humber.'

'A new home for the Citroën,' Rosie said. 'You haven't

seen much of Cottisbourne, have you? What with Prospero keeping you busy. At least you can see it from up here. The lights are lit on the airstrip this evening – can you see them? The planes must be out.'

Rosie pointed down the hill. Bluff followed the path of her finger and nodded. For a few seconds they stood together in companionable silence, both watching the silent airfield. It was so peaceful tonight that it seemed almost ridiculous to imagine that this was a world at war, but somewhere in the night, Prospero was scheming. Somewhere not that far away.

'You can even see some of the Park from up here,' Rosie told him. 'See where all those trees are, down there? You can see the huts poking through. There're the grounds ... the folly ... the stream that runs through the bottom ... The house is over there. You can see that big circle – it's the top of the drive.'

'Tell me a story about the theatre,' Bluff said suddenly. 'Something that makes you smile.'

He didn't want to think about the Park or Prospero tonight.

'Gosh, where do I begin?' Rosie said. 'When I was a child, I thought everyone's parents dressed up and pretended to be other people. I was very confused by the idea that actually not everyone's parents do. Or that not everyone lives in boarding houses. It was very odd coming here ... I still sometimes feel like Driver Sinclair is a role I'm playing. But you want a happy story, don't you?'

Rosie knew exactly what story to tell him, and she glowed with the joy of her memory. 'Well ... when everyone really felt their money troubles a few years back, Mummy and Daddy had a cancellation. It was a great shame, but the town had been very badly hit with a couple of big factories closing down and everyone losing their jobs. The theatre hadn't sold enough tickets. And do you know what Mummy and Daddy said? *We're going to do it anyway. You don't have to pay us.* So we loaded up the van, and off we went. Everybody mucked in. The cast were put up for free in people's houses, and we didn't charge for the tickets, and do you know, night after night we had a full house for *A Midsummer Night's Dream* and a standing ovation! It was fantastic. And it was such a lovely production. So fun and colourful. And we even added to the Players – a brilliant carpenter who made amazing sets, and a very talented young actor who was with us for a year before he went off to the West End. We had such a marvellous time. Oh, you would've loved it, Blu— Major-General.'

'Bluff,' he said with a smile. 'But *never* Torquil. Just out of interest, who *does* fund the company? Do you work with producers or does it all come from the Sinclairs and your ticket sales?'

'Bluff? Well, if you say so, Bluff. Hello, Bluff! I'm Rosie.' She held her hand out to shake. 'And as for the Players – it's mostly ticket sales and Mummy and Daddy twisting arms here and there. We've had producers a few times, though, but Mummy and Daddy are very particular about who they'll work with, you see.'

'Hello, Rosie, splendid to meet you.' Bluff shook her hand. 'How do they feel about Major-Generals who are also Sirs and have no experience whatsoever of producing plays, but are very keen to find out?'

'I don't think they've ever met any!' Rosie said. Was this real? Was Bluff proposing to work with the Cavendish Players? 'Would you like to, truly? Oh, there's a lot of producers who won't listen to Mummy and Daddy, and that's when the trouble starts. They insist on their pet actor playing the lead or what have you, and it never goes well. One producer insisted on his fiancée playing the lead, and she had a squeaky voice like Minnie Mouse! But if you're willing to learn from all their years of experience, then ... well, I'm sure they'd love to work with you!'

Bluff beamed at that, his face lighting up as he told her, 'The army's been good to me, but I've seen enough of the worst the world has to offer. I think an Allied victory might be an ideal curtain call, don't you? Time to leave the stage, as they say. Maybe I'll learn how to be wayward again.'

Rosie knew that no one at Cottisbourne Park would believe she could have heard what Bluff had just said. The stern senior officer, planning for a career in theatre? And who among them would ever believe that Bluff had once had a wayward side?

'I think it's a marvellous idea,' Rosie told him. 'You've seen some horrible things lately, not to mention had them happen to you. You deserve the chance to unleash your wayward self!'

'Father won't be happy,' he chuckled. 'But I don't think he'll object too much. I've served my time and he always did like an evening of Shakespeare.'

'Oh, we'll win him over to the cause, I'm certain!' Rosie said. 'You can't be the good son Bluff all your life. Why not rebel a little after everything you've done?'

Rosie had a suspicion that Bluff had seen things that would make the fire tonight look like nothing.

'Do you recall HMS Dasher going down last year?' he asked quietly. 'That was Prospero's doing. I was on board.'

'You were on board?' Rosie blinked in surprise. 'I heard something about it from Professor Hale. Something about an explosion inside the ship, and all those poor people were killed, and they have no idea what caused it. But ... it was Prospero?'

Bluff nodded. 'I can only tell you because you signed

Wyngate's damned *addendum*.' He spat the word out as though it was obscene. 'There were families on board, not that you'll read about them in any of the newspapers. Senior informers on the Axis bastards, double agents, pen pushers who dared to go against their paymasters and come over to our side. We promised them we'd get them out, whatever it took. *I* promised them.' He looked out over the landscape again, then closed his eyes and took a deep breath. 'It took months, Rosie, and every day of it I was ready for a knock on the door from the Gestapo. I was the one behind enemy lines, *I* was the one communicating with Britain and all the time, Prospero was keeping the Führer fully briefed on our plans. There's no way Germany cracked the code we were using; we changed it every week. Prospero *had* to be operating on our side and passing the information back.'

'You were behind enemy lines?' Rosie was amazed. Although on reflection, it made sense. He knew how to play a part. 'I had no idea there were families on the ship. How awful. How absolutely awful, and how bloody dreadful of Prospero to send them to their deaths! Oh, Bluff... you must've been terrified. And I'm not surprised you're so determined to track Prospero down. Not after living through that.'

'It wasn't an explosion in the hold, whatever the ministers claim.' He met Rosie's gaze. 'She was torpedoed. A bloody U-boat sitting out there off the Firth of Clyde, waiting for us ...'

Rosie shivered as a chill went through her. 'Prospero told them you'd be there. Prospero signed their death warrants. Are you any closer to working out who it is? I have my hunch, but I don't know if you'd agree.'

'I've one or two ideas.' Bluff scrubbed one hand back through his hair. 'The sea caught fire that afternoon, Rosie, but it seemed as dark as midnight. Concussion, you know, fractured the old skull, I'm afraid. And I was there in the water, freezing, bleeding, and all I could think of was that girl who'd been Portia on the most perfect summer evening. I could still hear her voice and there in the haze there was a light ... *how far that little candle throws his beams*. And I held onto it and somehow, I swam until a little boat – the light I'd seen – picked me up. The next time I opened my eyes, it was a week later and I felt as though I'd been hit by a train.'

Over the years, people had told Rosie how much her performances had meant to her, but no one had ever told her something like that. That she had given someone something to cling to in the darkest moment of their life. She was humbled, more than she could ever say. She blinked away tears.

Rosie took his hand.

'I'm so glad you were spared,' she whispered. 'And I'm so glad ... so, so glad, that my performance meant so much to you. What a beautiful evening it was. And we'll have ones just like it again once this is all over. We *will*.'

'We intercepted a message from him straight to the Berghof. Prospero was celebrating those deaths, none more so than the families we'd lost. He used our own code to send it, just to be sure that we'd know what he was saying if we *did* intercept it. Prospero revels in the chaos he causes.' The thought of it was sickening. Rosie could barely comprehend it. 'But we'll get him, we owe it to everybody he's betrayed. It was you who gave me the strength to not give up that day, Rosie, and I never expected to have the chance to tell you.'

'Thank goodness it did,' Rosie said. 'Otherwise who will bring down Prospero? Such a callous man. So arrogant. So proud of all those deaths. And now Professor Hale's added to the list, and you nearly were and even little Nancy – because that fire was Prospero's work, wasn't it? Who else could've done it?'

'It's Prospero.' There was nobody else it *could* be. 'And he's running scared. At first light I'm going to the barn to see exactly what he was trying to destroy with the fire. He won't have any luck if he tries again tonight, some of the lads from RAF Cottisbourne very kindly agreed to stand sentry.'

'Dare I say I secretly hope he *does* try, and he ends up having an argument with a bayonet?' Rosie remarked. 'So who have you crossed off your list, then?' Rosie started to count off the suspects' names on her fingers. 'Professor Swann, Dr Brett, Professor Jones, Mr Chandler, Dr Stuart and Mr Fleet. I saw Sid – I mean, Mr Chandler – helping to put out the fire. He looked genuinely shocked. I'd be very surprised if he'd started the fire. And Dr Stuart was helping as well.'

Bluff nodded. 'And you probably haven't heard that our chess-loving Professor Jones managed to slip in his bathroom this morning and break his ankle. I doubt he was capable of climbing into a hayloft and committing arson.'

Rosie winced. 'Poor chap! I doubt he's been capable of very much.'

'Fleet, on the other hand, presented himself at sickbay this morning with a considerable splinter in his hand.' He raised an eyebrow. 'Professor Jones mentioned it in passing when I visited his hut to see how he was faring. They were both seeing the medics at the same time.'

'A splinter?' Rosie tutted. 'I saw he had a bandage on his hand at church earlier. Well, that's rather suspicious, isn't it? You know what, Joe has a thing for Lil, the barmaid at The Boar's Head. She's always flirting with the pilots, not with him, and he sits there at the bar mooning at her while she chats to the pilots. You don't think ... if he was Prospero, could be casually trying to pick up information about the airbase as well, perhaps? He's just hoovering up everything he can.'

'It's a distinct possibility.' Bluff pinched the bridge of his nose again. He looked tired, and she could only imagine how much his head must still be thumping after the attack last night. 'Chandler, Stuart and Jones have fallen to the back of the pack as far as I'm concerned. I'll be focussing on Brett, Swann and Fleet from here.'

'That narrows it down, at least,' Rosie mused. 'And of those three, the only one who's ever been near the barn is Swann.' She stoked Bluff's arm. 'You need a good nap.'

'I shouldn't have let you come out tonight,' he whispered. 'But I'm glad you did.'

'I'm glad too.' Rosie hugged his arm. She looked up at him, at his soot-smeared face and his ruffled hair. Cottisbourne Park's very own hero. 'Look at us, up here on the hill, with the whole world in front of us. Can't be bad, can it?'

'There's something I should tell you, Driver Sinclair.' Bluff's tone was serious again, though there was a mischievous light in his eyes. He lowered his voice and admitted, 'I only speak three-and-a-half languages. Whatever must you think of me?'

'Only three-and-a-half? How can you show your face at the Park?' Rosie chuckled. 'Do you know, I'm *terribly* impressed.' And she was. And not just because Bluff could speak three-and-a-half languages.

Rosie gazed up at him. Did she dare take a chance?

She rose up onto her toes and brushed her lips against his cheek.

'A kiss for a hero,' she whispered.

He smiled and asked, 'Was it the three languages that did it? Or the half?'

'Oh, as much as I'm impressed by all that,' Rosie said, gazing at Bluff as the moonlight danced in his eyes. 'I think it was rescuing a little girl that impressed me most of all.'

'Would you allow me to escort you back to your quarters?' Bluff took Rosie's hand loosely in his. They linked their fingers together, as though it was all instinct. 'Or maybe chance another kiss?'

Rosie couldn't stop smiling. He was such a gent. 'I'd very much like you to escort me back to quarters. And I'd also rather like another kiss.'

Very tentatively, Bluff dipped his head and pressed his lips to Rosie's. The kiss was gentle – gentlemanly, really – exactly the sort of kiss she would have expected from Major-General Sir Kingsley-Flynn of H Cav.

And his moustache tickled just a little, but Rosie would've been disappointed if it hadn't. She returned his kiss just as softly, but as gentle as it was, Rosie was aware of a powerful pull deep within her, bringing her and Bluff together.

'After the war,' he whispered, 'would you let a fledgling theatrical producer take you dancing?'

'That would be marvellous,' Rosie replied, whispering her reply close to his ear. He smelt of woodsmoke from the fire, and that distinguished scent of sandalwood that he always carried with him. 'Then we can go and see a show!'

When the lights come on again.

Chapter 16

Even with blackout blinds on the windows, Rosie never slept much at this time of year. When she woke up, a rush of joy ran through her.

Bluff. Dear, lovely Bluff!

She lifted the blind and looked out across to his room, wondering if he was awake yet. The heavy curtains that hung at his window were slightly parted and the sash window had been lifted. Then, as Rosie paused, she heard the sound of whistling drifting across the courtyard from Bluff's open window.

That Old Black Magic.

She rested her elbows on the window sill, wondering if she'd catch a glance of him. He really was the most marvellous chap, and their kisses had been divine. Should she feel as she did after so little time? But then she'd heard of couples meeting at a dance for the first time who had proposed before the night had ended. And they couldn't have exchanged more than a couple of words.

Suddenly, the curtains across the courtyard opened and there was Bluff, his tie loose around his open shirt collar. He held a cup and saucer and at the sight of Rosie, lifted the cup in greeting and mouthed, 'Good morning!'

Rosie waved and mouthed *Good morning* in return. She knew she couldn't shout across the courtyard, but it was so tempting. Then she had an idea.

She left her post at the window and took down the *Merchant of Venice* poster from her wall. Then she returned and held the poster up so that he could see it. Bluff replied with a beaming smile and a thumbs up. Then he put his cup and saucer down on the window sill and offered her a silent round of applause.

Leaning out of the window, Rosie took a bow, then she held the poster aloft and pointed to it, then pointed to Bluff. *For you,* she mouthed, but she wondered if he would make out what she meant.

Me? Bluff mouthed, pressing his hand to his chest. *For me?*

Rosie nodded, a stage nod that could be seen up in the gods. *For you,* she mouthed again. Then she rolled it up, stuck it under her arm like a swagger stick and stood to attention. Bluff replied with a sharp salute and a grin.

Thank you, he mouthed. Then he tapped his watch before pointing to the barn and mouthing, *twenty minutes?*

Rosie nodded. She shaped her thumb and forefinger into a *C* then turned her hand round to make a *U.* And in case that had mystified him, she mouthed, *see you!*

And this time, his answering salute was just a little more louche. Bluff was in a good mood, it seemed, and Rosie knew why. Despite the threat of Prospero, there was still good in the world, and they had carved out a little bit of it for themselves. Together they would bring him in.

★ ★ ★

Twenty minutes later, Rosie was in her uniform, heading for the barn. She dreaded to think what sort of mess it would be in, and hoped that no unknown treasures had been lost in the fire. At least she'd found Portia the puppet in time.

When the barn appeared before her, Rosie took in the

sight of the wrecked building. She'd seen enough of them during the Blitz, but the fire damage to the barn hit home. She'd spent so much time in the place, after all, and her friend had lost his life in there. And so, nearly, had Bluff and Nancy.

The end of the barn where the hayloft had been was a blackened hole, and half of the roof had gone, the tiles falling in, Rosie supposed, as well as shattering all across the soaked ground. The far end from the hayloft looked relatively intact in comparison.

'Major-General?' Rosie called, knowing she couldn't be overheard calling him *Bluff*.

He had to be here somewhere, she couldn't imagine Bluff would have sent the men from RAF Cottisbourne off until he had arrived to relieve them. In front of her was the Citroën, blackened with soot, but miraculously undamaged. Professor Hale would've been pleased about that.

'Up in the hayloft, Driver,' Bluff called and she heard his feet descending the ladder. 'Did you bring the car keys along?'

Rosie patted the Citroën's bonnet before spotting Bluff. She held up the keys. 'Of course!'

'I couldn't get off to sleep last night,' Bluff said as he reached the floor. 'And I was thinking over what young Nancy had said. Ghosts in the hayloft. *Voices*.'

'Bound to be a draught, I'd imagine.' But from the look on Bluff's face, Rosie's mind began to turn. 'You think something was going on? Someone was talking in here?'

He nodded and dropped his voice to a conspiratorial whisper. 'Clicks and voices. It's a radio, I'm sure of it.'

Rosie rushed her hand to her mouth in surprise. 'Good Lord, I wouldn't be at all surprised if you were right! A radio ... of course. No wonder Prospero's been so obsessed with this barn if they were running a radio in the place.'

'He set the fire *in* the hayloft. Prospero's a desk man, no idea in the field at all,' Bluff told her. 'Last night's fire was proof of that. It was panicked and ill thought out.'

'Hard to get away quickly if you're up in the hayloft and you've set a fire there?' Rosie nodded. 'It doesn't surprise me, to be honest. They're all very ... cerebral here. They might speak umpteen different languages and be a calculus whizz, but ...'

'But they're not soldiers. Not like us.'

'So Prospero decided to burn the place down to hide the evidence. No radio, no mole.' Rosie gasped, as the clues began to stack up. 'And that's why Prospero killed Professor Hale in the barn! It seemed like such an odd place to do it, but doesn't it make sense if Professor Hale was onto them?'

'And up in the hayloft too,' he reminded her. 'I'll wager he'd heard something he shouldn't. I'll wager he saw Prospero's face too, that's why it had to be a bullet. Our mole didn't have time to set up an *accident* like my bang on the head.'

'What a dreadful business, someone stalking about the Park with a gun.' Rosie tutted. 'So let's see ... Professor Hale knows there's a mole working at the Park. He hears the voices and clicks in the barn. Maybe he'd popped in to have a look at the car for some reason. And he knows what those sounds mean. He's found Prospero's lair. And Prospero knows the jig is up ... and ... Oh, poor Professor Hale.'

Bluff nodded, then asked, 'Do you have a hammer in your toolbox, Rosie? We need to get that wall down.'

'Of course.' Rosie went to look for her toolbox, splashing through the sooty puddles. Fortunately, she kept it at the end of the barn that had been least affected by the fire, and she returned to Bluff with it. 'Here you go. Shame it got scratched, but no one's tools can be pristine forever, can they?'

He looked down at the hammer and grimaced. 'What've you been bashing with this?'

'I didn't do th—' Rosie froze. A thought had come to her. 'Hell's bells! Prospero used my hammer! To do what? They tried to burn down the barn, maybe to destroy the radio … do you think they might've smashed the thing up first?'

'Let's get the door barred, just in case.' Bluff hurried to the doors and pulled them closed. He dropped the bar into place, securing them against any unwanted visitors. Rosie's heart was racing as she watched. They were about to catch a glimpse of Prospero's lair.

Rosie went over to the wall, wondering if she could spot anything, a handle or a tell-tale crack. Her excitement building, she ran her hand along the soot-caked wall, but found nothing. Her fingers came away dirty with the stuff and she recoiled.

'Up to the hayloft, Driver Sinclair.' He held out his hand. 'Let me take the hammer. There's the ladder to climb.'

Rosie passed it to him. 'Here you are.'

Then she went over to the soot-covered ladder. She put one hand on the ladder, then glanced down at her skirt. Bluff followed the path of her gaze and cleared his throat.

'I shall go first, of course.'

'Thank you,' Rosie said, and stood aside. Thank goodness he understood her dilemma, without causing her any embarrassment. He straightened his cap, tucked the hammer into one pocket of his tunic and ascended the ladder to the smokey hayloft. The smokey hayloft where somebody had made a bed.

Rosie followed. She watched Bluff's highly-polished shoes

ahead of her, and marvelled at how he had transformed himself from the dishevelled hero of the night before to an immaculate senior officer again.

She pulled herself into the hayloft and carefully got to her feet, mindful that the floorboards might be damaged. She didn't bother brushing the stray wisps of straw from her skirt as her hands were too dirty.

The bed of straw and the blankets had long gone, and above them the roof was open to the sky.

'He started the fire here.' Bluff gestured to a jagged crater in the boards, through which Rosie could see the floor below. Bluff pressed his hand to the walls, which the fire had burned jet black. 'And he's an amateur in the field so I would say that he set it right in front of the place he hoped to destroy.'

But the junk that had been piled up in the hayloft had collapsed under the flames and the jet of water. If there was something hidden behind it, Rosie struggled to see how they'd find it.

'It's hollow.' Bluff rapped his fist against a portion of the blackened wall. 'There must be a door under all this mess, but Lord knows where.' He rapped again. 'Let's see what he's trying to – step back, Rosie, just in case – hide!'

And as Rosie stepped away, Bluff swung the hammer into the fire-weakened boards.

He wielded the hammer as easily as if it weighed little more than a feather. Rosie held her hands up to her face as wood splinters burst through the air and her eyes stung as dust and soot shot up.

'Gosh, this place is ready to collapse!' she remarked. 'Found anything?'

The hammer landed again, sending the wall caving

inwards. Bluff peered into the gap and whispered, 'Oh, I'll say…'

Rosie stepped carefully across the boards and joined him at the hole. She couldn't see much, but as the dust settled and her eyes stopped stinging, Rosie saw pieces of metal in the darkness.

She wasn't sure what she was seeing. It looked like a typewriter, but much bigger, with more rows of keys than she'd ever seen on a typewriter before. And beside it, there lay the wooden body of a radio with a half-moon-shaped dial, and what looked like an aerial.

But the whole lot was a mess, bashed about with something heavy.

'Well, now we know what happened to my hammer,' Rosie remarked wryly.

'A rotor machine,' Bluff murmured. 'A lot more sophisticated than anything we have here. It looks like a modified version of Swann's Endeavour machine – or it was, before Prospero took a hammer to it.' He looked at Rosie. 'Nobody at Cottisbourne beyond me and the men of hut two knows that this machine exists, Rosie.'

And with that, the list of suspects dwindled to one.

'Professor Swann…' Rosie whispered. She shivered as she glanced at Bluff. 'So that's that. We tell Wyngate and… gosh.'

A noose would look quite different to Swann's usual Saville Row ties.

'Wyngate's on his way from London,' he replied. 'He'll be here within the hour or so. Until then, let's keep this to ourselves. The Endeavour code comes direct from the Berghof itself, but it changes constantly. Our boffins can't keep up with it.' Bluff stepped over the ragged wood and into the secret room. 'But this looks like it's a step beyond what Swann's achieved for hut two.'

Or what he'd admitted he'd been able to achieve for hut two. If he was Prospero, he wouldn't want the Allies to decode what was coming direct from the führer, would he?

Rosie carefully followed. There was no danger of her snagging her stockings as they were a mirage created with stage makeup.

'What a shame it's in such a state,' Rosie said. 'If I understand, if that thing worked, we'd actually eavesdrop on Hitler.'

'Wyngate's bringing some of Whitehall's boffins down with him. They were going to look over the cyphers our suspects have been working on, but I think they'd be better employed repairing this bit of kit,' he replied. 'A shame we can't ask Professor Swann or his team, but that's a risk we can't take.'

'No, it's not.' Rosie crouched down and stared, fascinated at the exposed workings of the machine. 'Do you know who makes these? Our car and motorbike factories roll out all sorts of things these days. I wonder if this came out of a German car factory? You know, the funny thing is, the inside of this thing looks a lot like a gearbox. See the discs? And this thing here, this key on the front links up with this lever here. It's like a clutch!'

Bluff went down on one knee, peering at the typewriter-like keyboard, then casting his gaze up over the smashed lampboard that was still partially affixed to the back of the machine, though the wooden surrounds were splintered and bent.

'I believe they make a part here, a part there, so nobody quite understands how they all go together until the boffins get hold of them.' He blew over the keyboard, sending a cloud of dust scattering. 'It's bigger than the one in hut two. A few more bells and whistles. Unfortunately, codebreaking isn't my area of expertise.'

Rosie peered behind the damaged Endeavour machine and spotted a grey box behind it with what looked like metal screws on top of it.

'Ah!' Rosie chuckled. 'I thought so … it's powered by a car battery! This really is an astonishing piece of kit.'

'I expect fingerprints are too much to hope for, but if the Whitehall chaps can get this working…' he glanced at Rosie. 'Who knows what it'll tell us?'

Rosie thought of the Citroën, of the parts she'd dismantled and put back together again. She hugged Bluff's arm – for who would spot them inside a hidden wall cavity? – and said, 'Bluff, this thing is built like a cross between a typewriter and parts of a car. I got that old Citroën going. I reckon I could fix *this*.'

'We can't do anything until the ministry bods arrive, but when they do, how would you like to work on it with them?' He chanced a kiss to Rosie's cheek. 'I have no doubt you could put this back together in no time.'

'Are you sure?' Rosie bit her lip, amazed at the trust he put in her. 'I'd love to. And not just to make myself feel important – I'm *certain* I can help. I wouldn't say so unless I was sure. I wouldn't jeopardise the war effort.'

'My authority doesn't extend as far as Mr Wyngate,' he admitted, 'but if I have anything to do with it…' Bluff put his finger to his lips.

Rosie didn't move. All her senses were on alert. Had someone come into the barn? She listened out for footsteps, but instead she heard voices. Men. One sounded rather patrician, and she realised it was Swann. The other spoke with a very different sort of accent.

Mainland Europe. Eastern, perhaps. Poland. That's it. Swann is talking to one of the Polish codebreakers.

Behind the barn.

'...an accident, nothing more,' Charles Swann was saying, his voice hushed. 'Honestly, nobody suspects a thing, least of all that dunderhead from bloody Horse Guards!'

Rosie glanced at Bluff. What would he make of being called a dunderhead?

'But what if they find out?' Bartosz asked, his voice strained. 'Will not people go in there and try to find what caused the fire?'

Bartosz.

Rosie should've guessed. He'd been standing there at the front door of Cottisbourne Park on the day Hale was killed, beside the blood-covered Professor Swann. Then he'd run. And why? Because Bartosz had something to hide.

'The fire was an accident,' Charles said, but was that true or simply what the official story was going to be? There was nothing to place Charles Swann here, after all. 'This evening, I can show you the folly. It's perfect. I don't think anybody's been there in years.'

'Yes, show me it,' Bartosz said, his tone brightening. 'It is further away, isn't it? Not too close.'

'On the edge of the estate. Safely away from nosey urchins and bloody actresses,' Charles laughed. 'And hopefully without any dead—'

'Major-General!' A sharp voice split the morning quiet. *Wyngate.* 'Kingsley-Flynn, where are you, man? Your damned secretary's still eating breakfast and you've gone AWOL!'

'He moves fast!' Rosie whispered.

She heard movement from outside, the sound of grass swishing. Charles and Bartosz must've heard Wyngate and were on the run.

'The men from the ministry usually do,' Bluff chuckled and stood. He held out his hand to Rosie as downstairs, Wyngate hammered on the barn door. 'Madam, may I?'

Rosie took his hand. 'Of course.' As Wyngate went on hammering, Rosie was reminded of the unseemly direction his questioning had taken. 'Gosh, he won't think we were in here being saucy, will he?'

Bluff shook his head. 'Not when he sees what we've found.' Then he raised his voice and called, 'I'll be with you presently, Mr Wyngate!'

Rosie allowed Bluff to guide her to the ladder, then climbed carefully down. She wiped her sooty hands on a handkerchief, which she suspected would never come clean again, then tried to dash away the straw that was clinging to her uniform. The last thing she needed was for Wyngate to suspect that she and Bluff had been carrying on in the hay. Not that much was left of it after the fire.

'We'll move the Citroën when we've spoken to Wyngate,' Bluff whispered. 'She'll be a lot happier living in the garage under her caretaker.'

Rosie nodded. 'Professor Hale was trying to find her owner, and until he did, I thought it was best to leave her in here and not stake my claim. But now … well, things have changed somewhat, haven't they?'

'In all sorts of ways.' Bluff dusted down his tunic and straightened his cap so minutely Rosie couldn't see any difference whatsoever. But that was very Bluff. 'Right, let's get the door open.'

Rosie helped Bluff lift the bar, not that he needed her aid. The door creaked open and Wyngate was there outside, awaiting them, with a group of men standing rather stiffly in old tweeds and flannels. One of them was even wearing a smock. The groundsmen. Giving the sort of intense stares from under their flat caps that could discover a secret at one hundred paces.

'Good morning, sir,' Rosie said.

'Driver Sinclair, Major-General.' Wyngate lifted his hat to them. 'Special delivery from the Department of Works as requested, here to take care of your fire damage under the auspices of your Tommy, I believe.'

'Mr Wyngate.' Bluff gave a nod of greeting. 'The fire has caused some rather worrying structural damage to the hayloft, which is why I called you Works chaps in. We'd like your expert opinion if we could?'

'Very worrying indeed, sir,' Rosie added. 'Quite surprising, by all accounts.'

Wyngate clearly understood the charade and followed Rosie and Bluff across the barn, pausing only to throw an admiring glance at the car. Bluff climbed into the hayloft, followed by the man from the ministry, with Rosie bringing up the rear. He *must* be making the best of black market clothing coupons, she decided as she followed his immaculately polished shoes up towards the hayloft. Either that or things were very lax in the petty cash and expenses section of the War Office.

'Watch out for the floor, sir,' Rosie warned him, as Wyngate's shiny shoes took him across the scorched floorboards. 'Rather dicky now after the fire.'

'Not really dressed for it, Mr Wyngate,' Bluff observed. Rosie somehow managed not to chuckle at his remark. He stepped aside and gestured towards the wall that he and Rosie had opened. 'A hidden room. This seemed like the easiest way to get in given the hurry, but one assumes there's a door mechanism somewhere.'

'Quite an impressive piece of kit in there, sir,' Rosie said under her breath. 'Someone's been very busy indeed. Seems like our friend was very close to finding their hidey-hole, don't you think?'

'My God.' Wyngate's voice was a whisper, somewhere

between awe and horror. He took a pair of leather gloves from his pocket and stepped into the secret room, his gaze fixed on the shattered machine as though it might be about to rear up and bite him. 'This is an Endeavour machine, or something like it. I've never seen ... what *is* it?'

Wyngate pulled on the gloves and crouched beside the machine, but Rosie got the distinct impression that he wasn't any more of an expert on such things than Bluff.

'Driver Sinclair's a whizz with mechanics,' Bluff told him. 'I think she'd be a boon to your chaps when it comes to putting this back into some sort of working order.'

Rosie grinned at Bluff, and enthusiastically told Wyngate, 'It appears to be put together using similar principles to a gear box. I've extensive experience working on car parts, and I can assure you, I would have little difficulty mending it.'

He glanced up at her, narrowing his eyes as though considering it for a moment before he said, 'That's very decent, Driver, but I've brought some of Whitehall's finest with me today. I'm sure they'll soon have her singing.'

Rosie shrugged. She knew she could do it, but what could she say against a man like Wyngate? 'Well, I suppose so, sir. I'm sure they'll manage, as long as they know how to strip a gearbox.'

'And if they find that they don't, Driver Sinclair will be delighted to show them,' Bluff told him. Wyngate regarded him rather sternly, then rose to his feet, dusting his gloved hands together.

'I'll have my lads gather up the parts and take them inside to start work,' he said. 'Meanwhile, Major-General, you can give me a full debrief on exactly what's been happening. Driver Sinclair, you're dismissed.'

But Bluff cleared his throat and said, 'With respect, Mr Wyngate, Driver Sinclair has been an invaluable part of the investigation. She's signed the addendum, I'd like her to be present at the debriefing.'

Rosie nodded, and smiled sweetly at Wyngate. 'I'm more than happy to,' Rosie assured him.

'Of course, Major-General,' was Wyngate's surprising reply. 'I'll set my boffins to work on the machine and we'll meet in your office. You've both done very good work here. We're closing in on Prospero.'

Chapter 17

Once again, Rosie sat on her comfortable chair, with Wyngate on the ordinary wooden chair. Bluff looked nothing short of stately as he sat behind what had once been Hale's desk, assured as he addressed the man from the ministry and went through their findings.

He was careful to start with the list of six suspects, and explained to Wyngate how he had whittled it down until one name, and one name only, stood out from among the six.

Professor Charles Swann.

Swann chasing Nancy off from the barn, Swann discovering Hale's body, Swann having access time and again at every stage of his career to cyphers that were passed to the Nazis to allow them to decrypt crucial Allied code. If all of that didn't seal it, there was the small matter of the modified Endeavour machine in the hayloft. It might have been battered into pieces, but it was still based on technology that less than a dozen people in Cottisbourne had access to. And the man who knew the technology best of all? Charles Swann.

Wyngate listened to Bluff's report in silence, but his face grew paler with every new revelation and Rosie could hardly blame him. She doubted that anyone had imagined at the start of this investigation that it might name one of the most senior men at Cottisbourne Park as a Nazi spy.

'Swann's father...' Wyngate murmured eventually. He lit

a cigarette and whispered, 'He's earmarked as a future PM. A real highflier.'

'But couldn't he be making use of that?' Rosie said. 'On the surface, he might seem the least likely suspect, and he knows that, and he hides behind it.'

'Prospero is the most dangerous mole we've ever investigated,' Wyngate admitted. 'He's straight onto Jerry as soon as we've cracked a cypher so we're always running just to catch up. He's branched out in the last few months though, but we didn't know exactly how. He's been intercepting American and Russian messages that aren't coming via Cottisbourne and passing them back to Germany too. Driver Sinclair, could that machine you found be capable of doing that?'

Bluff nodded slowly, then said to Rosie, 'A machine that speaks multiple languages. Doesn't that sound like someone we know?'

Assuming Swann's polished tones, Rosie said, '*I can speak five languages...*' She nodded at Wyngate, hoping he wouldn't mind her impression of their prime suspect. 'I think it could. I think that's what the gears might be about. It would make sense, wouldn't it? If say first gear was German, and second gear was English, and on and on.'

'I need to telephone number 10.' Wyngate took a long pull on his cigarette. 'It may be a long call. Can I use your office, Major-General?'

'Of course.' Bluff nodded. 'And Rosie and I will go and look at the folly we heard Swann and Zalewski discussing. If I may, Mr Wyngate, today is the first time I've had any cause to suspect Dr Zalewski's involvement. He'll need considerably more investigation.'

Wyngate plucked his cigarette from between his lips and said, 'Oh, you can count on it.'

Rosie felt a twinge of guilt. Bartosz and the other Polish

codebreakers had left their families behind, their lives, and goodness knows what their loved ones were facing. And now Bartosz, who was in a comparatively safe place, was about to be arrested.

But then he'd overstepped the line. A man was dead, and Bluff and Nancy had nearly faced the same fate. No one could be overlooked.

★ ★ ★

Rosie led the way as she and Bluff strode through the grounds towards the folly. 'It's so out of the way. I should've thought of it before! But I just never go there, so ...'

He seemed quiet, chewing away at the stem of his pipe as they walked away from the house and deeper into the rolling grounds of Cottisbourne Park. Rosie wasn't surprised that he was so preoccupied though. A man might go to the gallows because of the discoveries they'd made, maybe more than one man, but if Charles Swann was Prospero, he'd thought nothing of condemning thousands to death when they had committed no crime at all.

As they hurried, Rosie spotted a figure up ahead.

'That's Caroline,' she whispered to Bluff. 'Oh, poor girl. How on earth will she fare when she finds out about her brother?'

'We say nothing,' he reminded her. 'I know it's difficult, Rosie. I'm sorry.'

'Morning!' Caroline shifted the large box she was carrying into the crook of her left arm and waved. 'Isn't it a beautiful day?'

Rosie nodded. Faced with Caroline, Rosie felt guilty for her role in the downfall of her brother, but what else could Rosie have done?

'Gorgeous! It'll be a lovely summer,' Rosie said with a smile she didn't really feel.

'And I'll be spending this lovely morning doing running repairs on the bombes in my humble little hut and a few bits Charles needed,' Caroline said good-naturedly. 'Whilst you lucky ducks enjoy the sunshine!'

'Official business, Miss Swann,' Bluff assured her. 'It just happens to be official business on a glorious day.'

'It's all important work!' Rosie said. 'I'll see you around, Caroline. I wouldn't want to keep you.'

With another wave Caroline pottered off, leaving Bluff and Rosie to continue on their way. It was a long shot, but perhaps Caroline might even flourish without Charles there to tease and cajole, to remind everyone that he was the professor and Caroline was nothing more than the *little sprat*. Rosie wasn't convinced though. Caroline had a blind spot where her brother's faults were concerned; this would probably hit her harder than anyone.

'Has to be done …' Rosie thought aloud.

They carried on, heading over a wide lawn and through a thicket of trees. A jolt went through Rosie when she saw the silhouette of a man among the trees. As they got nearer, she realised it was Dr Brett, spreading his picnic blanket on the ground.

'Hello, Dr Brett,' Rosie said brightly.

At the sound of Rosie's voice Dr Brett jumped. He clasped one hand to his heart and exclaimed, 'Good heavens, you gave me a fright! I've never seen another living soul here before.'

'Your secret is out,' Bluff replied with a smile. 'Don't let us disturb you, Dr Brett.'

But Brett looked distinctly disturbed. He was already gathering up his picnic blanket when Bluff and Rosie turned away. Rosie pointed to the small but elaborate building ahead, a little house with columns at its front, and a row of classic statues along the edge of its roof.

'There it is,' she said. 'Of course, you saw it last night from up on the hill, and today, well, here it is. A piece of Italy dropped into Sussex. You know, they say that it really was from Italy, and someone who lived at the Park long ago fell in love with it, bought it, and had it transported back to England stone by stone!'

'I don't like to be that chap,' Bluff said, 'but we do have a folly back at the old pile. I rather think you'd like it, though it wasn't imported from Italy. Family lore says that my great-grandmother built it. She was that sort of lady.'

'What a wonderful story! You'll have to show it to me one day.' Rosie beamed at him. Imagine, a boyfriend who had his own folly. 'I'm afraid to say we only have a shed back at Sinclair Acres! I hope you don't mind.'

'Why would I mind?' he asked, returning her smile. 'I rather fear you'll think our family home is a bit of a gloomy old pile. Of course, if I'm leaving the barracks life behind, I *will* need a home to call my own. You'll have to help me find the perfect place for an impresario.'

'You should have a lovely mews house up town!' Rosie enthused. Then she added, 'I should hope there's a few left, despite everything. You could even move into the folly! When I first saw it, I did wonder if it was possible to live in it. But I should imagine it'd get rather lonely, being out on a limb.'

The honey-coloured stone and white marble of the folly gleamed in the morning sunlight. For a moment, Rosie half fancied that she could really be in Italy. Not that it was somewhere she *actually* wanted to be at that moment.

Rosie led Bluff up to the French windows, but when she tried the handle, it was locked.

'Oh, why didn't I think to look for a key?' she sighed. 'What if there's only one and you-know-who has got it? Then again... we don't necessarily need a key.' Rosie plucked a pin from her hair.

'We make an excellent team.' Bluff held out his palm. 'You have the hairpins, I have the lockpicking skills.'

Rosie held onto the hairpin. 'Who's to say I don't have lockpicking skills too?'

She took out another hairpin, ignoring the tress that fell to her shoulder. Rosie crouched down in front of the lock and began to find her way inside it and learn its workings with the pins. 'I did go to school *sometimes* when I was a child, but it wasn't always easy for my parents to find a place for me. Often, I was left to my own devices in the theatre. I learnt all sorts of things, and one of the more unusual lessons I learned was from a member of the Players who had led a rather shady path before becoming a thespian. Lock-picking! We were devils, unlocking everything we could find!'

'Driver Sinclair, you have my apologies,' Bluff assured her. 'I can see I have a lot to learn about my leading lady.'

Rosie looked up at him, chuckling. She felt the lock giving inside as she poked and twisted the pins. 'Give me a second... It's an old lock, it's a bit of a tough nut to crack, this one!'

'Does that mean it hasn't been used for a while?' Bluff raised one eyebrow. 'Or does Dr Brett's love of seclusion extend to follies too?'

'It's a bit rusty. I can feel it grinding against the hairpins,' Rosie explained. 'It's old, that's for sure, but I couldn't say if anyone's used it recently or not.' Finally, it gave, and Rosie rocked back on her heels as the lock clicked. 'Open sesame!'

Bluff helped Rosie to her feet, then took hold of the door handle and turned it. The door opened easily, the hinges making no sound and Rosie knew immediately that they weren't the only recent visitors to the folly. Someone must have been here, but that wasn't a surprise if Charles had earmarked it as a new ops room.

'Anyone here?' Bluff called into the silence.

'Hello?' Rosie's voice echoed from the dark veined marble floor and the bare stone walls. But of course, there was no one there.

At the centre of the room stood an elaborate stone vase with the vine-wreathed head of Dionysus carved on its front, with heavy clusters of grapes. Perhaps it had served its time at Roman feasts. The rear wall of the folly carried on the theme, with three painted panels of cavorting Romans in flowing robes, holding golden goblets aloft.

'You could have quite the party in here, couldn't you?' Rosie whispered.

'Just like an officers' mess I used to know,' Bluff murmured. He looked up into the vaulted ceiling, where motes of dust swirled in the sunlight. 'But rather less lively.'

Up above them, well-fed cherubs drifted across a blue sky on fluffy white clouds.

'I'm not quite sure where Swann would hide his machines,' Rosie mused. She wandered over to the vase and peered over its edge. 'It's not like it's got a lid. And I doubt it'd all fit inside. Gosh, I don't know.'

A breeze stirred the trees outside, the rustling leaves disturbing the silence for a moment. As Rosie ran her gaze over the back wall, she spotted something.

'Bluff, come over here a second.' She headed over to the back wall and stopped in front of one of the panels. Bluff followed, and Rosie gingerly held out her finger and prodded the panel. It gave under her pressure. 'Oh, I saw it move in the breeze! Very cleverly done. You wouldn't think it was cloth, would you? We need to have a look behind these. I wonder...'

Rosie stepped back. The panels were set inside a frame and when she traced her fingertips down the side of one of them, she felt hinges.

'This one's hinged,' Rosie said. 'I expect the others might be too. It's like a door!'

'How would one open them?' Bluff mused to himself. He looked towards Rosie as he stepped forwards and ran his fingertips down the edge of one of the panels. 'Is this some sort of obscure hidden switch affair or shall we start with a good old sharp penknife?'

'Oh, let's go with a penknife!' Rosie urged him.

Bluff took a penknife from his pocket. With a click of his thumbnail, a keen blade arced out from the pitted wooden handle and Bluff pressed it into the edge of the frame, at the point where the panel met the wood. He worked carefully, no doubt so the silk panels wouldn't be damaged, and Rosie watched, impatient to see what was hiding in the folly. Long seconds passed before she heard a dull click and Bluff said, 'That's done it.'

He turned the knife, catching the tip of the blade behind the frame. Then, with a slow step backwards, Bluff opened the panel to reveal what lay behind it.

'I hope it's not just some mouldy old cushions for garden chairs behind here,' Rosie said.

She peered in over Bluff's shoulder and was astonished by what she saw in the little secret room beyond.

A machine, in bits.

But not smashed like the ones in the hayloft, no, this was in pieces because it appeared to be in the throes of being built. Cogs and gears had been set into a frame, with a panel of keys lying on the floor beside it, as if it was waiting to be screwed onto the front. Rosie spotted the usual bits and bobs to be found in any workshop – tools, some nails and screws, a small tub of glue. The very ordinariness of the process made the horror that the machine could unleash somehow all the worse.

'Prospero's going to carry on!' Rosie gasped. 'Got rid of the old machine, and here he is, building a new one!'

'Let's put things back as we found them and let Wyngate know,' Bluff said. 'I doubt Prospero will risk a visit in broad daylight.'

Chapter 18

Rosie and Bluff returned to the house. Cottisbourne Park was waking, as if it was just another day, the grounds busy with groups of codebreakers heading to their huts from the canteen. But for Rosie and Bluff it was anything other than an ordinary day.

They headed to Bluff's office, where they had left Wyngate to call Number 10. Rosie wondered what it must be like, to be entrusted with such an important telephone number. Bluff knocked once at the door then opened it without waiting for a reply. Wyngate had finished his telephone call, it seemed, and was standing beside the window that looked out over Cottisbourne Park. He was paler than ever, an air of distraction about him.

'Mr Wyngate?' Bluff said. The effect was immediate and Wyngate seemed to catch himself before he jumped. Rosie could see that he was startled though, as if he had been entirely lost in thought. Bluff must have noticed, but he didn't comment. Instead he was immediately all business, sparing Wyngate any awkwardness as he launched into an update on what they had found at the folly in the grounds.

Rosie watched as Wyngate's eyes widened at the news.

'I suppose it's not surprising,' Rosie remarked. 'He might've smashed up his machines that were in the hayloft, but he's not giving up that easily.'

'We'll be sending some very sensitive cyphers via

Cottisbourne Park in the next month or so,' Wyngate told them. 'Relative to events on the continent. We can't afford there to be even a whisper of a leak, that's precisely why the Prime Minister wants them to go from here. You've got the best cypher men in the business. Uncrackable, so they tell me.'

No wonder Wyngate looked so pale. And no wonder he'd put her through the wringer that day he'd interrogated her in the scullery.

'And yet we've got Prospero building his own Endeavour machine in the folly,' Rosie said.

'Not for much longer,' Bluff assured her. 'You discussed the sensitivity of the matter with the Prime Minister?'

Wyngate nodded. 'I did and he was precisely as happy about it as you might expect. But he recognises, as we all do, that difficult decisions have to be made. Mr Churchill has asked me to monitor Professor Swann today, to build up a picture of his movements. At the first sign of anything untoward he'll be arrested, but we have to hope he'll in-criminate himself. The discovery in the folly makes that far more likely. I'll put some men on it.'

Rosie glanced at Bluff with a quick smile. Then she said to Wyngate, 'Was Mr Churchill concerned about Professor Swann's family? His father being very important, I mean?'

'It's a concern,' was Wyngate's clipped response. 'One that my colleagues will deal with.'

'So, what are Rosie and I to do with ourselves today?' Bluff asked. 'Business as usual?'

But Wyngate shook his head and said, 'I want to go through every second of everything that has happened this week, Major-General. You too, Driver Sinclair. We need to have a clear account of the evidence against Professor Swann. I've a feeling we might need it.'

Rosie settled in her chair and they began. They carefully put together a timeline, which made Charles' guilt all too obvious. There was the fact that he had raised the alarm when Hale was shot, and had appeared covered in Hale's blood. Then he shouted at Nancy to keep away from the barn and complained about her presence at the Park. He had been so belligerent about Bluff's presence, and made no bones about the fact that he felt Bluff was intruding and blocking his God-given right to direct Cottisbourne Park. Charles hadn't appeared at the barn when it burned and his colleagues came together to help. His multilingual abilities seemed to tally with the fact that the machine appeared to be capable of producing communications in several languages. And finally, that overheard conversation with Bartosz.

Wyngate recorded it all in a small notebook, bound in black leather. He wrote quickly, silent as he took down Bluff and Rosie's recollections. Only when Bluff had reached the end of his own statement did he ask, 'Mr Wyngate, might I make a suggestion?'

'Of course,' Wyngate nodded.

'If and when Prospero is in custody and the machine is in working order, we should use it to our advantage.' He glanced at Rosie, warming to his theme. 'We know Prospero's codename. We have his radio so we may already know the frequency he uses and if we can get the Endeavour machine working and understand his modifications, we can use it. I'm sure Germany will cotton on eventually, but perhaps a few confusing messages might be in order? It'd put the high command in a hell of a tangle if their man at Cottisbourne tells them he has the where and when of Operation Overlord.'

Operation Overlord?

183

Rosie looked from Bluff to Wyngate and back again. She had never heard of it and had no idea what Bluff meant. Was this why the pressure really was on to identify and stop Prospero?

'You've signed the paperwork, there's no reason to keep you in the dark,' Wyngate said, darting a glance in Rosie's direction. 'Invasion plans, Driver Sinclair. That's all I'm empowered to tell you.'

'Invading …?' Rosie tried to read their faces, but neither man so much as twitched. But she had a hunch. After all, Wyngate had mentioned something about events on the continent. 'Allies invading mainland Europe – soon?'

'That's all I'm empowered to tell you,' Wyngate repeated firmly.

'Well,' Rosie said, 'I can see why this business about Prospero is so—'

She nearly jumped out of her skin as someone knocked on the window outside. Rosie couldn't see them at first, just a figure lost in the ivy that framed the window, but then they moved to stand in front of the glass. A man appeared, wearing small pebble glasses. He had a Fair Isle jumper under his jacket, knitted in a fiendishly complicated pattern.

'Mr Wyngate!' he called. Wyngate leapt to his feet, his face thunderous as he opened the window.

'Come round to the bloody office,' he told the man. 'You might as well be standing there with a loudhailer!'

'Sorry, sir!' The man hurried off.

Rosie fidgeted with the paperweight on the edge of the desk, a piece of glass that looked like a sea anemone.

Then there was a knock at the office door, followed by the voice of the man from the window again. 'Mr Wyngate!'

'Oakley!' Wyngate bellowed. 'Come in!'

The door opened and Oakley appeared, blinking. He stared at Bluff rather nervously as he came into the office and closed the door behind him.

'Sir, we've run into a problem,' Oakley told Wyngate. Wyngate was silent, his lips thinning as he nodded the man on. 'We're rather flummoxed by this new bit of kit. We've seen Endeavours before, but nothing like this. There's gears and whatnot and ... obviously, with plenty of time, we'd crack it eventually – a week or two, perhaps – but how much time do we have?'

Wyngate scrubbed his hand over his face as he said, 'A day or two, Mr Oakley.'

'Oh, right. Crikey.' Oakley stared down at the floor for a moment, then a smile came to his face. 'I say, I know just the chap who'll sort this out in a jiffy! Professor Swann, he works here, doesn't he? He's an expert when it comes to Endeavours.'

'He's indisposed.'

As Wyngate spoke, Bluff cleared his throat. He looked not to Wyngate, but to Oakley, and asked, 'Is it a cypher man you need or would a mechanic be better suited to the job?'

'Mechanic,' Oakley said with a firm nod. 'That thing looks like a gearbox, only none of us know much about them.'

Rosie could see that Wyngate had taken Bluff's hint and she held her breath as she waited for the verdict. Wyngate settled his gaze on her for a long second, then decided, 'Driver Sinclair, you're up.'

'Thank you, sir.' Rosie got up from her seat.

Oakley looked rather surprised, then he gestured towards Rosie's cap. He must've spotted the MTC's emblem on her cap, a tyre with two crossed spanners. His face split into a broad smile.

'Oh, thank heavens for that!' Oakley said. 'This way, madam. England hath need of thee.'

'Good luck, Driver.' Bluff looked prouder than anyone she'd ever seen. 'Show them how it's done.'

Rosie saluted. 'Don't worry, sir. I will!'

Chapter 19

Oakley led Rosie to a spare garage in the former stable block, just a couple of doors along from her room.

Two of Wyngate's groundsmen were busy in front of the garage, one raking the cinder path, the other ineffectually snipping at an encroaching hedge.

Guards, Rosie realised.

Her heart raced at the thought of what she was now part of, and the trust that Bluff and Wyngate had put in her. She felt like a real codebreaker girl now, like her friends.

Inside the garage, several folding tables had been put together and the remains of the Endeavour machine and the radio from the hayloft had been laid out with care. Working with pliers and tweezers, Wyngate's boffins were trying to put it back together again, although one of them had clearly given up and was leaning against the wall smoking.

Oakley introduced Rosie to the surprised men, but very soon Rosie had been absorbed into the team. Using a chalkboard, they explained to her the workings of the Endeavour that they understood – the rotors, the lightboard, the plugs, the mirror and the keyboard. Then they stood aside and passed Rosie the chalk so that she could explain how a gearbox worked – the wheels, pinions and shafts.

'And now all we need to do is work out how it all fits together.' Oakley sighed. 'And as for those little drums that come with this one, I haven't a clue what they do!'

Rosie had never in her life built what was, in effect, a three-dimensional jigsaw puzzle that didn't come with a picture on the lid. The chalkboard was covered in scribbles – a technical drawing one moment that was replaced seconds later by a scrawled equation that Rosie couldn't make head nor tail of.

What was already a complicated job was rendered all the more difficult thanks to the condition of the machine. But what was bent was made straight, what was dented and scratched was repaired, and what was reduced to bits was soldered back together. One of the team worked in the corner fashioning a new wooden frame, and another tweezered lengths of hairlike wire into position on a board. But as the light began to fade, so too did their enthusiasm.

Oakley shrugged. 'I rather think we ought to call it a night.'

The hum of activity died away, and Wyngate's boffins slouched off.

Rosie stood in the yard, yawning and stretching. She looked up at Bluff's window, wondering how his day had gone.

'Driver Sinclair.' Bluff's voice sounded from the entrance to the courtyard. 'Would you join me for dinner?'

Rosie smiled to hear his voice. She turned and gasped in surprise. He was wearing a fitted red jacket decorated in gold that caught the last of the daylight, and dark fitted trousers with a red stripe on the leg. Her khaki felt rather dowdy in comparison.

'How could I possibly say no?' Rosie replied, and hurried across the courtyard to him.

'Mr Wyngate has laid on a film for our highly valued Cottisbourne colleagues,' he explained. 'It'll be interesting to see who misses the show, don't you think? He's a tricky fellow, but he seems to be able to make things happen.'

She could already think of two particular codebreakers who would miss the show in favour of a trip to the folly.

Rosie linked arms with Bluff. 'You don't think anyone will mind, do you? If anyone asks, I shall tell them you're being a gentleman, nothing more.' She was very proud to be on his arm.

'I'm afraid the canteen's closed,' he lamented. 'But I managed to convince Beryl to prepare a special something before she knocked off. You can thank our Mr Wyngate again for having the right connections. Culinary, this time.'

'Is it a very special stew?' Rosie chuckled. She was enjoying her treat already.

'It is not.' They stepped into the echoing hallway of Cottisbourne Park, the lights low as the evening set in. 'How does roast chicken and all the trimmings sound?'

Rosie laughed in disbelief. 'Roast chicken? I can't remember the last time I had it! Oh, no wonder you've dressed up. This really *is* a big occasion!'

'One so rarely has roast chicken with one's girl,' he teased. 'And how better to lull Prospero than with a picture show and no sign of the dunderhead in khaki?'

One's girl.

'*Dunderhead.*' Rosie tutted. 'So rude! I felt offended on your behalf when I heard that.' As they walked along the corridor, Rosie whispered, 'It's almost as if we've been invited to dinner by the lady of the house. We'll open the door, and there they'll be in all their finery. And I won't know which knife and fork to use.'

'Madam.' Bluff opened a door. 'Our dining room.'

Rosie stepped inside. A round table set for two stood in the middle of the small but elegant room, a candle waiting to be lit at its centre. Beautiful old oil paintings hung on the walls. Cutlery glittered at each place and the long curtains were open to afford them a view of the grounds as they stretched away into the twilight.

'Oh, Bluff! This is the loveliest thing,' Rosie said. With the door shut behind them, she looped her arms around Bluff's neck and kissed him. 'Thank you. Thank you *so* much.'

Bluff touched his forehead to Rosie's and whispered, 'You deserve it. Can I escort you to your seat?'

'I'd love you to.' Rosie smiled at him. 'I've never been in a room like this before, only stage sets trying to imitate it.'

Arm in arm they strolled to the table, where Bluff pulled out one of the chairs for Rosie. Only when she was settled did he excuse himself, disappearing through a side door. Rosie has never expected anything like it. She had expected to be lucky if she got a helping of bloater paste on toast, yet apparently the ministry didn't only supply black market sharp tailoring, but roast chicken dinners too.

She laid her cap on the table beside her and straightened her tie. She wanted to look as smart as possible for Bluff. She couldn't remember anyone going to such trouble for her before.

When the door opened it was to admit Bluff, carrying a plate piled high with food in each hand. The aroma that met Rosie was one that she hadn't enjoyed in too long and her mouth watered. Cottisbourne Park rarely saw the like of a dinner like this. He put one plate in front of Rosie and one at his other setting, then asked, 'Wine, Driver Sinclair?'

'What a spread!' Rosie beamed at him. 'Oh, goodness, wine too, Bluff? Yes, please.'

'I've been in a few scrapes in my time.' Bluff crossed to the sideboard and picked up a bottle and corkscrew. 'And I always found that a hearty meal and a glass of good wine could do wonders. You've had quite the day – quite the week – you've more than earned it.'

'I rather think we both have! So much has happened...' Rosie leaned back in her chair. 'How was your day? Has you-know-who been up to anything?'

'Not yet.' Bluff pulled the cork from the bottle. How lovely to hear the pop of a cork again. 'Wyngate's got his men watching the folly this evening. Whitehall want him to hold off for a day or so, just to see if our man gives us anything extra. If he's got an ounce of intelligence though, he'll have spotted the coming and going and he'll sit tight.'

Rosie nodded. 'I hope he doesn't get up to anything. We're... well... a bit stuck with the machine. I'm in a room with some pretty enormous brains, and yet... well, we'll keep trying. We just have to work out how it all fits together.'

'And they're treating you respectfully?' Bluff filled the wine glasses. 'I want to know right away if they're not.'

'They are,' Rosie said gently. She stroked Bluff's arm. 'Thank you for asking. I'm part of their team. They treat me like an expert. They listen to me. Ask me questions. You know, at one point, I was explaining gearboxes in front of them like a teacher!'

'A toast to you.' Bluff raised his glass. 'The lady of the hour!'

Rosie raised her glass. 'Can I toast myself? I shall toast *you*. To the handsomest senior officer I've ever had the pleasure to meet!'

And it was a pleasure to spend an evening in this genteel dining room with him, enjoying the finest spread she'd seen in a very long time. It was a world away from the usual spartan efforts churned out by the hard-working ladies of the canteen and Rosie half-wondered if she'd fallen asleep and was dreaming. But it was real, she knew that, and that made it even more special.

'Beryl's done us proud,' Bluff commented. 'And Wyngate too. I have a feeling he may be looking to add to his team, you know. At Prof Hale's recommendation.'

'Me? Oh, I don't know...' But under her modest reply, Rosie rather liked the idea. Driving was all well and good, but after what had happened to Hale, Cottisbourne Park felt tainted.

'It's ... an interesting area to work in.' Bluff picked up his glass and took a sip. 'Before *Dasher* I was what they laughably call a *shepherd*, bringing people from behind the lines. It's dangerous, but it had its rewards. Now I'm a gardener and I really do see the worst of the worst. There's something particularly revolting about a traitor, isn't there?'

Rosie considered his words for a moment before she answered. 'Horrible. Two-faced, horrible rotters who undermine everyone around them and betray all the people they work with and live with every day. Such insincere liars. The temerity of you-know-who ... declaring he should be director. And why? Not because he wants to do good work for the war effort. Because then he'd be party to everything. The Nazis would win the moment he sat down behind Professor Hale's desk.'

'*Prospero*,' Bluff muttered. 'An apt codename, don't you think?'

Rosie sighed. 'The all-powerful wizard making his own rules on a little island...'

'Manipulating everyone ... yet our Prospero is about to get caught up in a tempest of his own making.' Bluff reached across to squeeze Rosie's hand. 'And we're going to make it happen.'

Chapter 20

Early next morning, Rosie was back in the garage again. All night, she'd dreamt of gears and lightbulbs and wires. And Bluff.

Powered by tea, Rosie got back to work with Wyngate's boffins. The wooden frame was soon finished, and wires were threaded in. They began to add the other parts, and Rosie tried to reassemble the gears. There appeared to be about ten different ways to fit them together and she'd tried each way about twenty times.

Rosie tried to work, but her thoughts wandered. She thought of Bluff in his mess dress, and how handsome he was, and what a lovely evening they had. She wished she could've been able to tell her friends about how wonderful it was. She thought of the braid twisted and plaited on his uniform and how it made the gold shimmer. She thought...

'Twisted. That's it! It's twisted!'

The boffins didn't know what she meant, so Rosie took to the chalkboard again and sketched out the vision she had in her head. The gears were twisted, not put together how she'd thought. She'd never seen anything like it before, but it made perfect sense.

Because how else could it work? Oakley had explained to her that whereas the Endeavour was usually used alongside a Bombe, the little drums that were inside this particular one seemed to be a miniature Bombe, wired into the machine.

It would tell the Endeavour what settings it needed, and that was why there were gears, it seemed, and why they were set up so idiosyncratically – to click everything automatically into place.

There was only one way to find out.

Sleeves rolled up, they got to work with their tools. Rosie felt the same glee she had when she'd worked on the car. There were parts and bits everywhere, but as the minutes ticked by, they each found their place. The twisted gears fitted.

Rosie had lost track of time. She'd forgotten to go to lunch and when she looked at her watch, it was the afternoon. Oakley set up the repaired Endeavour machine and the radio beside it, attaching them to the battery. An electrical hum vibrated through the hushed room.

'Shall we fetch Wyngate and the good Major-General?' Oakley suggested. 'I rather think they'll want to see this.'

Off Oakley went. Rosie wondered if he'd remember to use the door this time.

Only a few minutes later, Oakley returned with Bluff and Wyngate.

'Here we are,' Oakley said. 'We're ready.'

The two new arrivals regarded the machine in silence, as though it was taking them a moment to process what they were looking at. After a few moments Bluff asked, 'And the radio frequency? Is it still live?'

Oakley reached for the radio dial and turned it up. Morse code was coming in. Immediately, a couple of the team reached for notepads and pencils and started to write the letters and numbers down. Another began chalking them across the board.

Rosie didn't dare breathe.

Then the scribbling stopped but the Morse went on, relentlessly.

'They're repeating the message,' Oakley whispered to Rosie, Bluff and Wyngate.

The scribbling started up again, but just for a couple of characters.

Oakley grinned. 'Oh, dear, our German Morse operator has slipped up. It's like a fingerprint. We may well recognise who this fellow is!'

One of the team, a man called Lainson, came forwards. 'I know him all right. Let's put it through the Endeavour and see what it comes up with. If you're right about those drums, Oakley, and it being the machine's own internal bombe, then we might be in for a pleasant surprise.'

'Its own bombe?' Wyngate asked, unbelieving. 'How on earth does a machine this size incorporate a bombe?'

'Circuit boards, small drums, a unique gearing system ... dashed clever!' Lainson explained.

'Swann must be a damned genius,' Bluff whispered. 'What a waste.'

Oakley nodded to one of the team, who switched the Endeavour on. He started to input the Morse code and at the end of the message, pressed the switch that Rosie, on first seeing it, had compared to a clutch.

All the letters on the lightboard came up at once, and Oakley tugged at his hair in frustration. 'Oh, damn it, the fuse's gone!'

But then, something happened. Clicks came from inside the machine and the lights turned off. Then one by one they lit up for a moment before extinguishing.

Oakley clapped with glee. 'German-speakers, make yourselves known!'

Wyngate and Bluff exchanged a look and Bluff said, 'That would be us, Mr Oakley.'

'I believe Major-General Sir Kingsley-Flynn's German is a little better than mine,' Wyngate demurred. 'But only a touch.'

'Go on, sir,' Rosie stepped aside so that Bluff could take up the chair at the machine beside the operator inputting the Morse code. Lainson gave Bluff a notepad for his translation.

Rosie watched as Bluff worked, one eye on the machine as the letters glowed into life, the other on his notepad, where he was noting down the message in immaculate handwriting.

'Berlin sounds rather worried,' Bluff murmured. He stroked his hand over his chin and cleared his throat. 'Prospero. Advise on Operation Tempest. Was relocation and rebuild successful? Out.'

Oakley and his team gave Bluff a round of applause.

'No wonder they keep repeating the message!' Rosie exclaimed. She wanted to give Bluff a hug, but suspected now was not the time. 'Gosh, they *are* worried. And Prospero can't check in, so some poor chap in Berlin is hammering away at his Morse code … the same message again and again and again! What do we do, reply?'

Wyngate gave a sharp nod. 'We have to. Enough to settle their nerves, not so much we arouse their suspicions.'

'All right, Major-General,' Oakley said. 'Write your reply in German, we'll put the message through the Endeavour, and we'll get it out to them in Morse code.'

One of his team produced a case, smaller than a shoebox, and took a Morse keyer from it with a large black, bakelite button. Rosie had seen them at the Park before. He wired it into the radio and a light came on.

He gave Oakley a thumbs up. 'Ready, sir.'

'The major-general was one of our finest shepherds,' Wyngate told the rest of the gathering. 'And as one of our most accomplished gardeners, he knows exactly how these people speak. They won't see through him.'

Rosie clasped her hands as she watched Bluff. She was so proud of him. 'Good luck, sir,' she said.

Good luck, Bluff.

After a minute or two, Bluff said, 'I think this should be enough to buy us some time. I'd like your opinions before I translate into German.' He cleared his throat. 'This is Prospero. Tempest ongoing. Relocation successful. Rebuild in progress. Await further communication. Over.'

Rosie waited for the team's responses. There was silence as they considered for a moment, broken only by the same message in Morse code repeating again and again. Then they nodded as one.

'I think I speak for everyone when I say that's spot on, sir. Nice and simple,' Lainson said.

Wyngate's only reply was a tight nod, before Bluff pushed the pad across to the operator.

'There's your German,' he said. 'I'll let you take over from here.'

'Thank you, sir!' the operator said, and typed Bluff's message into the Endeavour.

One by one the lights came on and went out, encrypting the message. He wrote down each character that the machine threw out, then passed it to the man sitting by the radio, who rapidly tapped out the message in Morse code.

The incoming message stopped. The Morse operator tapped out Bluff's reply again. He paused, and tapped again. And again.

Then the incoming Morse started again, and the operator

wrote it down and passed it to his colleague at the Endeavour. He typed it in as before, and the decrypted German message flashed up on the machine for Bluff.

Bluff noted the letters on his pad before he read, 'Prospero. We await further communication. If KF suspicious, employ lethal force. Out.' He frowned, then looked back at the pad. When Bluff spoke again, he sounded almost comically put out. 'Hmm. Lethal force against KF? How very rude!'

Darling, I'm so sorry.

But she couldn't say it, so instead, she stood behind Bluff and squeezed his shoulder. 'Well, unfortunately Prospero didn't need a message from Berlin to encourage him to do that. What happens now?'

'We take this back to Whitehall,' Wyngate said. 'Major-General Sir Kingsley-Flynn's message will hold them at bay for a while at least. Our suspect did visit the folly last night, though it appeared he did no further work on the machine. I'll be placing him under arrest today, but my paymasters want the folly left undisturbed.'

'To flush out any accomplices?' Bluff asked. 'What's the cover story?'

'Officially, Swann is coming to London with us to share his expertise,' he replied. 'My men will stay here and monitor the folly. If Prospero *does* have an accomplice – his Polish friend, for instance – the second he goes in there to work on the machine and let the Fatherland know we've pulled Prospero in, I'll know about it.'

'Arrested *today*? Good,' Rosie said.

Things had moved fast. But Rosie was glad. Prospero was dangerous and he needed to be behind bars. *That* would take the smirk off his face. And as for Bartosz ... she had never liked Charles Swann, but Bartosz, as far as Rosie had known him, had seemed like a nice sort of chap. She could never have guessed he'd be involved in a Nazi operation to infiltrate British secrets.

You never can tell, Rosie thought.

'Driver Sinclair, do you know of a Doctor McAndrew?' Wyngate asked. 'Hut nine?'

'Oh, yes, Archie. He seems all right,' Rosie replied. 'He's a safe pair of hands. Mucks in with everyone else. Last time I heard, he was winning the tomato competition.'

Rosie bit her lip. *Tomato competition? Of all the things to say. Why would Wyngate want to know that?*

'He'll be caretaking here whilst Major-General Sir Kingsley-Flynn returns to London to deal with Prospero. I've worked with McAndrew before, he'll keep things ticking over.' Rosie's heart blanched. Bluff was being summoned to London then, presumably without her? Would he even return to Cottisbourne Park? 'Driver Sinclair, you'll be coming along too. You built this machine when our best chaps couldn't and presumably the major-general won't object to having a driver for the journey back?'

Bluff shot Rosie a rather twinkling glance, then said in his usual formal tones, 'No objections whosoever, Mr Wyngate. Driver Sinclair, perhaps you could instruct Doctor McAndrew on the care of Professor Hale's tomato plant in your absence?'

Rosie smiled at Bluff. A trip to London with Bluff. He wasn't being taken away after all. 'I will, sir, although I rather think Dr McAndrew has been keeping an eye on it already. He's a good egg.'

'I'll speak to Downing Street about the schedule,' Wyngate said. 'For now though, Driver Sinclair, would you be able to instruct my chaps on the dismantling of the machine? You'll be putting it together again in London.'

Rosie turned to look at the Endeavour, in its wooden frame with its keys and lights and rotas. What a daunting prospect. But Rosie could do it, she knew she could.

She nodded to Wyngate. 'Don't you worry, Mr Wyngate. It's in safe hands.'

Chapter 21

While Wyngate and Bluff headed off to arrest Prospero, Rosie helped to dismantle the machine and the radio. It was a much easier job than putting it together had been. With the help of Oakley and the team, she stowed it in the back of their van. It said *Radio Rentals* across the side, cover Rosie assumed in case someone should happen to look inside.

She moved the Citroën out of the barn. It looked rather sad with its patina of soot, so she wiped its windows. Then she moved out the Humber and put the Citroën into the garage where it would be safer than it had been in the barn.

Rosie went up to her room and packed, an easy task as she didn't need much more than her uniform. Still, she put her nicest dress in her suitcase just in case. She hadn't had a night away from the Park in a long time, and she waved to her room as she left it. She'd miss it.

Rosie loaded her suitcase into the boot, then she sat inside the car, drumming her fingers on the steering wheel in anticipation as she waited for Bluff and Wyngate to arrive with their quarry. At the first sight of them emerging from the house, she jumped from the car ready to open the door for Bluff and to load his luggage, but she hadn't expected the sight that greeted her.

Professor Swann was walking between Wyngate and Bluff. Though any casual observer would see nothing untoward in it, Rosie knew better. Charles was under arrest, though there were no handcuffs to suggest it and nothing to warn any accomplices that he was in such dire straits. His face was white as milk though, the colour completely gone from him and he clenched and unclenched his fists as he walked, his fingers fidgeting. Rosie couldn't quite tell if he was furious or sick with worry. Perhaps it was something between the two.

She gave Bluff and Wyngate a salute as they arrived. One of the military policemen, now in uniform, had brought Wyngate's car up alongside Rosie's, ready to take their prisoner. He opened the passenger door, and gave Wyngate a whip-crack salute.

'Sir!' he barked.

Rosie saw someone approaching from the house. A cry tore the air and she realised it was Caroline.

Poor devil, Rosie thought.

'What's happening?' Caroline asked frantically as she hurtled across the gravel. 'He hasn't packed his things! Where're you going?'

'Professor Swann's needed in London,' Wyngate told her. 'There's nothing to worry about.'

Rosie gave her an encouraging smile, hoping she could calm Caroline's panic. A smile to tell her that all was well. But Charles was her brother. Of course she could tell just by looking at the man that something was amiss.

'Telephone father,' Charles hissed. 'Tell him—'

'Professor Swann,' Bluff warned. 'You'll be able to—'

At that moment, Swann suddenly turned and landed a punch squarely on Wyngate's jaw, sending him sprawling. Then he dashed towards Rosie and the Humber, knocking her aside as he leapt into the driver's seat and slammed the door.

The military policeman abandoned his post and quick as

lightning ran round to the front of the Humber, planting his hands on the bonnet and glaring at Charles through the windscreen.

'Get out!' Rosie yelled through the car window at the wild-eyed Charles.

She grabbed the door handle and pulled, but Charles must've locked the door as it wouldn't budge. The engine roared into life, and Rosie was forced to let go. Even the military policeman thought better of being mown down and skidded out of the way.

The car tore off down the drive as Bluff bellowed after it, 'Don't be a fool, Swann!'

Rosie stared after the car in disbelief. 'What do we do? Go after him?'

'Citroën!' Bluff called, already running towards the garage as Wyngate clambered to his feet. Caroline was still standing there in silence, then she gave a sob and fled back into the house.

Rosie ran after Bluff. 'Are you sure? I've not taken her out for a run before!'

'Is there petrol in the tank?' He was already opening the garage doors. 'You know these roads better than anyone!'

'There is,' Rosie replied, her words catching in her throat. 'I know every lane and shortcut for miles around!'

Maybe that might make a difference, even though Charles had a head start.

She ran to Bluff's side and helped him open the heavy wooden doors. As soon as they were open, she pulled the key out of her pocket, which she still had from moving the car earlier. She ran to the driver's door and got in, then leaned across to open the passenger door for Bluff. She couldn't imagine him sitting in the back seat today.

Bluff leapt into the car and pulled the door shut as

Wyngate's sleek black car sped past the entrance to the courtyard in pursuit of Swann. Surely one of them would catch him.

Rosie had thought her first trip out in the Citroën would be a gentle tour of the local beauty spots. Instead, she followed Wyngate at speed as he headed off down the drive after Swann. The old car surprised her, not protesting at all as Rosie put her foot down.

'Where d'you think he's going?' she asked Bluff.

'I doubt he knows himself,' he replied. 'But if he wants to get himself shot, he's going about it in the right way.'

The Citroën bounced along the drive, then Rosie turned sharply as they emerged onto the main road.

'He's heading into the village!' Rosie exclaimed.

The Humber was travelling at a dangerous speed for the narrow roads, Wyngate's car easily matching it for pace. If they went on like this through the twisting lanes that surrounded Cottisbourne though, someone would end up in hospital.

Rosie slowed down and the gap grew between the Citroën and Wyngate's Jaguar. She couldn't bear the thought of hitting someone. But what if Prospero got away? Many more people would die. Reluctantly, she sped up again.

'Please no one get hurt, please no one get hurt...' she repeated under her breath.

Within moments, the familiar cottages on the edge of the village appeared. Rosie had barely time to register them as they sped past, the women chatting over their garden hedges a blur. Thank goodness there was no one else on the road.

But at that moment, Rosie noticed a cyclist up ahead, someone in overalls coming the opposite way. They wobbled on their bike and went straight into the hedge, waving their fist as the cars went past. Rosie felt terrible going against everything she had learnt in her MTC training. *Careful and courteous* had been their watchwords.

This was anything but.

The village itself passed in a flash, but Prospero showed no signs of slowing. Where would he go?

Up ahead, there was a sharp turning, and just as Rosie wondered if Prospero would chance it, he did. He turned too fast for Wyngate, but Rosie was ready and followed Prospero into the narrow lane that was squeezed between two fields. The Humber's tyres threw up dried mud from the road, sending it pattering against Rosie's windscreen. She glanced quickly behind and saw Wyngate now following her.

'There's a crossroads up ahead,' she told Bluff. 'I have no idea which way he'll go!'

Charles spun the wheel and with a squeal of tyres, the car lurched right at the crossroads. For a moment the wheels spun and it looked as though he was about to lose control, but somehow, he managed to wrest it back.

'Get alongside him,' Bluff urged and Rosie caught the glimpse of a revolver in his hand. 'He's going to kill himself if we don't stop him.'

Rosie's throat was dry with alarm, hoping against hope that there wasn't another vehicle coming their way. She managed to gain on Charles and with the accelerator flat on the floor, they were neck and neck. Bluff wound the window down and levelled the gun, then pulled the trigger. There was a bang and suddenly the Humber was no longer alongside them, but sloughing off the road and up the embankment of grass that ran alongside the churchyard, its front tyre already deflating.

Rosie pulled over, the Citroën's brakes complaining with a squeal. Gripping the wheel, her heart hammering as hard as if it was trying to escape her chest, she heaved great lungfuls of breath.

Prospero wouldn't be driving anywhere.

'Excellent work!' Bluff told her as he threw open the door and got out of the car, the gun still held before him. Charles had pillowed his arms atop the wheel of the Humber and his forehead was resting on them. As Bluff wrenched open the driver's door, Swann folded his arms, sat up straight and lifted his chin into that imperious tilt.

'You don't need the gun,' he told Bluff. 'Do I *look* like a hoodlum?'

'One can never tell,' was Bluff's reply.

Chapter 22

Rosie was billeted in a tall, old building in a road that ran from the Strand down to the Thames. She had her own room, but it was small, with a view of a tiny courtyard full of dustbins. If only her friends from Cottisbourne Park could've been here too, they would've had a laugh about her scenic London view.

Other women came and went, some in their best dresses as they went out in a cloud of perfume. Rosie assumed they worked in the various government buildings around Whitehall. And where all that perfume came from, she couldn't imagine.

Rosie wasn't given very long to settle in before she was called to the War Office. There, she was ensconced in a plain, windowless room in the bowels of the building where she was to rebuild the Endeavour and the radio.

This time, it was much easier to reconstruct it, but Rosie and Oakley with the team took their time. She still couldn't believe she was in London, and she wasn't much looking forward to the evening if the bombers returned.

Nancy would envy her, that much was true, and as Rosie worked on the machine, she wondered if Nancy's mother was somewhere in this very building. As she and the men Wyngate had brought to Cottisbourne painstakingly reconstructed the Endeavour machine, she wondered what Bluff would be doing now he was back in London. Would it be military drill or meetings with Wyngate and his seniors? Rosie suspected the latter.

There was a knock at the door and when it opened, there was Bluff. He was carrying a tray of steaming teacups.

'Good evening,' he said to the assembled group. 'I thought you hard workers might all welcome a cup of tea.'

'Oh, thank you, sir!' Rosie smiled. She was so glad to see him, and so glad that the real Bluff never pulled rank and would happily serve the tea.

'Wonderful stuff!' Oakley put down his screwdriver, then flexed his fingers. 'We're getting along with this reconstruction,' he told Bluff. 'Nearly there!'

'The MTC's loss is Special Operations Executive's gain, eh?' Bluff put the tea tray down on a desk. 'I hope they've put you in appropriate barracks, Driver Sinclair?'

'Not too bad. It's just off the Strand. I ...' Rosie stared. *Good Lord, he's wearing jodhpurs.* She looked back up at Bluff. 'Have you been out on a horse?'

Bluff looked rather apologetic. He rubbed the back of his neck and admitted, 'Only after a three-hour meeting in a windowless room. And everyone at the meeting was smoking a pipe.'

'Well, I'm glad you got some fresh air,' Rosie said. 'I hope those three hours in that meeting weren't too horrible.'

He shook his head as he assured her, 'It was necessary, let's put it that way. Our man's in custody and I'll be talking to him tomorrow.' Bluff lowered his voice to a whisper. 'I understand he's with his father at the moment.'

'Oh, I see,' Rosie replied. 'I hope he's not going to try and wriggle out of it.'

'We'll see.' Bluff looked across the workshop and asked, 'How much longer do you think you'll need?'

'Another half an hour, an hour at most,' Oakley told him

as he took a teacup from Bluff's tray. 'Why, would you like to borrow the newest member of our team, Major-General?'

'Unless you'd care to join me for dinner at the Café Royal, Mr Oakley,' Bluff replied. 'In which case I can always ask them to pull up another chair.'

'No, I think I shall have to refuse,' Oakley replied. 'Driver Sinclair, you've reassembled the Endeavour's gearbox. We only have the radio to finish now. London is yours!'

'If you're sure you can spare me,' Rosie said. She smiled at Bluff. 'The Café Royal, you say, Major-General?'

But Bluff shook his head. 'No special treatment, Driver Sinclair, the Café Royal must wait for the Endeavour machine. Perhaps I could call at your billet in an hour or so?'

'Of course,' Rosie replied. As much as she wanted to go out on the town with Bluff, she was enjoying her work. She wanted to see the machines reassembled and working again. 'I'll see you there, Major-General.'

'I shall let you get back to saving the free world.' Bluff saluted her. 'Good job, team.'

Rosie and the team got back to work. Big Ben chimed the hour as they stepped back from the machine and realised it was working. No message was coming through on the radio, but the satisfying hiss of static told them that it was ready.

Rosie came up out of the basement. The sun hadn't quite set. She hurried along the pavement, back to her billet, and rushed up the stairs to her room past other women – some in their uniforms, some in their best dresses and others in smart suits.

Rosie tidied her hair and put on her best dress and the little red velvet hat that matched it. She wished she had some perfume, but hoped Bluff would like her make-up, even though she found it hard to tone it down and not look as if she was about to take to the stage.

She went back downstairs to the lobby where some other women were lounging about. Cars and people passed on the narrow street as she waited for Bluff. A black cab glided to a halt and the door opened. She watched as Bluff climbed out, changed into an immaculate khaki uniform, his cap tucked under his arm.

'Good evening, Rosie. You look wonderful!' He took her hand and gestured to the cab. 'After you.'

Rosie climbed in. 'What a treat,' she said to Bluff. 'It makes a change not to drive for once!'

'I thought we'd both earned dinner and a little bit of dancing.' Bluff closed the door and settled beside her. 'One doesn't get into a car chase every day. Even London cabbies don't manage that.'

The driver turned round in his seat. 'Car chase, mate? Nah, not on these roads.'

Rosie chuckled. She squeezed Bluff's hand. 'Dinner and dancing sounds like the perfect way to end the day.'

Chapter 23

Arriving at the War Office the next morning, Rosie wondered what the day would bring.

Hopefully no more car chases, she thought as she walked along the black and white marble floor. Paintings and statues showed great leaders in their pomp and the heroes of legendary battles. In one painting, the mounted troops seemed to leap out of the canvas, their horses' hooves roiling at the air. In another, a soldier with a muddy face and torn uniform held aloft his regiment's bullet-holed pennant. Another made her smile – an enlarged photograph showing MTC ambulance drivers in France. What a brave bunch of girls they'd been.

Behind every door she heard the furious clatter of typewriters and teleprinters, and everyone seemed to be in a rush.

Rosie's thoughts returned to the evening. One day, she'd be able to tell her friends about it. Bluff had been the perfect gent at the Café Royal, and he'd impressed her with his dancing. She hadn't wanted to leave his embrace, but the evening had ended and as they emerged onto the night-time streets, with signposts pointing to shelters, and couples wandering in uniform, Rosie remembered that they were at war. She hated saying good night to Bluff because what if the bombers came over tonight? What if...?

The night had passed without any raids, and Rosie hoped

they'd seen the back of them. But that, she knew, was wishful thinking.

The front of the War Office was so well-appointed and elegant, but Rosie was headed once more to the basement. She knew why – the modified Endeavour was unique and if the worst should happen and bombs struck the War Office, at least it would be safe below ground.

The task that morning was to draw up blueprints of the Endeavour. She'd never worked on blueprints in her life. Rosie was at the chalkboard again, sketching the twist of the gearbox, when a knock sounded on the door.

As Rosie glanced across to greet the new arrival, a dark-haired woman poked her head round the door, smiling a greeting.

'Would this be a good time for a visit?' she asked and Rosie caught an accent in her voice. American? Canadian, maybe.

'I can't see any objections,' Rosie replied. 'What do you say, team?'

Oakley nodded. He had gone rather pale and was trying to smooth down his hair as he stood with the rest of the team who had been seated round the table. 'Of course, Miss Layton, do come in.'

'Business as usual,' she beamed as she opened the door and stepped into the room. 'Don't mind us.'

Rosie turned back to the board. 'So here we …'

Silence had descended like a cloak of snow across the room, and she looked round and couldn't quite believe her eyes. If only she could've told the girls about *this*.

'Good morning, sir,' she said, and saluted Prime Minister Winston Churchill as he walked into the room.

'Good morning.' Churchill inclined his head in acknowledgement. 'Continue, madam, I've no wish to distract you.'

Rosie nodded. She went to point to her sketch on the board with her piece of chalk, but she couldn't go back to pinions and wheels without saying something first.

'If I may, sir,' she said. 'There's a little girl I know who always asks me if I'm going to see you when I come up to London. She wants me to say hello to you. So ... *hello*, Prime Minister. From Nancy.'

The room seemed suddenly very quiet, the air still. Had she committed some terrible faux pas, Rosie wondered? Was this simply not done in London? Perhaps she'd be put on the next train home for daring to be quite so familiar with the formidable prime minister.

'Well.' Churchill nodded slowly, then met the greeting with a smile. 'I'd be most grateful if you would convey my greetings back to Nancy. Miss Layton, perhaps we might send a short note to the young lady?'

'Of course,' his secretary said. She made a quick note in her pad, then gave Rosie a nod.

'Thank you, sir. She'll be ever so pleased.' Rosie steadied herself, still reeling at what she had said, and returned to her description of the gear system. She drew a couple of lines on the board, and shaded in the area between them. 'Well, to continue with the particular design of the gears that we find in the machine, the twist is necessary in order to align the drums which consist of *this* Endeavour's onboard Bombe system.'

'And it would take a significant intellect to develop a machine of this kind?' the prime minister asked. 'I believe we've never seen its like?'

'Oh, a very clever person indeed,' Rosie replied.

'Ever so clever,' Oakley replied. 'I've never seen anything like it. I've worked on tabulating machines for many years, and I've never ever come across one constructed like this. It could only be designed and built by someone who has an intimate knowledge of both Endeavours *and* Bombes.'

Churchill stooped to peer at the machine, nodding thoughtfully. As he did, he asked, 'And now we have the machine, presumably we will be able to monitor the radio frequencies and put its technology to good use? Multiple languages, the major-general tells me. Quite remarkable.'

'Yes, sir, of course,' Lainson replied. 'We got a message through yesterday, as you may know, and we haven't picked up any further messages since we reassembled the machine here last night. And quite, it can cope with five different languages.'

Rosie heard an echo of Professor Swann's shameless brag. *'I speak five different languages!'*

A fat lot of good that would do him in prison.

'I understand that Major-General Sir Kingsley-Flynn is on hand should we receive a communication from Berlin.' Churchill straightened up and laid one hand on the machine. Rosie felt a swell of pride at the mention of Bluff's part in their achievement. 'Splendid work. Well done, all.'

He shook hands with everyone, and didn't seem put off by Rosie's chalky hand.

'It's been an honour to meet you,' she told him.

'And you, Driver Sinclair,' he assured her. 'Good day.'

As the prime minister took his leave, Miss Layton approached Rosie with her notepad open, a sharpened pencil poised over the page.

'If I could just take Nancy's name and address,' Miss Layton asked, 'for Mr Churchill's correspondence.'

Rosie smiled and gave her Nancy's details. The little girl was going to be very happy indeed at what was about to drop through her letterbox.

Chapter 24

At lunchtime, Rosie went to the canteen with some of the team from the basement. As she joined the queue, up ahead she saw the familiar broad shoulders of Bluff. She wasn't quite sure what the etiquette was. She couldn't very well shout his name, so she asked Oakley to hold her place in the queue, then she dashed up to Bluff.

'Hello, Major-General.' Rosie prodded his arm, chuckling. 'I hope your feet aren't too sore after last night. You'll never guess who I met this morning!'

'Driver Sinclair, good afternoon,' Bluff replied. He looked tired despite his smile, something distracted behind his eyes. 'Let me guess ... Was it His Majesty?'

'Almost! It was ...' Keen to amuse Bluff, Rosie stuck out her chest, her hand in one pocket as she pretended to puff a cigar. 'Can you guess?'

He dropped his voice to a whisper and asked, 'Mr Churchill?'

'Yes, well done!' Rosie laughed, but Bluff still looked rather sad. 'Oh, you poor chap, did you not sleep very well? It's so quiet in Cottisbourne, isn't it? And so noisy all night in London. Are the other soldiers terribly rowdy?'

'Not in the major-general's corner of Hyde Park barracks,' Bluff assured her. 'Would you like to eat lunch in my office, Driver Sinclair? There's something I'd like to discuss with you.'

'I'd love to.' Rosie smiled gently. He had something on his mind and she felt rather awkward for foisting her silly Churchill impression on him.

'I telephoned the sickbay at Cottisbourne Park this morning,' Bluff said as they waited. 'Joseph Fleet told the nurse there that he'd fallen off his bike, hence the splinter. That's the problem with this job, you see, makes a chap suspicious of everything.'

'Fell off his bike?' Rosie rolled her eyes. 'It wouldn't surprise me – he rides down to the pub on it, then wobbles back.'

They waited in line for their lunch and, each armed with a sandwich, headed for Bluff's office. She followed him along the busy corridors, where everyone they passed met Bluff with a respectful nod or even a salute. The War Office building was vast, bigger by far than Cottisbourne Park, and the deeper into it that they went, the more splendid their surroundings became. The wide corridors, which bustled with administrators and civil servants, began to narrow and grow quieter, the paintings on the walls growing grander and when they saw soldiers now, they wore medal ribbons and the stars that allowed Rosie to pick them out as senior ranks. Though none were as senior as her major-general.

'Sorry it's a bit of a trek.' Bluff opened a door. 'My office.'

As Rosie stepped inside, she felt as if she was entering a gentleman's club. Not that she'd ever been in one, but this was how she'd imagined them to be. Polished dark wood panels rose halfway up the walls, filling the room with the scent of beeswax, which had mixed in the air with tobacco from Bluff's pipe. Long windows looked out onto Whitehall, and above the fireplace was a huge canvas showing what looked like Wellington trotting rather proudly on horseback before his men. One of them held a golden Napoleonic eagle on a broken staff, symbolising, Rosie supposed, the victory at Waterloo.

A large wooden desk had centre stage, but evidently Bluff didn't do all his work there, as two dark green leather armchairs stood in front of the fireplace, with a gramophone beside them.

Bluff put his plate down on the desk. He held out his hand to Rosie and asked, 'How was Winnie?'

Rosie took his hand, then rested her head against his chest, as if they were still dancing at the Café Royal. 'He was very nice. I made a fool of myself though and told him *Nancy says hello!* But he didn't seem to mind. He's going to write her a note. And aside from that... he seems rather impressed about the Endeavour. Isn't that grand?'

'It's wonderful.' Bluff put his arm around Rosie's waist and held her close. 'Wasn't last night a perfect memory? Much-needed, I'd say.'

'Oh, it really was!' Rosie lifted her face to Bluff's and gently kissed his lips. 'I hated saying goodnight to you, you know. I didn't want to wave you off.'

'I didn't like bringing you to London,' he admitted. 'Oh, it's nothing compared to the Blitz, but... I'd rather you weren't in the capital when the Luftwaffe are looking to teach us a lesson. You're a very brave woman, Rosie. I've known lifelong soldiers who could learn something from you.'

'Am I brave?' Rosie chuckled. 'I just sort of... do what I need to do. Is that what's troubling you, being here in London? I shall be all right. I'm only on the second floor in my billet – I haven't far to go to get to the shelter.'

'They're frightfully poor shots this time round. They've forgotten what bullseye looks like.' Bluff kissed Rosie's hair.

'I spent the morning with Professor Swann. It's left me troubled.'

'I'm not surprised, you poor thing,' Rosie replied. 'I can't imagine it's nice sharing the same air as a traitor.'

But Bluff said nothing for a long moment. Instead, he settled his cheek against Rosie's hair, holding her until he eventually murmured, 'Something about it doesn't feel right. Usually, I have a sixth sense and … It's Swann, you see. I just don't get that sense.'

Rosie needed a moment to process Bluff's words. They'd been so sure. They both had. They had been convinced of Swann's guilt, and now the Earth seemed to have shifted on its axis.

'You … you mean you don't think he's Prospero?'

'No,' he whispered. 'No, I don't.'

'Gosh …' Rosie said. 'What can we do, Bluff? What the heck can we do?'

'We'll start by eating lunch,' was Bluff's very pragmatic reply. 'I need to talk it through with you. You were there at Cottisbourne, you know Swann. It just feels … *wrong*.'

'He was covered in our friend's blood,' Rosie reminded him, as they each took one of the armchairs. 'It makes him look rather guilty, I'd say.'

Bluff nodded. 'Swann's version of events is that he was out getting some fresh air when he heard a gunshot. His first thought in finding the prof was to try and resuscitate him, which is how he ended up in that state. Of course, it's an obvious lie, but … Prospero has escaped capture for four years, Rosie. It's rather lucky for us that he managed to get himself covered in blood on the day I arrived.' He shook his head, anguish on his face. 'But of course, Wyngate would say that it's because Prospero's never panicked before. And panic has made our methodical spy chaotic.'

'I would've said that Swann is the sort of chap who *never* panics,' Rosie said. 'But then, we both saw what happened when he stole the Humber and tried to escape. *That's* a man who's panicking. But if he's not Prospero, why run off like that?' Rosie bit into her sandwich and thought for a moment before asking Bluff, 'Have you told Wyngate that you're not sure about Swann?'

'He ran because he was terrified. Oh, he sits there with his nose in the air playing the part, but I can tell that he's petrified,' Bluff said. 'And when I told him that we'd pieced together his machine and even had a brief chat with Berlin, he looked at me as though I was speaking another language. He might just be a hell of an actor, but I don't think so. You're the only person I've told so far, I wanted to get my thoughts in order.'

'That's intriguing ...' Rosie tapped her chin in thought. 'You see, he's such a big head that you'd think he'd be incapable of not showing some sort of glee at what we've found out about Prospero. But his surprise ... his complete lack of recognition ... it does rather sound as if he genuinely hasn't a clue about any of this.'

But the circumstantial evidence told them differently. A vast field had been whittled down over the years to just half a dozen. Six men who were entrusted with the secrets that Prospero later shared to his Nazi paymasters, six men alone who fit the profile of their quarry, who had the clearance and skills to be the brains behind Operation Tempest. And of those six, the only one who evidence had placed in the barn, let alone covered in Hale's blood, was Professor Charles Swann. And Professor Charles Swann was the genius who had decoded Endeavour.

'Wyngate and his people believe Swann decoded Endeavour as a decoy.' Bluff put his plate down and stood.

He crossed the office to a bureau and took out a brandy decanter and two glasses. 'To us, he's the boffin working on the uncrackable code. Meanwhile, he's laughing behind his hand with Jerry and making sure that whenever we crack one cypher thanks to his machine, they've already moved onto the next. It was something one of your code chaps said the other day though…'

Bluff poured out the drinks and brought them back to the armchairs. His expression was thoughtful, as though he was still making sense of his ideas.

'He said that the Morse code operator had a fingerprint, as if one might almost get to know them.' Bluff held up his glass. 'I had one of Swann's Endeavour machines delivered from hut two and I'd like you and your team to take a look at it. I don't think it looks like it was built by the same person at all. For all Swann's linguistic and codecracking skills, I'm not entirely sure the chap's a natural engineer. It's unwieldy, nothing like the kit we found in the hayloft. And it doesn't feel like a decoy. Perhaps we discounted the other names too easily.'

Rosie thought back to Dr Brett, who had been so alarmed when they'd found him in the woods by the folly. And what about Joe and his splinter? Could he have got it from lurking in the barn, or had he just got it by falling off his bicycle?

Rosie sipped the brandy. 'The Endeavours they use in that hut are their tools. Like my spanners and wrenches and things. You leave your mark on them. It's rather like trying to use someone else's pen, or wear someone else's shoes! I think you're right. And I'm sure the team will be perfectly capable of making any comparisons and the differences between the two machines.'

He nodded. 'I'll have the machine sent over to your workshop this afternoon. I just need Swann to tell me what he's afraid of. There's something he's hiding, I can see that, and I just need him to tell—'

The door of Bluff's office banged open and a furious voice bellowed, 'Whatever in the blue blazes d'you think you're up to, you damned scoundrel?'

Rosie almost dropped her glass in fright.

There in front of them stood a grey-haired, puce-faced man in pinstripes, a gold watch chain glittering across his stomach. He tilted his chin up at an imperious angle, and Rosie had the oddest sensation of déjà vu.

Until she realised she hadn't met this man before, but had definitely encountered his son. The resemblance was uncanny, as if she was seeing the future Professor Swann through a crystal ball. At least, if he didn't end up with his head in a noose.

Bluff bolted from his chair to intercept the new arrival with an exclamation of, 'What the devil, Swann?'

'Why the hell have you arrested my boy?' Mr Swann barked. 'The son of a cabinet minister, treated like a common thief! How *dare* you?!'

'I've arrested no one,' Bluff told him with a calmness that Rosie wasn't sure she could've mustered in the face of such fury. 'I've simply done my job.'

'Not arrested anyone?' Mr Swann's face turned several shades redder. 'So why is my son in a cell? Tell me that, eh? And if that's what doing your job is, then what a damned shabby show!'

Rosie wondered how he could've known. Surely Professor Swann's arrest had been done in secret. But then, he wasn't just *any* professor but the son of a minister. Somehow, the news had got out.

'Minister, please,' Bluff tried to reason, but Rosie could see fresh anguish in his eyes. Did he really believe that Charles might be the wrong man? 'Believe me, this isn't what I wanted. I have to go where the evidence leads me.'

'Evidence? I bet you don't have the tiniest scrap!' Mr Swann stalked towards Bluff, jabbing his finger in the air. 'I know what this is all about. *Let's embarrass the minister! Let's weaken the government! Let's stage a military coup!* Well, I won't allow bounders in uniform like you to use my son as a political pawn!'

Military coup?

The Swanns really didn't like or trust the military, did they?

'How dare you?' Bluff's voice had taken on an edge that Rosie wasn't sure she liked the sound of. But it was hardly surprising. He'd narrowly escaped the Dasher's sinking with his life and she couldn't imagine the risks he'd taken time and again behind enemy lines, only to stand here in Whitehall and be accused of something close to treason.

'How dare I? How dare *you*?!' Mr Swann protested. 'My son has worked tirelessly since this bally war broke out, reduced to living in a shed, abandoning all the research he was working on in college ... and you *arrest him?* He's the most English of Englishmen!' Mr Swann's lip puckered. He was a blustery, entitled patriarch, but through it, Rosie could see the evident pain he must feel. Bad enough to discover your son has been arrested; even worse that he might be a traitor to everything Mr Swann stood for. 'Have you seen his overarm throw? *Have you?* Tell me how a man capable of playing cricket like that could even *consider* undermining his country?'

'Minister, I am asking you *politely* to leave this office.' A little *too* politely, perhaps.

'I'm not moving until you tell me what's going on!' Mr Swann raged. 'My son's not a spy! He can't be! How could you *possibly* understand the sort of work he's involved in? It must be a mix-up. It must. Somebody's blundered, and it's not *me*, and it's not *my* son!'

Bluff shook his head and told him, 'You know I can't engage in this conversation, Minister.'

Mr Swann inhaled and seemed to calm a little, his face returning to a less vivid colour. He painted on a forced smile and in the suave tones of an experienced politician, he said to Bluff, 'No doubt this can all be smoothed over with the minimum of fuss, what?'

'Out!' Bluff commanded. So even he had his tipping point, Rosie realised. 'Or by God, Swann, I'll put you out!'

Mr Swann narrowed his eyes, then he turned and headed for the door. Just as he was leaving, he looked back over his shoulder and said, 'You haven't heard the last of this. You and your little friend.' He gave Rosie a pointed nod, then slammed the door behind him.

'Just as charming as his son...' Rosie whispered.

Bluff pinched his thumb and forefinger to the bridge of his nose. He shook his head and murmured, 'I just can't be sure...' Then he shook his head again, as though to clear it. He drew in a deep, fortifying breath and told Rosie, 'We have to be better than him. And we have to get this right. As soon as your team has any conclusions on the difference between the machines, call me in. We're going to solve this, Rosie, you and I.'

Rosie reached for his other hand. 'Don't let Mr Swann shake you. We'll call you in as soon as we know anything. And don't worry, we *will* work out what's going on.'

Chapter 25

Back in the basement that afternoon, the blueprints were put aside as the Endeavour from hut two arrived. It had been driven up by two of the military policemen who had still been at Cottisbourne Park, watching for any accomplices.

Oakley and Lainson carefully removed the outer shell of the new machine, then they opened up the machine from the hayloft.

Two columns had been drawn on the board, and one by one each column began to fill as the similarities and differences between the machines were noted down.

In some ways they were identical – but only as far as the standard configuration of an Endeavour went. It became obvious to the team that the tweaks made to the machines were quite different.

Could that mean they were made by different people, or that Swann had covered himself by deliberately building in the differences?

Rosie peered inside. There were no drums or gears in the newly-arrived machine. It was far less modified than the hayloft machine. As the team discussed the technical differences, Rosie spotted something. Only a little thing, but perhaps it made a big difference.

'Could I mention something?' she asked, not wanting to disturb them.

'Of course, Driver Sinclair!' Oakley said. 'Spotted anything?'

'The way the wire's finished off,' she replied.

The team looked bemused, clearly unsure what she meant.

'If you're wrapping a wire around a pin, you'll do it one way and stick to it. It's like casting off your knitting. Everyone has their favoured way. But look...' Rosie pointed inside the hayloft machine at a point where a wire had been twisted, then over to a similar point in the new machine. 'They're mirror images of each other. I'd almost wonder if the hayloft machine was worked on by someone who's left-handed, and the new one by a right-handed person. Or vice versa. But it doesn't look like the work of the same person, does it? And why would you deliberately change the way you tighten a bit of wire? Look, over and over and over again...' Rosie beamed as she pointed back and forth between the two machines. It was so obvious now she'd spotted it. 'It's different!'

Laughter broke out in the team.

'Bravo!' Oakley said, clapping.

'Trust an MTC girl to spot that!' Lainson chuckled. 'And you know, now you've mentioned it, look at how they've nipped off the plastic covering from the wire. The hayloft machine's is straight across, but hut two's is at this angle, and that angle... it's rather sloppy in comparison, don't you think?'

'Yes,' Rosie replied, thinking of Bluff's word. 'It's rather like a fingerprint, wouldn't you say? Let's get the major-general down here.'

Rosie rang Bluff's office. 'We've found something,' she said.

'I've got Wyngate with me,' he replied. 'We'll be down directly.'

225

'See you very soon, sir,' Rosie said, and put down the phone.

She went over to the board and sketched the different ways the wire had been worked. She was very pleased with her discovery, but then she thought of Charles sitting in his cell and wondered what on earth they'd do with him.

When Wyngate and Bluff arrived in the workshop, Rosie and her team led them through her findings. She saw Wyngate visibly pale as he listened, his lips drawing thinner with each new discovery. This might not be enough to exonerate Charles Swann, but it seemed like enough for a good defence solicitor to work with. If Charles *had* a defence solicitor, that was, and if they were ever allowed to see these machines and learn of the differences between them.

'We can get other machines Swann's built over the last few years,' Wyngate told them as Rosie's impromptu presentation reached its conclusion. 'The team can take them apart and see if there's a pattern, but if there is …'

'Prospero is still out there,' Bluff concluded. 'And we have to catch him before he gets word of Overlord.'

'We need to listen for any messages.' Rosie gestured towards the Endeavour from the hayloft. 'If Prospero was capable of making this, then he'll have no trouble putting together even a basic machine to make contact again with Germany. We might catch communication between them.'

Bluff nodded. 'We'll get monitoring on it.' He looked to Wyngate and said, 'I doubt Prospero hasn't jumped to another frequency now he knows his machine's been taken out of the barn.'

'At least we've got somewhere to start from,' Wyngate replied. 'A needle in a slightly smaller haystack.'

★ ★ ★

226

Once Rosie's shift had ended, she went up to Bluff's office. She sat in one of the armchairs, a whiskey in her hand as a record played on the gramophone. She almost felt cosy, until she remembered that the man in the cell wasn't Prospero. And that the bombers might fly over.

There was a delicious sense of order in Bluff's office though, despite the tape on the windows and the threat from the air. Here it seemed as though little had changed in a hundred years or more, everything as solid and dependable as Bluff himself. They talked about the theatre and life before the war, as well as the promise of the future after it, when Rosie would tread the boards again and Bluff would make his first forays into showbiz. It didn't seem like a dream when Bluff spoke about it in his Sandhurst tones, and Rosie let herself forget Prospero and the invasion Wyngate had told her about. Here, in the dying light, everything was peaceful again.

If Bluff became a producer and worked with the Cavendish Players, then all sorts of marvellous things could happen. Her parents could retire – at least, from running the group. They'd always perform, even if they lived into their nineties. And she and Bluff could work together. And that really would be fun. Much more fun than worrying when the army deployed him who knew where.

'Won't we have a wonderful time?' Rosie smiled at Bluff, who looked happier now as they sat and talked.

'We will,' he agreed. 'There's a whole world for us to see. And all of it wants to hear from the Cavendish Players.'

'I should hope so too!' Rosie chuckled. She left her chair and perched on the arm of Bluff's. She slipped her arm around his shoulders and brushed her lips to his hair. 'Don't worry, I'll hop down sharpish if someone should come in.'

He gazed up at her and promised as the telephone began

to ring, 'I'll send them out with a flea on their ear if they try it.'

'Loucheness in the War Office – what fun!' Rosie stared reproachfully at the telephone, and got off the arm of Bluff's chair so that he could answer the call. He kissed her cheek then made his way across the office to the desk and picked up the receiver.

'Kingsley-Flynn,' was his abrupt salutation. 'Ah, Mr Wyngate. Working late again?'

Wyngate.

Rosie followed Bluff to his desk. *News?* she mouthed.

He nodded and said, 'I see. And that was this evening?' There was a pause. 'Doesn't that strike you as odd, Wyngate? Yes, that's exactly my thought too.'

Rosie's eyes widened. What was happening?

'Keep me informed, Wyngate,' Bluff said. 'Goodnight.'

'What is it?' Rosie asked him, excited.

He put the receiver down and said with just a hint of disbelief, 'They've arrested Dr Zalewski at the folly. The oddest thing though, nobody has laid a finger on the machine we found hidden in there. Apparently, he was just ... sitting.'

'Just *sitting?*' Rosie frowned. That really was odd. 'Was he in the main room, or was he in the secret room at the back?'

'The main room. They left a couple of triggers on the hidden doors and they hadn't been opened,' Bluff said. 'Nobody's been in since Wyngate's men.'

'What was he doing, admiring the view?' Rosie shook her head. 'He was definitely up to *something* with Professor Swann. God knows what. Maybe they're raiding the stores. Is there a demand on the blackmarket for fuse boards and wires ... what else is there? Pencils and notepads? Hardly worth doing, and Swann's family aren't strapped for cash, so I can't imagine he'd run the risk for a few quid here and there. And why risk his neck stealing a car and peeling off in it?'

He shook his head and said, 'Whatever it is, he's not telling. Oh, he's saying he's innocent but that's all he's giving us.'

'*I'd* say I was innocent if I was rounded up by Wyngate's burly military coppers!' Rosie gave Bluff a hug. 'But it seems significant, doesn't it? I feel like we're getting closer and closer to the truth.'

Bluff nodded. 'And if he *is* innocent, I won't let him hang. No matter how bloody minded he is.'

'I suppose there's no law against sitting in a folly, but...' Rosie shook her head. 'If only those two'd just admit to what they're up to.'

'I'm seeing our Polish chum tomorrow,' Bluff said. 'I don't suppose you've any plans for di—'

And the telephone jangled into life again.

Rosie pouted. She wanted to tell him that no, she didn't have any plans, but it seemed that dinner would have to wait.

He picked up the receiver again and said, 'Kingsley-Fly—when?' Bluff shot Rosie a glance. 'We'll come straight down.'

The machine. A message had come through on the machine, Rosie was certain of it.

All thoughts of dinner fled as Rosie and Bluff hurried down to the basement workshop.

Oakley and the team were waiting for them and as soon as the door closed behind them, he started to explain in a whisper as Morse code bleeped from the radio.

'We went through the frequencies. All quiet until...! We've put the first message through the Endeavour. Major-General, if we might have the benefit of your linguistic expertise once more?'

Bluff picked up the pad and read, 'Prospero. New frequency confirmed.' At that he glanced towards Rosie and the team. 'Stand by for message from Rienzi. Twenty-two hundred hours. Out.'

'Rienzi? That sounds Italian to me,' Lainson remarked.

'It's one of Wagner's operas,' Rosie explained.

'Ten o'clock,' Oakley said. Then he tugged at his hair in frustration. 'Oh, lord, what time? London time or Berlin time?'

'Berlin,' Bluff said with certainty. 'Talk to your chums in monitoring. I want the airwaves scoured back and forth, up and down until you find Prospero. He'll be waiting for that message and I'm damn sure he'll reply. We need to catch that reply and keep that frequency monitored night and day so we know where they're moving to next. We have a chance to listen in to Prospero and his paymasters, we can't miss it.'

'Of course, sir!' Oakley said. He dashed to the telephone in the corner and put his call through.

Lainson cracked his knuckles. 'And now we wait...'

It was the biggest breakthrough they'd had so far, Rosie realised. Prospero moved frequencies at a rate of knots, but if they could find him out there, they could follow him as he jumped from one broadcast to the next. Finding the radio still tuned in despite its destruction had been a lucky break, and they couldn't afford to waste it. Now they would be riding on their quarry's coattails until he made another mistake.

Bluff looked at his watch and said, 'I make that an hour from now. If no one has any objections, I'd like to take Driver Sinclair along to the mess for supper.' He inclined his head, the picture of a gracious officer. 'And you chaps get some decent nosebag on me. We might be in for a late finish.'

'Very decent of you, Major-General,' Lainson replied, and the rest of the team nodded.

'Supper in the mess will be lovely, sir,' Rosie said, although she'd never been to a mess before, and certainly nowhere as grand as the War Office.

The mess? Am I dressed for the mess? Will they even let me in?

'Driver Sinclair.' Bluff touched her elbow very lightly. 'After you. And I apologise in advance if I spoil supper with my attempts to puzzle out the identity of Rienzi.'

'It's more interesting than talking about the weather,' Rosie assured him.

Up they went, back through the building, the plain concrete of the basement giving way to the grand decor of the War Office above stairs. She didn't take Bluff's arm, but every now and then she pretended to walk too near him by accident and brushed her fingertips against his hand.

★ ★ ★

Returning to the basement after dining in the plush surroundings of the mess was quite a contrast. And as they'd eaten, Rosie had glanced about the room, wondering how many of the other diners knew what she and Bluff were working on. Indeed, what secrets were *they* working on that Rosie would never know about?

But they were all working for the common good.

Except for Prospero. Whoever they were.

And at least the bombers had held off. Maybe they'd be in for another quiet night.

The workshop was buzzing with activity. The Endeavour and the radio had been given centre stage and the team were gathered around it. Rosie noticed a spare chair among them, which she assumed had been left vacant for their resident German translator. Another board had been brought into the room and one of the team was frowning as he chose his piece of chalk. This was important business, after all.

There was no sign of Wyngate and Rosie wondered if he was with the new prisoner, the Polish codebreaker who had gone to the folly simply to sit. She wondered too about Charles Swann and his father and about Caroline, who must be waiting at Cottisbourne in confusion, unless the furious cabinet minister had plucked her from her role. She wouldn't even be able to tell anyone why she was so upset either, because the arrest of Prospero would certainly be a state secret. It was still no match for sibling intuition, it seemed.

'Do we have monitoring standing by for that reply?' Bluff asked as the clock ticked on. 'They might only have a matter of a minute or two to tune into Prospero. We don't know when we'll get another opportunity like this.'

'They're ready,' Oakley assured him. 'They've brought in everyone they could find. Called in people who'd just got home from their shift. They're using multiple devices and have been doing a deep sweep for the past hour. If Prospero so much as sneezes, they'll know about it.'

Bluff nodded. 'And what of the voice our young informant heard in the hayloft? I'm assuming that was a stopgap until the machine was up and running?'

Lainson nodded. 'Absolutely. Once Prospero had got it all working, there'd be no need for any voices over the air. Everything comes in, and out, in Morse code. Far more secure.'

'So she heard...' he narrowed his eyes, thoughtful, 'Frequencies?'

'Oh, yes,' Oakley said. 'They broadcast frequencies. In German, of course. Very short messages, which they'd hope no one would've spotted and been able to trace. Prospero would've been told ahead of time when to listen out and on what frequency from his handler. Then all he'd need to do is tune in at the right time, and it comes through the radio.

And there might be other information, about the correct setup of the machine – so no wonder he took a hammer to it. Once Prospero had all the necessary information, he went from voice to Morse code and he'd stick with it.'

It was only then that the reality of how lucky Nancy had been struck Rosie. She'd been in the barn at the very moment when Prospero was gathering information direct from Germany. If they'd happened upon each other, she had no doubt that the mole would've thought nothing of doing to Nancy exactly what they did to Professor Hale.

That little girl should get a medal.

'Sixty seconds.' Bluff knitted his hands behind his back. 'Let's see what our friend Rienzi has to say.'

As one, the team glanced anxiously up at the clock on the wall as the hands moved closer to nine o'clock. The radio hummed and the empty static seemed to become more and more intense as time ticked on.

Finally, just as the clock told them it was nine, a message started to come through on the radio. Heads down, two of the team were writing down the Morse code. They were the only people in the room who dared move at that moment. They carried on, then both looked up at once and nodded.

'It's repeating now. Here, put this through the machine.'

The notepad was passed across to the operator at the Endeavour. As before, he inputted the letters and numbers and the Endeavour flashed into life, each character decrypted into parts of the message from Berlin.

Another operator wrote these down, then passed the finished message to Bluff to translate.

'There you are, sir,' he whispered.

This time the message repeated a third and fourth time, but Bluff was already working on his translation as the dots and dashes of the Morse code terminated. The room fell silent, the only sound now that of Bluff's pencil scratching across the paper. Eventually he cleared his throat and began.

'Prospero. Stand by for message from Rienzi. Message begins. My friend, thank you for your kind birthday regards. The occasion was a splendid one, marked with all ceremony by the *Volk.*' At the word, he glanced up from the page for a second. 'Perhaps you shall celebrate with us next year, my loyal friend. Message from Rienzi ends.'

Who was this Rienzi, telling Prospero about their birthday? They sounded very self-important. It wasn't much of a message.

'But that wasn't the end of the broadcast.' Bluff tapped the pencil on the page and cleared his throat, then went on. 'Prospero, advise latest findings on invasion at earliest opportunity. Repeat, advise latest findings on invasion at earliest opportunity, by request of Rienzi. Over.'

'Invasion?' Rosie went cold. Prospero had got wind of Operation Overlord. But perhaps not the details. 'Oh, heavens. At least he hasn't told them yet. That's something, isn't it?'

Rosie hated the thought of all the personnel waiting for their moment to invade, only for the entirety of the Führer's ranks to be waiting exactly in position for them. They would annihilate the landing parties and with them all hope of a swift end to the war.

'He won't know yet, and this is all the proof we need that Prospero – or an accomplice – is still broadcasting.' He threw the pad and pencil down on the desk. 'I've never taken down dictation from the Führer before.'

Hitler? The messages were from Hitler?

Rosie stared at the radio in disgust and astonishment, as if she'd suddenly spotted a thick layer of grime all over it, and the static was the buzz of corpse flies.

'Bravo, Blu— Major-General,' Rosie said, patting him on

the shoulder. 'Goodness ... the words of Hitler himself, right here in the basement.'

The room had fallen silent again, as though the simple act of translating his words had cast a pall over the team who had worked so companionably together.

After a second or so Bluff picked up the pad and paper again and said as though he were a schoolmaster, 'Show us your working out, Kingsley-Flynn. Adolf has a bit of a soft spot for Wagner and where does Rienzi come from? *Wagner.* Our man in Berlin has celebrated another year older and woe betide anyone in the Fatherland who didn't roll out the red carpet and toast his damnable name. *That*, lady and gentlemen, was a message from Herr Hitler to his loyal and dear friend, *Prospero.* Which is precisely why it reads like a postcard from a provincial clerk.'

'Prospero, receiving messages directly from the Führer ...' Rosie shivered, horrified that placid Cottisbourne Park could harbour an enemy of such magnitude. 'There can't be many spies who receive that dubious honour, can there?'

He shook his head and glanced towards the phone. 'And we should know soon enough if our boffins caught Prospero's reply. If they did, then we have our frequencies and we can listen in to our heart's content.'

The telephone rang soon afterwards. Oakley picked it up before the first ring. He scribbled down the message, nodding as he went. Then he put down the telephone.

'They netted Prospero's reply,' Oakley told them, with a wobble of excitement in his voice. His gaze wandered to the door. 'It's coming through on one of the teleprinters down the corridor. We'll have it shortly.'

Someone knocked on the door and Lainson answered. A woman in uniform briskly handed over a sheet of paper and was gone.

'Here it is!' Lainson said.

Rosie caught sight of a string of meaningless letters and numbers printed on the paper, which Lainson handed to the operator at the Endeavour. He typed it in, and one character at a time flashed up on the lampboard, the decrypted German message. As the lights were illuminated, Bluff noted down the letters until the message concluded and he could read it to them.

'My esteemed Rienzi, it is my dearest wish to celebrate with you next year and to toast a well-deserved victory at long last. Information gathering on Overlord continues. Forgive forthcoming delays and short-term reliance on this frequency. Second relocation and rebuild was necessary and is ongoing. Over.'

Rosie grimaced. 'What a bootlicker. But it's quite a long message – at least it seems long to me. Does that mean there might be a chance now that the signal can be traced? Hopefully before they find out anything else about Overlord, that is.'

Bluff looked to the rest of the team for the answer. 'If Prospero's stuck on this frequency for a while, what do you think? Or is *Cottisbourne Park* the best result we can hope for?'

Oakley stroked his chin. 'Could well be … if they don't change frequency. Cottisbourne Park is a big place. It could even be that they're in the village somewhere – someone else's barn, or up the church tower, perhaps! But it gives us the best chance yet to get a *precise* location. Imagine getting your mitts on Prospero just as the devil's in the middle of broadcasting!'

Bluff gave the barest hint of a smile and murmured, 'Just imagine.'

Chapter 26

Bleary-eyed, Rosie lifted her head from the pillow. Someone was knocking at her door. She glanced over to the window, but she couldn't hear the wail of air-raid sirens. So why on earth was someone knocking?

The knock sounded again and a female voice whispered urgently, 'Driver Sinclair, wake up!'

'I'm awake!' Rosie called, though she didn't feel it. She stumbled across to the door and opened it, to see a woman standing there in an MTC uniform like Rosie's. The familiarity of the uniform made her feel slightly less unnerved, but even so, it was the middle of the night. Surely something was wrong. 'What's happened?'

'Driver Anderson,' the woman replied. 'You're to report to Mr Wyngate and Major-General Sir Kingsley-Flynn at the War Office as a matter of urgency. I'll wait for you to dress.'

Rosie nodded. *Get dressed. I'll get dressed.*

She closed the door and hopped about in the dark trying to find her clothes. At least all those years in tiny dressing rooms had made her neat when it came to laying out her things. She dressed as fast as she could, and after taking out her pins, combed through her hair. It sprang back into shape and she put on her cap. Then she looked at her watch and the luminous hands told her it was half past two.

Rosie followed the MTC driver down the stairs. She was too alert to feel tired, wondering what was up. She nearly went round to the driver's door out of habit, before remembering that for once she was a passenger. Driver Anderson opened the back door and Rosie climbed in. The engine growled into life once more and they were off, driving through the nighttime city on their way to Whitehall. She had never seen the streets so dark, the facades of buildings shimmering phantoms in the dimmed headlamps of the car. At that moment, it seemed as though the whole world was asleep, but somewhere in the night Bartosz Zalewski and Charles Swann awaited their fates. Somewhere in the night Prospero was sleeping soundly, dreaming of a victorious future.

When the War Office came into view, Rosie steeled herself. Something serious was going on for her to be roused at this hour, and to be sent a driver. Something that couldn't wait until she arrived at nine o'clock.

The driver went round to the car park behind the building and Rosie and Driver Anderson got out. It was only the luck of the draw that they were in their current positions. How easily it could've been the other way around, Rosie assigned to the War Office in London instead of Cottisbourne Park.

Driver Anderson led Rosie into the War Office. Even at night, the place was just as busy as it was during the day. Rosie followed the driver up the grand white marble staircase, and along a corridor to an enormous pair of double doors. She knocked.

'I'll leave you in the major-general's hands.' Driver Anderson smiled as Bluff opened the door. 'Good night, Driver Sinclair.'

'Goodnight. Safe driving,' Rosie said. She smiled at Bluff. 'Hello, Major-General.'

'Sorry to drag you out of bed, Driver Sinclair,' Bluff said. She wondered if he had been to sleep, but it didn't look like it. Dark circles ringed his eyes and he stifled a yawn as he told her, 'This couldn't wait until breakfast.'

'So I see,' Rosie said.

She stepped into the room and was confronted by what almost looked like a dining room in a well-appointed home. The space was dominated by a huge polished wooden table, which matched the wooden panels around the walls. A portrait of the Duke of Wellington, arms folded, was hung in pride of place on the mantelpiece.

And beneath it, an accidental mirror image with his arms folded too, was Wyngate, seated at the table. He looked exhausted too.

'Good morning, Mr Wyngate,' Rosie said.

'Driver.' He gave a sharp nod, then took a cigarette packet from his pocket and flipped it open. Seeing it was empty, he crumpled it in his fist and threw it onto the table. 'I hear you've been taking messages from Berlin?'

Rosie glanced at Bluff. 'Not personally, but yes, I heard the messages come in. It's incredible, really, to think that Prospero receives messages from Hitler himself.'

'Tea.' Bluff handed Rosie a cup and saucer from which a narrow plume of steam rose. 'Take a seat, Driver. You'll forgive Mr Wyngate's gallows humour, it's been a very trying evening one way or another.'

Rosie gratefully sipped her tea, then she sat down beside the place that Bluff had apparently marked out for himself, his pipe waiting for him in an ashtray.

'That would've been a rude awakening. Woken at two to be chucked in a cell!' She grinned at Wyngate. 'I'm not Prospero, I promise. I can't speak any German, for one thing! So ... what's happened?'

Bluff took his seat. He picked up his pipe and asked, 'Would you say you were particularly close to Dr Zalewski?'

Where on earth is this going?

Rosie shook her head. 'I wouldn't say so, no. I've had to drive him sometimes when he's been on official business, and we've chatted, but, you know, only about the weather and that sort of thing. He helped out with costumes for the panto, but I have to say, there were so many people working on that show that I really didn't have time to speak to everyone. He'd always say hello if we were passing, but I wouldn't say he was a particular friend.'

'That's the odd thing.' Bluff weighed the bowl of his pipe in one hand. 'He's asking to speak to you, Rosie. How do you feel about that?'

'*Me?*' Rosie nearly spilled her tea in surprise. 'Why on earth does he want to speak to me? I ... I don't know ... if you want me to go and see him, then I will, but ... I don't have any experience in these things. Apart from the time the Players performed at Holloway jail. I wouldn't want to get it wrong.'

'There's no question of you going in alone,' Wyngate snapped sharply. 'This is a potentially very dangerous man. You'll have me or the major-general with you at all times.'

Rosie couldn't imagine that Wyngate's brusque manner would convince anyone to tell their secrets, especially after what looked like far too long without sleep. He was positively bristling with nervous energy.

'If you're willing to see him, it might be helpful,' Bluff said. 'Just let him talk. We want to know what he's got to say, no matter how inconsequential it might seem.'

'Even if he just wants to talk about the panto.' Rosie nodded. She'd joined the MTC to do her bit, and if that meant talking to a suspected spy in the early hours of the morning, then that's what she'd do. 'All right. You'll come with me, Major-General, won't you?'

Bluff glanced to Wyngate, who gave a nod.

'Of course,' he replied. 'But I'll let you do the talking.'

Rosie took a final sip of tea. 'Righty-ho, let's find out what's on Dr Zalewski's mind.'

★★★

The contrast between the elegant boardroom and the cells below couldn't have been greater. Gone were the wood panels and oil paintings. Instead, the walls were whitewashed brick, with the occasional poster reminding the inhabitants that *careless talk costs lives* and to *dig for victory*.

Not that anyone would be digging vegetable patches down here. They were more likely to be dreaming of digging tunnels to escape.

No scent of beeswax met Rosie, just the smell of disinfectant and fear. Wyngate walked ahead, Bluff at her side as the corridors narrowed and the elegant chandeliers that hung in the vast offices and marble-floored lobby were replaced by stark electric lights.

'If he tries to draw you into games, the major-general will intervene,' Wyngate informed her. 'I don't want you to speak if you don't have to. You're there to listen.'

'Dr Zalewski has asked for Driver Sinclair for a reason,' Bluff replied. 'I have no doubt that she'll know what the situation calls for, Mr Wyngate. Trust her. Professor Hale did and so do I.'

Wyngate glanced over his shoulder, his gaze flicking over Rosie. He gave a curt nod, then looked away again.

Was Wyngate put out that Bartosz wanted to speak to her? It seemed so.

A guard in a grey uniform unlocked a grill that blocked the corridor, then another guard on the other side led them past a row of heavy-looking doors, which Rosie assumed were the cells.

The guard took a large bunch of keys from a chain at his waist and unlocked one of the doors.

Bartosz was on the bench that ran across the back wall of the cell, curled up in a ball, a grey blanket around him.

He looked up with red-rimmed eyes, and Rosie assumed he hadn't slept. But there was something drawn and sad about his expression as well that made her wonder if he had been crying.

The door clanged shut behind them, and Rosie instinctively pressed her back to it, as if somehow she could vanish out of the cell. She'd never seen somewhere so miserable and hopeless.

Bartosz unfolded himself and sat on the bench.

'You came,' he said, his voice small. 'I didn't think they'd let you.' He looked Bluff up and down, as if he was wondering why he was there.

'I asked for the major-general to be present,' Rosie told him. 'There's nothing you could say to me that he can't hear.'

'You're welcome to have a solicitor with you,' Bluff told Bartosz, his manner surprisingly gentle. Rosie couldn't imagine Wyngate being half so delicate in his approach. 'We just want to know the truth, Dr Zalewski.'

A slight smile came to Bartosz's lips. If he'd believed, like everyone else, that Bluff was a stern, unbending officer, then he'd just been surprised.

'But the truth ... I am still in trouble if you know the truth. Only ...' Bartosz gestured to the walls of his cell. 'Only I am put in a different cell. The questions I was asked ... you think I am a spy. And you think Charles is also.'

'There is a spy at Cottisbourne, there's no doubt about that,' Bluff explained. 'The evidence points to you and

Professor Swann, but evidence can be misleading. I'm not interested in anything other than stopping that spy before he does any more damage. Please, Dr Zalewski, tell us what you know.'

'You hang spies, don't you?' Bartosz wiped at his eyes with the corner of his rough blanket. 'I suppose it is better to be in a cell than hanged...'

'What have you and Professor Swann been up to, Doctor?' Rosie asked him. He looked so dejected, so scared, that Rosie relinquished her spot by the door and crossed the room to crouch down in front of him. 'You wanted to tell me, didn't you?'

He nodded. 'Because you are an actress.'

Rosie glanced back at Bluff for a moment. Was it something to do with the panto? Had Bartosz and Charles run off with the takings that were supposed to go to the Red Cross?

'I was. I'm not at the moment, though,' Rosie said kindly. She took Bartosz's hand. It was grimy from being in the cell and she did her best to pretend that it wasn't.

'You know, there are all sorts of people in the theatres, aren't there?' Bartosz said. 'You know lots of people, don't you?'

Rosie still wasn't sure what he was getting at. Was he hoping she'd introduce him to Vivien Leigh or Merle Oberon?

'Lots of people, yes,' Rosie said. 'All sorts of people.'

Bartosz shivered. He closed his eyes, as if getting his strength up, then he said, 'Then you have met ... you have met...' He stopped and opened his eyes, unshed tears caught in his lashes. 'Men like me. Men like my *zabko*. Charles.'

Men like me.

Suddenly it made sense. Everything made sense. No wonder they wouldn't confess to the truth.

'You and Charles are lovers?' Rosie asked him.

Bartosz nodded quickly. He gripped Rosie's hand.

'Yes. You know, I got a place at Oxford before the war. And... and when things started to get bad, and the cryptographers back home passed the British their work on the Endeavour, I was asked to go to Cambridge – by Charles. He needed a Polish mathematician to help with the sections in Polish. Of course, we had important things to do, but even as we worked... I sensed that he was like me. And I was right. And my *zabko* is so very handsome... and... we became lovers. Then we were sent to Cottisbourne. Not to the same hut, but even so... I was so happy because it meant that I was near my *zabko*. But there are so many people, the Park is so busy... we met in the barn, you see, when no one else was around. Do you see? For all these years we have kept it a secret. And I did not want to tell. But what choice do I have? I cannot see my *zabko* dead.'

Bluff drew in a long breath, then asked, 'The bed in the hayloft was yours?'

Bartosz chuckled sadly. 'It was. Our little sanctuary. My *zabko* got some blankets, some good ones, from home. You know, in Cambridge, Charles told everyone that he and I worked through the night. But... that was not working so much. In Cottisbourne, we could not spend the night together, but we could have a half hour sometimes in the barn. Rosie, you have no idea, the times me and my *zabko* were stuck up there and you were working on the car! And we would hope you would not climb up. And the little girl, Nancy, she nearly found us. That was why... I am sorry Charles shouted at her. I told him not to – she is little, she misses her family, and I miss mine. But he was scared we would be found out.' Bartosz sighed. 'And now, look, I have to tell you anyway.'

'Professor Swann hasn't told us any of this. He's been very self-possessed and I'm afraid that hasn't helped with his pleas of innocence,' Bluff said. 'When he heard you'd been arrested, it was the first time Wyngate and I saw anything resembling emotion. If what you've told us is true, Doctor, it changes everything.'

Bartosz's face crumpled and he sobbed into his blanket. 'My *zabko* ...' He whispered something, which Rosie realised was probably Polish. Then he said, 'It *is* true. But I don't know how I can prove it to you. Look in my things. My books, at Cottisbourne Park. There is ... Shakespeare's poems. His sonnets. Charles gave it to me for Christmas. He wrote in the front, a little message, and he put it into code. It made me smile very much when I read it. Will that prove it?'

'It'll help.' Bluff reached out and patted Bartosz's shoulder. 'But we need Professor Swann to corroborate what you're saying. I'm going to ask you some personal questions, Doctor Zalewski. I'm not trying to be invasive, but I need to be able to ask Swann the same questions and hear the same answers. You understand?'

Bartosz nodded. With an embarrassed smile, he said, 'I do. I understand. What do you want to know?'

Bluff would know what to ask, Rosie reasoned, because spies must come with cover stories. But she couldn't see anyone concocting a cover story that could be as ruinous as this one. Would the two men end up in prison anyway?

'Three things.' Bluff counted them off on his fingers. 'Firstly, where did you go for your first meal as a couple – not as colleagues? Second, what gifts did you exchange last Christmas? Finally, I want to know – and I'm sorry to ask this, but it's not something you could be coached on – what have you and Professor Swann discussed about your future together?'

Rosie got up from the floor and dusted down her skirt as she sat down on the bench next to Bartosz. Bluff didn't seem shocked or disgusted. He didn't react as she knew some men would've done at a revelation like Bartosz's. He was as pragmatic as ever.

Bartosz picked at the hem on the blanket. 'You know, it is odd to speak of this. For we have never spoken to anyone about it. It has always been a secret. So ... our first meal as a couple? Charles took me to a café. It is called Fitzbillies. And we had buns.' Bartosz spun his finger round, and finally found the word he was looking for. 'Chelsea buns!'

Rosie smiled. 'Good choice! I like a Chelsea bun, too.'

'And Christmas ... last Christmas, I gave Charles a scarf. Judith in my hut, she knitted it, in return for my chocolate ration. And Charles, he gave me a book about British birds.' Bartosz laughed, and it echoed oddly in that cheerless place. 'The pictures are so pretty in it. And as for our future?' Bartosz shook his head. He was melancholy again. 'Pah, what future is there for men like he and I? We talked about Cambridge. He said he could get me a post there, and we could ... we could live in the same house and no one would think for a moment that anything was ... how does he put it? *Untoward*, that is it.'

Rosie hoped with all her heart that they would get their future. But if they went to prison, would any college want them?

Bluff nodded. 'Is there anything else at all that you'd like to tell us or that you think we should know, Doctor?'

Bartosz stared at the wall for a moment, then said, 'I want you to know that he and I are in love. I want you to know there is nothing wrong in how we feel. And yet, for all that, I know you must report what I have said, and I know that once you do, he and I will be moved to another prison. I know there will be no Cambridge for us after that. I know all this.' Bartosz shrugged, resigned. 'You must do what you have to do.'

'May I ask Dr Zalewki a question, sir?' Rosie asked Bluff. Bartosz's story had almost completely convinced her. But there was something she wanted to know the answer to. Bluff nodded, so Rosie turned to Bartosz and asked him, 'Why were you in the folly, Bartosz?'

He chuckled for a moment before saying, 'Because I am a sentimental fool. When the barn burned down, we lost our bed. And so we decided we would meet in the folly. And after Charles was taken away, I still went. I got inside, and I sat down, and I thought of my *zabko,* and I wished I could be with him. And you know, my wish almost came true. Because just as I was about to leave, all those men came in and arrested me. And they brought me here.' Bartosz tapped the wall. 'I pretend that my *zabko* is in the next cell, and I tap out messages in Morse code to him.'

'My only interest is in apprehending our mole.' To Rosie's surprise, Bluff extended his hand towards Bartosz. 'If what you've told me is true, I'll do what I can to ensure this goes no further. I can't make you a promise yet, but to lose two talented codebreakers over their private affairs would seem rather foolish when we're looking to win a war.'

Thank goodness Bluff wasn't small-minded.

Bartosz enthusiastically shook Bluff's hand. 'Thank you, thank you, Major-General!' He shot up off the bench, took Bluff's face in both hands and planted a kiss on each cheek. 'You know, I will tell off my *zabko* for the rude things he said about you! You are a good – you are a great man! And Rosie ...' He turned and kissed Rosie's cheeks too. 'Thank you, thank you! When you are in the theatre again, I will come and see your show! I promise! *All* your shows!'

'You'll be more than welcome, Bartosz,' Rosie said.

'One thing Professor Swann should know.' Bluff's smile was mischievous. 'Every time he called me a dunderhead, my left ear itched. There's not much I miss.'

Bartosz gasped. 'You heard him say that? I am so sorry. You must have been glad to put him in a cell!'

Bluff admitted with a chuckle, 'I've been called worse. Try to sleep, Doctor. I'll do what I can.'

'I will try.' Bartosz nodded. He sat back down on the bench and kneaded his lumpy pillow. 'I will sleep much better now.'

248

Chapter 27

In the corridor outside the cells, Rosie glanced at Bluff. There was a lightness about him that hadn't been there before Bartosz's revelation, even though he looked grey with tiredness.

'You haven't had any sleep yet, have you?' Rosie asked him gently.

'Does it show?' He leaned against the wall and tipped his head back. 'What a bloody tangle.'

A guard was standing nearby. In case he could overhear them, Rosie said, 'Just a bit. I had no idea. But the pieces fit together now, don't they?'

'I'll have to tell Wyngate tonight,' Bluff told her. 'But if those two fellows are involved in this, I'll turn in my medals. There's not a chance of it.'

'I wonder what Wyngate will say...' Rosie brushed her hand against Bluff's, hoping the guard wouldn't see. She was worried that he looked so exhausted. 'And then you're going to get a good night's sleep.'

'That'll happen when we've got Prospero under lock and key. Instead we're back at square bloody one.' He patted her arm. 'Let's go and see the man from the ministry.'

They went back up through the building to the grand boardroom where they had left Wyngate. Rosie wondered if he'd managed to get any more cigarettes, because she was sure he'd need them when he heard what Bartosz had revealed.

Yet to her surprise Wyngate took the news calmly. Rosie detected the slightest arch of one eyebrow, but other than that, he barely reacted.

'We'll speak to Professor Swann tomorrow,' was his conclusion. 'I need cigarettes and sleep before I even try to tackle this. And I need to update the PM.'

'Will you have to tell him that Professor Swann and Dr Zalewski are ...' Rosie hesitated before saying, 'Lovers?'

Wyngate kicked his feet up onto the polished table. He crossed them at the ankle and regarded the shiny tip of one shoe before he decided, 'I expect so. That'll be an interesting conversation.'

'But won't they get into trouble?' Rosie asked. 'I think Dr Zalewski was ever so brave telling us.'

'Not if I have any sway,' Bluff said. 'I think it'd be a shocking waste of resources to take two of our best boffins out of service over a personal affair like this. If we can clear them, we need them back at Cottisbourne.'

Wyngate continued to inspect his shoes, silent. Seconds passed until he eventually said, 'Agreed. If we threw everyone in the Scrubs for it, half of Whitehall would be in handcuffs.'

Rosie gasped. 'Goodness me! Well, when you put it like that ...! By the way, I'm glad I could help. I never thought I'd end up visiting a prisoner in a cell in the MTC, but it's funny how things turn out, isn't it? Goodnight, Wyngate.'

'I'll see you both here tomorrow at nine,' he replied. 'Goodnight, Major-General. Goodnight, Driver Sinclair, and good work today.'

Good work? That meant a lot coming from the man who'd interrogated her in a scullery.

Rosie and Bluff wound their way back through the

building, the elaborate marble staircase a stark contrast to the miserable cells in the basement.

'Will Driver Anderson drop us off?' Rosie asked Bluff.

'I'll let her know you're ready to head back to barracks,' Bluff said. 'I think I might go for a bit of a stroll. Clear my thoughts before I get my head down.'

'But it's the middle of the night,' Rosie said, surprised. 'What about the curfew?'

He smiled, almost apologetic when he said, 'SOE privilege.'

'I don't suppose that privilege extends to chums, does it?' Rosie wasn't ready to say goodnight again just yet. 'I'm not sure I'll get back to sleep again without stretching my legs. If you don't mind having company, that is?'

'Driver Sinclair, I would love it.' Bluff offered his arm. 'Would you care to join me?'

Rosie took his arm, glad of the adventure. She wanted to put her memory of the cells far behind her. 'Of course. Where are we wandering to?'

'Would you like to see the London home of the Buckinghamshire Kingsley-Flynns?' It sounded like a tease, but what if it wasn't? 'From the outside at least. If we go in at this time of night the housekeeper's likely to appear with a shotgun!'

Housekeeper?

'Is this a jape, and you're *actually* going to take me to Buckingham Palace?' Rosie chuckled. 'Go on, show me where your family live.'

Together they strolled out into the spring evening, arm in arm. The sky was still dark, but soon it would begin to lighten and London would wake to another day. It seemed surreal to recall the last few days, with visits from Churchill and messages from Hitler, but strolling through the warm night with Bluff, everything somehow made sense.

'Aren't we lucky, coming outside for fresh air?' Rosie said, her voice hushed. 'I do feel bad for everyone cooped up inside. Poor Bartosz and Professor Swann. It's not surprising that Swann ran off in the Humber, is it? He must've thought that he and Bartosz had been found out.'

'Wyngate told him he was under suspicion of spying,' Bluff told her. 'I think he just went into a blind panic. When I mentioned Zalewski's name in questioning, he was adamant that Zalewski was an innocent man. If nothing else, Swann was loyal to a fault. He should've spoken up. Lord knows, we're all men of the wor— well, present company excepted, obviously.'

'You took it in your stride,' Rosie said. 'You didn't go all funny like *some* men do when they hear about … you know. You didn't get angry or run off. I'm glad you didn't. It makes me like you all the more.'

'I saw things in Europe that I could scarcely credit one human being could do to another, Rosie.' Bluff looked down at their joined hands. He lifted them and kissed Rosie's fingers. 'Swann and Zalewski are doing no harm, so let them be. It's another little candle in the dark, isn't it?'

'Exactly. Two people who just want to be happy.' Rosie smiled at him and said, 'And together. You know, in the Cavendish Players, we sometimes had chaps like them, and Mummy and Daddy always said, *we're a family, and we love you all.* They never judged. And for one or two of those men, the Players were the only family they had.'

'They were fortunate to find that family, and we're very fortunate to have found one another,' he smiled. 'Where do you envision my little mews house, Rosie? When all this is done, of course.'

'One of those little streets that's in the middle of everywhere, but you'd never know it because it's so quiet,' Rosie told him, warming to her theme. She could just picture it, too. Everything neat, but colourful. Like Bluff. 'And you'd live near a park, definitely. Maybe … maybe somewhere like Marylebone, or Bayswater?'

'With Ken Palace on the doorstep? Very me,' Bluff beamed. 'I'd like a nice little garden. And a horse stabled at Hyde Park, naturally.'

'*Very* you!' Rosie chuckled and admitted, 'I'm so sad I missed you on horseback. One day, perhaps. You'll have to teach me how to ride. Mummy sat me on a horse when I was little. She said I should at least be able to sit on one without falling off, in case I was wanted for a period film! Suffice to say, that hasn't happened.'

What a thought, being taught to ride by a senior officer of the Household Cavalry. Rosie would never have even imagined such a thing, yet here it was likely to come true. And in Hyde Park, no less. She couldn't imagine what her mother would say.

'I'd like to live in London,' Rosie told him. 'But not all the time. I suppose I'm so used to wandering about the place. But then there's always so much happening in London, it would be hard to be bored, I imagine. And all those theatres on your doorstep too!'

'So a place in London and somewhere in the country for weekends? *Very* Kingsley-Flynn,' Bluff chuckled. 'I take it you won't need the moat, maze and room for an opera festival?'

'No, I'll pass on that!' Rosie pictured Bluff leaning against a fence with honeysuckle twining up it, his pipe in his mouth. And herself on the step. 'I'd like to live somewhere like Cottisbourne. I dare say you might find it rather dull, though!'

'Dull? If I'm spending my weeks in London and launching my post-military theatrical endeavours, a country retreat will be just what I need!' Bluff paused. He turned a little and took Rosie's hand. 'A little cottage in Sussex. Roses and honeysuckle in the garden? I've seen enough darkness in the last five years to last a lifetime, Rosie.'

Rosie grinned at him. 'I was picturing just the same thing! Isn't that *wonderful?* Oh, Bluff... gosh, we haven't known each other very long, but it seems like we have!'

Bluff lifted Rosie's hand and pressed a very courtly kiss to it before he said, 'It rather seems like we have.'

Emboldened, Rosie said, 'This isn't just a passing fad, is it? I feel very much as though...' She wasn't sure how to phrase it without terrifying him. But then again, Bluff didn't strike her as the sort of man who was scared of much. 'As though we'll see a lot more of each other.'

'A *lot*,' Bluff agreed, studying her face with a soft gaze. 'I look forward to discovering what our future holds.'

'I'm so glad you think so too! I'd feel rather foolish if you'd said, *Nonsense, I'm a soldier, I'm off to find another girl!*' Rosie chuckled as she looked around at the grand square they had arrived in. 'But then, you're not like that, are you?'

'Lord, no,' Bluff assured her with an apologetic chuckle. 'After five years smuggling folk from behind enemy lines and rooting out traitors on home soil, I'm ready for a rather more sedate future. And there's only one girl I hope will be a part of it.'

'Your Portia?' Rosie asked him, and leaned in to kiss him. But she paused and said, 'Are we allowed to kiss here? It's awfully grand.'

Tall, white Georgian houses that looked like Buckingham Palace in miniature rose up against the night sky. All their blackout curtains were drawn and the windows were taped up, but it didn't reduce from the square's grandeur. Was this where Bluff had meant to take her? Did his family really have a house here?

'I should bally well hope I'm allowed to kiss my Portia on Belgrave Square,' Bluff said with a knowingly lofty toss of his head. 'We've had a house here for two hundred-odd years!'

'Two hundred years?' Rosie stared at him in amazement. 'But … surely that means you're the only people who've ever lived in the house? Oh, Bluff … and there was me saying you ought to live in a mews house! Silly me – you wouldn't want one after living here, would you?'

'This old place?' Bluff jerked his thumb towards the house that stood immediately behind them. 'It's a twenty minute round trip just to make a cup of tea and a chap can't sneeze without a butler appearing with a freshly pressed hand-kerchief. But my own little mews house with a gramophone, a garden and you? That sounds perfect to me.'

'Oh, doesn't it just?' Rosie wrapped her arms around him. 'We don't need butlers and housekeepers, do we? We'd be just as happy wherever … gosh, we're talking as if we're going to be married!' She looked up at him. He was still smiling. He seemed to like the idea.

'It wouldn't surprise me at all,' was his gentle reply.

255

Chapter 28

As Rosie got ready to go back to the War Office, she wondered how odd it was going to be, seeing Bluff in such formal surroundings. They'd as good as proposed to each other the night before. They hadn't known each other long at all, she knew that, and it wasn't as if they'd run to the nearest jewellers for a ring. But still, they had talked about it, and it seemed so wonderful that Rosie couldn't tell herself that it was a bad idea. They wanted the same things, and the prospect of spending the rest of her life with Bluff made Rosie's heart light.

On her way out, one of the girls in the billet complimented Rosie on her make-up, but she wasn't wearing any. She was glowing with happiness and hoped Wyngate wouldn't remark on it. Because what would a man like him think to her and Bluff being a couple?

Despite her lack of sleep, Rosie didn't feel tired. There was the future to think of now, a future that felt far more real and attainable than it had in a long time. But for that future to happen, they had to get back onto the trail that would lead them to Prospero.

Rosie went into the boardroom, where Wyngate and Bluff were waiting.

'Good morning,' she said to them and saluted. Bluff looked as though he'd slept as well as she had. Gone were the dark circles, his eyes sparkling anew. Wyngate looked rather a little less fresh than the two of them, but he was as well groomed as ever despite the tiredness in his gaze.

'Driver Sinclair.' Bluff rose to his feet and returned Rosie's salute. He gestured to the tea service on the table and said, 'Help yourself, Driver. It might be a long morning.'

Wyngate greeted Rosie with a nod, his attention taken by the contents of a folder that lay open on the table before him. It contained a thick sheaf of papers, atop which were the blueprints Rosie and her team had drawn up in their workshop.

Rosie poured herself some tea, and helped herself to a thick shortbread biscuit, the like of which she hadn't seen in ages. She ate it as carefully as she could, conscious that it would spill crumbs all over the plush table.

She gestured towards the packet of cigarettes on the table in front of Wyngate. 'I see you got some ciggies,' she said, trying get him to chat.

'Are you always so interminably perky?' Wyngate asked. 'Or is it just for my benefit?'

'Mind your manners, Mr Wyngate.' Bluff leapt gallantly to Rosie's defence, earning a *harumph* in reply. 'I'll remind you that but for Driver Sinclair's skills, we wouldn't be sitting here with the ability to listen in to Prospero as though he's transmitting straight into the War Office. That's certainly something worth smiling about.'

Rosie grinned at Bluff. 'Thank you, Major-General,' she said. 'And yes, Mr Wyngate, I'm quite a cheerful sort of person, really. Especially when I get to eat a biscuit like *this*.'

Good, I'm glad I annoy him, she decided. *Especially after he grilled me in that bloody awful scullery.*

'Well, here's something else for you to smile about.' Wyngate tapped one elegant fingernail on the blueprints. 'I've appraised the Prime Minister of Zalewski's revelations and he's of the opinion that it places us in a very invidious position. Obviously if what he claims is true, it creates a potentially embarrassing situation for everybody concerned.'

'Just a little.' Rosie put down the remains of her biscuit and told Wyngate, 'I had the pleasure of meeting Professor Swann's father. He's very concerned about the idea of scandal, and how it might affect the government. If Swann and Zalewski were prosecuted ... that could present a problem not only for Mr Swann, but lots of other people, couldn't it? And to be honest, I half-wonder if he already has an inkling that his son might be homosexual. Perhaps this wouldn't be the first time Mr Swann's had to deal with a brewing scandal.'

Wyngate arched his eyebrow and said, 'Perhaps you might be right, Driver Sinclair.' And Rosie knew then that she *was*. 'Given the current situation in Europe and the need to keep up morale at home as well as starve Jerry of anything they might turn into propaganda, the ministry feels that pursuing a prosecution over the close friendship of the two gentlemen concerned wouldn't be in the interest of any of the parties concerned.'

'A splendid decision,' Bluff said approvingly.

'Prospero is still broadcasting.' Wyngate closed the folder. 'If I'm satisfied that Swann and Zalewski are innocent of any treasonous activity, I have permission from the highest authority to release them. They'll return to Cottisbourne Park and be provided with cover stories wherever necessary. I can't make that decision unless Swann swallows his over-inflated bloody pride and tells me something other than the fact that his father'll have me cleaning toilets after the war. That isn't going to get him out of here.'

Rosie mastered her threatened splutter of laughter.

'Perhaps it's your manner,' Bluff ventured. 'You have a

very ... direct approach. Swann doesn't strike me as a chap who would respond well to interrogation.'

'Goodness me, no!' Rosie picked up her biscuit again. Before she bit into it, she added cheekily, 'You didn't quiz him in a scullery, did you, Mr Wyngate?'

He fixed her with a look that was somewhere between bewildered and withering before he said, 'I'm very glad you're on *our* side, Driver Sinclair.' With that, Wyngate knitted his fingers atop the closed folder. 'Mr Churchill is very impressed by how easily you winkled a confession out of Zalewski last night. Against my better judgement, he has suggested that you be present this morning when Major-General Sir Kingsley-Flynn and I speak to Swann.'

'Mr Churchill himself suggested that I ...' Rosie brushed the biscuits crumbs off her fingers. She felt rather proud about that. 'That's quite a surprise, I must say. It goes without saying, I'm very happy to help again.'

'We need him to corroborate Zalewski's story to the last full stop,' he told them. 'One wrong detail and everything falls into question. Frankly, I want this finished so we can get on with the important business.'

'In that case, might I suggest that Driver Sinclair approaches Professor Swann?' Bluff suggested. 'You and I haven't got anywhere, Wyngate, and the prime minister clearly respects Rosie's methods. What harm can it do to let her talk to him with us present?'

Wyngate tutted, then barked, 'Fine. But I want to see results.'

Rosie, ignoring Wyngate's sharpness, smiled at Bluff and pushed back her chair. 'Well, I'm ready. Are you two?'

Bluff was on his feet in a moment, setting his cap firmly on his head and Wyngate scooped up the folder as he stood. He leaned across to snatch up a biscuit and said, 'If this starts to go wrong, Driver Sinclair, you relinquish the interview to me or the major-general. Agreed?'

Rosie nodded. 'Of course. Joshing aside, Mr Wyngate, I do know how important this is. It's ever so serious and we can't nab the real Prospero until this is done and dusted.'

They headed back down to the basement, but this time, instead of going into a cell, the guard led them into what Rosie realised was an interview room. A scratched, but solid table stood in the middle of the room, and chairs sat either side of it.

It was time to find out what Professor Swann would make of the words of Dr Zalewski, the man who claimed to be his lover.

The air felt pregnant with anticipation as two sets of footsteps echoed along the corridor outside. They drew closer until the door opened and Charles Swann entered, a uniformed guard behind him. Rosie couldn't help the gasp of surprise she gave at the sight of him, because she had never seen Charles looking anything less than immaculate. He looked as though he hadn't slept for days, his skin grey and his eyes red, set in dark hollows of exhaustion. His clothes might have come straight from Savile Row, but the man wearing them looked like a ghost.

Was it because of his lover's arrest?

Once again, she wondered how far he would've taken his outraged silence. Would he have gone to the gallows to save Bartosz?

'Good morning, Professor.' Rosie smiled at him, even though she was steeling herself for his typically brusque response. Then again, did he have the energy to be rude and superior anymore? 'I hope you don't mind, but I wondered if we could have a chat?'

'Is this where we've come to?' Charles pulled out a chair

and sat down. He folded his arms. 'You've got the Girl Guides interviewing innocent men now, have you? You've done very well out of those little liaisons with our Major-General, Miss Sinclair. What a promotion, eh?'

'I'm *Driver* Sinclair, thank you.' Rosie sat down as well. 'I want to try to help you, Professor Swann. If we're going to talk about liaisons...' She looked him steadily in the eye and didn't say anything more. He matched her gaze, his blue eyes bright despite his obvious exhaustion.

'Dr Zalewski asked to speak to Driver Sinclair yesterday,' Bluff said. At the mention of his lover's name, Charles swallowed. It was the smallest gesture, but Rosie noticed it. 'I think you know what he told us and I can assure you, you're unlikely to hang for it. I wouldn't want to hang as a Nazi spy just to save my pride.'

'I had no idea you two had known each other so long,' Rosie said, conversationally. 'He's ever such a nice chap. It must be so difficult for him, with his family back in Poland. I'm glad he's got you.'

'And yet you're ashamed of him,' Bluff sighed. Charles' gaze darkened and dropped away, focussing on the pitted top of the table between them. 'He's not ashamed of you, Swann. He's risked everything to save your skin, but you won't do the same for him, will you? Would you let Zalewski go to the hangman to save your precious name?'

'That's not how it is,' Charles whispered.

Rosie smiled gently at him and asked, 'What does *zabko* mean?'

Charles' lips twitched into a smile, then he shook his head as though trying to clear it. He brought his hand up to cover his mouth and stifled something that sounded almost like a sob.

'Don't,' he whispered.

261

Rosie reached across the table and took his other hand. 'Bartosz wanted to speak to me, because … well, because he knows that in the theatre people aren't all that stuffy and we're not so worried about reputations and that sort of thing. We're in the business of entertaining people. *Happiness.* I grew up around men like you and Bartosz and no one ever told me that … that there was anything wrong with two men, or two women for that matter, being in love.'

He shifted in his seat, leaning forward just a little to confide, 'I'm not ashamed of him. I couldn't be.'

'You love him, don't you? And I'm sorry that I was in the barn so often, working on the car. If I'd known, I would've …' Rosie held his hand a little tighter. 'I would've moved the car somewhere else and given you space.'

'Barty doesn't deserve …' Charles swallowed again. 'I'm not a spy, Driver Sinclair. But I'd give up my repu— no. I'd give my life for him.'

Behind Rosie, Wyngate sighed. Not a sigh of sentimentality, but of annoyance. She prayed that he wouldn't speak and break the spell that seemed to be hanging in the air between her and Charles Swann, and he didn't. Instead, the room fell silent again.

After a little while, Rosie said, 'Bartosz said you met in Cambridge. That he was sent from Oxford to help you with the research on the Endeavour that had been sent from Poland. I've performed a few times in Cambridge. It's such a nice place. You must've enjoyed showing him the sites.' Thinking of Bluff's three questions that he'd put to Bartosz, she asked Charles, 'Did you take him somewhere lovely to eat when you first became a couple? Somewhere very Cambridge?'

He nodded and there was that smile again, sad around the edges.

'He was so excited to see Cambridge.' Charles' smile grew a little more mischievous. 'Well, can you blame him after being stuck at Oxford? It was the first good thing that'd happened since war broke out. Such a kind man. If you know Cambridge, you must have been to Fitzbillies?'

'Of course!' Rosie chuckled. 'I went every day and bought a bag of cakes for the cast and the staff at the theatre!'

'If you haven't tried their Chelsea buns, they're a must,' Charles confided. And just like that, he'd confirmed Bluff's first question. 'Barty was absolutely addicted to them after our first trip there. I used to warn him he'd turn into a Chelsea bun if he wasn't careful!'

'Oh, I thought I'd have to have my costume taken out after all the Chelsea buns I had from there!' Rosie laughed. 'You know Bartosz helped on the panto, of course? I suppose Christmas must be difficult for you ... if you want to spend it together, but you can't be seen to do so?'

Charles shook his head. 'Not particularly. Cambridge has a wonderfully forgiving eye when it comes to chaps like us. *Confirmed bachelors* is what you'd hear, or simply *firm friends*.' He smiled and admitted, 'There are a lot of confirmed bachelor friends at the colleges. I heard this week that Barty was to be given a permanent role at St Vinny's with me, but I never had the chance to ... we'd have been together, and not just this Christmas. Every Christmas that came after it too.'

Another of Bluff's questions was answered it seemed. 'Had you asked them to get Bartosz a job at Cambridge, then?' Rosie asked him, just to be sure.

'Yes. He's an absolute whizz,' he replied. 'His understanding of Shakespeare's sonnets is remarkable. Such a sensitivity. I gave him a book of them with a little silly coded note inside. It's something Caroline and I used to do as children ... For all my languages, I've never understood poetry like Barty.

All days are nights to see till I see thee. Beautiful, don't you think?'

'Oh, very,' Rosie replied, grinning because Charles had just unwittingly confirmed another thing that Bartosz had told them. 'You know, Professor Swann, I think everything's going to be all right.'

She glanced back at Bluff. He scratched his neck, holding her gaze, and gave an almost imperceptible nod.

The scarf.

'If I have to go to prison for what Barty and I share, I will.' Charles lifted his chin. 'But please, keep his name out of it. That's all I ask.'

'I hope that won't happen,' Rosie told him. 'But I understand why you want to protect him. He clearly loves you very much. He told us what he gave up so he could get you a Christmas present.' Rosie thought of Judith, powering away with her knitting needles with Bartosz's chocolate ration beside her. The funny thing was, she remembered Judith knitting a scarf while they rehearsed the panto, her eyes on the script and not her needles. Rosie'd had no idea who it was for or what it had cost.

'Oh, Barty and his chocolate!' Charles chuckled affectionately. 'When he told me what the scarf had cost, I told him *it must be love*, he wouldn't give up his rations for anything else! I gave him a book of British birds and every time Barty saw one of them in the park he ticked it off in the book. We're hoping to spot even more over the summer.'

'You should've told us,' Wyngate said. 'You've wasted a hell of a lot of time, Swann.'

Rosie glanced round at Wyngate. 'You know why he couldn't. Because of silly rules about who grown adults can and can't fall in love with.'

Maybe she shouldn't have spoken like that to Wyngate,

but Rosie was deeply touched by seeing a whole new, un-expected side to Professor Swann. A man who, despite what the world might think, had a heart after all. Unlike Wyngate.

'Professor Swann, one more question,' Bluff said. 'Our mole, *Prospero*, has had access to codes and messages that only half a dozen codebreakers in the country can have seen, going back a couple of years. You were the last one of that half dozen whose name had to be eliminated. Can you think of any way that someone might have been able to intercept those messages? Someone with the intelligence to under-stand what they were looking at and how to interpret it?'

'I suppose someone with a bit of radio nous could listen in, but they'd have to be a bally genius to understand it,' Charles replied. 'Look, if you want proof of my loyalty, I can give it. When I was invalided out with a burst appendix the blood poisoning nearly killed me, but I kept working even at home. Ministry bods came along to the country pile and secured the library. Far nicer than any hut in the back of beyond. They brought all the radio and Endeavour kit along, everything I needed. If I was a traitor, would I really have done that? From the house of a future Prime Minister? I'd have to have had a death wish!'

Wyngate gave another of his long sighs and murmured, 'Stranger things have happened.'

Charles tutted. He looked towards Bluff and snapped, 'I wouldn't even let the Sprat come near and she haunted that bloody library like the spectre at the feast! Did your mole leak any of those messages? If he did, take me to the gallows now.'

'Yes, he did. But those were messages that other names on our list of suspects might have seen too. None of them were exclusive to you.' Bluff shook his head. Charles was lucky though. If one of those messages he had worked on at his ancestral home had been exclusive to him, it would have been damning evidence despite Bartosz. 'Professor Swa—' He was suddenly silent, then said with unmistakable urgency, 'Thank you, Professor, that's all.'

What had Charles said? Were they going to have a trip out to the Swann's house in the country?

'Mr Wyngate, Driver Sinclair, I think we're done here.' Bluff rose to his feet. He knocked on the door to summon the guard, apparently calling the meeting to a close. 'Thank you, Professor Swann.'

Rosie reached for Charles' hand to shake. 'One day, hopefully soon, we'll all have Chelsea buns again at Fitzbillies.'

The key scraped in the lock and the guard appeared. 'Come along, prisoner,' he said gruffly.

'*Professor Swann*,' Wyngate corrected the guard. 'A little common courtesy for an innocent man, if you please.'

The guard eyed Charles suspiciously. 'Am I taking him back to his cell, or to the counter so's he can have his belt and shoelaces back and hop off home?'

What a humiliating experience this was for the usually elegant Charles Swann.

'Back to his cell for now,' Wyngate said as Charles closed his eyes and took in a deep breath. 'But I expect he and Dr Zalewski will be helping with the war effort again by tomorrow.'

'Right you are, then.' The guard nodded to Charles and said, suddenly as polite as a maître d', 'If you wouldn't mind coming along this way, sir, please. Can I get you and the doctor anything? Another pillow perhaps? Cup of tea?'

'Oh, a cup of tea would be very welcome indeed,' Charles said as they left the interview room. 'And some toast if you could. Granary bread would be splendid.' At the door he paused and turned. 'Driver Sinclair, Major-General, I owe you both an apology and my thanks. I hope you'll accept.'

'I accept,' Rosie said. Teasing him, she added, 'But only as long as you don't call my clever man a dunderhead again.'

Charles' eyes widened, but he said, 'I give you my word.' Then he smiled and added, 'Be careful, Wyngate, or she'll have your job by tomorrow.'

The guard chuckled. He'd evidently encountered Wyngate before.

'Goodbye, and good luck,' Rosie said to Charles.

'Thank you, Professor,' Bluff said. Then Charles was gone, a new lightness about him that Rosie wasn't sure she'd ever seen, even before he was arrested and brought to Whitehall.

Some people had more secrets to carry than most.

Rosie said to Bluff, 'A penny for your thoughts, Bluff. No, wait, I'll give you a whole shilling!'

'Caroline,' was all he said.

'Does she know about her brother and Bartosz?' Rosie asked him. 'I don't know. I expect she doesn't.'

Bluff closed the door and told them, 'Caroline Swann is Prospero.'

The room was cold, but Rosie felt even colder. She repeated Bluff's words in her head, and they didn't change.

Caroline Swann is Prospero.

'Bluff, darling, you're ever so tired,' Rosie reminded him. 'You're not making any sense. Caroline's not Prospero! What do you mean?'

He couldn't mean what he was saying. *Surely.* Caroline was her friend. Nice, kind, sweet Caroline. She wasn't a spy. She *couldn't* be a spy. Because if Caroline Swann of all people could be a spy, then the world was a more frightening place than Rosie had ever realised.

'Don't be absurd,' Wyngate spat. 'Get your head together, man! Can you hear yourself?'

'She's not even a man!' Rosie exclaimed, leaping to her friend's defence, but as soon the words came out of her mouth, she doubted herself.

How did they know Prospero was a man? They didn't. They'd only assumed so because Prospero was a male character in Shakespeare's play, and Bluff's hit list of six were all men. And hadn't Rosie played the principal boy in the panto while Professor Hale had played Widow Twanky? The spy's codename meant nothing.

'She doesn't have to be.' Then Bluff pulled open the door and shouted, 'Swann! Swann, wait!'

'Yes, Major-General!' the guard called.

There were footsteps and the jangling of keys. Whistling. *Whistling?*

Why was the guard whistling when so much was at stake?

'Here he is,' the guard announced, as he reappeared in the doorway with Charles. Then, having deposited the prisoner, he left, closing the door behind him.

'What is it?' Charles looked terrified. 'Has something happened to—'

'The codes you and your sister used to make up,' Bluff cut in, 'You never used them to encode messages for us, did you?'

'We were children, Jerry would've cracked them in a second,' Charles replied. 'Perhaps I did, without thinking, but they would've been heavily modified. Every code went through a second pair of hands to ensure it was watertight.'

Bluff nodded. 'But when you were ill and working in the library, who was the second pair of hands?'

'I've no idea.' Charles frowned. 'Usually we'd pass them to a colleague, but Daddy brought them to Whitehall and ensured they went to one of the team for verification. Then

they'd come back to me for implementation and transmission.'

Daddy.

Trying to sound casual, Rosie asked, 'Would he have asked
your sister to help?'

'I doubt it,' he replied. 'Not that he wouldn't think she was
capable. When Daddy struggled with the *Times* crossword
over breakfast, the Sprat was always the one with the answers.
Very keen brain. Probably the best at Cottisbourne.'

'Other than you?' Wyngate asked in a dry tone. Charles
caught it and smiled.

'Better even than me. But don't tell her I said that, will
you?'

He was jealous of her intelligence. That's why he'd made
her life so miserable.

And all of that subterfuge, all of the lies, had been to
protect his lover.

And now they knew Prospero was very clever indeed.
That machine, no one had seen anything like it. But then,
being clever was one thing – having the dexterity to build
something like that required other skills. And Caroline just
didn't.

An image was prodding its way into Rosie's mind and she
finally saw it. Caroline, carrying a box of machine parts. The
woman who said she didn't work on the machines had told
her she was going to run repairs on the bombe.

She'd slipped up. The mighty Prospero had blundered.

'Charles …' Rosie asked him. He raised an eyebrow, waiting for her to go on. 'Have you ever seen Caroline tinker
with things? Old clocks or watches? The workings in a
jewellery box maybe?'

'She's not terribly mechanically minded,' he replied. 'She
used to tinker all the time and I'd tease her, tell her no chap

wants to marry a girl with oily hands. No harm in it, but I rather think she took it to heart.'

Rosie couldn't help but think of Bluff. He didn't seem to mind her having oily hands. But then … hadn't Charles just told her that, quite possibly, Caroline *did* have the technical skills of Prospero after all?

'She might have carried on tinkering, you know, out of your sight,' Rosie suggested. 'And you'd be surprised just which chaps *do* like a woman with oily hands. I suppose once you went off to boarding school, you didn't see very much of Caroline?'

'Only in the hols. You don't think— oh no,' he laughed and shook his head. '*The Sprat*? Not a chance!'

'Why not?' Rosie asked him. 'You've just told us she's more intelligent than even *you*. The mighty Professor Swann!'

'Caroline! She was born to be a clergyman's wife, she isn't a *spy*!'

'Oh, Charles!' Rosie shook her head, laughing at her own deceptive preconceptions as much as his. 'That's just it! That makes her the *perfect* spy! Because no one would ever, ever suspect her!'

Wyngate knocked on the door to summon the guard. He told Charles, 'We're going to keep you here until we've looked into this. If it *is* your sister, it's vital that she thinks she's home free because you're sitting in prison—'

'How did she know?' Bluff asked quietly, realisation dawning on his face. 'Nobody at Cottisbourne knows you were arrested, but she came flying out in tears. She's monitoring the phone lines, isn't she? She's been one step ahead of us all the bloody way!'

Rosie gasped in horror. Of course, Caroline had. 'There's no other way. She just appeared, bawling her eyes out! Oh, we've been so dim!'

The guard opened the door. 'Got your tea ready for you, sir,' he said to Charles as he led him away. 'Do come this way.'

'I've got to make some calls,' Wyngate told Bluff and Rosie. 'Head back to your office and I'll be with you as soon as I've got an update.'

Chapter 29

Rosie and Bluff headed back up the stairs, Rosie taking them two at a time to keep up with Bluff. She didn't want to believe that she was friends with Prospero, but every thought that came into her head merely underscored the very real possibility that self-effacing Caroline Swann was a spy.

And a murderer.

Rosie wasn't sure what was the hardest thing to accept. She felt hollow, the suspicion of Caroline's betrayal and duplicity an abhorrent shock.

As soon as the door of Bluff's office closed behind them, he took Rosie's hands in his and said, 'She took everyone in, Rosie. I don't think the prof ever even mentioned her name.'

'Even Professor Hale ...' Rosie shook her head. 'And we're sure, aren't we? We're definitely sure it *is* her? I'm sorry, it's just that she's my friend, and ... it makes sense, but at the same time, it's not easy to accept.'

'And it rests on Swann's father. I need to hear him tell me that he showed her those cyphers instead of bringing them to Whitehall.' Bluff squeezed Rosie's hand. 'Let's go through it all and make sure this puzzle fits together. This *has* to be right.'

Rosie and Bluff sat in the armchairs, drinking tea and writing up what they knew as Bluff's pipe filled the air with its aromatic smoke.

Caroline was intelligent enough and adequately gifted at

mathematics to have gained a post at Cottisbourne Park. But in addition to that, her own brother, a Cambridge professor, had admitted that she was brighter than him. There was no question that she was clever enough to be Prospero. And not only that, but she had toyed with codes and encryption from childhood.

She had lied about her skills with machines, but had slipped up. And Rosie wouldn't have been surprised if the machine parts they'd spotted Caroline with, which she had claimed were for the bombe, were in fact destined for the rebuild of Caroline's modified Endeavour machine.

So that covered her abilities.

Then there were her opportunities. On the surface, Caroline was such an inoffensive person that wherever she went in the Park, people would smile, or not notice her at all. The perfect spy. Who could say how often she had gone to hut two on the pretext of visiting her brother? Who knew what scraps of intelligence she might have acquired?

And what about her brother's sick leave, when Caroline had been in the family home with him – at the same time as all that sensitive material? Rosie remembered Caroline's tales about the old house and she told Bluff about the priest holes and near-invisible servant passages, stairways and doors that Caroline had hidden in as a child. No doubt she had used them again as an adult as she sought after her brother's messages. Messages that she could read because her father had used her to verify that the cypher Charles designed to encode British messages would be uncrackable for the Axis spies.

And it would have been, if Caroline had not become one of the very spies they were hoping to perplex. Once she joined the staff at Cottisbourne Park, the Nazis found themselves with one of the best-connected moles in the country. But for Professor Hale, nobody would ever have known it was Caroline Swann.

And but for Caroline Swann, Professor Hale would still be alive.

As Rosie got up to pour more tea, a thought came to her. She had been so focused on the *what* and *how* that she hadn't stopped to think of it. But now she did.

'It all makes sense, apart from one thing.' She passed Bluff his recharged cup and asked him, 'Why? Why has Caroline betrayed her own country?'

'Because she's the Sprat. Charles' little sister, *born to marry a clergyman* whilst her brother's flying high at Cambridge.' Bluff took his pipe from between his lips. 'But Prospero conducts the tempest.'

'So, this is about power ... for someone who has none.' Rosie shook her head sadly. 'What must she think of me? I'm ... I was so fond of her and now I feel as if all along she was laughing behind my back. The stupid actress who barely went to school ...'

But Bluff's look told her that he didn't agree. 'Or the engineer who got Prospero's machine up and running when Whitehall's finest couldn't?'

'Well ...' Rosie shrugged. 'Not so stupid after all, then. We might've underestimated Caroline, but she's *really* underestimated us!'

'And as soon as Wyngate gives us the go-ahead, it'll be back to Cottisbourne to collect Caroline Swann.' Bluff took a sip of tea. 'I think the prof would be proud.'

Rosie held up her tea cup. 'To Professor Hale,' she said. Bluff lifted his teacup and echoed the toast as across the office, the telephone jangled into life.

Wyngate?

'Kingsl— we're on our way.' He put the receiver down

and turned to Rosie. 'Prospero and Germany are on the radio as we speak. An exchange, *live.*'

Rosie almost ran for the door still holding her teacup. She left it on a bookcase by the door and hurried out into the corridor.

Once again, she worked her way through the elaborate maze of the building and she and Bluff arrived in the workshop again.

Oakley and his team were crowded around the machine and the radio, and as before, they had left a spare seat for Bluff, their translator.

The only sound in the room came from the radio.

Beep-be-beep-beep.

'The listening station boffins are tracing this, I assume?' Bluff asked in a whisper. 'I don't expect she'll keep the transmission open long enough, but ...'

Oakley looked over and nodded. 'We've got several stations on the lookout. Let's just hope he ... *she?*' His eyes widened behind his glasses.

Meanwhile, the operator at the Endeavour – the machine Rosie now knew her own friend had modified in order to betray her country – began to type in the characters that had come by the intercepted Morse code.

The lampboard illuminated character by character as the Endeavour decrypted the message in German. As it did, Bluff worked on the messages already received. Rosie watched his hand move across the page, telling the tale of Caroline Swann and her betrayal of everything they were fighting for.

The messages kept coming. Rosie wished she understood Morse code. She wished she could speak German. But she had to remind herself that if it wasn't for her, the Endeavour wouldn't now be decrypting the messages flying between Berlin and Cottisbourne.

'She knows about Overlord,' Bluff muttered as the pencil nib snapped. He held out his hand for a replacement, then went on with the translation as the messages stopped.

Was that long enough?

And with that, the radio fell silent.

The question remained, how much did she know about Operation Overlord? And how much had she told? Rosie gripped her hands, her knuckles turning white.

Oakley looked over at the phone. He'd have to make the call. He swallowed. 'You chaps crack on, I'll see if we've got anything.'

He went over to the phone and turned his back on them, as if he was preparing himself to deal with his embarrassment if he didn't receive good news.

'This might take a minute or two,' Bluff told them. He met Rosie's gaze and told her, 'Prospero's planning to run.'

'What?' Rosie exclaimed in dismay. And they were so close to catching her. Who knew what mayhem Prospero would stir up if she got away? Rosie wrung her hands. 'We've got to stop her! We can't let her get away!'

'Any word on that trace?' He called. 'Did they get her or didn't she give us the time?'

Oakley turned back to face them. He neatly put down the phone.

'News, chums! They've got a location.' Oakley nodded. 'Cottisbourne Park. Not the main house or the huts. Looks like the messages were broadcast from the folly.'

'She got her replacement machine set up quickly,' Rosie remarked. 'I'd be impressed if she wasn't selling us out to the enemy.'

'The bloody folly!' Bluff said in realisation. 'As far as she's concerned, Prospero's in prison. Nobody's going back to that folly because there shouldn't be anything left to find! We've got her this time!'

Cheers rang round the room from people who, Rosie suspected, were too quiet to cheer all that often.

'Will Wyngate send his soldier coppers back to Cottisbourne to arrest her?' Rosie asked.

'We need him out of his meeting,' Bluff replied. 'Because this is time we can't afford to lose. Shall we hear what Prospero and Germany have been saying to each other? She's not planning to stay at Cottisbourne for long.'

Rosie nodded. 'Go on. What did that conniving…?' *Cow*. Rosie bit back the insult. 'What's she been saying to her friends?'

'Broadcasting in the morning; I'll wager Germany know this means something's amiss. The opening message is just Prospero putting a call to make sure they're receiving. When she knows they are, she begins.' Bluff cleared his throat. 'Confirm Ariel apprehended and will hang. Operation Tempest stage two to commence. Request safe passage immediately. Over.'

'She's given her brother a codename…' Rosie shook her head. 'And look at how coolly she takes the prospect of him being hanged! My God… he's been a terrible brother to her, but *hanging?*'

'And Germany reply,' Bluff went on. 'Prospero. Rienzi must confirm commencement of stage two. Advise need for immediacy. Over.'

'Hitler himself has to give permission?' Rosie was shocked all over again by Caroline's subterfuge. Her gentle, kind friend was in league with the devil.

'There's something in this next message that will chill the blood of any of our coding bigwigs.' Bluff looked down at the page again. 'Have isolated frequencies unique to Britman.

Overlord commences July. Request listening and cypher station in Berlin. Fully manned. Prospero to oversee. Over.' He raised his eyes, then explained, 'Britman is Mr Churchill's personal cypher. We'll be changing it in roughly sixty seconds now we've seen this, but she's hooked onto the most closely guarded and watched frequencies in the country. *July*. There's nothing she doesn't know if she knows that. The date can and will be changed. If Jerry's expecting us in July, we'll make sure we take him by surprise. Nancy wasn't wrong with her talk of ghosts, she's like a bloody phantom; invisible and missing nothing.'

'Oh, hell!' Rosie swore, no longer caring if people thought she wasn't a nice young lady. 'She's going to lose us the war! They'll be goose-stepping down Whitehall if we don't stop her! And she wants her own bloody listening and cypher station? Oh, she's got a nerve! She's got a bloody nerve!'

'And this is where we were lucky. She repeated the message twice and I'd hazard a guess that whoever's sitting on the other end of this went scurrying off in a panic to get old Adolf out of bed,' Bluff said with a meaningful look at the clock, which was nearing midday. 'Our young lady has a direct line to the very top.'

'How she must love being so important,' Rosie sighed. 'She's got what she wanted … but my word, it's horrid to think of all those people she's trampled underfoot to get there.'

'One assumes Hitler holds her in high regard, given the final message from Berlin.' Bluff turned the page and read the translation there. 'Prospero. Rienzi confirms operation Tempest stage two. Safe passage granted. Pick up from the appointed place at zero hundred hours. Listening and cypher station established and awaiting Prospero. Message from Rienzi begins. My loyal friend, the Fatherland thanks you. I look forward to our first dance. Message from Rienzi ends. Over and out.'

'*First dance?*' Rosie grimaced as if she'd encountered a bad smell. 'Right, they're picking her up at midnight. So that's something. By ... by what? A boat? Where's the *appointed place* when it's at home?'

Bluff shook his head before saying, 'And she closes with a very simple, *Message received and understood. Heil Hitler. Out.*'

'*Heil Hitler.* I'll give her Heil Hitler, the bloody ...' Rosie clenched and unclenched her hands. 'What do we do? How do we know where they're collecting her? It could be *any-where* on the south coast!'

'Not just the south,' Bluff pointed out. 'Charles' car's still at Cottisbourne. She's got a good fifteen hours, but there's the small matter of petrol, of course ...'

'And she's so ...' Rosie chose her words carefully. 'She doesn't stick out. No one's going to notice anything strange. Can we warn the police to look out for the car?'

Bluff nodded and rose from the chair. He seemed filled with a fresh energy, like a bloodhound tracking a scent.

'I'm bloody tempted to jump on her frequency and tell Berlin that the pick up's aborted, but we can't risk making them suspicious.' Bluff snatched up the pad. 'Let's see what Wyngate has to say.'

Chapter 30

Rosie and Bluff emerged from the stairs that led up from the basement just in time to meet Wyngate. He was lighting one cigarette from the dying embers of another, something nervy in his movements.

'Oh, I'm glad we've bumped into you,' Rosie said, surprised to hear herself say the words. But there was no place for personal quibbles at the moment.

'You've heard then?' Wyngate asked. 'The call came through when I was leaving the PM.'

'Yes, we heard the message come in,' Rosie told him. 'She's planned a rendezvous early tomorrow morning.'

'What?' Wyngate barked. 'A rendez— she's gone, Driver Sinclair. Dr McAndrew reports that Miss Swann didn't arrive for her shift this morning. Nobody's seen her since lights out and she was gone before breakfast. To complicate matters, it looks as though there's a missing evacuee in the village too, last seen in the grounds of Cottisbourne Park last night.'

'Nancy.' Rosie grabbed for Bluff's arm. She couldn't hold herself up. She could barely breathe. 'Nancy. She's got her, hasn't she? Caroline nearly killed her in the barn fire. Oh, God, we've got to find them! We've got to!'

'It's all right,' Bluff said gently. 'She's an adventurer, you know that.'

Bluff took Rosie's hand as Wyngate assured them, 'We've got men looking for them both all over the area. Your pals Sarah and Maggie know all Nancy's favourite haunts. Don't panic yet, Driver, I hear the little girl's got a bit of a reputation for roaming.' He glanced over his shoulder then confided, 'Her mother's in administration here. I'd rather we say nothing. Walls have ears.'

'Oh, silly girl … what has she done?' *Come on, Rosie, she's probably got into the garage and she's playing with the Citroën again.* Rosie smiled at that thought and kept it close to fend off her worst fears. 'Good idea. She doesn't need to start worrying yet.'

'The PM wants an update from you both,' Wyngate told them, sweeping past them and heading for the foyer of the building. 'This morning's messages and what our next move is. By this time tomorrow I want that bloody woman sitting in my cells whistling *Horst-Wessel-Lied* and wondering where it all went wrong!'

Somehow, Rosie followed him with Bluff, though she barely knew how. A sea of people parted as they went through the busy foyer, but Rosie barely saw anyone. She kept thinking of Nancy playing in the car, imagining a trip to the seaside, and she wanted to believe more than anything that that was exactly what Nancy was doing at that moment. Anything else was too awful to imagine. Nancy had never suspected Caroline – no one had. She wouldn't know what danger she was in.

They walked down Whitehall, just another group of people in uniforms and civvies, past monuments to wars that had ended long ago. Rosie nearly stumbled over a sandbag, and cursed herself for not paying more attention. They crossed the road, the traffic stirring up dust and grit, and the next thing Rosie realised, she and Bluff were following Wyngate down a side street, with a Georgian terrace at its end.

And then Rosie realised.

'Downing Street...' she whispered to Bluff.

'If it looks a bit of a bombsite inside, that's because it very nearly was,' Bluff replied. 'Had one come down on Horse Guards a couple of months ago that took the plaster off the PM's walls and blew his windows clean out.'

'Close-run thing.' Rosie remarked. 'Let's hope those bombers don't come back and try to finish the job.'

The police standing outside evidently recognised Wyngate, but still asked for their ID cards before letting them inside.

Rosie hadn't known what to expect, although the thick carpet underfoot that seemed to swallow all sound didn't surprise her. Portraits of former prime ministers hung along the walls, and Rosie wondered what on earth they'd make of what was going on. Here and there she could see suggestions of the damage left by the bomb, with cracks in the plaster and splinters in the wood, but it must have paled in comparison to Horse Guards itself.

As Wyngate led them through the building Rosie heard the occasional snatch of conversation and the hammer of typewriter keys, but the place seemed oddly quiet. Perhaps everyone was in the War Rooms these days, she reasoned, safe deep below ground.

'Good afternoon,' Miss Layton smiled as she emerged from a door up ahead. 'Mr Churchill's waiting in his office. Tea?'

Rosie nodded. 'Yes, please.' Although she immediately wished she'd said *no*, because wouldn't it be embarrassing to spill tea in front of Churchill?

'Please, Miss Layton,' Bluff smiled. Wyngate said nothing. Instead, he rapped on the closed door in front of them. Bluff looked down at Rosie and offered her a fortifying smile, then quickly dashed a kiss to her cheek when Miss Layton turned to go.

A voice from within bid them enter, and as soon as Rosie

saw Churchill sitting behind his desk, she reminded herself that he'd wandered into her workplace too, and that she shouldn't be scared. She smiled at him, wondering if he'd remember her, but then she spotted a figure standing by the window, his shoulders hunched. He looked familiar, and when he turned Rosie realised why.

It was Mr Swann, his face grey now instead of dark red. All the wind had been knocked out of his sails, and he nodded his greeting to them as they entered the room.

The pleasantries that were exchanged as they were seated made Rosie think of meetings with theatre managers, when one wrong word could be the difference between a booking or a polite refusal. Yet the matters they were about to discuss were of far more importance than the schedule of the Cavendish players. Bluff held the notebook containing the translations in his lap, and it seemed so unremarkable to say it held such secrets.

Just like Caroline.

'Mr Wyngate has appraised me of the unfortunate new developments in these matters, but I understand new messages have been received,' Churchill told them, casting a glance in Swann's direction. 'Major-General, please read the translations.'

And there in the office, as Miss Layton served tea, Bluff read out the messages that had been sent from the folly at Cottisbourne Park and the replies that had been received from Berlin.

Mr Swann's complexion turned greyer still. It was bad enough discovering a friend was a spy, but Rosie couldn't imagine how it felt to discover your own child was one.

'What a wretched mess,' Mr Swann said. He picked up his cup and sipped, but didn't seem to take any pleasure in it. 'I don't suppose we have the slightest idea where this *appointed place* is? And I need to make it absolutely clear that the information she may have on Overlord has *not* come from me.'

'Forgive me if I'm overstepping, Mr Swann,' Bluff said, 'but there is one piece of the puzzle missing. Miss Swann may well have been listening and watching from within the walls of your country estate during her brother's illness, but there remains the question of the cypher used to encode the initial messages Prospero leaked. Miss Swann wasn't in the ministry's employment at the time of Prospero's first activities and was never involved in encoding, only decoding. Sir, did you show your daughter the cyphers Professor Swann entrusted with you for delivery to his colleagues for verification?'

Mr Swann's mouth slowly opened, making him look for all the world like a ventriloquist's dummy.

'Let me see.' He put his cup and saucer on Churchill's desk, the china rattling. 'I ... I ... did. She's my daughter. She's a clever old stick. I ... I told her it was important. Confidential. It needed to be done fast, and I knew she was capable of it. I just didn't know she was capable of everything else that she's done. She's my *daughter.* How could I possibly distrust her?'

Bluff nodded, then asked, 'And this was before she was employed by the ministry and had signed the Official Secrets Act?'

'Yes,' he admitted, his head bowed. Then he tilted up his chin and said, 'Look here, she's a bright little thing, and I was lining up a job for her in just that sort of work. She and Charles used to play with codes when they were children. Someone gave Charles a codebook for Christmas, you see. I knew she'd be signing the Act eventually, it was just a matter of time. I didn't think ... she's so quiet, so obedient and

284

good, I couldn't possibly have even *guessed* that she would betray us all. Everyone of us sitting in this room, everyone in this street, this city, this whole country. If I'd known, I would've … I would've …' He raised his hands and clenched them in mid-air, and Rosie was glad that whatever he was about to say, he thought better of, and left it unsaid.

'She joined the ministry the following month,' Wyngate informed them, his words clipped. 'You should've waited.'

'Do you think that would've made any difference?' Mr Swann rubbed his hand over his face. 'She would've done it anyway. And I know, I should've followed protocol, I should've passed it to Whitehall. But I didn't. I was trying to be quick, and I was worried about Charles. He had a close squeak with that illness, and I was out of my mind with worry. But let's not rake through old coals. It won't help us now. If only it could.'

'We have the option of hijacking the frequency and telling Berlin Prospero's calling off the pickup,' Wyngate told them all. 'If we do that, we risk losing her. And the girl, if they're together.'

'I think that should be our last resort, Mr Wyngate,' the prime minister replied. From behind his desk, he regarded Swann in silence for a few seconds. Rosie wondered what was going through his mind, but she didn't suppose she'd ever truly know. Eventually he nodded and said, 'Miss Swann has absconded from Cottisbourne Park for her meeting with her German friends. Major-General, as our trusted gardener, what do you propose should be our next move?'

'I'd like to ask Mr Swann if there's anywhere he can think of that might have significance for his daughter,' Bluff said, looking to Swann. 'A place where she might arrange a rendezvous?'

Swann stared at the desk in front of him for a moment,

then shook his head. 'We have friends here and there on the coast, but it's unlikely she'd call in on anyone, don't you think? I honestly couldn't narrow it down to just one spot, I'm afraid.'

And Rosie thought of Nancy again, and the fire in the barn.

'I'd like a list of names and addresses,' Wyngate said. 'Unlikely or not, Mr Swann.'

'All right. I'll be as quick as I can.' He reached inside his jacket and produced a notebook, and started to scribble in it.

How long did they have? Rosie tried again to think of anything, anything at all Caroline had said about places here and there, but thanks to Rosie's itinerant life in the Cavendish Players they'd talked about so many towns and villages over the few years she'd known her that nothing came to mind.

'We're so close,' Rosie said. 'So close. We can't let her get away now.'

Chapter 31

Swann handed over the names and addresses to Wyngate, and the list vanished to be scrutinised. There was nothing more to be done. Oakley and his team monitored the radio. Even though Prospero had flown and any further messages were unlikely, they had to do something.

'Just in case, you never know!' Oakley had said.

But it was very difficult not to feel defeated. To have come this far and have Prospero slip away, with who knew what information about Overlord, was galling. So many lives depended on them tracking her down, but where did you start with someone like Caroline? She was a blank slate.

Rosie napped in one of Bluff's armchairs, hoping she'd come up with something if her mind was fresher. It was comforting hearing Bluff come and go as she dozed. But what about the future that had seemed within touching distance early that same morning? What future would any of them have if Caroline spilled her secrets to the enemy? And what future did Nancy have if she'd been snatched away by Prospero?

Rosie slept fitfully, drifting in and out of sleep at the sound of Big Ben's chime or a slamming door somewhere in the building. At some point Rosie must have sunk into a deeper slumber though, because Bluff's hand was on her arm through her dreams and he was gently whispering her name.

'Rosie,' he said softly. 'Darling, wake up.'

Rosie opened her eyes and blinked up at Bluff. For a moment, her mind was clear of all worry and fear, but in seconds her previous thoughts returned, and she felt guilty for sleeping on the job. 'I'm sorry. Have I been asleep for ages?'

'Just a little while,' Bluff assured her, but the lengthening shadows told Rosie otherwise. 'I would've let you sleep, but I've just been told there's a Miss Nancy Thomas waiting downstairs. Apparently, she's asking for me by name.'

Rosie chuckled with relief. 'That's my little friend Nancy! Oh, thank heavens, she's all right. Although what on earth is she doing in London?'

'More to the point, how did she get here from Cottisbourne?' Bluff offered Rosie his hand and helped her to her feet. 'I could do with a few more with her initiative in the army.'

'She's a remarkable child.' Rosie stood now, but didn't let go of Bluff's hand. 'Perhaps she's come to see her mother, but wanted to say hello to you as well. She was homesick, poor little thing.'

They were still holding hands as they made their way through the building, which still bustled despite the encroaching evening. Even with Caroline out there and waiting to make her escape, the knowledge that Nancy was safe gave Rosie a new impetus. If Nancy had come to London, there was still hope for Prospero's arrest, she told herself.

They were taken into a waiting room, which was more elegant than most living rooms. People in uniforms and civvies were waiting, some peering over their newspapers at the small interloper.

Nancy was easy to spot. The only child in the room, she had Portia on her knee and her gas mask around her neck.

One sock had rolled down, and both her plaits had nearly unravelled.

'There she is, and in one piece!' Rosie waved to her and called, 'Nancy!'

Several heads turned, and Rosie heard a distinct *harrumph* from one quarter. But she didn't care. Nancy didn't seem to either and she leapt down from her seat and executed a sharp salute, which Bluff and Rosie returned.

'Major-General, Driver Rosie!' Nancy announced. 'I'd like to report a spy!'

This wasn't just a game, Rosie was certain of it. Nancy wouldn't have come here – however she had managed it – just to engage in make-believe.

'Major-General,' Rosie said to Bluff, 'shall we take our young recruit to your office?'

Bluff nodded. He asked the woman seated behind the reception desk, 'Would you arrange for some supper to be sent up for the young lady, please? And fresh tea for us.' She responded with a nod and then the trio were off through the corridors of the War Office, with Portia dancing alongside.

'How did you find your way here?' Rosie asked her, as they went up the grand marble staircase again. She wondered what it looked like to a child like Nancy. Perhaps she was picturing Cinderella sweeping down it in a glittering gown.

'On the train,' Nancy explained. 'I just stuck close to folk and nobody noticed I wasn't supposed to be there! It's easy when you're a spy. Is this where Mum works?'

What a resourceful little girl.

Rosie glanced at Bluff. She could tell from his expression that he shared her sentiments.

'Well, that was ingenious of you,' Rosie said. 'Although maybe you should let your Gran and Grandpa know the next time you do that. And yes, your mummy *does* work here. Would you like to see her?'

'Would I!' Nancy exclaimed. She looked around, taking in the chandeliers and the portraits, the bustling civil servants and uniformed officials. 'I didn't know if you'd come to London, but I guessed you must have and I thought if you weren't here, I could ask for Mr Churchill instead.'

'Wise thinking indeed,' Bluff said with a nod of approval. 'And you're here to report a spy?'

At that, Nancy pressed a finger to her lips and whispered, 'I'll tell you when we're alone. Careless talk costs lives, Major-General.'

They reached Bluff's office, and Rosie wondered if Nancy would feel nervous, but she seemed more excited than anything else.

Once the door was safely closed behind them, Rosie asked her, 'So, Agent Nancy, what have you got to tell us?'

'Caroline Swann is a Nazi spy.' Nancy said it so matter-of-factly that it was almost comical. She settled herself in one of Bluff's armchairs and added, 'She's done a runner, and I've got the evidence to prove it.'

Bluff darted a glance towards Rosie and asked, 'Do you know where she is, Nancy?'

Nancy gave a decisive nod. 'She caught the lunchtime train to Southend. Took her bike and a satchel full of paper and left this behind in the folly.' From her coat pocket, Nancy produced a handwritten envelope, which she held out to Bluff. He took it and withdrew a single sheet of paper from within.

So Caroline had taken the train from Cottisbourne to London, then picked up a connection to Southend. Rosie could picture the wide, marshy coast ... Something was stirring in her mind, but it wouldn't come into focus. She glanced over at Bluff, wondering what was in the envelope. 'What does it say?'

'To whoever finds this,' Bluff read, 'I am sorry. The shame of my brother's arrest has broken my heart. The happiest days of our lives were spent in our little boat on grandmama's loch and that's where I'll rest. Please don't try to find me. The waters are deep and I wouldn't want anyone to put themselves at risk searching for a Sprat. Tell Charles he isn't to blame and I forgive him for his betrayals. I have light in my heart, because I know I'm going to a better place.'

'Bare-faced liar. How dare she?' With effort, Rosie reined in her anger. She didn't want Nancy to see it. 'Setting us all up to go haring off to Scotland, and pretending she could be so upset by someone committing all those acts of betrayal that are all down to *her*...! Well, Nancy, thank goodness you spotted her. There's no way she's going to Scotland if she got the train down to Southend!'

'And think of the time we'd have wasted searching for her up there if not for Nancy.' Bluff put the letter down on his desk. 'What else did you have to report, Driver Thomas?'

A knock sounded at the door and for a minute or so the debrief had to wait as Nancy's supper of sandwiches arrived, along with fresh tea and a glass of lemonade. Bluff passed the little girl her meal and she set it on the arm of the chair, preferring to tell her tale before she ate.

'There was a lot of coming and going at the folly from the groundsmen so I knew something was up, especially when Bart and Swann both got spirited away,' she explained. 'I kept an eye on the place and last night, when all them *groundsmen* had cleared off in a van, who do I see going back in but Caroline, with a box filled with bits of kit. She came and went a couple of times and while she was away, I snuck in to see what she was up to, but there was nothing there.

The next time she went in with a box, I counted to twenty and I followed her.' Nancy widened her eyes and told them, 'No sign of life, but I know she's not a ghost. I could hear noises in the wall again, like someone building something. Metal and tools and that.'

'Remarkable,' Bluff murmured. Nancy nodded and took a bite of her sandwich. 'She must've considered it safe once *Prospero* was in a cell and the folly had been cleaned out. As soon as our boys left, she moved back in.'

'So I stayed there all night right through to this morning and that's when I heard it. Morse code.' Nancy nodded to herself. 'Not ghosts at all. I wanted to tell Mr McAndrew, but his secretary told me to clear off. I went back down to the folly and saw her pin that note to the door. Then she took off on her bike, so I grabbed the note and followed her. She bought a ticket to Southend, so I got on the train and came straight here.'

'Good heavens, Nancy!' Rosie was astounded at how determined and resourceful the child had been. 'You've done very, very well to have found all that out, and to bring the letter with you as well. I know it must've been a surprise to find out what Caroline was up to, seeing as she was our friend, but she kept it so secret. Nobody could've known. You did well to tell us.'

Nancy beamed, but her smile faded into a frown as she realised, 'So if her brother isn't a spy, that means he really is just a grumpy old whatsit!'

Bluff didn't quite manage to catch his smile before he replied, 'Does anyone else at Cottisbourne suspect Professor Swann and Dr Zalewski have been apprehended as spies, Nancy? The official explanation is that they're assisting with a project here in London.'

'Oh, they've all fallen for that hook, line and sinker,' she

292

grinned. 'But I saw him crash Rosie's motor into the verge. Something had to be up, didn't it?'

'You saw...?' Rosie chuckled. 'You really do get everywhere in that village! Where on Earth were you hiding?' She nudged Nancy playfully and said, 'You should've come and helped me change the tyre! No... I'm only joking.' And she kissed the top of Nancy's head.

Bluff clapped his hands together and said, 'Right-o, I'm just going to pop along the hallway to make some telephone calls. Nancy, you stay here and enjoy your supper. Rosie, would you mind staying with her?'

'Of course, I don't mind at all,' Rosie said. 'Portia and I will put on a little show for Driver Thomas to say thank you.'

Not that Rosie wanted to encourage Nancy in her scrapes, but she was such an independent little girl, and without her, they would've been haring about after Caroline at the wrong end of the country.

Rosie entertained Nancy with Portia. She felt hopeful now that they'd stop Caroline in time, and that the future she and Bluff had talked about would happen after all. Prospero's chances of getting to Germany and passing on the details of Overlord had drastically shrunk, all thanks to a little girl whose socks wouldn't stay up.

There was a soft knock on the door, and a woman's voice hesitantly called, 'Nancy? Nancy, are you there?'

'Mum!' Nancy exclaimed as she darted from the armchair with such speed that she nearly fell over her own feet. She raced to the door and pulled it open, flinging herself into her mother's arms.

Nancy's mother – who looked for all the world like an older version of the little girl – picked her up and whirled her round. Then she brought her close and hugged her, pressing her lips to Nancy's hair.

'Oh, you've grown – you're getting too big for me to do that now!' She chuckled as she set Nancy back on her feet. 'Dare I ask what you're doing here, darling?'

'I'm helping to catch a spy!' Nancy wrapped her arms around her mother's waist and hugged her again. 'Have you heard from dad?'

'Catch a spy?' Mrs Thomas laughed. She didn't sound incredulous, which made Rosie wonder just what Nancy got up to. 'I have, and he's very well. He's going to send you a letter.'

The telephone on Bluff's desk rang and Nancy glanced over her shoulder. For a moment Rosie had the feeling the little girl was going to answer it, but she didn't. Instead, she continued to cling to her mother like a limpet.

Rosie went over to the desk. Employing her most cut-glass tones, she picked up the telephone. 'Hello, Major-General Sir Kingsley-Flynn's telephone, Driver Sinclair speaking. Who may I ask is calling?'

'Rosie, it's Bluff.' He sounded chipper too. 'Wyngate and his chaps are on their way to Southend as we speak. I've managed to track down Nancy's mother too, so expect a visit soon.'

Rosie looked up from the telephone. Nancy and her mother were still hugging.

'Oh, she's here, and they're ever so happy to see each other again! Thank you, Bluff,' Rosie said. 'And Wyngate was quick off the mark, too. Gosh, I'll be so relieved when this is all over.'

'I'm just waiting to speak to the PM and I'll be right along.' She could hear the smile in Bluff's voice when he added, 'I didn't expect Wyngate to be quite so accepting, but it was the note that did it. Nancy's quite an operative!'

'Wasn't she good? I don't want to encourage her running

off, but then again, I'm not sure she needs encouragement,' Rosie said. 'I'm sure your chum Winny will be pleased when he hears we're finally onto her.'

'I don't doubt it. And I've spoken to the worried grand-parents and they're worried no longer,' Bluff replied. 'I'll see you in a little while, Rosie.'

Rosie put down the telephone. She made Nancy's mother feel at home, pouring her a cup of tea. Mrs Thomas sat on one of the armchairs with Nancy on her lap as the little girl tucked into her sandwiches and lemonade.

Rosie leaned back in the chair, feeling at one with the world. Not something she'd felt very often since the war had begun.

Minutes passed and the skies grew darker, but inside all was light again. Nancy stopped chattering only to eat, filling her mother in on life in Cottisbourne, but Rosie noticed that she never gave anything away about Caroline Swann or her brother. *Careless talk*, as the little girl had reminded Bluff.

Eventually Rosie heard Bluff's heavy tread approaching, followed by another pair of feet. The door opened and Bluff stepped into the office, politely tucking his cap beneath his arm on seeing Nancy's mother. At the sight of him, Nancy gave a beaming smile, but it turned into a gape of disbelief at the sight of his companion.

'Miss Nancy Thomas,' Churchill said, holding out his hand. 'I'm so pleased to meet you at last.'

Chapter 32

Rosie was fairly sure that Churchill hadn't expected to receive a personal performance from a puppet on his visit to Bluff's office, but stranger things had happened. He took it in good part, and seemed quite taken by the little girl who had helped to catch a spy.

Well, at least Rosie hoped that was what Wyngate and his team were close to achieving by now.

Just as Portia took her bow, a sound started up that sent alarm through Rosie. A sound she'd dearly hoped not to hear while in London.

Sirens.

A bombing raid's coming.

Bluff and Churchill were on their feet at the first wail of the siren. The prime minister shook Nancy's hand again and told her, 'Alas, Driver Thomas, duty calls. The major-general will see you all safely to the shelter. It's been a pleasure to meet such a conscientious agent.'

'You can count on me, sir,' Nancy beamed, offering her habitual salute. Then she took her mother's hand and told Bluff, 'Ready!'

Nancy's mother gave her daughter a strained smile. She was trying to hide her trepidation from her daughter, Rosie knew. 'Let's get you and Portia nice and safe downstairs,' she said, as gently as if she was talking about tucking them into bed.

And with that, they abandoned Bluff's office and headed for somewhere safer.

Doors opened and closed along the corridor, and the sound of brisk footsteps mixed with the wail of the sirens from outside. Rosie's stomach gripped and twisted with fear. She reached for Bluff's hand.

'We'll be all right, won't we?' she said to him. Her usually strong voice sounded small.

'Nothing to worry about. I won't let any harm come to you,' Bluff assured her as they descended the stairs. She thought of the vast Admiralty Citadel along the road and wished vaguely that they were safe in its reinforced walls. The ornate War Office felt oddly vulnerable sitting in its prime Whitehall position.

The shelter was lined with concrete, and the space was filled with benches. It was practical and utilitarian to a degree that clashed with the wedding cake grandeur of the elaborate building above them.

A lot of people squeezed in, and the War Office's regulars looked relatively unfazed at having to return to the shelter. Rosie had felt safe in Cottisbourne with her friends, but at the thought of the bombers flying over, unwelcome memories of the Blitz returned to her.

She snuggled against Bluff as she remembered how her ambulance had squeaked and bumped over the damaged roads. She recalled her fear when she'd once lost her way in the blackout with an injured patient in the back because several roads she'd come to know quite well had simply disappeared.

She tried to think instead about the people she'd helped to rescue, the slings she'd made from tea towels and bits of torn curtain, the laughs she'd had with the ARP wardens when she'd towed their mobile canteen.

Nancy settled on her mother's knee and Bluff put his arm around Rosie's shoulder. He drew her close and kissed her hair, then whispered, 'What do you think? Is there a play in this?'

'I'm sure someone's already penning one as we speak,' Rosie replied, trying her best to sound chirpy. 'How about *Lady Windermere's Gas Mask*?'

'All about a stuffy old major-general who never forgot an actress he saw one summer night.' He rested his cheek against Rosie's hair. 'And never expected to see her again?'

'Yes! And how she ended up being his driver, and they became awfully fond of one another.' Rosie smiled up at him and tapped the tip of his nose. She whispered, 'And of course, whenever her friend comes on stage, the audience boos, because *they've* seen what she's been up to in the hayloft.'

'Awfully fond indeed,' Bluff replied. 'I can't wait for you to drive us to the seaside in the Citroën. We'll have fish and chips and paddle in the shallows.'

There was a hollow bang in the distance and the light trembled off for a second before illuminating again. A bomb must've dropped, but not too close.

Not too close. That's all right. Not too close.

Although it had been far too close for someone.

'And eat candy floss. And watch the Punch and Judy show!' Rosie pictured Bluff with his trousers rolled up and started to laugh. In fact, perhaps he'd be in civvies. 'Do you know, I've just realised, I've never seen you out of uniform.'

Bluff chuckled and said, 'Indeed you haven't! That day will come when you least expect it.'

'Maybe at your window in your pyjamas!' Rosie chuckled saucily, but then she realised that once Prospero had been arrested, Bluff would have no further reason to be at Cottisbourne Park. The thought left her feeling empty. 'Bluff, are you going to be at Cottisbourne for a little while? Or will they send you somewhere else?'

Thud.

Another bomb.

Even Bluff glanced up at that one, though when he resumed their conversation, he gave no trace of concern.

'I don't know yet,' he admitted. 'But I lost my driver, you know, or she would've brought me to Cottisbourne in the first place. She married a farmer and got into the family way.'

'Bit difficult fitting behind the steering wheel, I'd imagine, with a bun in the—' Rosie stopped. Maybe theatricals didn't mind such talk, but she wasn't sure about the serious folk at the War Office. 'So do you think they might transfer me so I'd be driving you? That would be smashing, wouldn't it?'

'Let's see what our chap in the sharp suit says first,' he whispered. 'You might be destined for bigger things than driving me.'

But Rosie wasn't sure she wanted *bigger things*. Once the war was over and everyone could go home again, she'd be back on the stage. She'd felt safe at Cottisbourne Park – at least she *had* until Hale's murder, and would feel safe again once they heard from Wyngate that Caroline was tucked up safely behind bars. She liked her little room above the garage, and she looked forward to her visits from Nancy, and the Park was such a friendly place, and the village was lovely. Although she knew that wherever she went, Sarah and Maggie would always be her friends. They'd become the sisters she'd never had.

But she nodded anyway. Because she'd been lucky, really, and if she was called upon to leave the Park, then she knew she should. Others had made far greater sacrifices than she had.

'Oh, yes, let's see,' Rosie said.

Nancy's mother gently rocked her daughter. Rosie couldn't imagine how hard it must be to keep chipper when she was no doubt as worried as everyone else. 'We'll go for a walk tomorrow, would you like that? We can go for a row on a boat in the park. Do you remember we went with Daddy when he was last on leave? We'll buy him a postcard of the Serpentine and send it to him. He'd like that, wouldn't he?'

Rosie pictured her own postcards on the wall of her room, and how she and her friends had crowded round and talked about the places they'd all been to, back in a world where they could go almost wherever they wanted. Sarah had talked with excitement about walking on Exmoor and picnicking beside a stream, and Maggie had recalled her holidays on the Yorkshire coast, paddling in the surf and eating fish and chips.

And in Rosie's mind, a beam of sunlight came in through the window and struck one of the postcards on her wall. Rosie peered closer, and closer, and saw a broad beach stretching away from marshes that were turned to gold by a sunrise and there, in the midst of it, a large square stone.

And at once she realised where Caroline was headed.

Prospero's Throne.

'Bluff, I know where she's going to be picked up! I know where the appointed place must be! It's up the coast from ... *where she went.* There's a beach and there's marshes, and there's a big stone that looks like it's just dropped there from somewhere else. It's almost like a throne.' She glanced around at the other people in the room. They seemed to be occupied by their own thoughts. Rosie cupped her hands around Bluff's ear and whispered, 'Prospero's Throne. She talked about going there as a child!'

Bluff nodded once, then whispered with urgency, 'Cycling distance from the station, would you say?'

'Yes, I'd say so,' Rosie replied. 'We did the summer season near there once, we went to the bay on an afternoon day off!'

'And how hard to find is this place? Is it going to say *Prospero's Throne* on any map that Wyngate and his men are using?'

'No! It's not called anything.' Rosie told him. 'It's in the marshes, not far from Burnham where people go sailing. There's a tiny little path, not really big enough for a car, and you have to go through a bunch of fir trees to reach it. It won't be obvious to them at all. Oh, why didn't I think of it before?'

'Come on!' Bluff patted Rosie's hand. 'We need to at least try and get a message to Wyngate. Nancy, Driver Sinclair and I are needed in the War Rooms. You're in charge.'

Nancy saluted and said, 'Yes sir!'

Her mother smiled, but even so, there was concern in her gaze as she said, 'Be careful, you two.'

'Don't worry, we will,' Rosie said as she got up from the bench and followed Bluff. Together they left the shelter and made their way along a dimly-lit corridor. Somewhere someone was leading a cheery singalong and Bluff reached for Rosie's hand.

'We're only going to pass a message on,' he assured her as he took a bunch of keys from his pocket and unlocked a door. 'Then back to the shelter. We're under the slab, there's nowhere safer in England.'

Rosie tried her best to be brave. 'Right! We'll be fine, won't we?'

Bluff paused and met Rosie's gaze. 'I promise,' he whispered, then placed a gentle kiss on her lips.

Rosie hadn't expected what was behind the door. Maybe a small office with someone sat behind a desk, but instead she was confronted by an operations room. It was just like she'd seen in some of the news reels they sometimes showed at the Park. Telephones rang, the room was filled with people hurrying here and there, and in the middle of the room a crowd of people in uniforms stood around a map, pushing objects that looked like large counters across it with long sticks.

They were monitoring the path of the bombers, and Rosie admired their detachment. She wasn't sure she could be quite so calm given that those very same bombers were overhead.

A dozen hands flew up in salutes to Bluff and he returned them as one as he asked a uniformed woman, 'Urgent message for Wyngate. Which clerk?'

A hand came up, and Rosie saw a woman with the neatest hairdo she'd ever seen, in a uniform that was only bested by Bluff's for neatness.

'That's me, sir,' she said, coming forward.

'We've an urgent message for Wyngate,' he told her. 'Driver Sinclair can pinpoint Prospero's location. If we can see a map, she'll be able to provide coordinates.'

'I'm sorry, sir,' the clerk said, 'but Mr Wyngate told me he'd be out of contact until after midnight. He said he might call in before then, though – we might just be able to get the message to him in time.'

Rosie asked for a map of south-east Essex and the clerk disappeared for a moment, then returned, already unfurling a roll of paper. She spread it flat on a table and weighted it down in the corners, then she passed Rosie a pencil.

Her heart racing, Rosie leaned over the map and found Southend-on-Sea. Then she followed the coast round from Shoeburyness, east towards the marshes around the River Crouch.

She found the spot.

The land was threaded with creeks and rivers, with a scattering of farm buildings, but there was nothing else there aside from a plantation of firs that must've been planted to provide shelter from the sea.

The stone that rose up from the marsh was marked on the map, but it hadn't been given its name.

Rosie circled it.

'There you go. That's it. That's called Prospero's Throne.'

The clerk checked the coordinates with a long ruler, then jotted them down.

'We'll keep the lines open and hope Wyngate calls in.' She patted Rosie's shoulder. 'Chin up. We'll get Prospero, never fear!'

'I hope so,' Rosie whispered. 'I really do.'

But what if Wyngate didn't think to go to that lonely part of the coast? Prospero would get away, and with her would go the plans for Overlord, straight into the hands of the enemy.

Rosie looked back at the map. Then she glanced at Bluff. Was he wondering the same thing?

No, she shouldn't even entertain the idea. But she could drive. She could handle the roads. What if she and Bluff went to Prospero's Throne?

'Can I take this?' Bluff tapped his finger against the map. He was already folding it before the clerk had a chance to reply. 'Do you have the keys to the Humber, Rosie? We can't risk her escaping. Not now we're so damn close.'

Rosie knew he didn't need to remind her about the air-raid going on above them. They'd be taking a risk driving out of London while the bombers flew over, but this was the only chance they had.

'I've got the keys.' She smiled at Bluff. 'And I'm ready.'

Bluff held out his hand for the keys as he said, 'I'd rather you were in the shelter. It's not safe outside.'

'It's not safe for you, either.' Rosie stood a little taller and reminded him, 'I'm trained for this. I drove ambulances during raids in the Blitz, and I'm sure the Luftwaffe were busier then, than they are tonight.'

And that was before the question of Bluff actually finding the hidden spot, if he could. For a long moment Bluff held Rosie's gaze, then he finally nodded.

'Driver Sinclair, you're a brick. A trip to the armoury then off we go.'

Chapter 33

Once she was behind the wheel, Rosie's nerve had nearly failed her at the threat of the bombers overheard. She forced herself to ignore the thrum of the engines and the thuds as the bombs hit home.

Rosie tried not to think too much about the weapon Bluff was carrying. She had admired his apparent sangfroid in the armoury, selecting a gun with as much ceremony as if he had been collecting a parcel. Rosie had decided to go without. She'd never handled a gun before, and didn't want to add an extra unknown factor to the pot.

She didn't want to think about what he might have to do with it, but who knew what Prospero might do if they caught up with her in time?

As they drove through London, Rosie had to take a couple of diversions where roads had been closed off. It reminded her once again of the danger of driving in an air raid, but it was nothing like the hellish, fiery cityscape she'd seen at the beginning of the war.

It seemed to take forever to leave the outskirts of London, but finally they reached the Essex countryside and the road that would take them to the North Sea coast. Rosie felt a lot safer now, but it was a long way to drive in near-darkness.

The car carried them at speed. Rosie tried to think only of driving the car, and not the enormity of what lay ahead.

It's only a trip to the seaside.

Before the main road could take them into the tangle of Southend, Rosie turned off. They were now on country lanes bordered with scrubby hedges that struggled to withstand the cold blasts from the North Sea. The land was flat, and when Rosie cranked down her window a little, she could smell the salty tang of the sea air.

'We're getting close,' she whispered, as if somehow Caroline might overhear. 'It's time for the map.'

'My cue,' Bluff smiled as he unfolded the map. He struck a match and held it over the surface until he had found their location, then blew out the flame. The car was lit by the moon now, but the bombers that had roared above were silent. It was a small comfort, at least.

'Thanks.' Rosie leaned across and kissed his cheek, then carried on.

She took the turning and after several yards they left the lane, heading into a track that led through pines. The dark branches disguised their approach. She pulled off the track, behind the wreck of an old farm building among the pines, and stopped.

Rosie looked at her watch. The luminous dial told her it was getting close to midnight.

'A bit of proper soldiering,' Bluff said with what she suspected was forced cheer. He was worried, but Rosie intuited it was for her rather than the confrontation that awaited. 'You're not going to stay here, are you?'

'I'm coming with you,' Rosie said. 'I've been here before, I know the lie of the land. Trust me, Bluff, I won't do anything stupid. Besides...' She reached into the pocket on the door and her hand closed around a piece of cold metal. Rosie produced the heavy spanner and showed it to Bluff. 'Should it be needed. I might not know what to do with a gun, but I *do* know how to use one of these.'

306

They got out of the car. The only sound was the lapping of waves on the beach, and the soft whisper of the pine trees as a breeze shivered through them. The moon lit the sea ahead, the trunks of the pines silhouetted against the silver glow as Rosie and Bluff crept towards the inlet that led from the sea. There was no sign of life, but Caroline Swann could appear and disappear as mysteriously as a phantom, Rosie had learned that over the past few days. The sea was calm as a millpond and if any vessel was out there, it was lost in that vast expanse of darkness.

'It's very peaceful,' Bluff whispered. There was a rueful note in his voice when he said, 'I wonder how long that'll last.'

Rosie took Bluff's hand as they waited, hidden behind the last row of trees beside the inlet. The square bulk of Prospero's Throne rose up through the mud before them, ancient and unyielding. It stood at the mouth of the inlet, as stubborn as Canute.

'Might it get a little dicey?' she asked him. *Silly question.* Why else was he carrying a gun?

'I hope not.' His hand tightened around hers. 'The invasion ... I'll be deployed with it, Rosie. It's all hands on deck.'

Rosie pressed her eyes closed, trying to stop the tears that had started to rise. 'Gosh. I ... I should've realised. But I'd thought ... I'd thought ... you'd stay here.' She opened her eyes and glanced up at him. She couldn't bear the thought of him going into enemy territory. 'You'll be home soon, though, won't you? You won't be away long?'

'I'll be back before you know it,' he promised. 'I've got the most wonderful girl waiting, you see.'

'Would that be me?' Rosie grinned, cheekily. She looked over at the horizon. There were a couple of vessels, small dark shapes against the waves. 'And if you need a driver over there, you know you can rely on me, don't you?'

'I wouldn't think of anyone el—' Bluff fell silent. He raised his hand and pointed out towards the sea, where a single flame flickered in the darkness. It blinked in and out of sight, the pattern too deliberate to be anything other than a signal. Bluff whispered one word. '*Prospero.*'

It was as if the air had heard him, as a breeze rustled through the trees at that moment, and sent the water rippling.

'She's here, then, somewhere...' Rosie whispered. She turned her head, but could only see the trees and the great flat expanse of the marsh and the sea. But Caroline had to be here. Her traitorous friend.

In the darkness the signal came again, closer each time as the little boat drew near. Soon Rosie could make it out and it seemed a humble vessel in which to brave the waters of the North Sea, a fishing boat that had seen better days. It stood to reason though, one would never imagine that the Führer would send such a craft to retrieve his most valuable spy. And that was precisely why they had. Out there in the night, this little vessel would pass unnoticed.

Bluff lifted Rosie's hand and kissed it, then released her. He reached down and drew his holstered gun, then took a small step forward.

Rosie pressed her cheek against the rough bark of the tree, her heart racing. Her hand felt so empty without Bluff's, but she could still feel the warmth of his kiss.

'Good luck...' she whispered, as the breeze shook the branches again. Movement in Rosie's peripheral vision caught her eye and she saw a slight figure in a long overcoat, a satchel thrown over one shoulder, and a lit candle illuminating her path. The figure held one hand over the flame, returning the signal of the boat as it turned into the narrow inlet and began its final approach.

Prospero.

Rosie bit back the sudden rocket of anger that shot through her.

How dare she. My friend. A traitor. A murderer. And now she's trying to get away!

'Miss Swann!' Bluff announced, the gun levelled at her. 'It's over.'

The candle fell away and Rosie realised too late that the hand with which Caroline had obscured the flame wasn't empty. In the light of the moon Rosie saw a flash of light glint off the barrel of a small pistol and when Caroline pulled the trigger, the *crack* split the night in two.

Rosie ducked behind the tree, then peered around it. Bluff was lying on the ground, motionless.

She's shot Bluff!

Dismissing any worries that Caroline might turn the gun on her, Rosie ran out from her hiding place towards Bluff.

'Bluff! Bluff! Are you all right?' she called.

Rosie knelt down beside him in the mud, frightened to touch him. He was on his back, unmoving, a dark stain spreading across his uniform from the tattered hole in the shoulder of his tunic. She barely had time to take it in before she felt the cold metal of Caroline's gun barrel against the back of her head.

'Stand up,' Caroline instructed as her foot lashed out to kick Bluff's gun towards the mud. 'I like you, Rosie, I don't want to shoot you. I didn't want to shoot the old prof either, but I had to.'

Rosie got up very carefully. She held up her hands, as she had done once in a play.

'You've … you've killed Bluff …' Rosie's lip quivered. She

wasn't sure that Caroline had, but she couldn't risk Caroline taking another shot at him just to make certain.

'I don't think the world's going to miss one more soldier, do you?' Caroline asked brightly. The boat had reached the shore now and two men were disembarking, dressed as though for a night's fishing. 'Don't worry, Driver Rosie, they have cars in Germany. Theatres too!'

Caroline was going to take her to Germany.

Rosie sniffed back a tear. She didn't want to go. And she couldn't leave Bluff lying injured or worse in the mud.

'What if I don't want to go?'

'I shoot you and my chums here dump you both in the sea.' She waved a happy greeting to the sailors. 'Guten abend! Ich bin Prospero und das ist meine freundin, Rosie!'

The sailors waved back.

'Guten abend, Prospero!' one of them called.

Then Rosie saw it. At first she wondered if it was a buoy she hadn't noticed before, just slightly out to sea. But as Rosie watched, the silent shape seemed to grow, rising up out of the water.

It was the tower of a submarine.

And still it rose, the great, dark bulk of the vessel now breaching the waves, like a whale emerging from the deep. Rosie froze in horror.

A German sub? It can't be!

But then she looked again. A flag was rising from the tower, and when it caught the breeze, Rosie saw the face of the Jolly Roger grinning out at her.

It's one of ours!

'Mein Gott!' one of the sailors shouted. 'Ach nee!'

The gun barrel was still pressed to Rosie's head, but Caroline heard the steel in her voice when she whispered, 'I'm sorry, Rosie. I would've loved to take you with me.'

A lamp on the submarine's tower strafed the coast, and finally fixed on the fishing boat in the inlet. As it did, Rosie heard a click from the gun as Caroline's finger tightened on the trigger.

Rosie pressed her fingertips to her eyes, and drew in a long sob. Hoping she had convinced Caroline that she was crying with despair, Rosie dropped her right hand, and snatched the spanner from her pocket. She repressed her revulsion at what she had to do.

Knowing it was either fight or be shot or taken to the last possible place on earth she wanted to be, Rosie spun round and walloped Caroline around the head with the spanner.

As the spanner made contact, a shot rang out and Caroline's left leg seemed to go from under her. Then she crumpled under the combined assault of Rosie's spanner and Bluff's bullet. As Caroline hit the ground Bluff lamented, 'Never was any damn good shooting left handed!'

The two sailors looked back at the submarine then, as one, they reached for their holstered guns and threw them onto the ground. They raised their hands in surrender and one of them called, 'Wir geben auf!'

'Thank heavens for that!' Bluff stood with some effort and holstered his gun. He pressed his hand to the wound in his shoulder. 'Bloody good show, Rosie. Are you all right?'

'I am – now I know *you're* all right.' Rosie crouched beside Caroline and in the bright light from the submarine quickly checked her over. Then she picked up Caroline's gun, holding it with distaste as if it was a week-old kipper. 'She's out cold.'

'Miss, excuse me?' one of the sailors said in halting English. He pointed to Bluff. 'We can help your friend?'

And then Bluff was in full flight, addressing the duo in fluent, fast German. Soon they were laughing like old pals, their mirth ringing on the air as the two men went back to the boat. Bluff sank down to sit on the ground, his hand clamped to his injured shoulder.

'First aid kit,' Bluff told Rosie, nodding towards the men. He held out his hand to her. 'Poor lads are half-starved. They're in no hurry to see the Fatherland again for a while.'

Rosie knelt in the mud next to him. She started to unfasten his belt. 'Let's get this tunic off you and we can check the wound. How are you feeling? Any faintness?'

'I'm a British soldier,' he replied as he let her help him out of the mud-spattered tunic. 'I'm never faint.'

Rosie heard shouts from beyond the trees and moments later there was Wyngate flanked by half a dozen military police. He took in the scene at a glance as Caroline began to stir. She clapped her hand to her mouth, stifling a wracking cough and tried to push herself to her knees. The mud seemed to hold her fast though so there she lay, coughing into her palm.

'Get the cuffs on our spy and put her in the car,' Wyngate instructed. 'Then give the sub the signal. I don't think we need those boys to hang about any longer. Driver, Major-General, sorry to miss the show.'

'Don't hold out for a repeat performance,' Rosie quipped. 'Blu— the major-general's been shot in the shoulder. Prospero's taken a bullet to the leg and a spanner to the head. And the sailors have surrendered and gone to get their first aid kit.'

The sailors came forward, holding up their hands, the first aid kit dangling from one of their hands. Wyngate offered them a careful nod and whispered to Rosie, 'I don't think I'd take on a T-class either. Or an actress from Weston-super-Mare.'

The military police had Caroline on her feet, her hands

cuffed behind her back. Her weight was supported by two officers and blood trickled down her right shin from the graze left by Bluff's bullet. It was lucky for Caroline that he was a poor shot with his left hand, Rosie reflected. Despite her limping gait and the mud that slicked her coat and hair, Caroline no longer looked like the meek young woman Rosie had known. Instead there was something different about her. A cool self-possession that even her brother would have struggled to achieve.

'It looks as though Rienzi will be dancing alone,' Bluff told her. 'Good evening, Miss Swann.'

'Goodbye, Major-General. Goodbye, Rosie,' Caroline replied. Then she smiled and added in a coquettish purr, 'Heil Hitler.'

As the words left Caroline's mouth her whole body seemed to grow rigid. Then her eyes rolled back in her head and she let out a strangled cry that ended only when she slumped against her captors, the last breath going out of her with a choked, agonised gasp.

'She's dead!' Rosie stared at the unmoving figure, sagged between two military policemen. A sob rose up in Rosie's throat. Despite what Caroline had been, and what she'd done, the last thing Rosie had thought she'd ever see was the spy die in front of her with no warning at all.

Suicide pill. That has to be it.

'That's saved the courts a job,' Wyngate observed as though there was nothing unremarkable about what they'd all just witnessed. 'Major-General, do you require an ambulance?'

Bluff looked down at his tattered shirt, slick with blood, then shook his head.

'We've an excellent sickbay at Cottisbourne,' he assured Wyngate. 'They're more than capable of dealing with a scratch.'

313

Chapter 34

They arrived back in Cottisbourne just as the sun was coming up. Rosie had driven as carefully as she could, trying not to jolt Bluff around too much. The sailors had made a good job of patching him up for the journey, and they had waved happily as the military police led them away.

When Rosie pulled up by the garage at Cottisbourne Park, she pictured Caroline in floods of tears as her brother was taken away. Tears that hadn't been real.

Rosie sighed. Who would've ever thought it of Caroline, the spy who had deceived almost everyone and had nearly got away?

'I hope Nurse won't mind us waking her up early,' Rosie said. She came round to the passenger side and opened the door, then held her arm out for Bluff. He took it and gingerly climbed out of the car, leaning his weight on her.

'She should've stood trial,' he said. 'But perhaps this is justice enough.'

Rosie nodded. 'She didn't get away. We stopped her, you and I. You, and I, and Nancy. We stopped her, and she never got to pass on the plans for *you-know-what.*'

Rosie looked up as another car pulled in. Wyngate had arrived.

'Get this man to sick bay, Driver,' Wyngate told Rosie as he opened the car door. 'I'll see you both in the major-general's office when he's had that shoulder looked at.' He strode across the gravel towards the house, dropping his voice to a whisper as he passed. 'Good job, chaps. Very bloody good.'

When Rosie was sure he was out of earshot, she whispered to Bluff, 'My word, praise from Wyngate! We must've done something right.'

She helped Bluff over to the sickbay, arriving just as the nurse did.

The nurse examined him and determined that the bullet had passed through his arm and that nothing had broken. But it was a large flesh wound and she told him that he would need to go on sick leave from active service for at least six weeks. The wound was dressed, a clean uniform was delivered from Bluff's room by one of the military police and soon he was as immaculate as ever, even with one arm in a pristine sling.

'Desk duties only!' she called after him as they left.

'I'm so sorry you were shot, Bluff,' Rosie said. 'But I rather think that's worked out surprisingly well!'

'Desk duties,' Bluff murmured, shaking his head. 'I should be there with the lads when they go in. It isn't right, Rosie.'

'You've done your bit. If you hadn't confronted Caroline, those lads would've had a hell of a time.' Rosie smiled at him. 'And given how secret this all is, they'll never know. But *we* will.'

Bluff smiled, then dotted a kiss to her cheek.

'We will,' he whispered.

They reached the house and went down the paneled corridor to Bluff's office. It was too early for Jean to be around so Rosie went to the door and knocked.

'Mr Wyngate?' Rosie called. To her surprise, Wyngate opened the door to admit them. He looked as though a weight had been lifted from his shoulders, just as Rosie felt.

With a sweeping glance over Bluff's sling, he asked, 'You're on desk duties for a while then?' When Bluff replied with a nod, Wyngate gave a narrow smile. 'Oh, I'm sure Mr Churchill will find plenty to keep you busy.'

'I'm sure he will,' Rosie said. She and Bluff each took a seat. 'I don't suppose ... has Caroline's family been told? I'm sorry ... I know I probably shouldn't care, but she used to be my friend.'

Wyngate leaned back against the desk and folded his arms. For a moment he was silent, then he said, 'Miss Swann went for a walk yesterday morning in the woods behind Cottisbourne Park. She sat to watch the sunrise and simply fell asleep.' He took off his hat and laid it on the desk. 'A congenital condition, I believe. The end was very peaceful. Her family will be informed later today.'

How coolly he talked about that imaginary death.

'And they won't know the truth? That she took a suicide pill?' Rosie asked.

'Miss Swann was a valued member of the Cottisbourne Park family. Without her expertise and dedication, we would all have been the poorer.' He cocked his head to one side. 'But the war effort continues.'

Bluff gave a careful nod. 'What of her brother? And Dr Zalewski?'

'Ten languages between them and a wealth of cypher skills,' Wyngate replied. 'We'll be moving Dr Zalewski into hut number two. Complementary abilities, you know. They've been working in Whitehall on a secret project, but they'll be back later today. We're having a shake up at Cottisbourne Park. A Mrs Thomas will be joining the administration team at special request of the PM too.'

'Nancy's mother is coming here? Oh, that's the most wonderful thing!' Rosie said. 'Poor Nancy was so worried ... They might not be back home, but at least they'll be together.' She tapped the side of her nose. 'And of course, Charles and Bartosz have been working very hard in Whitehall. I'm glad they're coming back. You might be surprised, Wyngate, but … I enjoyed working with you. Even though we didn't get off to the best of starts.'

'Driver Sinclair, Professor Hale believed you'd be an asset to my section and in many ways, he was right. In others … I don't know if you have the ruthless instinct it requires.' It didn't sound like a criticism to Rosie though, and she was rather pleased to hear that she wasn't ruthless enough for Mr Wyngate. 'But Major-General Sir Kingsley-Flynn will have a hell of a lot of people to vet once we're safely strolling up the Champs-Élysées. I can't offer you a role in my section, but I think you would bring a certain pluck to the major-general's division in Whitehall. If that's of interest, report to Mr Jeffreys at the War Office a week on Monday for your induction.'

'Does Mr Jeffreys bear a striking resemblance to you, Mr Wyngate?' Bluff asked, but the only reply was one of those narrow smiles.

'Well … I don't know what to say. Other than thank you!' She glanced from Wyngate – or was it Jeffreys? – to Bluff. 'Would you like me to be on your team? I've loved driving these past few years, but if I can turn my hand to something else, then I'd be more than happy to.'

Bluff smiled and assured her, 'I'd be very happy for you to join us, Rosie. We make a *very* good team.'

★ ★ ★

In the afternoon, Sarah and Maggie arrived to meet Rosie. They came bearing sandwiches they'd saved from lunch for her, and Rosie wished she'd been able to bring them something in return from her travels.

'It's so awful, poor Caroline popping her clogs like that,' Sarah said. 'But the three of us will always be friends, won't we?'

'We better had,' laughed Maggie, as she handed out the rock buns she'd smuggled out of the canteen. 'I don't share my contraband cake with just anybody!'

Rosie nodded. 'We will.'

Wherever in the world I might go.

Rosie was so glad to see her friends again, but it'd been a long night. Sarah and Maggie got back to work, leaving Rosie to catch up on her sleep. She woke up just as evening began to fall, and got out of bed to peer out around her curtains.

Her first thought was for Bluff, wondering how he was getting on with his wound. The sash window and curtains of his bedroom were open, a low light bathing the room beyond. There on the sill, its light flickering, was a candle stub.

How far that little candle throws his beams ...

He was awake.

Rosie hurried to put on her dress. Not her best, as that was still at her billet in London. She picked up the poster from her performance in Gloucester that Bluff had carried with him for so long, then she hurried across the courtyard to the house. As she was crossing two figures entered the courtyard, but Rosie didn't care if anyone saw where she was headed.

And then she realised who it was.

Charles and Bartosz.

At the sight of her Charles froze for a second before the two men approached. As they drew level with Rosie he said softly, 'I owe you an apology, Driver Sinclair. I truly am sorry. If not for you ...'

'It's all right,' she whispered. 'Really, it was Bartosz. He asked to speak to me.'

Bartosz smiled, his eyes sparkling. 'But who else could I have told? And the major-general, he was kind too. I'm just so happy to be here again, and working with my *very* good friend, Professor Swann.'

'Give the major-general our very best,' Charles asked. 'I know now that I'm the only dunderhead at Cottisbourne Park.'

'I will!' Rosie said. 'Goodbye, you two. I'll see you around.'

She waved to them both as she hurried on into the house and up the stairs to Bluff's room.

She knocked on his door. A few seconds passed before it opened and there was Bluff, in the civvies she'd teased him about in what seemed like another lifetime. It had never occurred to Rosie that the first time she saw him out of uniform would be in his pyjamas and a dressing gown of deep blue paisley silk, but this week had brought a lot of surprises. He still wore the sling, Rosie was pleased to see, but he looked none the worse for his experience.

'Hello, Rosie,' Bluff smiled. He glanced back into the room, where soft music was playing from the gramophone. 'Will you join me for a glass of the good stuff?'

'I'd love to.' She nodded towards his sling. 'How's the wound, soldier?'

Bluff glanced towards his shoulder and gave a one-sided shrug.

'Oh, you know,' he deadpanned, 'Nothing that'll keep H Cav down.'

Rosie chuckled. She knew he wouldn't tell her that it was twinging and sore.

'Just a scratch, of course,' Rosie said. She held out the poster to him. 'I got you a get well soon present.'

'I'll have it framed and hung in pride of place in my new mews house.' Bluff took the poster and unrolled it. He gave a warm smile as he cast his glance over it, then rolled the sheet again and put it down atop the dresser. 'Thank you very much, Rosie. For all sorts of things.'

Rosie put her arm around his waist and laid her head against his good shoulder. 'You don't have to thank me, darling.'

'I do,' Bluff murmured as he closed the door and wrapped his arm around her. He rested his lips against her hair and whispered, 'You're a dashed special sort of girl, Rosie Sinclair. I've never met anyone quite like you.'

'And I've never met anyone like *you*.' Rosie began to sway in time to the music and without meaning to, she and Bluff were gently dancing in his room. 'It's not quite the Café Royal, but we're both here, and you're almost in one piece, and that's what's important.'

'Who needs the Café Royal?' asked Bluff. 'It couldn't be better than this.'

Epilogue

Rosie and Bluff had returned to Cottisbourne, working on intercepting messages that went to and from Hitler's bunker in Berlin. There was no more talk of Prospero or Operation Tempest, no mention of birthday celebrations and the loyalty of the *Volk*, and there was precious little talk of dancing either. The invasion had not been stopped despite Caroline Swann's best efforts. Rienzi's reign was coming to an end.

And the last few messages had come through.

Rienzi was dead, and although Dönitz replaced him, he was hardly in a position of power. Day by day, messages came in, as across Europe, his remaining armies surrendered.

A week after Rienzi's death, the war in Europe was over.

The codebreakers at Cottisbourne Park threw homemade streamers and danced in the huts. Someone found some balloons, they pooled their resources for some treats, and they held a party in the grounds. The celebrations were the loudest Cottisbourne Park had seen in a long time and Rosie laughed as her friends cast off their cares, drinking beer and dancing with their colleagues.

But Rosie wasn't in the mood to be raucous. She thought of Hale and wished he'd been able to live to see this day. And she suspected Bluff was thinking the same, about all his lost friends who would never come home.

While the party went on, Rosie and Bluff took the

Citroën, the car that Hale had been so fond of, out for a drive.

On their way through the village, Rosie spotted Nancy and her mother, Portia tucked under the little girl's arm. Rosie tooted and waved, and they waved back. Nancy had excitedly told her the news that her father was finally on his way home, and she couldn't have been happier. Not so long ago she'd wondered what tomorrow would bring, but now the world seemed to be slowing down. They were a long way from normality, but Rosie could sense its glimmer on the horizon like the sun rising on a new day.

Rosie drove them up to the place where she and Bluff had ventured on the first night he'd arrived in Cottisbourne. They were the gardener and his driver then, but they were so much more than that now.

They climbed over the wall and sat down beside Romeo and Juliet, the two stones named by Hale. Below them, Cottisbourne and the countryside around it lay out before them in the golden summer light.

Rosie rested her head on Bluff's shoulder. 'I won't lie, there's been times when I thought we'd never see this day,' she said. 'But we have. We both have.'

Bluff put his arm around Rosie's waist and gently held her to him. He drew in a deep breath of fresh air, then said, 'I forgot to mention, I found the owner of that mysterious Citroën you've poured your heart and soul into.'

'Well done you!' Rosie chuckled, then she looked over her shoulder at the car and said, crestfallen, 'Oh … I suppose they'll want it back?'

'It belonged to the father of the lady who gave Cottisbourne Park to the war effort. Unlike you, that lady has no interest in motorcars and was happy to sell,' He kissed her cheek and whispered against her ear, 'She's all yours, darling.'

'Really? Oh, darling, thank you so much. What a wonderful gift!' Rosie squeezed his hand. 'Today has just been one piece of good news after another! And now, I suppose... now it's over, it won't be long before you hang your uniform up for good?'

'And the curtain goes up on our first production.' Bluff sounded excited at the prospect, but over the past year they'd made such plans that she hardly blamed him. And now they were going to be a reality. 'Are there any rules on producers fraternising with leading ladies?'

'Oh, yes,' Rosie nodded. 'You have to give me *lots* of hugs and kisses, and I'll give you lots in return. And we have to live in a mews house, too, of course!'

'What about producers marrying leading ladies? Any rules against that?'

Rosie shook her head. 'None at all. And you know, I don't even have to give up my job if I become a married woman. No one gives a fig in the theatre if the actresses are married or not.' Rosie lifted his hand and brought it to her lips. She adored Bluff, and now that the war was over, their life together could properly begin. 'You know, Bluff, I've been thinking... we've seen a lot of each other over the past year. Worked closely, gone dancing, had the occasional kiss. We've even met each other's parents, and I think it's time I made a decent major-general of you. What do you say, darling? Will you marry me, Bluff?'

It wasn't often that Bluff was speechless, but Rosie seemed to have achieved it for a few seconds at least. He broke into a beaming smile and said, 'Miss Sinclair, I can't think of anything I'd rather do. Am I to assume that you've already selected your bridesmaids?'

'Of course, who else but the codebreakers girls?' Rosie stroked Bluff's cheek, gazing at his dancing eyes. She sighed happily and said, 'Oh, I love you, Bluff!'

'I love you, Rosie,' he said gently. 'My leading lady.'

**If you enjoyed *The Codebreaker Girls,*
you will fall in love with Ellie Curzon's
heartwarming and romantic WW2 saga...**

Can they find love in the darkest days of war?

It's 1944, and **Florence** is a talented engineer in
the Women's Auxiliary Air Force, patching up
planes to make sure that the brave Spitfire pilots of
Cottisbourne airbase return safely day after day.

When she befriends the new squadron leader – shy,
handsome **Siegfried** – it seems that romance might
blossom under the war-torn skies. But Florence is
nursing a broken heart and a terrible secret, which
might destroy her one chance of happiness...

Meanwhile, a new plane is being developed that could
turn the tide of the war, but Florence fears there is
traitor is in their midst, putting Siegfried – and the
whole country – in terrible danger. Can Florence
save her Spitfire boys, and her own heart?

Order your copy now!

Milton Keynes UK
Ingram Content Group UK Ltd.
UKHW040110041023
429898UK00003B/111